4—

Praise for Lorie O'Clare's previous novels

"The best book I've read this year!"
—*New York Times* bestselling author
Lora Leigh on *Tall, Dark and Deadly*

"O'Clare [writes] page-turners filled with well-developed characters, and sparkling, sharp-witted dialogue…and attraction so strong you can feel it!"
—*Romantic Times BOOKreviews*

"Gripping." —*A Romance Review*

"Ms. O'Clare has written a gritty, dangerous, and sexy story. The action starts on the first page and doesn't let up until the last. *Tall, Dark and Deadly* is a page-turner packed with sensuality and suspense. You won't want to miss this one."
—*Fallen Angel Reviews*

"Intriguing [and] highly stimulating…a fantastic blend of mystery and suspense." —*All About Murder*

"The passion and steamy sensuality are great, as are the action and emotion." —*Romance Reviews Today*

D0050284

CLACKAMAS BOOK EXCHANGE
10655 SE 42ND AVE
MILWAUKIE, OR. 97222-5251

Play Dirty

LORIE O'CLARE

St. Martin's Paperbacks

NOTE: If you purchased this book without a cover you should be aware that this book is stolen property. It was reported as "unsold and destroyed" to the publisher, and neither the author nor the publisher has received any payment for this "stripped book."

This is a work of fiction. All of the characters, organizations, and events portrayed in this novel are either products of the author's imagination or are used fictitiously.

PLAY DIRTY

Copyright © 2010 by Lorie O'Clare.
Excerpt from *Get Lucky* copyright © 2010 by Lorie O'Clare.

All rights reserved.

For information address St. Martin's Press, 175 Fifth Avenue, New York, NY 10010.

ISBN: 978-0-312-37215-6

Printed in the United States of America

St. Martin's Paperbacks edition / October 2010

St. Martin's Paperbacks are published by St. Martin's Press, 175 Fifth Avenue, New York, NY 10010.

10 9 8 7 6 5 4 3 2 1

To my three wonderful sons, who are more supportive of my writing than anyone. The sound of my fingernails tapping on the keys has lulled them to sleep as long as they can remember. And they've told me they love the sound of it because it sounds like home. They are my best critics, even though none of them have read my books. But they read the blurbs because they want to know about the action. They are my best promotional team, and just all around three incredible young men. I love you Andy, Jonathan, and Luke.

To My Dear Readers,

There is always something dangerous hovering around the title "bounty hunter." Over the years, our history has depicted them as treading the fine line between working for the law and working against it. Movies have presented bounty hunters as good people and bad people. We have examples like the Dog, who depict bounty hunting as a moving experience and a chance for the person being hunted to start anew. There are also movies which turn bounty hunting into an almost comical line of work.

Real bounty hunters vary from the type who work closely with the court system and chase those who don't show up for court dates, to the kind who work out of their homes, are licensed private investigators, and quite often have more than one line of work to make ends meet. Hollywood has glamorized a line of work that in reality is dangerous and requires an incredibly large amount of patience.

The few bounty hunters I visited with declined to have their names mentioned here. They shared their experiences, some of their stories being exciting and others rather boring. What I did notice was a similar type of personality in each of them, which helped me mold Greg, Marc, and Jake's personalities. These are men who aren't shy. They are in good shape and have a solid conviction to find out what they need to know about you. Each man I spoke with never broke eye contact and had an insight that allowed them to know more about me than I offered while speaking with them. They are patient, quiet, and good listeners. Needless to say, it wasn't hard to mold incredible heroes after seeing how those who choose to be bounty hunters behave.

Greg King is a strong giant of a man. There isn't a woman around who can break his convictions. Except, of course, the one lady that Greg has loved since he was a boy. He has strong morals and doesn't break the law, but knows it well enough to use it to his advantage. Greg's passed those traits on to both of his sons.

I look forward to introducing you to the King family. These men are powerful, determined, incredibly tall and muscular. The Kings know they can't hide well in a crowd but also use their size and strength to their advantage in ways you can only imagine until you've read these books. What impressed me most about Greg King and his sons was their undying devotion to the women they fall in love with.

You'd think a man who is so powerful, physically on top of his act, willful and determined would demand a submissive woman. The Kings all believe that is the right type of lady for them. The fates have another life in store for them. Their women might not be as physically strong, but they are definitely strong of mind. Haley King is just that type of woman.

I know you'll love Haley. I sure do. She is stubborn, determined, and knows how to control her man. So please, enter the world of bounty hunters with me, get to know the Kings, and I think you'll find you've made good friends who will stay with you long after you finish reading this story.

Lorie O'Clare

Chapter 1

Greg King loved not having to worry about getting a warrant. But if he shot to kill, he would face murder charges. He really did hate some of the laws on the books.

Keeping his Glock pointed to the ground, he hit the street, humidity causing his shirt to cling to him like a second skin. It wasn't even light out yet. It would be another scorcher, tolerable only if he nailed the fugitive they'd been tracking since 2:00 A.M. before the sun got too high in the sky.

And they said life would be boring once he retired from the LAPD.

"Marc, you in place?" he hissed into his Bluetooth.

"Yup," Marc whispered in his ear, sounding somewhat winded. "Stationary and ready for fireworks."

"Jake, what's it like out front?"

"All quiet. He's still in there." Jake's anxious tone sounded as if he was running high on adrenaline.

But then, weren't they all? It had been one hell of a night.

"I'm going in," Greg informed his sons.

Marc and Jake both loved the kill, although technically no one died. Or they weren't supposed to. Greg and his sons were only paid when they brought their prey in alive. A dead fugitive was no good to the bondsman who'd hired them or, in this case, bondswoman.

Greg knew the craving to make the bust, bring down the fugitive, and slap on those cuffs ran strong enough in his blood that both of his boys would get high from the adventure just like he did.

What he did was dangerous and Greg would never live through one of his family dying because of his livelihood, but Marc and Jake insisted working at his side. Despite Greg's protests, both of his sons had proven to be quick studies and had overcome every obstacle Greg had thrown at them in an effort to make them choose another line of work. Today they were almost as good as him. Both his sons were built like him, well over six feet and incredibly muscular. Their appearance intimidated the not-so-hardened criminal, which always worked to a bounty hunter's advantage.

Pulling all-nighters like this never got old. Dealing with the bureaucratic red tape that forced him to wait on judges' signatures and stalling until he got the go-ahead from his senior officers had gotten old as hell. Those days were behind him now. Being a bounty hunter allowed him freedom to do exactly what he planned on doing right now, and would have killed to do for the past twenty years.

Greg cut between the dilapidated house and the house next door to where Charlie Woods supposedly lived, moving silently in spite of his size. Size did matter. No one would convince him otherwise. But Greg knew how to move without disturbing a soul, even though he stood six feet, four inches. There was no reason to wake the entire neighborhood simply because Pedro Gutierrez thought he could jump bail and make a run for it. Charlie was a known member of the Hell Cats, a gang Pedro had once belonged to, and according to reliable sources, Pedro was hiding out at Charlie's. Greg wouldn't learn the truth by simply knocking on the door.

He reached the backyard and hurried across the lawn, slowing when he reached the metal screen door. He kept his gun down, pulling the door open with his left hand, then braced it with his body as he turned the handle on the door.

"Are you in?" Jake demanded, his whispered question sounding as if he stood right behind his father.

Greg took his hand off the doorknob and adjusted the earpiece so his son wasn't yelling in his ear.

"It's locked," he growled, having half a mind to shoot the fucking doorknob off the door. "I'm trying the windows."

"We're coming in through the front," Marc decided, breaking in on the conversation.

"Like hell," Greg said, keeping his voice to a barely audible whisper. "He's fucking armed and dangerous. We're working against a ticking time bomb. You two wait for my go-ahead."

Already he was around the back of the house, edging his way to the nearest window. It was probably a bedroom window and quite possibly where their guy might be hiding out. Greg stared at the dark window—blinds, possibly curtains, or even a mattress—that was making it impossible to see inside. The storm window was up, though, and the window wasn't so high off the ground or too small that he couldn't haul his large frame through it if he moved quickly. The element of surprise was his only advantage right now.

"Go ahead and call in backup," Greg told Marc.

"I'm on it," he announced.

Greg didn't bother asking if that meant they were already on their way, or not. Backup would get here when they got here. Greg wasn't waiting.

Sliding his gun into his holster, Greg pulled out his pocketknife and flipped it open. It wasn't the kind of knife most fathers carried around with them. The razor-sharp blade would cut through the metal of the screen frame if he wanted it to. Instead, he sliced the screen, imagining their fugitive would probably try suing if he owned this dump and charge Greg for breaking and entering plus vandalizing his home. It wouldn't be the first time.

Maybe Greg didn't get the protection offered when he had worn the uniform and he had to be careful how he went about making his arrests. But at least today red tape was something he would slice through with his handy little pocketknife. He ran his own show these days. All that mattered was that the bonds company got their fugitive and Greg got his check.

He sliced the screen, starting in the top left corner and gutting it down the middle, then cutting along the bottom until the screen peeled to the side for him. Greg reached through it, feeling it scrape his damp flesh above his leather glove, and pushed the window up. It lifted with a whiny squeak, obviously complaining from lack of use.

"I'm heading in," he whispered to his sons. "Move now!"

More than once in his life, living in Los Angeles, people had asked if Greg were a professional wrestler. His size didn't bother him, and it wouldn't slow him down now. Snapping his pocketknife shut and sheathing it in the leather case attached to his belt, Greg hoisted himself through the window, feeling the wooden frame of the window rake over his shoulders and then his legs. He fell to his side on a dirty wooden floor and immediately pulled his gun, forcing his eyes to adjust quickly to his surroundings as he looked around.

Other than a box spring and a bare mattress, there wasn't any furniture in the room. Crumpled fast-food bags and crushed beer cans gave the room the appearance of being one big trash dump.

"Did you hear that?" a man asked from the other room.

"Sounds like we have company." The thick Hispanic accent sounded just like Pedro Gutierrez, a well-known drug lord and arms dealer who'd been arrested last month and had failed to show up for court yesterday afternoon. His probation officer couldn't find him and the bondswoman was getting nervous.

It was a stupid move on Pedro's part. He obviously didn't check the statistics before deciding to run. No criminal ran from Los Angeles and got away. This was Greg's town and he was too good. His track record spoke for itself.

"Who the fuck is back there?" the man roared, obviously not afraid at all of the boogey man in a dark bedroom.

Nor did the man turn on the bedroom light as he stormed in, which was just fine with Greg.

"Hello, Pedro," he said calmly, pointing his gun straight at the man's face.

Pedro apparently had no manners. He didn't return the greeting, but instead hauled ass toward the other end of the house. Greg charged after him, feeling the house shake from the two of them running through it.

It wasn't a long hallway, but Greg didn't catch the shadow that appeared from the bedroom across the hall in time. He saw the baseball bat, heard the whoosh when it swung through the air.

"Son of a bitch!" he yelled, turning and raising his arm. He braced himself for the pain that shot across his shoulder and down his spine. The bat hit the side of his neck, just above his shoulder, with enough driving force to knock Greg against the hallway wall.

"Fucking hell!" he roared, although the words damn near caught in his throat when his windpipe smashed closed, stealing his breath and racking every inch of his body.

Hitting the wall with the other shoulder didn't make matters any better. The intense headache he'd probably have to deal with the rest of the day slammed into his brain instantly.

A dark, burly-looking man bellowed something that didn't sound very friendly in Spanish and Pedro responded, their guttural slang difficult for Greg to translate. Especially when pain ransacked his body and a ringing started in his head as he slumped against the wall. The burly motherfucker shoved Greg out of the way, causing him to lose his footing, and then bounded after Pedro, leaving Greg to hold up the slimy wall.

At least he hadn't been shot. Maybe the two men weren't armed. His body hurt like fucking hell, but he'd have to worry about that later. Reaching for his neck, he cringed from the intense pain that shot down his arm. There wasn't any blood, though.

"I didn't give up a night's sleep so you could give me a

migraine and get away." Greg cursed, using the hallway wall to push himself to his feet. It seemed his legs were heavier than usual when he tried running after them, and he damn near fell on his face. "Tough it up, King," he ordered himself.

They couldn't get far. His boys were out front and on the side of the house. Unless they'd already entered. He was in the living room, staring at the open front door, when he heard gunfire.

"Son of a bitch!"

Haley would never forgive him if one of the boys were seriously injured, or worse, injured while working a job.

Greg ignored the pain and ran out of the house, not having to worry about his eyes adjusting this time. It wasn't much lighter outside than it was in the house, but the pain made everything blur. Flashing reds and whites gave the front yard a surreal look. It was odd that moments like this caused him to think of his estranged wife.

"You have the right to remain silent," a young rookie Greg didn't recognize said as he continued shoving Charlie Woods toward a squad car. His tone was harsh and full of himself, as if he'd been the one chasing Pedro all night.

"Dad!" Jake yelled, hurrying across the yard.

Greg noticed Marc talking to Margaret Young, one of the bondswomen whom the Kings worked with on a regular basis. Jake reached Greg's side, grabbing his arm on his injured side.

"Where's Pedro?" Greg demanded, grabbing his son's arm and holding on to it, probably tighter than he should have.

"We got them," Jake said, not complaining even if Greg's hold on him was painful. "Are you okay?" he asked as Marc headed across the lawn to join them.

"I nabbed Pedro," Marc announced, giving his dad a quick once-over. Although Marc was the oldest at twenty-five, Jake stood an inch or so taller. Both were built like their old man, although at the moment Greg didn't feel incredibly intimidating, as many claimed the three of them appeared when standing together. "Charlie Woods was with him and they're reading his rights to him right now. Margaret has one more for us if you're up for it. Apparently this one was nabbed at the same time as Gutierrez and missed his court date yesterday afternoon, too."

There were squad cars up and down the street, their lights flashing and lighting up the whole block. Greg and his sons might have done all the grunt work, but the uniforms loved being there for all the glory. Greg had years of putting more of these hoods behind bars than he cared to count. He didn't need to slap handcuffs on some punk to know he was good. If any of the older boys had been here for the bust, they would have treated Greg with respect. Greg no longer cared about lawyers downplaying his work or courtrooms where facts were twisted. His job ended when he turned in the perp, then it was on to the next hunt.

Greg barely heard his son describe their next perp as he stared at a woman who stood down the street, partially hidden in shadows. His head and shoulder were pounding, causing a ringing sound in his head. He ignored the pain. She shifted, crossed her arms, and studied him. It was as if tunnel vision kicked in and all he saw was the woman returning his stare.

She wore a pale pink jogging outfit and tight spandex that hugged her small waist, making her full, round breasts look even larger. Her skin was tanned and her light brown hair cut short, shorter than he remembered it, and it was kinky from the humidity. So, Haley wasn't a blonde anymore. Interesting. Would her hair still feel as soft between his fingers?

Six years might have passed, but he would know Haley if it had been sixty years and a hundred people stood between them. Her hair was a different color than it used to be, and she dressed in an outfit she wouldn't have been caught dead in before, not too revealing but more youthful looking. It looked damn good on her, too. The jogging outfit hugged her in all the right places and showed off her soft curves and breasts.

She wasn't a small woman, but she had always felt tiny next

to him. It aroused his strongest protective instincts, and even now, he wanted to walk down the street, snatch her up, and hide her somewhere while he stood guard. No matter how many years dragged on he would never trust anyone else to keep her safe.

No one understood why Greg King had an impeccable record as a bounty hunter yet couldn't track down his wife who disappeared without as much as a note explaining her actions. Greg didn't need a note. The world could go ahead and think the love of his life had slipped through his fingers. He knew the truth, and although he had never liked it, he had lived with it. Haley hadn't given him a choice.

He doubted Haley thought she would be gone this long. Greg willed her to be closer, to see deeper into her eyes. Did she regret that stupid fight as much as he did? They'd never been given time to make up.

"Dad? What gives?" Marc was talking, but Greg didn't catch a word of it.

He tried stepping around his sons, needing to be closer to Haley. He didn't want her to disappear, no matter how justified her first disappearance was. At the same time he didn't want his sons to be distracted from their work. If Haley was in trouble, emotions would only make it harder to help her. And why else would she be here?

"Go get the details from Margaret," he said gruffly, waving them off as he tried circling around them. Every instinct inside him demanded he grab her, learn her problems, fix them, and never let her go again.

"Already done." Marc remained by his side, holding papers that Greg hadn't noticed in his hand before now. "Jason Wilson, thirty years old, Caucasian, six feet and two hundred pounds. Bail was set at fifteen grand just like Gutierrez."

"If these two were buddies, Wilson might not be too far from here," Jake said, sandwiching his dad as he stood too close on Greg's other side.

"They weren't buddies." Greg shot his younger son a harsh

glare as he stopped walking, knowing neither would give him a moment's peace if he didn't give them something to keep busy and distract them long enough for him to get around the squad cars and have a moment to learn why Haley was here. "Wilson and Gutierrez were drug lords, each controlling his own neighborhood until both were set up."

"If they were narked out, Wilson might have gone after whoever squealed on him once he bailed out."

Greg quit staring at Haley, who'd yet to pull her gaze from his, and scowled at his older son. "Their informant is well on his way into a witness protection program. You don't take out two men who basically controlled most of the city and believe you can walk the streets safely after that. Not to mention, this is information both of you should know already."

"Are you sure you're okay?" Marc changed the subject to avoid the lecture.

Pedro Gutierrez was cuffed and walked between two cops. His buddy Charlie Woods already sat in the backseat of a squad car. Pedro paused in front of Greg, blocking his view of Haley. Greg didn't give a rat's ass what the guy might have to say. But as Greg moved around Jake, searching for Haley, Pedro started ranting, his menacing tone probably enough to scare many.

"He said he can help you nail Jason," Marc said under his breath. Marc stiffened and balled his hands into fists when Pedro spoke again. Whatever he said, Pedro knew it affected Marc. His cruel sneer was damn near the ugliest thing Greg had ever seen. "Dad," Marc hissed.

"Did he just say something about Mom?" Jake asked under his breath, every inch of him tightening defensively.

"He just said if we don't capture Wilson, by tomorrow we'd be able to find him with your wife."

Greg snapped his attention from his older son, past Pedro, who continued sneering. Before Greg allowed his brain to talk him out of it, he stormed around his sons, ignoring the curious looks from the circus ring of cops and onlookers. He was fluent in Spanish, and he'd damn well find out what Pedro meant by his bold accusation.

Margaret stepped in front of Greg before he noticed her. His focus was on Pedro and the officers escorting him to the squad car.

"I gave all the specs to Marc." Margaret frowned at Greg. "Everything okay?"

He fought off the urge to physically move her and bound after Pedro. The asshole spoke about Haley as if he knew she stood across the street. Greg shot a desperate look to where Haley had been standing. She was gone.

"Greg?" Margaret asked.

"Nothing. Everything is fine." Something close to panic hit him, creating an urge to race down the street, tear the neighborhood apart if needed. Haley had been standing right there!

The officers assisted Pedro into the squad car. Greg searched the curb across the street. He didn't see any signs of Haley. And he knew he hadn't just imagined her. He hadn't taken that hard of a blow to the head.

Margaret waved him off, pulling her cell out and taking a call as she headed to her car.

Jake and Marc once again moved in around him. Greg ignored them, searching the other side of the street, taking in each person who stood watching the scene.

"Mom's been gone for six years. If you don't know where she is, there is no way scumbags like these would have a clue." Jake looked to his dad for understanding. "Unless, of course, you *do* know where she is."

Pedro was now secure in the backseat of the squad car. Haley was gone, disappearing without a trace, but something told Greg this time she wasn't really gone.

"No, I don't." Anger surged through him with such a vengeance it made Greg stagger. His boys misinterpreted his actions and assumed he might be hurt worse than he was letting on.

"We'll head back to the house, run a profile on Wilson, and see if we can't narrow down his possible whereabouts online before heading back out." Marc tried pretending he was in charge sometimes, and even managed to sound like he knew what he was doing. Truth be told, he was one hell of a bounty hunter, as good as his father. "It might not hurt for you to try and catch a couple hours of sleep while we research him," Marc encouraged, trying to herd his father to the car.

Greg didn't fight Marc but headed to the Avalanche, leading the way and jiggling his keys in his hands as his sons walked on either side of him. He scanned the street, the usual scene following a bust in full progress. None of that impressed him. If Haley was in town, and appearing at a bust, something was seriously wrong.

Greg couldn't count the many sleepless nights he'd spent staring at his ceiling trying to figure out why Haley had done what she did. There had been other options, other ways the situation could have been handled. Granted, her testimony had resulted in one of the most horrendous drug dealers in history getting life without parole. Haley had broken up her family to save other families from losing loved ones to drugs. It was a sacrifice Greg wasn't sure he could have ever gone through with and he hadn't forgiven her for being strong enough to leave him.

He blamed her for agreeing to enter the Witness Protection Program. It tore him up to this day that he'd not told her he loved her before she'd left. And all because of a stupid fight. They'd had fights before, but this one had been a doozy. Even so, they could have worked through it. She had been everything to him, and still was. Every day he saw her in their boys. Her things were still in their home. Haley was in the air he breathed, in his dreams at night, and in his thoughts during the day more than anyone would know.

He didn't care how many years went by. He knew his wife as well as he knew himself. Haley might possibly be the only person he'd ever met who was more stubborn than he was.

She was also a good detective. And she'd never worn a badge. Today he wasn't too stubborn to tell her that.

He slid behind the steering wheel, knowing it'd be smart to let one of his sons drive but not really caring. He swore there was a grapefruit sprouting from the nape of his neck, and the throbbing pain was pissing him off as much as Pedro's promise that Wilson would find Haley. One of those scumbags would die before they touched Haley.

"You two work up an MO on Jason Wilson." Laying out the game plan helped Greg focus so he could drive. "I'm going to figure out if there's a reason Pedro mentioned your mother."

"He said that to piss you off so you'd bring Wilson back in," Marc decided. "He figures if he's going to rot behind bars, so is Wilson."

"Probably." Greg would have believed that if he hadn't just seen his wife across the street.

"Where you going?" Marc asked, sitting shotgun.

"Just checking something out." Greg turned the corner at the end of the block. Haley couldn't have gotten too far, unless someone was waiting to give her a lift. He headed around the block, looking up and down the street when he turned. She wasn't anywhere.

"What are you checking out?" Marc pressed.

Jake leaned forward, parked in the middle of the backseat with his hands resting on either front seat. "What are you doing, Dad?"

"Shut the hell up, both of you!" Greg wasn't explaining his actions to either one of them. Ignoring the tense silence that followed, he continued scanning the streets, even driving past Charlie Woods's house one more time. Haley was gone, as if she'd never been there in the first place.

Chapter 2

It was hot and humid as hell, yet Haley King shook as if she were freezing to death. It took several tries to get the key card to slide behind the doorknob to her hotel room.

After all these years. Lord, after all of these years.

Greg had seen her. And God, she had seen him!

She entered her hotel room, the door closing on its own behind her, and dropped her purse and key card to her room on the king-sized bed. A wave of comfort and security hit her when she heard the door click locked. No one would find her here. She was safe, for now.

"Okay, breathe," she ordered herself, pacing the length of the room several times before stopping and staring at herself in the mirror.

Her hair was cut short, and her natural light brown color instead of the platinum blonde it had been during the years of her marriage. Even now, six years later, she sometimes did a double take when looking at her reflection. Who the hell was she?

You're Hannah McDowell. And had been ever since entering the Witness Protection Program. Testifying against Perry Pierre had been the toughest thing she'd ever done in her life; well, the second toughest. Leaving Greg and her boys was the hardest thing she'd ever done. She'd left to protect her family, and was returning to protect herself. U.S. Marshal Arnold Summers might disagree, but she hadn't taken time to ask for his opinion.

And now she was back.

My God, Greg was as magnificent now as he had been six years ago. He was muscular, tall, and in perfect shape. No, he was in even better shape than she remembered. And Jake and Marc—her babies! They were all grown-up and looked just like their father. All three of them were so perfect.

Why hadn't she seen Greg as perfect six years ago?

It was their fight. My God, it had been bad.

There had been occasional fights over the years, but none of them as bad as this one. She'd seen a side of Greg she'd never seen before and hadn't liked it one little bit. He'd been a damned hypocrite supporting all her criminology classes and her self-defense classes, and listening to her speak repeatedly over the years of the day when she'd be a private investigator. When the time came to make her dream a reality, Greg had thrown a fit. It hadn't been fair bringing up his mother. It had been even more unfair for him to tell her he wouldn't be able to live wondering if she'd taken a bullet on the job that day. Even when she'd told him she'd lived that very life as his wife for years with him on the police force, Greg hadn't backed down. But when he'd demanded, sliced his hand through the air, and informed her how it would be, as if he owned her, she'd lost it. Haley didn't remember all the names she had called him, but she still heard the loud bang of the door in her memories when she had slammed it shut all those years ago and walked out on him. She'd testified the next day and willingly agreed to enter the Witness Protection Program later that afternoon. Her anger over their argument fueled her ability to go through with it. Not once had she dreamed she'd be gone this long.

Six years changed a person. Greg would probably be different today. Haley knew she was. For one thing, she was now the private investigator she'd only dreamed of being six years ago. There had been a half-block's distance between them when she'd stared into his eyes early this morning, but she swore his possessive look was still there. Today he would have to accept who she was. He just had to.

Not for the first time, she came to the conclusion that the Witness Protection Program had saved their marriage instead of destroying it. Greg had been working fifty-plus hours a week and she had been doing about the same. She had loved teaching but had loved her detective work even more. No one had known what she was doing. Well, they hadn't until she had gone to the precinct containing the school where she'd been teaching. Even then Greg hadn't been alerted. It wasn't his precinct. Which was why he'd been shocked as hell when she'd told him how she'd nailed a major drug dealer and that her testimony would put him away for life.

She swallowed emotions that rose in her throat and caused tears to pool in her eyes. It had been wrong not to tell him about her undercover work with that precinct and she'd never had a chance to apologize.

Six years! Everyone she knew in LA believed she'd walked out on her husband and boys, outraged that Greg was more in love with his work than with her. Now she was back, and she had to see him. Haley had done some snooping, confirmed that King Fugitive Apprehension was working a bust. All she'd wanted was to see his face, to see him in the flesh.

And damn! Had she gotten an eyeful!

He'd worn a muscle T-shirt and his body definitely gave credit to the name of the shirt. There wasn't enough shirt to hide the perfect specimen of man who wore it. Greg looked incredible, the epitome of perfection. Haley had stared at thick slabs of perfectly chiseled, heavily built-up muscle. It was as if he'd been carved, each cut painstakingly molded so there would be no faults. She knew if she'd been able to touch him, every inch of his body would have been harder than stone. Tight bands created precise lines across his stomach that were plainly visible under his shirt. Greg gave new meaning to a "six pack."

His arms were smooth, round curves and his shoulders taut ripples of roped muscle.

Heat had spread throughout her and she couldn't look away. Greg hadn't been this distractingly well built when they'd been together. He looked the way she imagined warriors from a darker time might look. Greg had always been larger than life and strong. Today he looked as if he spent an hour in the gym each day. There was another thing that Haley had noticed. Greg sure hadn't looked pissed off to see her.

Taking the stand against Perry Pierre had been a death sentence. The look on Perry's face when she'd shared with the court what she knew, what she'd seen, was enough proof to send him to prison. The sneer Perry gave her showed he believed he could kill her, whether behind bars or not.

Haley remembered the look on Greg's face when she told him she would testify, which meant disappearing as well. Perry's twisted glare didn't bother her half as much as Greg's blank expression. He'd shut down, agreed she made the right decision, and not touched her again. Today, though, when he looked at her, he had looked . . .

"Hungry," she mused, talking to her reflection.

Taking on Greg was one thing, but there were also her sons. She hadn't said anything to them before she left, nothing other than their usual morning chatter as they started their day. If she had inquired a bit deeper into their personal lives, their girlfriends they had that week, or what they had wanted to do the following weekend, Marc and Jake hadn't seemed to notice. She remembered walking with them to the driveway and watching Jake leave for school and Marc for work. That was the last time she had seen her beautiful boys.

Until today.

"None of this," she ordered herself. It had been the hardest, most soul-crushing move she'd ever made. There'd never been a moment's doubt that leaving had saved all their lives. It had broken her heart, but if she had stayed and been shot, or witnessed one of her sons or Greg being shot as a result of her testimony, the pain would have been worse.

Haley headed over to her laptop, booted it up, then entered the password-protected Web site. "You did the right thing then and you're doing the right thing now. Stay on track. You've got work to do."

Her boss, John Payton, had disappeared three days ago. Maybe it was coincidence that his disappearance happened around the same time Perry Pierre died in prison. Either way, Pierre's death freed her, and her boss's disappearance worried her.

It was time to leave behind her life as Hannah McDowell. The Witness Protection Program usually recommended keeping your first name and changing the last, therefore keeping the same initials. It was said that made it easier to assume a new name.

Haley had chosen Hannah, the name she and Greg would have given their daughter if they'd ever had one, and McDowell, the maiden name that her grandmother had changed to Dow when she became an American citizen. Two names Haley and one other person on this planet would know and understand. Her and Greg.

Haley stretched across the large bed and fished her cell phone out of her purse. She would try calling John again. At the same time she checked her boss's e-mail on the password-protected site. Usually he read it daily, but none of it had been opened. John hadn't been online.

"Pick up; pick up," she whispered, listening to the rings while staring at the in-box for Payton Investigative Services.

None of this made sense. John wasn't answering his personal cell phone, and he hadn't checked e-mail in the past few days. In six years he'd become more than her boss. He'd become a dear friend, her mentor, and the only family she had while living in Nebraska. She didn't like thinking it could all be ripped out from underneath her, again.

"Damn it," she hissed, dropping her phone next to her on the bed and adjusting her laptop while moving to the next page that normally showed his agenda for the day. It was blank. "Where are you, John?"

It wasn't like him. John was a man of routine, strolling into the office an hour later than she every morning and smelling of the cigarettes he claimed not to smoke. To many, he might appear uptight and eccentric, but John wasn't either. He was intelligent and an incredible detective. For six years Haley knew where he was almost every hour of every day. He had been addicted to his calendar and had insisted he and Haley—although to him she was Hannah—always knew where the other was at all times. Disappearing for any amount of time wasn't like him.

John had hired her as a secretary when she'd moved to Omaha, Nebraska. The Witness Protection Program had advised a different line of work. But as Haley had argued, this *was* a different line of work for her. She'd been a teacher's aide. Haley gave up her heart and her soul when she'd entered the program. It kept her a bit closer to Greg, being in a similar line of work. She'd taken classes and had some experience that she put to good use over the years she'd worked for John.

Something had blossomed inside Haley while working in John's office. She did bookkeeping and answered phones but also did fieldwork. John treated her like a partner. Haley wouldn't have been surprised if there were times John forgot she was a woman. He was so focused on his work.

No matter the years that passed slowly, or how fulfilling her work was, the emptiness inside her never went away. Haley had kept up on Greg and her sons' lives the best she could. Her heart broke every day, all over again, as she continued living without them. She would return to them. There wasn't any doubt in her mind. When she did, Haley wondered if they'd pick up right where they'd left off. If they did, it would mean fighting all over again about her working alongside Greg, hunting by his side, and knowing the adrenaline rush as they brushed with danger time and time again. Haley wasn't going to give up investigating. Nor would she ever give up on Greg.

When John took the case for Roberto Torres things began changing. That was when the trouble started. Haley was sure of it. She sighed, ordering herself to focus, and opened a fresh browser page. Haley pulled up Torres's MySpace page, knowing Roberto used it to pick up women behind his wife's back. Roberto was a prick, a scumbag, and a lowlife. He was proof that even nice midwestern towns such as Omaha could house weasels. She hadn't liked him the moment he'd entered John's office, looking at her as if she were fresh meat and groping her the first time her boss turned around.

She didn't need John's protection, and Roberto quickly learned that. The first time he'd tried copping a feel of her breasts, Haley had smacked him across the face hard enough to leave a red mark. From that point forward, he pouted every time he saw her, as if that would make her come around. It was also during that time, a couple months ago, when John grew distracted, not listening when she spoke to him, which wasn't his normal behavior at all. Something had been on his mind, but he wouldn't tell her what it was.

"If only you'd confided in me," she complained, her stomach growling, although she doubted she could eat anything right now. "Why did you have to be so damned secretive about the Roberto Torres case?"

John was gone. Roberto showed up the other morning, demanding to see him, and she'd told him John had a doctor's appointment. Something told her Roberto already knew John had disappeared. After Roberto had left the office, she'd found the letter.

She glanced at her purse, where the single piece of paper was folded and stuffed in an evidence bag she'd snagged from the office. John had outsourced some of their evidence instead of paying for his own equipment, Haley couldn't match a fingerprint. If there were prints on it, there was only one man she trusted. Greg.

The image of him standing in that front yard popped back into her head. His muscle shirt had clung to his body, and so much man made every inch of her quiver with need that she'd waited too long to satisfy. He hadn't been so incredibly sexy when she'd left him, had he? Was it possible living without him for so long made him even more appealing to her? Haley hadn't thought of herself as one of those wives who was tired of her husband. Far from it. They fought. Everyone fought from time to time. It made making up so much more fun. And damn, they had a hell of a lot of making up to do.

She squirmed, the ache deep inside her turning to a nagging pressure as she sat on her bed. "Concentrate, Haley," she scolded herself. "Put the pieces together." She didn't have all the pieces though. She was sure of it.

Haley stared at her purse. She didn't need to pull out the baggie to know what the letter said. Its message was engraved in her brain.

You can run but there is nowhere to hide.

Was the message for John? If so, she was positive he'd never seen it. Roberto had to have delivered that letter. It was on the edge of her desk, facedown, after he left the office. She would swear it wasn't there before he arrived. Did that mean it was for her?

After sitting at her desk for three days without John coming to work, Haley had made a tough decision. Like John, she had no family in Omaha, no one to answer to, or who would miss her when she left. She'd printed a note for the office door that said: "On Vacation," locked the place up, and left.

Hannah McDowell could travel. She could reserve a room or an airline ticket. But if somehow John was in over his head on this latest case that he wouldn't discuss with her, then he'd put a mark on Hannah's head, too. She needed to know what happened to John before going public and announcing him a missing person. Until she had answers, going to the police, and putting Hannah McDowell in jeopardy, was a risk she wouldn't take.

If there was one thing Haley knew, it was how to get through a crisis situation. She'd left the office, headed home to her one-bedroom apartment, packed as much that would fit in her suitcase, and stuffed all of her personals in an overnight bag. She'd put the suitcase in her trunk, waited an hour, then carried out her overnight bag and set it in her passenger seat with her purse. Taking advantage of evening rush-hour traffic, she'd driven through the city and kept going. Two days later she was in Los Angeles, her hometown.

If everything was okay, John would have called by now, wondering why there was a sign on his office door. He would want to know where I was, she thought. He hadn't called. No one had called her. But then, other than her landlord and John, no one knew her personal cell phone number. Not the utility companies or any other businesses in Omaha that had required a phone number when she filled out a form. She used the same fictitious number for all forms, and made a point never to do anything that would merit needing to be called.

It was a simple life, fulfilling with her work, yet lonely as hell. Burying herself in cases helped keep the emptiness from eating her alive. It was fulfilling helping solve a crime or finding a missing person. Yet longing for her family persisted. She wasn't supposed to know Perry Pierre was dead. If she were, someone would have called and told her the program was no longer necessary. Was it just coincidence that John had disappeared at the same time that Pierre died?

Sliding off the bed, Haley walked over to the heavy curtains covering the windows. She pulled them back just far enough to peer outside. From the fifth floor she could see over the roof that shaded the entrance to the hotel. Cars idled underneath, their drivers either hurrying inside or seeking valet parking. Beyond the flat roof, the interstate looked pretty hectic, even at this hour. She was back in LA, though. Traffic was always insane.

Maybe she should head out for a bit. There wasn't anything to do here. She could answer John's e-mails, make a show that his practice was business as usual. But until she knew for sure there was still a business or if John was even alive, answering queries or scheduling appointments seemed rather pointless.

So now what? Would she simply saunter up to her old home and ring the doorbell? Or should she just walk on in?

It had been six years.

"What if there is another woman?" Just voicing the thought brought on an unexpected surge of violent daydreams. She'd rip a woman's hair out if she dared touch Greg. "God! Quit it," she snapped, dragging her fingers through her own hair. From what she could tell from keeping an eye on Greg, there were no women. He would keep his personal life out of the public eye, though.

She shoved the aggravating thoughts out of her head, or did her best to anyway. Haley pulled the curtain shut and headed for her suitcase. She'd been in Los Angeles a full day. It was time to hang up her clothes and turn her hotel room into a temporary home, since she'd reserved it for a week, then do what she came here to do—get answers.

After a shower and changing her outfit three times before deciding what to wear, she applied just a small amount of makeup, nothing flashy. Her shoulder-length hair was almost dry when she put a few curls in it and appraised the final picture in the mirror. She went for a casual look, not too sexy. At forty-five, she would never pull off the bombshell look Greg used to claim she held when they were younger. Working out regularly helped keep her tummy flat. If she had a weakness, it was her vanity. Looking good mattered to her as much as not missing any clue in an investigation.

"Not too shabby," she told herself, turning and surveying the side angle. Her tan Capris and cream-colored sleeveless blouse showed off her figure, but the outfit was also comfortable. She slipped on her tennis shoes and grabbed her purse. "At least a drive-by."

Although soon she needed to make contact. She'd researched and learned what bonding companies Greg was working with, and public records showed what court cases were no-shows. Follow that up with an anonymous call to KFA this morning, and she'd learned he was out in the field. Haley narrowed down several addresses and had lucked out, finding Greg at the first address she had driven by.

Maybe parking and walking down the street to get a better look wasn't the smartest move. She hadn't expected Greg to be standing in the front yard, doing nothing. Now he knew she was in town and if she didn't make contact, he'd hunt her down. Haley preferred hunting to being hunted.

The valet brought her car around and winked when she tipped him. No one gave her a second look or acted peculiar around her in the lobby or in front of the hotel. It was business as usual with travelers hustling around her, concerned only with their own affairs.

Haley slipped behind the wheel of her running car, relieved to be ignored, then froze when her cell phone rang. She almost knocked everything out of her purse retrieving it, nervous anticipation causing perspiration to soak her skin. She flipped open the phone and stared at a number she didn't recognize. She should send it to voice mail. She didn't even know the area code.

"Hello," she uttered, knowing she wouldn't be able to stand missing a call, then learning it was something important.

"Hannah," a male voice said.

"Who is this?" She didn't recognize the scratchy, husky-sounding baritone. Her heart pounded painfully as it moved into her throat.

"It's John, Hannah," he said.

"My God, where are you?" she practically yelled, ignoring the honking car behind her as she sat in park and gripped her steering wheel so hard that it hurt. "What number is this? What's happened?" The questions rushed out of her. "Do you know how worried I've been?"

"Hannah," John interrupted, not sounding at all like himself.

She didn't say anything, her imagination going nuts with possible reasons why he sounded so bad. Maybe he'd been tortured or kidnapped and questioned for so many hours he'd lost his voice, or possibly he'd been taken somewhere and abandoned, or perhaps he escaped and had been walking endless miles until he found a Good Samaritan who let him use a phone.

"Go home," he told her, bringing all of her thoughts to a halt. "Don't try to find me, or to run."

"John," she cut in, his words not making any sense. "What are you talking about? I can't run the office without you there."

"Go home, Hannah. Do as I say." He sounded as if he wanted to say more but didn't.

"Where are you?" she demanded. Something wasn't right, but she needed real proof John was in trouble. Her gut said he was. Although if he weren't, she'd kick his ass until he regretted the moment he decided to take off and leave her to go insane worrying about him.

"Promise me you'll go home, Hannah," he told her, ignoring her question.

"I'm not promising anything until you tell me what the hell is going on." Suddenly she was mad. John had a lot of nerve calling her after disappearing for three days and thinking he didn't have to offer some kind of believable explanation. "You've got a lot of nerve taking off like this and not telling me."

"I didn't take off," he began, but his words were cut off.

A strange sound came through the phone and her flesh crawled. Dead silence followed, making her wonder if he'd hung up. She pulled the phone from her ear long enough to confirm they were still connected. Something definitely wasn't right. John wasn't the kind of man to whine or cry out if he was hurt. Unless maybe he'd been tortured for so long his reserve was shattered.

"John?" she whispered, terrified to learn the truth. Her fingers were so damp she could barely hold the phone to her ear.

"Do as I say, Hannah," he finally said.

"John, what's going on?" she whispered, a mixture of terror and anger gripping her. It took her a minute to realize that once again a car behind her honked, demanding she move. "Please, tell me," she urged, keeping her voice calm when she wanted to scream.

"Go home. There's nowhere to hide." He hung up, the click so loud in her ear she jumped.

"Oh God," she murmured, tears burning her eyes and the world around her blurring so badly she couldn't see to move the car or get out of it.

She damn near screamed when someone tapped on her car door window. "Ma'am, are you okay?" a concerned bellhop asked.

Haley banged her knee against the steering wheel. Her cell phone slid out of her hand and fell somewhere by her feet.

"F-f-f-ine. I'm f-f-f-ine," she stammered, not bothering to roll her window down and waving him away.

"If you've changed your mind about going anywhere, I'd be more than willing to park your car again for you," he offered, still leaning and peering into her car.

She needed to regain her composure, which was harder to do with him gawking at her through the window. Haley shifted her car into drive and moved it forward, leaving the bellhop standing in the middle of the circular drive looking after her. She pulled the car to the end of the drive and parked it again, dragging in a deep breath but shaking so terribly she needed a minute before she could drive.

"My phone," she announced to herself, leaning forward and struggling against her steering wheel while dragging her fingers over the floor until she found it. Picking it up, she flipped it open again and pushed the numbers to place her next call. It was already ringing when she put it to her ear.

There wasn't time to prepare what she would say when someone answered. "Greg King," he answered, his deep, soothing baritone washing over her and creating a warmth inside her that she wasn't ready for.

"Who is this?" he demanded.

Haley opened her mouth but then froze. She couldn't speak to him on the phone. What the hell had she been thinking?

She snapped the phone shut, closing it as he said something else, although she didn't catch what it was. He hadn't changed his personal cell phone number. Haley stared at her phone, holding it in her palm, then glancing out her window when a car drove by. The bellhops stood at the curb. If she stayed here much longer, they would come check on her again. And the luxury hotel that up until a few moments ago had seemed so safe and comforting to her now seemed as dangerous as everything else in her world.

Something was wrong with John. He was alive. Wherever he was, his kidnappers hadn't blocked his number. It was a common trick used to antagonize whoever was being called. More than likely John had called from a track phone. The area code probably didn't match wherever he was, although she'd trace the number as soon as she could to verify. The number intentionally wasn't blocked to let her know they didn't view her as a threat. It was an insult. She would have to show whoever had John that they'd judged her poorly.

"Well hell," she sighed, staring at her phone for a moment before sliding it into her purse. She hadn't blocked her number when she'd called Greg. He hadn't called her back, but he now knew her private cell phone number. "He'll call unless you call him back."

After taking several deep, cleansing breaths, she put her car into gear and headed out onto the street, merging in with traffic. Greg didn't call her back. But he would. Trouble was brewing all around her; she needed her head on straight if she was to figure out what the hell was going on. It would be smart to seek Greg out soon so she'd be at the advantage and as prepared as she could be. If she waited for him to call her, she'd be caught off guard whenever he did.

The possibility existed that he didn't want to get back with her. After all, if he recognized her this morning, and if he'd learned where she lived for the past six years, then he would know her area code. He would know she was the one who had called him just now. And he wasn't trying to return the call, to force her to talk to him after all these years. She drove in silence, barely noticing the traffic. She was confused, worried, and angry.

Her gut told her how it was. And her gut was usually right. Greg was staring at his phone right now, trying to figure out why she'd just called. He missed the hell out of her and couldn't wait to see her. Haley had to believe that was how it was, or she'd go nuts.

Chapter 3

"Greg, are you awake?" Natasha King, Greg's niece and KFA's office manager, stuck her head in around his bedroom door. "There's someone here to see you."

"I'm busy." Greg had set his computer up so he faced his door and anyone entering his bedroom couldn't immediately see his monitor. It gave him the two seconds necessary to close anything he didn't want anyone else seeing.

"She said she went to high school with you and Aunt Haley." Natasha wrinkled her nose, knowing it was taboo mentioning Haley's name in his home.

No one brought up his wife. Greg thought about her constantly, but conversations about her were too difficult, too complicated. There were days when it was damn hard allowing everyone to believe he didn't know where she was. Not one day had passed since his wife left when he didn't know exactly where she was.

Greg switched back to the Google Earth program on his screen, focusing on the small house where Haley had lived in Omaha, Nebraska, for the past six years. He didn't close out the other screen, though, the reverse lookup program he'd just used to determine who owned the cell phone number that had just called him.

Hannah McDowell.

It was less difficult today knowing Haley was so far away than it once had been. But the protector in him, the controlling edge that ran hot in his veins, wouldn't allow a day to pass without making sure she was okay, safe, and not dating anyone. Today that part of him that needed to know she was all right boiled out of control inside him.

"What's her name?" Greg glanced at his cell phone, which he'd put back on his desk next to his computer. Why did Haley just call him and hang up? Was it a sign, a message he was supposed to figure out? Or had something else caused her to hang up without speaking?

"Samantha Wilson. She says she is Jason Wilson's sister," Natasha told him.

"What does she want?"

"She wants us to bring in her brother."

"She wants her brother back in jail?" Greg frowned, seriously not wanting to deal with this right now. "Have Marc or Jake talk to her."

"She insists on talking to you."

Greg focused on his phone. They were already planning on going after Jason Wilson. But his sister showing up, asking them to bring him in, didn't make sense. Greg might have taken a bang to the head, but he wasn't that out of it. Family didn't help him bring in fugitive relatives. They fought him, helped hide their relatives, and lied through their teeth to prevent him from putting their loved ones back behind bars.

Drug lords were trying to skip town, and probably the country. Family members of fugitives usually wanted to cry on his shoulder. But Greg wouldn't be able to think straight until he understood what Haley was up to. He glanced over his monitor at his niece. Greg had never thought much of his deadbeat brother. Natasha, his only child, was perfect in every way: a college graduate, a black belt in karate, and absolutely gorgeous. Greg often thought of her as the daughter he never had.

"She's not going to leave until you speak to her." Natasha crossed her arms over her chest, giving her uncle a look that told him she wouldn't leave him alone until he talked to Samantha Wilson.

"Fine. I'll talk to her," he conceded, glaring at his phone as he slid his office chair away from his desk. He fingered his private cell for a moment before leaving it on his desk as he headed out of his room.

There were days when he missed Haley so much he couldn't think straight. There were also times when he hated her for going after one of the biggest drug lords on the street at that time. Sometimes he hated himself for not packing up the boys and going with her into the Witness Protection Program.

Greg and Haley had fought about her testifying for weeks before she had decided to do it. She'd told him she couldn't live with herself if Perry Pierre walked and continued shoveling deadly drugs into the school system. Their boys had been nineteen and seventeen when she had left and she'd told Greg there were so many other children out there as good as their boys who deserved a shot at life without drugs.

Haley had possessed his heart every minute she'd been gone. There were days he didn't want to continue without her. Especially right now. Haley was here in LA. He didn't want to deal with MOs, potential clients, or anything else other than heading out the door, hitting the streets, and finding Haley.

Images of her standing on the curb in the shadows of dawn filled his head. She'd looked good. Really good. Hot as hell. Greg had dated a lot right after Haley left, primarily because he hoped she would get jealous and tell the Witness Protection Program to go to hell and let him protect her. His amateur sleuth of a wife would have kept an eye on him just as he did with her. It hadn't taken long to forget other women and bury himself in work, not having time or interest in any lady who came around. None of them had looked as sexy as Haley had this morning.

"This is Samantha Wilson," Natasha said with a wave of her hand as Greg followed her into the office.

He studied the woman who turned from one of the many

windows that lined the walls. The blinds hanging over them were opened, letting in the sun and offering a full view of the street out front. Still distracted by thoughts of Haley, he stopped just inside the doorway of the renovated enclosed front porch to his home that now served as the KFA office.

"I saw you bring in Pedro Gutierrez this morning." Samantha Wilson extended her hand, her long, bright pink fingernails looking like tiny weapons pointed directly at him. Her halter top and short shorts barely covered her bronzed, well-maintained body. It looked like she worked hard and had paid decent money to have a perfect body at her age. And she didn't have a problem showing off as much of it as she legally could. High-heeled sandals helped display her long, slender legs.

"Did you now?" Greg shook her hand, barely remembering the woman who claimed to have gone to high school with him. She looked like so many women her age, overly made up and trying too damn hard to look ten years younger, when her own age was more attractive to most men.

"Yes, I did." Samantha paused when Marc and Jake entered the large office. The flicker of interest in her green eyes was a bit too obvious as she watched Greg's sons the way a cougar watched her prey before pouncing and devouring. "I want you to find and bring in my younger brother, Jason Wilson, the same way you brought in Pedro."

Marc and Jake stopped in their tracks, gawking at her. She offered Greg a triumphant smile, as if she believed none of them would turn her down. Maybe she didn't understand that normal people tried to protect their relatives and keep them out of jail instead of trying to put them behind bars.

"When did you see me this morning?" Greg asked.

"I was across the street when you chased Pedro out of his home. That was so brave and daring of you," she purred, then looked around the glass-walled office. "Where is Haley? You two are still together, aren't you?"

For someone who knew enough about him to find him on

the job, Samantha made a show of not knowing where his wife was. Something was seriously wrong with this picture.

"She's not here," Greg said, unwilling to elaborate if Samantha wanted to create an image of herself as a cold, heartless, stupid woman. "And you were at Pedro's?" he pressed. "I don't remember seeing you. Were you dressed like you are now?"

"No. I still wore my pink jogging suit," she offered, giving him too wide of a smile for it to appear sincere. "I swear you saw me. You looked right at me. I thought you would come talk to me. Although, I admit, if you had you would have caught me blushing like a schoolgirl knowing the great Greg King remembered me after all these years." She dragged her painted nails down her chest to her breasts, as if encouraging all eyes to look there.

Somehow she'd learned about Haley being in town. That knowledge alone piqued his interest. Her very satisfied grin made her look as if she believed she'd backed him into a corner. Samantha believed that telling him that she had been wearing Haley's outfit this morning, and had been in the exact same location, would be enough to make him jump through hoops to do whatever she wanted. She knew why Haley had been standing there and thought toying with Greg would get her what she wanted. Greg didn't like this game and had no intention of falling for her bait.

"I didn't see you," Greg said bluntly. "I'm sorry if you expected a reunion earlier this morning, Samantha, but we were a bit busy."

Samantha looked away first, licking her lips and taking her time eyeballing every inch of his sons, while sucking in a deep breath and showing off as much cleavage as her skintight halter top would allow.

"Call me Sam," she breathed, giving him the same once-over she had just given his sons. "I'm sure you're incredibly busy, but you really have to find my brother. I'll pay you very well for your time."

He would also bet she didn't want her brother back in jail

but came here using that line in order to gain some other kind of information. His head started pounding worse than it had a few minutes ago. Samantha, or Sam, looked more interested in fucking his sons than she did in convincing Greg to find her brother. She knew Haley had been across the street this morning. Greg needed Sam out of there so he could figure out the connection.

"We take most of our cases from bondsmen," he said, and walked over to the double glass doors that were open to the public during business hours. "Maybe you should hire a private investigator." He reached to open the doors and escort her out of his office.

"I do believe you're a licensed private investigator," Sam announced, grinning triumphantly as she waved her fingernails toward the certificate hanging on the wall behind Natasha's desk. "Bondsmen give you, what? Ten percent of the bond? So you would get fifteen hundred dollars for bringing in my brother, since his bond is set at fifteen thousand. I'll give you two thousand right now and another grand when you turn him over to the police." She opened her purse, pulling out her wallet, then opening it, showing off a thick stack of bills. "That's twice the income you would make from a bondsman."

"That isn't necessary." Greg shook his head and crossed his arms over his chest. He couldn't begin to think what this woman had to do with Haley.

Sam turned her hungry look on him, her lashes heavy with mascara. They fluttered as she dropped her gaze to his shoulders and arms, almost looking as if she were sizing him up. The only way he'd get her out of his office was to throw her over his shoulder and toss her out. The thought lost its appeal when he considered the fact that she might enjoy it a bit too much. But the sooner Sam left, the sooner he could learn more about Haley, and why Sam knew she was at the scene this morning.

"We don't have time to take on another client. Our rules are first come, first served. Now if you would like to make an appointment." Greg stalked across the office to Natasha's desk, where she sat watching them warily.

Jake and Marc kept their eyes on him, too. Only because he was lying to Sam as much as she was lying to him. His sons would stay quiet. They understood, or at least thought they did. He didn't know Sam well enough to know if she was a good actress or a pawn. Greg needed to know the real reason why she had just walked through his door. Greg wanted her gone but really wanted to know why she came here believing she could toss lies at him and he'd believe them. Either she hadn't done her research or whoever sent her here was an idiot.

"The rules are, there are no rules." Samantha quoted a headline that was framed next to his certificates on the wall behind Natasha's desk.

"There are always rules," Greg snapped. He didn't agree with the article that stated he had switched careers so he could break the rules and still get his man, but Haley had clipped it, framing it since it was about him. It was written by a jealous reporter, encouraged by city officials who believed Greg was more dangerous out of uniform. Like the laws of Los Angeles suffered because he dressed in jeans and a T-shirt these days. "Some people may feel they're more powerful if they can bend the laws designed to make this country great, but I'm not one of them," he informed Sam, hearing himself repeat what he'd told his wife years ago when she had hung the article about him on the wall. "What you're really saying is you're willing to break the rules. I'm curious to know why. Why are you really here, Ms. Wilson?"

"It's Sam. And like I would tell a cop I'm going to break the rules." Sam brushed her light brown hair off her forehead. She was sweating, which made her tanned skin glow. She tugged her halter top and covered the glimpse of her flat belly as she pulled it over her shorts. The material went taut over her large breasts. "And I'm telling you the truth," she stressed. "I want you to bring in my brother."

"I never said you weren't telling the truth," Greg said,

yanking her attention from his sons back to him. "You pointed out the article, not me." He continued across the room to the door leading into the rest of his home, the door with the sign on it that said: Private.

"Why do you want us to find your brother?" Marc leaned against Natasha's desk. He watched Sam with alert blue eyes as she moved to the large windows that overlooked the ocean. Marc didn't give her time to answer but pressed further. "We're not cheap, and most family members like their relatives to be out of prison, not behind bars. Your brother missed his court date. He's already done time and now is looking at facing another sentencing if convicted of current charges he may, or may not, be guilty of. Apparently going back to prison doesn't appeal to him, so he's run. Why do you want him back behind bars?"

"My brother is out there, hiding in the streets!" Sam wailed, spinning around and causing her shoulder-length light brown hair to fan over her golden shoulders. Her confident expression suddenly turned frantic. "He won't survive and I don't want him dead. You would all do anything to protect each other. I'm the same way with my family. He won't be in prison forever, but he'll be alive. He was an idiot to run. He needs to be incarcerated where he's safe."

"Safe from whom?" Jake asked the question that was at the tip of Greg's tongue. Narrowing his gaze on Sam, fists at his sides, Jake lowered his voice. Either he was going for intimidation or he was trying to prove he was the cockier, wilder, and more dangerous of the King boys. "We only hunt on the side of the law," he added.

"You've got to trust me. I'll pay whatever price you say," she pleaded. There was too much urgency in her tone. If she picked up on all of them noticing, it possibly explained why she blew out a breath, noticeably relaxing, and smiled at Greg. Her white teeth glowed against her tanned face. "You would do the same thing if one of your boys were in the predicament my brother is in." She nodded to Marc and Jake, her high heels clicking against the hardwood floor when she walked between the two of them. "Jason is only safe behind bars; otherwise they'll kill him. Tell me where to sign, or whatever you do to get the ball rolling, and I'll pay you whatever amount you say."

"You're going to tell me why your brother is safer locked up than he is roaming the streets." Greg watched a flicker of emotion dance in her green eyes. "Who sent you here, *Sam*?" he demanded, stressing her first name.

It didn't surprise him when she didn't respond right away, or look surprised by the question. "I'll pay you twice whatever you were about to charge me for you not to ask me that question again," she said finally.

"Not interested. It was good seeing you again, Sam. Sorry we can't help you."

As persistent as she'd been, Greg was surprised when she left without more of a fight. He was also relieved. More than likely Sam would head back to whoever sent her and share the conversation she had and gain more ammunition to return with at a later date. Another time, he and his sons might have followed her. Greg didn't care about Sam as much as he did Haley. He headed out of the office before Marc, Jake, and Natasha gave him the third degree. The kitchen still held on to the heavy aroma of the chili they'd made the night before. After pouring coffee, he started for his bedroom when his younger son appeared in the doorway.

"Okay. Explain to me why you just turned down all that cash?" At twenty-three, Jake still didn't show an ounce of drive toward doing anything serious with his life. The boy loved money, though, and all the things he could do with it. "No bondsman would pay us half what she is offering to bring in her brother."

"We make good money," Greg reminded his son and blew on the steaming coffee.

King Fugitive Apprehension had one of the best reputa-

tions in California. Greg was proud of the business he'd built
from scratch after retiring from the LAPD. Most cops when
they retired got potbellies while sitting around drinking beer
and swapping stories with other washed-up cops. Greg knew,
even when he was still wet behind the ears and their future
glowed with excitement and dreams of their golden years,
that he wouldn't take retirement easy. Haley had wanted to
be part of KFA, something they got to the point of arguing
about daily. He wouldn't risk losing her. The thought of Haley
taking a bullet sickened him. It was rather ironic that in the
end, he had lost her because of her craving for detective
work, just not how he'd feared he would.

Greg was damn good at reading people; it was second nature after being a cop for twenty years. He had never guessed
Haley was playing private dick in the public schools.

If he had, he would have stopped her in her tracks. Haley
didn't know she had been following one of the deadliest drug
dealers in the city. Greg had had a few run-ins with Perry
Pierre before he'd been arrested thanks to Haley's carrying a
wire. He had been a sick, evil motherfucker, who was also incredibly intelligent and had enough crooked lawyers working
on his side to keep him out of Greg's grasp. Perry hadn't anticipated that an innocent-appearing teacher's aide would be
his downfall, though. Greg downed more of his coffee, aware
that he had ignored his son while he got lost in his thoughts.

Marc pushed his way through the doorway and around his
younger brother, who was taller and bigger than he was. Marc
had more of his mother's features and was as much a lady-killer
as his brother.

"She's gone. But she'll be back." Marc walked over to the
refrigerator. "I say we hunt down her brother. And yes," he said
before Greg could point out what he'd just said to Jake, "she's
lying through her perfectly straight, white teeth." Marc pulled
out bacon, eggs, and butter, holding them to his chest when he
straightened. "Pedro and Jason didn't show up for court, and

were ready to run. Something is going down, and I think Sam knows what it is. It's got her scared to death and she is crying out for help."

"Yup," Greg said, continuing to sip his coffee. It wasn't an accident that Sam Wilson had sauntered into his life after all these years. She wasn't across the street at Pedro's this morning. Which meant she knew Haley was there. Which meant someone had told her Haley was there. Greg stalked back to his bedroom, not saying a word to his sons. He needed answers.

He didn't waste time. Closing his bedroom door, he grabbed his phone. Greg pushed the buttons to call back the number that had hung up on him earlier.

His fingers clamped around the phone as he held it to his ear and listened to it ring, once, twice, three times. It continued ringing, not going to voice mail. Greg's insides tightened, the throbbing in the back of his neck and exhaustion from being up all night not holding a flame to the overwhelming sensation eating at him that he needed to find Haley right away.

She didn't answer. He paced his floor, trying to see the entire picture when he only had a few puzzle pieces to work with. Sitting at his desk, he went over the paperwork Margaret Young had left them. He did a search on Jason Wilson, then Googled Samantha Wilson. He paced some more. Nothing he pulled up helped him, or lessened the headache that was threatening to turn into a migraine.

Grabbing his phone, he dialed Haley's number again. He wasn't sure how many times the phone rang before his office door suddenly swung open. Greg spun around, ready to unleash his frustrations on whoever dared barge in on him. He ended the call, slamming his phone down on his desk.

"The door was closed for a reason," he snarled at his older son, daring Marc to come back at him with a snide remark. Greg had a lot of energy all of a sudden that needed a channel; knocking his son down a few notches when he simply cocked an eyebrow at him sounded like a damn good idea to him.

"She's back," Marc said.

Greg leapt for the door, for a moment believing his son was talking about Haley. Sanity barely kicked in when Greg heard Sam talking in the outer room where Natasha was still at her desk. He gripped the door, making a show of closing it. Marc shifted his weight from one leg to the other, not moving but watching his father.

"And that merited barging in on me?" Greg muttered under his breath.

"I thought so," Marc said slowly, sounding unusually calm and in control, which made him even more aggravating. "Sam just told me Mom was in danger."

Greg needed to strike out. If he could just hit something, destroy it, possibly he would then be able to wrap his mind around the events crashing in around him one after the other. Nothing pissed him off more than someone else having more information than he did. And he wasn't being given enough time to learn what was going on. Damn Haley for not answering his call. She had sought him out. Something was wrong. She better have a real good reason for not answering when he called her back.

"Dad," Marc said, holding on to that annoyingly calm tone of his. "Dad," he repeated, touching Greg's arm.

Greg turned from Marc and pounded his fist into the wall. Jake stuck his head around the almost-closed door, pushing it open far enough to peer at both of them.

"We cool?" Jake asked.

"Do I look cool?" Greg snapped.

"No. You look like you're ready to blow a gasket." Marc glanced at his younger brother before giving their father an appraising look. "Maybe you should sit down."

Greg took a deep breath and said, "I'm fine." The last thing Greg would have was his boys worrying about him.

Heading away from them and back to his desk, he glared at his cell phone, silently willing it to ring and Haley to be on the line ready with explanations as to why she was back in his life.

"Are you not going to talk to her?" Marc asked.

Greg scrubbed his head with his hand, peering at his sons as they stared at him, waiting for his go-ahead. As much as it tortured him over the years having Haley out of his life, his sons had suffered, too.

Your mother just tried to call me. The words were right there on the tip of his tongue. Marc and Jake stared at him, waiting for him to speak. No matter that his sons were grown men, they were still his boys. He wouldn't get their hopes up, and seeing their expectant expressions, Greg wouldn't destroy that by telling them something when he didn't have all the facts.

"Let's go see what this lady wants," he said, fighting for composure as he walked around his sons. If they thought he had something else to say to them and held back that was just too damn bad.

Greg entered the office, focusing on Sam Wilson. Although still decked out in her scanty outfit with her long, tan legs nicely shown off in the high heels she wore, when Sam lifted her gaze to his everything about her had changed.

"I can't go through with this," she whispered, her eyes welling up with tears as she spoke.

Greg wouldn't dwell on how many women had turned to him, tears in their eyes, and told him they couldn't take it anymore, only to turn traitor the first chance they got. In his line of work he'd seen it all.

He stood there, relaxing his features and keeping one thing in mind. Whether she knew it or not, Sam was a link to Haley.

"What can't you take anymore?" Greg asked.

"I was told to come tell you everything I said. I was told if I didn't, they would kill my brother."

"Who are they?" Greg asked, something telling him possibly for the first time she said the truth. He still didn't trust her.

A tear slid down her cheek, black from her eyeliner. It stained her skin as her lower lip started quivering and she shook her head. "I don't know," she said.

Greg wasn't in the mood for dramatics. "You don't know who told you to come over here," he muttered. If this was her attempt at acting, she really sucked at it. He'd seen a lot better.

"Why did you say our mom was in danger?" Marc stepped around his father, cutting in with his hands on his hips. "You'd be smart to tell us what you know right now."

Sam blinked, dabbing at her face with her fingers, and attempted grinning at Marc. Greg leaned against the edge of Natasha's desk, watching Marc take on this woman. He wouldn't have opened with questions about Haley. If Sam had already brought up Haley, she knew her to be an open wound with all of them. Marc just proved that by demanding to know why she'd spoken about his mom. Asking her anything about Haley would leave them vulnerable to lies and pain. Greg wouldn't give Sam that edge and something told him that that was exactly what she hoped to gain. Sam wanted to distract them with information, which would probably be false, about Haley. Now to find out why.

"I don't know a lot about her, but she must be in some kind of predicament," Sam said quietly. "Why else would they tell me to say I was at your crime scene?"

Greg accepted the mug of coffee Natasha offered him and watched Sam over the rim as he sipped. She looked away first, glancing down at her hands as she fidgeted and shifted her weight. Her entire persona had changed since she'd returned.

"Why would saying you were where we were make us think that had anything to do with our mother?" Marc asked.

Sam's green eyes looked rather bloodshot with her makeup smudged. She licked her lips and pressed them together, probably brainstorming for a believable answer.

"I was told to ask how Haley was doing, to pretend I didn't know she didn't live here." Sam actually blushed and focused on her fingernails as she continued, appearing apprehensive about continuing, almost as if she was worried about offending them. "And so when I was told to say I saw you this morning, and to tell you I wore a jogging outfit, and to say you looked right at me, I knew you probably saw someone." She glanced up, offering a small smile as she ran her finger under her eyes, removing the black smear that was there. "Could I get something to drink, please?"

If Greg asked Natasha to get Sam coffee, she'd just as soon pour it down the sink as oblige. His niece had no problem reminding any of them she was not their servant. Natasha didn't move when Greg walked around her desk, behind her chair, to the coffee pot. Sam smiled gratefully when he handed her a Styrofoam cup of coffee.

"Everyone thinks I'm an idiot, but I tell you, the only idiots are those who judge someone by how they look, and not by what's in their mind. Wouldn't you agree, Greg?"

"I'm more concerned with if you don't know who gave you your instructions, what compelled you to follow them?" Greg left her in the middle of the office and moved to lean against the window sill.

Natasha leaned in her office chair, watching Sam with a skeptical look on her face. Marc and Jake remained at the doorway leading into the house. Marc scowled, his arms crossed over his chest, and Jake leaned against the wall, his thumbs tucked into his jeans pockets. Sam might not have realized her actions but she was positioned so all of them could watch her, and gather their impressions. Each of them would see her at a slightly different angle. Greg would question his sons and niece later for their impressions of her.

"I told you already." Sam blew on her coffee. "They will hurt my brother if I don't do as they say."

"And you know this how?"

She shot him a pensive stare, watching him a moment before answering. "They told me he would die if I didn't come to you and say what they wanted."

All Greg gathered at the moment was that Sam wasn't an amateur. There probably wasn't a lick of truth in anything she said, which would mean they still didn't have a clue why she was here.

Sam drank some of her coffee, leaving a red lip stain on the cup when she held it in her hand. "My little brother isn't a saint, but he isn't a bad person, either. He made some mistakes and got caught, but now, in the hands of these people, he will die if I don't do as they say."

"And how do you know this?" Marc asked.

Instead of acknowledging Marc, Sam walked up to Greg and placed her cup on the desk next to him, then dug through her purse. She pulled out a piece of paper, which was folded in half, then folded again. Unfolding it, she held it up for him to see. Marc and Jake moved closer, focusing on the typed message on the paper. Sam pointed at the bottom of the message with her long painted fingernail.

"Jason told me once that if he were to really make it as a businessman in this town he would have to take down The Bird. The only reason I remember him saying that was because it sounded so weird. Why would anyone want to take down a bird? I figured out for myself that The Bird was a person and not a creature."

Greg focused on the letter. Everything she'd just told them was laid out numerically, in steps, as instructions of what she would say when she arrived here. The letter stated that if she didn't do exactly what she was told, she would never see her brother again. At the bottom of the page in tall, flowing cursive was one word—"Bird." Any criminal in Los Angeles knew the most dangerous, most successful hit man in the entire country was known simply as The Bird.

Greg needed to find Haley immediately.

Chapter 4

Haley shouldn't be here. It was stupid thinking that driving past the house where she and Greg had raised their boys, and where he still lived with both of them, would help her clear her head. After the quick drive-by, seeing a new-looking black Avalanche in the driveway and the porch now closed in, appearing to have been converted into another room, Haley refused to let herself drive by again. She'd kept going, passing the grocery store where once she'd known everyone who worked there, the small strip mall where she and Greg used to take the boys for ice cream and to rent movies. For such a huge city, the neighborhood where they raised their boys hadn't changed all that much in the years since she'd been gone.

"You're torturing yourself," she told herself when she pulled into the small, secluded parking lot and parked her car in a spot facing the football field.

It seemed a thousand years ago. Haley could still see Greg running across that field, the crowd cheering when he made a touchdown. He'd been her high school sweetheart, her husband, and the father of her children.

"He's still your husband." She swallowed the lump in her throat, wondering for the hundredth time how life would be now if she'd never left. She would have won the argument about working with him but where would that have gotten them?

Would it have brought them closer? Would he have driven them away with his overprotective nature?

Although at the moment, she would love it if he'd appear out of nowhere, yank her against that virile body of his, and make her promise never to leave him again. The thought made her smile, but then she laughed. Greg would never do that. There wasn't an ounce of mushiness in the man. His all-man, hard, and determined nature had always turned her on, but when she thought about it, those moments when she saw the man underneath all that hard muscle and he-man attitude were the ones she'd always cherish. Like when she'd birthed their sons. The look on his face, the way he'd stared from her to their babies with awe and admiration, all his defenses down, were moments she'd never forget.

There were other times. She remembered she hadn't seen this side of him until their first Christmas after they'd been married. Greg truly loved buying gifts for her, and the boys when they'd appeared in their lives later. Every Christmas this over-sized elf, full of mischief and surprises, surfaced. Haley was sure the first time she'd ever heard him giggle was one night when he thought he'd successfully hidden presents from her.

Greg also loved nature. He'd never come out and admitted it, but when he'd bought his first motorcycle and took her out for a ride, the peaceful expression that finally covered his face and erased all the tension from his body was an image she'd never forgotten. Those bike rides turned into family affairs when their boys were old enough to ride. Greg was so gallant, so manly, and so awesome with his traditional nature, she'd fallen in love with him all over again with each ride. He would sweep her into his arms when they traipsed across a meadow to the perfect picnic spot and came upon a creek. He would always help her onto his motorcycle before getting on himself. And even the small things, like making a plate for her instead of expecting her to make both their plates, had added up and made him the perfect man.

A perfect man she hadn't seen in six years. All for the sake of justice and insuring he and Marc and Jake stayed alive. Had keeping them alive destroyed any chances she and Greg might have to rekindle their relationship?

Lord. Haley pulled herself out of her meandering memories and stared at the football field another moment before getting out of her car. She hadn't given any thought to her direction until she realized she'd walked behind the field to a low piece of land that used to be secluded by a thick grove of trees. Instinctively, she patted the small handgun she'd slid into her pocket. It was hard to say when the trees had gone, but the apartment complex with the large fence differentiating its property from the high school's wasn't there when she and Greg went to school here.

Glancing around, she was pretty sure she wasn't trespassing. She was very sure the heat would soak her clothes with sweat and leave them stuck to her body and itchy. Already she felt drops of perspiration bead between her breasts. Her attention rested on the large cement slab, which was actually the top of a sewage reservoir. Haley hurried to it, finding herself in the shade of several trees remaining from the many that used to be here.

"It's the same place." A rush of excitement surged through her insides.

She sat at the edge of the cement, stretching her legs down the incline. Glancing both ways, she took in the length of the huge cement ditch that was actually a sewer runoff. Heat rose off the cement, and she stared in the direction where she knew there was a place kids would walk into an underground sewage tunnel. It had grossed her out as a teenager, although a lot of the kids would go there to get laid, or on dares. No one was around and she wondered if kids at the high school today still came here to hang out. More than likely not, with computers and cell phones having ended the need to find secluded areas like this to have uninterrupted conversations.

Right there, on the slab where she sat, was where Greg had

asked her to go steady. It was where he first kissed her. It was where they'd both said they loved each other for the first time. She adjusted herself, the metal of her gun already growing warm and her clothing not enough protection to keep it from irritating her skin.

"Haley." A deep voice behind her interrupted the silence.

Haley jumped, startled and instantly mad at herself for daydreaming. She leapt to her feet but lost her footing, and started sliding down the steep cement incline. "Stop!" she yelled, slashing out with her hand when someone gripped her from behind, lifting her off the ground. "Let me go! No!"

Powerful hands turned her around, but Haley shoved herself free and pulled her gun at the same time.

Haley stared into Gregs piercing blue eyes that were as radiant and compelling as she remembered. Her breath caught in her throat and she swore her heart stopped beating.

"You left to keep me alive and now you return to kill me?" Greg tilted his head slightly as his eyes drifted from her face to her gun. He wasn't smiling.

"No," she breathed, feeling a rush of heat that had nothing to do with the temperature outside, and she lowered her gun. "You startled me," she snapped, sucking in a deep breath. She'd done the right thing. Of all people, Greg would be the first to agree. She'd been overpowered from behind and there wasn't time to determine if they were friend or foe. She'd defended herself.

"What are you doing here?" he asked.

Haley slid her gun back into her pocket, then let her gaze travel up his body. She had a much closer view of all that muscle and intense, raw masculinity now than she had had this morning. He didn't wear a muscle T-shirt anymore, but instead a pullover, short-sleeved shirt, the kind she'd always loved seeing him in. It was solid blue, which accentuated those blue eyes. And it fit as if it were made for him, not too tight, but not so loose she couldn't tell muscles rippled and flexed underneath.

Her heart continually missed beats, and if he'd asked her what two and two was at the moment, she wasn't sure she'd be able to respond. She swore that along with more muscles, Greg seemed taller as well. And he'd been six feet five inches when she'd left six years ago. Greg was living, breathing proof there were men out there who most definitely improved with age.

"I asked you a question. Are you okay?"

Haley's mouth was too dry. She moistened her lips and met those incredibly blue eyes. Greg looked more irritated than happy to see her.

She blinked, needing to focus. The worst thing she could do was let Greg see that after all these years, he was her biggest weakness. She'd stood up to bad men before who were built like Greg, and a hell of a lot meaner. Nonetheless, his callous manner and penetrating stare made her heart swell painfully.

"You don't want me here?" she asked, managing not to let her voice crack. If her worst nightmares were about to come true, she'd be damned if Greg saw her break down and cry over it.

"I meant, what are you doing here?" He tapped his shoe on the edge of the slab cement. "Come here to reminisce, darling?" His voice deepened with his second question, and when she looked at his eyes again, the irritation was definitely no longer there. Instead something smoldered with heat she ached to embrace.

"I, well, I . . ."

Greg didn't make her suffer through trying to find an answer but pulled her into his arms, not saying another word. He held her against his virile body, lifting her so her feet dangled against his legs. When he kissed her, her entire world toppled to the side, taking her with it.

Haley couldn't think. It was as if every worry in her head, everything in her world, just disappeared and all that existed was those muscular arms wrapped around her and his warm body pressed against hers. Greg didn't ask permission, he didn't hesitate, and he didn't waste time devouring her, as if six years hadn't passed since they'd last seen each other.

There had been many nights when she'd dreamed of being

in his arms. Just as many nights were haunted with night-mares over the same man. She'd imagined their reconciliation being anywhere from incredibly erotic to cruel and bloody. Over the years Haley had contemplated whether a reunion would ever even occur. In her sane moments she couldn't imagine ending up with anyone other than Greg. He was her man. She'd returned to the spot where they'd often come to make love. During high school they always managed to find each other here. Haley had come there with hopes of clearing her head and Greg had found her once again.

But of course he would. She was his other half. They might have continued without each other for six years. But they hadn't truly lived.

He moved his large hand up her back, pushing her shirt higher and dragging his fingers through her hair. His touch ignited sensations that had been dormant for years, proving to her she was once again alive. He forced her head back so he could deepen the kiss and her insides heated to feverish levels. He cupped her ass with his other hand, lifting her even more and pressing her against all that hard-packed muscle. Her breasts swelled and ached, her nipples puckered as they were smashed against his steel body. Every inch of her grew hypersensitive, the nerve endings in her body growing acutely aware of everywhere he touched her. Need simmered and reached a boiling point before she could catch her breath.

Greg stroked her ass, his fingers brushing dangerously close to her pussy, which started throbbing almost painfully. A heavy fog of lust settled in her brain. She wanted him. Right here. Right now. Greg was her husband. They could make love. It wouldn't be wrong. There wasn't any reason to hold back, to break things off before they became serious. You couldn't get more serious than married.

That thought alone told her she needed to hit the breaks and fast.

"Wait," she gasped, turning her head away as sanity tried to slowly crawl through the sensual fog.

Haley managed to focus and immediately frowned at the incredibly satisfied expression on Greg's face. Her arms were clasped around his neck and she was holding on tight. God, she never wanted to let go.

"Put me down." She moved her hands over his shoulders, acutely aware of the rippling muscles beneath his shirt. When he relaxed his grip, she slid down the length of his body until her feet reached the ground. "That was one hell of a greeting."

"I figured it was best to get it out of the way." Greg took a step back, adjusting his blue shirt and stretching the fabric over roped muscle. He allowed his gaze to travel down her body. "Now, what's wrong?"

"Why do you think something is wrong?" A torrential wave of emotions attacked her, making it impossible to focus. There would be plenty of time, very soon, to figure out why John had left. She didn't want one intoxicating kiss to be the end of their initial reunion. "Do you think I would come running to you only if there was a problem?"

The corner of Greg's mouth twitched when his attention returned to her face. "That and a whole lot more, sweetheart. I plan on giving you everything very soon." His tone was low, heated and seductive.

And just like that, her body went soft as if preparing itself for him. She didn't know if she should run away or tell him to find the nearest room. He'd always had that kind of effect on her.

Haley looked away first, adjusting her shirt and combing her hair with her fingers in an effort to gather control. "And to think I was willing to make love right here."

His groan helped her regain a handle on the situation. She'd played this moment out many times in her head.

"But you're right. We should talk." She adjusted her capris and her sleeveless sweater again.

Greg's little half smile of his she used to find so damn sexy appeared. "Damn, babe, you really look good."

"Thank you," she murmured, feeling herself grow enflamed. She wanted him so badly she wasn't sure she could talk. "The first thing I noticed this morning was how much more muscular you are."

Something shifted in his expression she didn't understand, but disappeared almost immediately. "I've always loved your natural hair color. Did you change it from blonde to keep all the guys away?"

"Are you suggesting I wouldn't attract them looking like this?"

This time his growl was fiercer as he grabbed her. He tangled his long fingers in her hair until he held her head in place, tilting it back and gazing down at her. His free hand moved to her neck and he began stroking her tender flesh.

"You don't want to start a fight by telling me about all your old boyfriends."

"There are no old or current boyfriends."

"Good." Someone else might be nervous with a man the size of Greg holding her as he did. "I don't want to fight, Haley."

"Perry Pierre is dead," she blurted, and although all Greg did was blink, she knew it was information he didn't already know. "I'm sure we'll find time to fight at some point in our lives."

"So you're coming home?"

"Where else would I go?" She smiled up at him and watched Greg's eyes darken. "I've missed you and the boys."

This time when his lips met hers, he took his time savoring her. He still gripped her so she couldn't move her head. Haley wanted to push him to the ground, take over, and relearn every inch of his body.

She hated confinement, being controlled, and Greg would know that better than anyone. She didn't sense hostility, or even a challenge. Something told her enough time had passed that there might be small things about each other that were no longer foremost on their minds. Greg was the protector, the provider, and had always been determined to make sure her life was perfect with everything she needed. At least that was what he believed he had been doing. Haley saw that now so much clearer than she had six years ago.

Hopefully they were both a bit wiser, a bit more willing to hear each other. They'd been through a lot and she didn't expect everything to be back to the way it used to be without a hitch. Haley didn't want it back the way it used to be. She wanted it better.

One thing that was obvious. Greg was visibly a lot better than he'd been in several different categories. She ran her palm up the side of his arm, cupping his bulging muscles and squeezing slightly with her fingers. Greg was a rock, so solid and warm and every inch of him harder than steel. She did mean everywhere, too. There was no erectile dysfunction going on with this man.

It was terrible and she'd never admit it to a soul, but she didn't remember Greg being so large. Maybe he had her head pulled back, her neck stretched and poised for him to torture as he pleased, and her body molded against his, but that didn't prevent her from accurately feeling his cock as it throbbed against her stomach. He was thick, solid, and long. Haley remembered their love-making. No amount of years would erase her memories of the passion they'd shared. And Greg could satisfy the hell out of her, make her come hard enough that she'd almost passed out on more than one occasion. But his dick, nudging her while pressed between their bodies, offered wicked promises of sex so intense that just thinking about it made her more than a little light-headed.

For the first time, Haley was grateful Greg held her so securely. If her brain were a bit clearer, she might think he kept such a firm grip on her for fear she might disappear out of his life again. She couldn't blame him for that. It had been her choice to enter the program but that hadn't made her miss Greg any less. Now that he was here, with their tongues creating an erotic, sensual dance of silent promises and resurrecting passion that had been dormant way too long, she prayed he was back in her life for good.

Greg groaned, ending the kiss but continuing to place moist, hot kisses across her face, then down her neck. If she pressed, they probably could make love right here. It was hot, though, grass was itchy, and she wasn't a teenager anymore. They had beds, air conditioning, and hot showers for when they were through.

"Oh my God," she gasped when she meant to say they needed to come up for air.

"I can't get enough of you, Haley," Greg grunted, but quit kissing her and raised his head far enough for her to focus on his eyes.

"I'm not going anywhere." She smiled and searched his face. Maybe if they started talking about her boss, shifted things over to business, both of their heads would clear. "But there is something I want to discuss with you."

"What's that?" There was still a fog of lust over his eyes, and he focused on her mouth when he spoke. "Are you in trouble?"

"No." His question cleared her head, though, and she stepped backward. "Why would you ask me that?"

Greg dropped his hands and also stepped backward. His dick was still incredibly hard and impossible not to look at. It looked like it would be painful with it so swollen and pressing against his jeans. It was almost long enough to stretch past the button above his zipper, and as if aware of her watching, it pulsed, causing her to blink and her mouth to water. A hunger that had nothing to do with food swept over her with a vicious energy so powerful she almost staggered from the intensity of it.

"I need to know you've come back for me."

"Why would you doubt me?" She frowned at him. "I told you I found out Perry Pierre died in prison."

He studied her for a moment. If he questioned her just because he hadn't learned the news first, he would simply have to get over it. She was a damn good detective and part of maintaining that reputation meant always being on top of all current events.

"When did he die?"

"A week ago or more." She added quickly when he started

to speak, "And I just found out a few days ago. It was on a news site on the Internet."

"But you couldn't call, let me know you were coming home? Instead it appears you were sneaking around, checking everything out, as if something had you nervous."

It didn't surprise her Greg noticed everything and analyzed it all thoroughly before making any decisions. Even if he hadn't heard about Pierre, it wasn't as if it were headline news. Greg had always been perceptive of his surroundings and it was part of what had made him a damn good cop. She imagined he was at least as good a bounty hunter. His name was mentioned occasionally in Omaha, proof how solid and widespread his current reputation was.

"There is one thing. My boss is missing. He's been gone three days now, which is definitely not like him at all." She blurted the words out, then sucked in a breath. Speaking it out loud seemed to make it so much more official than just a hunch something was wrong. Although the phone call earlier seemed to prove something wasn't right.

"So you're back here to seek out help in finding your missing boss?" he asked, and he straightened, studying her with an attentive gaze.

"Are you trying to hurt me?" She felt a surge of emotions she wasn't ready for. Their initial reunion wasn't going to be fighting.

"Maybe," he admitted. "I never wanted you to leave."

"Which would have meant not testifying."

"You could have testified and stayed here."

It was the same argument they'd had last time she'd seen Greg, and for a moment she felt the last six years fade away and they were right back where they were, with him demanding she do things his way.

"Not according to the prosecutors. The U.S. Marshal believed I would have been killed if I didn't go into the program. He could have sent someone after you, Marc, and Jake."

"I could have protected you." He fisted his hands at his

side but then relaxed them, "I would never have let those bastards touch any of us."

She saw his pain, saw how her leaving tore at more than his heart. It had hit his pride with a blow he still hadn't recovered from.

"The past is done," she said, letting the fight in her dissipate. "I don't know where the future is headed, but this is my home." She met his gaze. "You're my home." She knew if she had stayed, protecting all of them would have consumed him. He might never have built the successful business he had now.

As she stared into his sky blue eyes it hit her that possibly John had disappeared because someone had figured out who her husband was. That thought made her sick to her stomach. Pierre wouldn't try hurting her from the grave, would he?

"You aren't going to run to me with a problem and then disappear again thinking you can handle it on your own," he informed her. "If you're back, you're back."

She turned to the cement ravine, squinting against the glaring sun that reflected off the cement. Where else did he think she would go? She'd lost his trust, and that knowledge hurt worse than anything else he could have said. Why couldn't he see she'd left to protect them? Why wouldn't he understand she was capable of protecting them, too?

Greg misinterpreted her silence as meaning she wasn't sure. "Tell me about your situation." His voice was like ice.

"A man's life is in danger. I knew he wouldn't just disappear and when he called me . . . ," she began, but then heard her words and knew she wasn't making any sense. "Greg," she said, sighing as she faced him. He held up his hand, silencing her.

"Slow down. Start at the beginning." Greg was all business, exactly the way she'd treat a hysterical client.

Their worlds weren't as far apart from each other as they possibly thought they were. When she turned around his arms were crossed against his chest. They were thicker than they used to be. Even back in high school, Greg was an intimidating person; his large size and dominating nature were enough to make most cower around him. He told her once his initial attraction to her was because she never cowered but treated him as if he were no bigger than she was. She stared at the trees behind him, needing to focus. She didn't need to prove herself. If she came across to Greg as disoriented, though, he would never understand they were equal.

"I'm not sure where the beginning is," she said, focusing on the days before John disappeared and how out of the ordinary his actions had been. He was another man she cared about a lot, and one who quite possibly was fighting for his life right now. "Three days ago my boss, John Payton, who owns Payton Investigative Services in Omaha, Nebraska, disappeared."

"You'll have to determine if he had any enemies, or if possibly the case he's currently working on went awry." Greg didn't give any indication if he already knew where she'd worked these past years.

"An investigator always has enemies," she told him. "It's a dangerous line of work."

He gave her a pointed look. "Yes, it is," he muttered.

She wouldn't mention how addictive that danger could be. Working with John over the years, feeling the craving to narrow in on the kill, helped her understand her husband possibly more so than she had in the years they'd been living together. She was as hooked on investigating now as Greg was.

"Roberto Torres," she said, and when Greg cocked an eyebrow she elaborated. "Roberto was John's latest client. He hired John to help him track a few people he was concerned about."

"How so?"

"That's just it. John and I worked all of his cases together. But with Roberto, there wasn't any paperwork, and John never wanted to talk to me about him. He wouldn't even let me do fieldwork on this case." She threw her hands up in the air. "I don't even know if there was fieldwork."

"You did fieldwork?" Greg seemed to grow before her eyes.

"And loved it," she purred, grinning when he scowled at her. "I'm going to get my private investigator's license."

"Why didn't you already get it?" he drawled, his features hardening as he stared at her with steely cobalt eyes.

"I couldn't become licensed as Hannah McDowell!" she yelled, aching to smack this obstinate attitude out of him.

"You believe this Torres person has something to do with your boss disappearing?" Greg dropped the subject of her licensing as if he hadn't cared in the first place.

"I have something that might confirm that one way or another." She could be all business, too. "Come with me." Haley moved around Greg, her skin tingling when she passed him as if electrical currents bounced off his body, charging hers and once again igniting the need inside her that she'd barely managed to reduce to a simmering state.

"Was your boss on the up-and-up?" Greg asked, falling in step with her as they walked alongside the football field back to her car.

His black Avalanche was parked next to her small Honda. She shaded her eyes with her hand when she squinted up at him, catching a view of the field next to them.

"Most definitely. John was one of those private dicks from the old school," she said. "He was a no-nonsense businessman. He'd given up chasing after cheating spouses and focused only on more serious cases. But he could smell a crook a mile away and called it without hesitating or caring if anyone disputed him. He was never wrong."

John and Greg were a lot alike. She shot him a furtive glance, catching him watching her, and directed her attention to the cars and the heat waving up off the ground as they approached.

"I take it he didn't ever show up for work without you knowing."

"I knew his schedule better than he did," she said.

Greg grunted but didn't comment. She walked around her car, unlocked it, and reached into the oven-like interior to pull out her purse. After wiping sweat from her brow and rubbing her hand on her Capris, Haley reached into her purse and grabbed the Ziploc baggie with the note inside.

"Roberto Torres had to have left this on my desk. It wasn't there when I got into work that morning, and I spotted it after he left. No one else was in that morning but him."

"Why did he show up?"

"He wanted to know where John was. I told him he had a doctor's appointment, but something told me he already knew John wasn't there. The note was on the edge of my desk. I used my scissors to pick it up and put it in the baggie. Roberto wasn't wearing gloves. If he left this note, his prints will be on it." She held up the baggie. "John always took his evidence bags down to the police station to be printed."

"If his prints are on file." Greg took the note from her, reading it and then frowning as he searched her face. "Where are you staying?"

"You don't know?" She couldn't help herself and fought a smile when he scowled at her.

"It's been a long night and even longer morning. I haven't taken time to find out."

He didn't look like he was exhausted. If anything, Greg looked incredibly pumped.

"At the Sheraton downtown. I've paid for a week," she offered. "Will you see if there are prints on this letter?"

"Yup," Greg said, heading around the front of his car to his truck, as if he would leave.

She'd witnessed his indifferent attitude toward others over the years, but Haley had never experienced it herself and she didn't like it. If it weren't for the kiss he'd nailed her with the second he saw her, she would swear the flame he had carried for her since they were teenagers had burned out years ago.

"There's something else," she said, her voice breathy. She wasn't ready for him to leave. After six years of Greg being out of her life she didn't want him walking away now with total indifference.

"What's that?" he asked, pushing the button on his keys and making his truck beep. He didn't turn to face her but instead reached into his car and started it. "Better start yours so you aren't sitting in an oven," he grunted, still not facing her.

Haley took the advice, once again leaning into the oven and sticking her key in the ignition and starting it. Already the metal around the keyhole was hot. Glancing up before getting out of the car, she studied Greg for a few seconds. She ached for him. They would start the ball rolling on John but she needed back in Greg's arms, to make love and bond them together once again. It hit her as she straightened how much she wanted Greg to acknowledge she was a good investigator. Why did she need his confirmation of her abilities? Abilities she already knew were excellent.

"What else do you have?" He'd managed to move around her car in the time it took her to straighten. His silent approach was just like that of a predator, in her case a deadly one.

Haley stared into his light blue eyes and swore she saw the same heat there that had always been in his eyes before.

"John called me earlier today." She fumbled with her purse, her palms so sweaty she could barely get a grip on her cell phone. Greg's overwhelming presence, as he stood so close to her but didn't touch her, damn near unnerved her when she pushed buttons trying to retrieve the number and time of the call. "He didn't sound at all like himself," she continued, finally pulling up the number and call time. She held the phone up to Greg. "It was the first time I'd heard from him since he disappeared."

His fingers brushed around hers. Holding her hand in his as he raised the phone closer to his face, he squinted at the screen. "What did he say?" Greg asked, his warm touch sending heat surging down her arm. Her insides quickened as her heartbeat started throbbing between her legs.

Haley cleared her throat and pulled her hand out of his. Greg pressed his lips into a thin line, fisting his hands against his hips, and waited for her response. The glare of the sun made it almost impossible to study his face, so instead she focused on the small amount of chest hair visible around his sleeveless shirt.

Her mouth was dry as hell when she spoke. "He told me to go home. He said not to run. He didn't sound right. When I told him I wouldn't go anywhere until he explained why he ran, he told me he didn't run. Then he made a strange sound, like he was hurt."

Greg's expression remained unchanged, as if he couldn't care less about what she was saying.

Haley shook her head. This was too hard to do. Haley shoved the phone into her purse, reaching for her door handle. It was so hot it almost burned her hand. But she couldn't stand here and talk to Greg about something that upset her as much as this did and watch his cold, indifferent expression. As soon as she put some space between the two of them, she could clear her head. Damn him anyway for kissing her like that.

"He told you to go home? Is that exactly what he said?"

Haley let go of the hot door handle, rubbing her hands as she sighed with frustration. "Yes, I'm sure. Very sure. He repeated it too many times. He kept saying, 'Go home. Don't run.' And right before he hung up he said there is nowhere to hide."

"Which is exactly what the note says," Greg said, glancing at his truck, where he'd left the note in the baggie she'd given him. "And he didn't say anything else? Do you think someone was coaching him on what to say?"

"Someone had to be. John doesn't speak in riddles. He is very cut-and-dry."

"And he kept telling you to go home."

"Yes," she said, crossing her arms and squinting into Greg's face. "He kept telling me to go home."

"Well, darling, you've done what he told you to do. You've come home." He held out his hand. "Let me see your cell again."

"What?" Haley frowned as she pulled her cell out again. "What makes you think that? John knows me as Hannah Mc-Dowell."

Greg took her phone from her and returned to his truck,

this time climbing inside behind the driver's wheel. Haley followed him, inching around his open truck door and the side of her car without touching any of the hot metal.

"You're not taking my phone, Greg."

"You're right. I wouldn't be able to reach you if I did that." He went to her recent calls. "Which number did he call you from?"

"The last call," she said.

He wrote the number on a small pad of paper, then handed her phone to her.

"John wouldn't have meant for me to come here," she told Greg, remembering the many stake-outs where they'd discussed their pasts. Her stories had never made John suspicious. "He never had a clue of any identity other than who I was while living there."

"John Payton was one hell of an investigator. His record was impeccable. If it had been otherwise I wouldn't have let you stay there."

"What?" Haley gasped. "You knew where I was and never tried to make contact?"

When he eased out of his truck, forcing her to step backward, he filled the space between the two of them. She couldn't pull away when he gently tipped her head back so they were looking each other in the eyes.

"Believe me, sweetheart, if any man had tried moving into your space, you would have known how little involvement I had with your life. I will always protect my wife."

"I kept an eye on the three of you, too."

"I let you go because you believed you were doing the right thing." For the first time his expression looked pained. "You're my wife, Haley, and until that changes, I will always watch out for you." He rested his hand against the top of her car door, holding it open for her while she stared at him.

"Thank you," she mumbled, praying their love for each other was as strong as it felt it was at the moment.

She slid into her car wondering how much of her life over the past six years he did know about. Did he watch her every time she went out on a date? Did he know when another man entered her home? Haley knew she wouldn't have been able to handle knowing if Greg had gone out with another woman. She'd never gone on a real date. Not in her eyes. There was never a man she wanted to start anything with.

"Greg?" she said, pushing the button to roll down her window when he closed her door.

Once again she had a mouthwatering view of his torso and flat stomach. She strained to look higher, past all that roped muscle bulging against the thin shirt he wore and into his smoldering gaze.

He didn't say anything but watched her, waiting for her to speak.

"I want to see Marc and Jake." Her heart constricted when a muscle twitched alongside Greg's jawbone, the same way it always did when something pissed him off.

"I'll let them know," he said after a moment.

"No. Please." She sucked in a breath, hating asking for permission for this. They were her sons, too. Hell, they were grown men. "Please don't say anything until I contact them. I'll do it soon. I promise."

Greg stared at her a moment longer and then walked around the front of her car and climbed into his truck, disappearing behind the heavily tinted window. A tear slid down her face and she slapped it away. She would get through this—somehow.

Chapter 5

"Why are you doing a search on Roberto Torres?" Marc leaned against Greg's desk, texting someone on his phone.

"Is he somehow related to Jason Wilson?" Jake stood in the middle of his dad's office, pumping twenty-five-pound weights in both hands as he brought them to his shoulders. "We've got one antsy bonds lady hounding Natasha. Why can't we find the bastard?"

"The picture is bigger than I originally thought," Greg told them, then jerked his attention to Jake's phone when it started buzzing.

A day had passed since Greg saw Haley and he felt as if he had walked alongside himself since coming home. In spite of showering, eating, and sleeping, he swore he still tasted her on his lips. Worse yet, every time one of the boys' phones rang, Greg's heart threatened to explode in his chest.

Jake put the weights down and reached lazily for his phone, glancing at the number before smiling at his dad. "My date for Friday night," he offered, holding the phone up in the air as it continued ringing.

"She means so much to you," Marc grunted, rolling his eyes when his brother took his time answering.

Jake just gave a broad, toothy grin while his blue eyes flashed in amusement. He looked just like his mother did when she didn't care how much she irritated Greg if she was having fun at something.

As he answered the phone, Jake saluted his father, lowering his voice to a soft growl when he spoke. "It's about time you called," he said instead of *hello*. "I've been waiting to hear from you all day." Then wagging his eyebrows at his dad and brother, Jake sauntered out of the room.

"I don't know where he gets that," Greg complained, rubbing his forehead as he returned his attention to his computer screen. Haley would throw a fit when she learned what a player her younger son had turned out to be. They'd been almost grown when she left, and she'd done more of the raising than he had. He had fumbled his way through as best as he could.

"Not from me." Marc shoved off of Greg's desk and walked around to where Jake had been standing, then picked up the weights and carried them to the rack where they belonged. "He's got some fucked-up notion he's in charge when he plays the ladies like that. Don't worry. The right girl will come along and knock him down to size."

"Maybe," Greg said, staring at the screen he'd just pulled up. "Would you look at this?"

"What?" Marc came back around the desk. "Who is it?"

"Roberto Torres. He isn't exactly a small fish in a small pond. The question is, what was he doing in Nebraska?" Greg read an old newspaper article he'd found that told of Torres being indicted for tax evasion and appearing in court with his partner, Marty Byrd. Greg flipped back to his search screen, typing in anything he could think of, but couldn't find a follow-up article that showed any convictions. "That was back in '93."

"So? What of it? Who are these guys?"

Greg leaned back, clasping his hands behind his head, and stretched his legs under his desk. Muscles cramped throughout his body. He needed to get away from the computer and move around some. How people managed to sit in front of one of these things all day baffled him.

"The name Roberto Torres came up the other day. I thought I'd see if he had any connections with Pedro Gutierrez, Charlie Woods, or Jason Wilson." Greg chose his words carefully, not wishing to lie to his son. He had checked to see if there was any association, but he'd doubted he'd find anything.

"And were there?"

"Nope."

"I've never heard of these men. How did you hear of them exactly?" Marc was giving him a speculative look when Greg glanced up at him.

"Just came up in conversation." Greg wouldn't be run through the wringer by his own son. "Something has happened recently. I can feel it. We've got too much sudden unrest."

"Because a couple of no-good punks skipped out on court dates?" Marc frowned at him. "Dad, I think you got hit on the back of the head harder than we originally thought."

"I'll show you hit on the back of the head," Greg growled, then glared at his son when he appeared impervious to the threat. "Sometimes, son, you need to take a broader look at the picture."

"And sometimes you need to learn when someone isn't telling you all they know," Marc shot back at him.

Greg should be proud, and any other time he would have been. His son was quick on his toes, and it was because Greg had done a damn good job of bringing him into the business.

It was the only reason his sons were in this line of work. No one else could have trained his sons and convinced Greg they wouldn't get their heads shot off. This was a dangerous business. He'd seen too many good men shot down in their prime. That wouldn't happen to any of his family. Not as long as he was around.

Greg pushed away from his desk instead of addressing the

comeback, and waited for Marc to move before walking around and stopping at the large windows that faced his backyard.

"I doubt you really want to know all that I know." Greg ignored his son when he rolled his eyes, and instead nodded toward his computer. Something had popped up while researching the information Haley gave him the other day. He didn't have a problem sharing it with his son. Marc was almost as good at analyzing a situation as Greg was. "But when I did a search on Roberto Torres, because of his line of work, I expected to find some connection to him and Gutierrez."

"You know the Internet isn't conclusive."

Greg nodded. "We'll put some feelers out on this, too. But I was rather surprised to see the name Marty Byrd tied in with Torres."

"Marty Byrd?"

"The Bird, as he's known, is one of the world's best assassins, if not the best." Greg's insides tightened painfully as he thought of The Bird being even indirectly connected to Haley. "I haven't heard his name come up in several years, but I don't doubt he's still doing what he does best."

"Killing people," Marc grunted. "So what is the connection between him and our local boys?"

"I'm not sure," Greg said slowly, staring out the window at their large backyard that ended with a wooden fence. Beyond it the ocean faded into the horizon. It was a captivating, breathtaking view that he didn't see at the moment. Instead, remembering previous encounters with Marty Byrd, he considered creating an MO. Something told him trouble brewed in the worst of ways and if he didn't remain alert and ready, it might do worse than bite him in the ass. "I know all you see are two assholes who thought they could skip out and get away with it," he said, running his hand over his closely trimmed hair as he studied his son's brooding expression. Marc might think his father was holding out on him, but he didn't have a clue how much Greg wasn't telling him. For now, it would have to stay that way. "Sometimes when certain events that might not appear related in any way happen at the same time it's wise to pay very close attention and step back, taking time to view anything that might seem coincidental at first."

Marc's phone rang and he pulled it out of his back pocket, staring at the number at the same time Jake appeared in the doorway.

"Dad," Jake said, the cocky expression he wore when he'd left completely gone. Jake looked so pale Greg took a step forward, fearing the worst as Marc's phone kept ringing.

"Who is it?" Greg asked Marc, pulling his attention from his youngest only long enough to catch his oldest scowling at his phone.

"I don't know the area code."

Jake told him, moving to his brother's side. "It's Mom. She just called me."

Greg hadn't expected it to happen like this. He hadn't given Haley the boys' phone numbers. Her investigative skills were top notch. But for the calls to come in while his sons were with him? The span of confused emotions on both of their faces ripped at his heart. He wanted Haley here in their home more than he wanted his next breath. Marc and Jake were an equal part of this family. Greg didn't have final say on bringing Haley home. As he studied his sons' faces, he saw with heart-wrenching clarity why Haley had wanted to call them. Haley couldn't come home without their approval, too.

"Hello." Marc spoke in a soft, deep baritone, the voice he usually reserved for moments when he really intended to impress whomever he addressed. He scowled at the floor, pressing his phone to his ear and holding the side of his head with his free hand. "Mom, hi," he added.

Jake stood next to him, suddenly looking so much younger, his green eyes bright with excitement as he studied his brother.

Haley spoke for a while, her words barely audible, as she gently offered a brief explanation for disappearing on her sons when they were teenagers.

"Mom, it's okay. You can give us all the details in person,"

Marc cut her off, offering forgiveness before her apology was even out of her mouth. "Are you in town?"

Haley answered while Jake nodded, apparently having already gathered that information from her. "We're going out to eat with her tonight. Or, at least I am if you don't want to."

"We'll come pick you up." Marc glared at his younger brother as if he were an idiot to think Marc would be left out.

"What?" Greg interrupted. His sons looked up at him as if they'd forgotten he was in the room. "You're not going out to eat."

"Wait, Mom," Marc said quickly, shooting his father a look to kill. "Dad, we are quite capable of making our own decisions where this is concerned," he hissed.

"That has nothing to do with it." Greg moved across the room and snagged the phone out of his son's hand before Marc could stop him. "Haley," he hissed, determined to gain control of this situation before it spiraled out of control. None of them understood the potential danger, because he hadn't told them. But Haley was back and *no one* would hurt her or take her from him again.

Marc moved on his father faster than he ever had before, snagging the phone back while a growl escaped his lips. The temper that flashed in his eyes would probably have terrified anyone else. Jake took a step forward, the tallest of the three. His anger was more obvious than Marc's although he didn't say a word. Greg wasn't fool enough not to pay heed.

"I'm not saying you can't see your mom," Greg told them, shifting his attention from Marc to Jake. It was interesting to see how eagerly they jumped for their mother and that there wasn't any ill will harbored over the years. Obviously his fear that his sons wouldn't accept Haley had been ill-warranted. He also saw it was even more imperative he protect all of them. Marc and Jake were so excited about their mom, they might not see danger that otherwise would be obvious to both of them.

"Damn good thing," Jake said angrily.

"Everyone listen!" Greg snapped, all too aware of the phone

Marc held in his hand and that Haley could probably hear him. "Your mother hasn't told either of you yet about her boss."

"What?" Jake said, his jaw dropping. "You've already talked to her?"

Marc's expression hardened further, his knuckles turning white against his phone when he placed it against his ear, not taking his attention off his father.

"When did you talk to Dad?" Marc asked Haley. "Yesterday, huh?" He gave his father an accusatory look. "Slipped your mind to mention that to us, Dad?" Marc sneered, but then dropped his gaze to the floor when Haley spoke, apparently informing her son she'd asked Greg to remain quiet.

"You three will have your dinner here at the house. Your mom is not prancing around town until I know what the hell is going on. I don't like the trouble I'm seeing and until I know it's not connected to your mom, she's keeping a low profile. That isn't open for discussion from any of you," he announced, then pushed his way past his sons and marched out of his office, leaving his boys alone to talk to their mother.

Greg hurried up the stairs and bounded down the hallway to his bedroom. Shoving his door open, he closed it behind him, then paced the length of his room. Too many emotions attacked to make sense of any of them. He scowled, his hands fisted at his sides, walking over to the glass doors leading to the patio off his room, then back to the entrance of his room, unsure if he wanted to hit the wall or send something flying.

Ever since he had seen Haley yesterday she was all that was on his mind. It had taken more effort than he'd ever needed before to try focusing on work, and even then he knew he wasn't thinking clearly. That made him vulnerable, putting him in a position to easily fuck up. Which in itself pissed him off. He wouldn't let Marc and Jake take her out for fear they wouldn't be on top of their act, yet he wasn't doing any better.

He'd known this moment would come. Haley would come home. She would take the Witness Protection Program seriously. Haley had always played by the rules. She'd been a good mom, impressing the hell out of him daily with her ability to love all three of them with everything she had even when each of them had been less than perfect. She'd taken on volunteer work when the boys got older and didn't need as much of her time. She'd taken classes at the local college, studying law and criminology. Even then, she was always there whenever he or the boys needed her. He should have seen then that her love for investigative work ran deeper than a hobby. It had been all Haley had talked about while taking those classes. She would challenge him with scenarios and test his factual knowledge, her face glowing as she laughed when she believed she'd caught him in an area he wasn't as well-versed as she.

Once he'd discovered Haley was living in Omaha, Nebraska, and working for a private dick, he'd caught himself several times marching out the door, ready to go after her and haul her home. He could have done it. Haley couldn't have stopped him. But she would have hated and resented him. Greg wouldn't be able to live knowing she didn't love him. The wait had been hell. He couldn't say how many times he'd died inside over the years while she had been gone. But the moment she could, as she'd promised him six years ago, she came back home.

"Dad?"

Greg realized he'd been scowling at the floor and stared at his closed door when Jake called out again.

"Hey, Dad!" Jake was louder and more determined.

He really didn't want to talk to either of his sons yet. Maybe after he got himself under control, figured out how best to keep his emotions from skyrocketing out of control every time the subject of his wife and the trouble she might be in came up. For six years he'd existed without Haley but only by prohibiting anyone from mentioning her. Haley was back. Everyone wanted to talk about her. All Greg wanted to do was stalk out his door, get his woman, and bring her home.

The raw instinctive nature to reclaim what was his and protect her to the death was damn close to tumbling out of control inside him.

"What?" he demanded, unable to keep the harshness out of his tone.

Jake's thick mop of curls was tousled when he pushed open the door and studied his father warily. "You cool?" he asked.

One look at his son's face and Greg let out a sigh, scrubbing his hair with his hand, and gestured for Jake to enter. "I'm fine, son. Promise."

"You're lying, but okay. Are you still mad at Mom? We'll understand if you need time." Jake blew out a breath, staring at the ground, then lifted his gaze to his father's. "Mom told us you didn't want her testifying. She pulled off one hell of a feat putting such a huge drug dealer behind bars. I have to admit, if I'd known six years ago why she was really leaving, I would have thrown a fit, too."

Greg spotted Marc standing in the hallway, his arms crossed over his chest. As excited as both of them were about her phone call, demons surged through both of them, tearing at them as fiercely as they ate at Greg.

"I'm not still upset with your mom." One look at the two young men staring at him and he knew honesty was the only way to work their way through this. "I didn't want her to go," he said quietly. "Your mom believed with all her heart the only way Perry Pierre would spend his life in prison was if she testified."

"Was that true?" Marc asked.

"Yup. She was their key witness."

Silence followed. Marc and Jake stewed over this knowledge, learning for the first time what Greg had years to come to terms with.

"Your mom came home because Perry Pierre, the drug dealer she helped put behind bars, died in prison," he said, feeling better as he talked about Haley with the two of them. "She told me her boss disapeared." With a few words he brought them up to date.

Jake didn't say anything and Marc looked up, their expressions showing Greg they hadn't heard any of this yet.

"Your mom is in trouble, boys."

It actually helped calm him down some when he explained, paraphrasing parts of it, and definitely omitting the part about kissing her senseless, all the details Haley had told him when he met her the day before.

"Is that why you were doing a search on Torres and The Bird?" Marc asked.

Greg nodded. Both Marc and Jake stood in the middle of his room now. He walked over to the glass doors and opened them, letting the ocean breeze spill into his room. The fresh air helped soothe his frantic urges that had attacked and left him feeling wired, although dragging Haley home still had an incredible appeal to it.

"Torres had been paying her boss a few visits before he disappeared." He wasn't sure why he voiced Haley's concerns when he had no proof, but he did. "Your mom thinks it's odd that Pierre dies, then her boss disappears."

Jake said dryly, "Definitely makes for some sudden excitement."

"It does sound like we'd be better off bringing her here. Although you wouldn't have had to worry, Dad. Nothing will happen to Mom when she's with us. You've got my word on that." Marc's usually bright eyes were a hard cobalt blue.

"I have no doubts there," Greg said, meaning it. All three of them cared for her as much as they always had. "What time are you going to get her?"

"Seven," Jake said. "But Dad, why is she staying in a hotel?"

Greg wasn't sure how much longer he could maintain his cool. A dark beast threatened to explode inside. He wanted Haley here now, in his bed, both of them branding the other all over again.

Marc studied his dad and actually looked as if he understood. "I say we bring her home."

"Your mom is being cautious." Greg couldn't have agreed with his son more.

There wasn't any way he could eat. Listening to Haley's melodic laughter, to Marc and Jake trying to outdo each other with anecdotes as they caught up on life, was sustenance enough. It was as if Haley had left on some extended vacation and was now being welcomed home with open arms and tears of happiness. No one brought up the Witness Protection Program, Perry Pierre, or her missing boss. They kept the conversation easy as if the four of them had entered into some pact agreeing not to upset each other.

"You better eat or you'll get a headache," Haley said, grinning and glancing at Greg, then looking pointedly at his plate.

Marc and Jake didn't say anything. Both had been laughing, but their broad grins slowly faded. Marc leaned back in the large chair that matched their patio table. Jake continued resting his elbows on either side of his plate, which had been well-cleared with only streaks of barbecue sauce left on it. Both of them looked observant, sharp, and attentive, as if anxiously anticipating the first interaction between their parents in six years.

Greg glanced down at the thick steak he'd grilled and the crisp foil still wrapped around his baked potato.

"This is awkward," Haley muttered, her laugh hesitant. "I'm sorry. That just slipped out."

As it should have, he wanted to tell her. Greg shot Marc a warning look when he opened his mouth, ready to come to his mother's aid and assure her there was nothing to feel awkward about.

"I'll munch on it later," he answered, lifting his gaze to hers.

Haley was actually blushing. For a moment he was carried back to their early days, in high school and right after. She'd always been outgoing, confident, but alone there were times when she'd taken their conversation too far, too personal. Greg had always balked, hesitating like the big dope he'd been back then. And she'd blushed. Just as she was now.

God! He was the luckiest son of a bitch on the planet. He decided to misinterpret the way she looked at him and sighed. "Fine, Mom," he said, making a show and rolling his eyes. "I'll eat my food."

Marc snorted and Haley looked away from him, giving her attention to her sons. "You two were pretty much grown when I left, or so I'd thought." She shook her head and sighed. "Look at you two. I guess it shouldn't surprise me how incredibly handsome both of you are." Her words continually caught in her throat, but she kept going, her emotions spilling out as she spoke. "You don't know how terribly I've missed all of you," she whispered and grabbed Jake's hand, who sat next to her.

Marc reached over and put his hand on both of theirs. Greg didn't need to see her face to know the tears were spilling. Marc and Jake's tortured expressions said it all. Barely a moment passed and she looked at him. Slowly she extended her small hand, with her nails painted a delicate pale pink and her fingers bare. Where was her wedding ring? He didn't dwell on that but looked into her moist green eyes and fell in love all over again.

"Haley," he growled, taking her hand but needing so much more.

Without asking he tugged, pulling her to him, chair and all. His sons were forced to let her go, but Greg didn't care. His woman. His wife. The mother of his two sons, who were incredible young men. Greg had waited for years and had been forced to endure the torture of waiting even longer once he knew she was back. He couldn't wait any longer.

With one more quick tug, Greg lifted Haley out of her chair and pulled her onto his lap, scooting his chair back as he did to make room for her to sit there. The way she cuddled against him, leaning against his chest as she pulled up her legs and draped one arm behind his shoulders, felt so damn good he was immediately hard as stone. Her lashes fluttered over her eyes and were clumped together with tears when she raised them to look up at him, a small smile promise enough of where their evening would end up. Every ounce of blood drained straight to his cock.

"They're just too damn cute at that age," one of his sons muttered and the two of them chuckled easily, then mumbled amongst themselves, getting rather crude as they speculated when they'd have to break the two of them up.

Haley was oblivious to the pain she put Greg in when she shifted in his lap, her soft bottom torturing him almost beyond his limit of control, as she straightened a bit. He rewarded her attempt to get comfortable on his lap when his cock danced in his jeans, tensing and throbbing as he poked her in the rear. Her look when she stared at him, their faces inches from each other, was positively evil.

"If you're doing this on purpose," he grumbled under his breath.

She didn't blush when she graced him with an incredibly innocent look. "Doing what on purpose?" she purred.

"Mom!" Jake complained, apparently believing he was coming to his father's defense. "I never would have guessed my own flesh and blood would be such a cruel tease."

"Whether I'm a tease or not," Haley informed him, wagging her finger at Jake, "is none of your business."

Jake had the good sense to appear appropriately chastised.

"Why aren't you eating?" she asked, shifting again, this time rubbing her rear against his cock and making it too obvious to be accidental.

Greg stiffened, and grabbed her hips to still her as he gave her a look she interpreted accurately. She quit moving. "Honestly, I feel as if I were on a first date with chaperones," he confessed. There wasn't another person on this planet he had ever been able to open up to so easily. With Haley, it just came naturally. "I'm sure I'll munch it all down here soon."

"I know what you mean," she said, leaning into him and wrapping her other arm around his shoulder. "I was nervous as hell coming over here and no matter how much I yelled at myself that I was simply going home, I couldn't get the butterflies to settle."

"And now?" he asked, resting his hand on her bare leg. It was so smooth, trim and warm. He bet every inch of her felt that way.

Again she shifted her head so their eyes were close. Haley stared into his eyes, her green pools so deep he could easily drown in them.

"I'm relaxing more," she whispered, and gave him a small smile.

"I think the two of them have earned some quality alone time," Marc announced, downing his beer and grabbing his plate as he slid his chair away from the table. "Come on, Jake, we're on kitchen detail."

"I'm all for you cleaning up," Haley said, her voice once again relaxed and cheerful. "But don't disappear once you're done. I want to talk to the two of you."

They nodded, both of them carrying as much off the patio table as they could and disappearing through the sliding glass doors into the kitchen. The moment they were alone, Haley once again gave him all her attention.

"I want some time to talk to the two of them," she explained. "Alone," she added.

"That's fine." He wanted alone time with her, too, and very soon. Six years might have passed, but he still understood the worried expression on Haley's face. He guessed what she wanted to say to them but fished anyway, eager to know everything on her mind. "They'll talk to you about anything, Haley. You know, Jake cancelled a date tonight to be here."

She laughed, her broad smile making her eyes glow. "I need to know in my heart that both of them sincerely understand, and forgive me, for leaving for so long. I can't go on, Greg, not until there isn't any doubt my sons don't harbor any resentment."

Greg pulled her to him and her mouth found his. He tasted

her steak and the beer she'd been nursing throughout their meal. When she opened up to him, sighing into his mouth as her body completely relaxed against his, he was quite sure he was experiencing a bit of heaven. His woman was in his arms, his Haley, the better and stronger half of him. At the moment he didn't have a clue how he'd made it through those six long years without her.

Marc and Jake made quick work of taking all the dishes in from their screened-in patio. It was dark beyond the taut screen stretched to form a wall and keep out all insects. Greg reluctantly helped Haley stand when she asked their sons if they'd escort her for a short walk on the beach. Both Marc and Jake raised eyebrows, curiosity kicking in, when he announced he'd stay here and watch the fort until they returned. His heart skipped a beat when Haley turned from them and almost threw herself into Greg's arms before leaving.

"Don't go anywhere," she whispered, and grinned up at him.

"Don't be gone too long," he warned her.

Greg didn't turn on lights as he walked through his house. He was disjointed in his own home, although for the first time in years the emptiness inside him, that invisible force he'd had to push out of his way just to carry out the simplest of tasks, was gone. If anything, as he entered the KFA office off his living room, he felt light-headed, giddy.

Damn. He felt happy.

The answering machine on Natasha's desk flashed at him, the blinking red light indicating there were messages. Greg pushed the button on the machine and stood in the dark, facing Natasha's desk as he listened.

"This message is for Greg King," a woman's voice said in a husky whisper. "This is Samantha Wilson and I'm staying at the Doubletree Hotel." She gave a room number and phone number. "Something has happened. I really must see you tonight. Please call me as soon as you get this message. I need you to come to my room." She sounded out of breath and desperate. It was the same way most women clients sounded when they wanted something from him.

Greg played the message again, writing down the phone number and room number as he slid into Natasha's chair behind her desk. He tapped the notepad with his pen, staring at the information. There was no way he would leave the house with Haley here, not that he saw any reason to go to Samantha anyway. Another thought hit him. Samantha wasn't trying to lure him away from his home because Haley was here, was she?

She had already confessed to assisting someone when contacting him initially. She was a pawn being used to get his attention, through seduction, or any means possible, to distract him. What was he being distracted from?

Already Greg knew she was capable of lying and capable of putting on an act to get what she wanted. He might never know the true Samantha Wilson, although admittedly, he didn't really care. As long as he learned what she was about, that was all that mattered.

The phone rang again as he stared at the notepad. He watched the light flash and shifted his attention to the answering machine when it clicked on. No one left a message.

Their house was fairly soundproof, especially the walls around the office and the rest of his home. It allowed for privacy and keeping his personal life just that—personal. With the office door open he heard Haley, Marc, and Jake when they entered the kitchen.

At the same time he saw headlights flash through the closed blinds across the room.

There were advantages to sitting in the dark. No one knew he was there. Greg came around the desk and moved one of the blinds in time to see a car pull in behind the Avalanche.

Occasionally, someone would show up at night, quite often with too much drama in their lives. The business hours were clearly posted on the door, the Closed sign in place, and the alarm set. Everyone he cared about in this world was here and

Greg would ensure their protection. He slid his keys out of his pocket and unlocked the top filing cabinet drawer, then pulled the spare gun out from under paperwork. He checked to see if it was loaded, tested the safety, and slid it into his back pocket.

The car parked and headlights turned off. Greg's insides tightened. There were more than a few times he could remember when a perp had walked up to the front door, rung the doorbell, and then shot, killed, and burglarized a home. It was the easiest way to enter without triggering the alarm. Although instinct told him this wasn't a burglar, that didn't ease his mind any.

Greg left the office and entered his living room, catching a peek of Haley and his sons leaning against the kitchen counter and talking.

That's when he heard the clicking of heels on the pavement out front. It was a determined, repetitive sound, which gave Greg a good indication of who his unwanted guest was.

Greg pulled on his shirt to cover the gun in his back pocket just as someone rapped solidly on the office door. Greg pulled the closed blinds hanging over the window on the front office door to the side. Sam looked up, startled, her mouth forming a perfect circle as her hand flattened on her chest. It was childish but there was a warped sense of satisfaction when he scared the crap out of her.

It was times like this Greg wished he was really good at texting. He would have shot his sons a message, giving them a heads-up and telling them to keep their mother in the back half of the house until he could get this bimbo out of here. There was no such luck, though. He would never master texting. Instead he flipped on the office light and opened the front door. The beeping from the security system activating would catch his sons' attention. Greg could picture Haley hurrying to check on him. Something told him Haley and Sam wouldn't be happy to see each other.

Especially with the slinky dress Sam wore that fell halfway down her thighs and hugged her slender waist as well as showing off her large breasts. Her legs were bare and the open-toed high-heeled sandals she wore looked rather uncomfortable. Greg took her in with a quick swoop as he held onto the door and blocked her entrance.

"It's dark," she purred. "Are you going to make me stand out here?"

"What are you doing here?" Greg didn't move.

"I left voice mail. You didn't call back." Sam stepped into Greg, dragging her fingernails down his chest. "Please let me in," she whispered, her voice turning soft and sultry.

"It's late, Sam. What do you want?" Greg stepped back but didn't move so she could enter.

Sam clutched her purse, suddenly looking awkward as she tried looking past him into the dark office.

"I thought I would try and find Jason myself," she began. "I got the impression you weren't taking me seriously." When she still didn't get a rise out of him, Sam sighed. "Please, Greg, let me come inside."

Greg remained quiet, letting her into the office. Jason wasn't in LA anymore or they would have found him. If she wanted to waste her time searching around town, Greg couldn't care less. She wasn't going to leave until she said what she came to say, though.

"I knew a lot of his friends, or umm," she said, hesitating as she turned in the middle of the office and batted her long, thick eyelashes at him. " 'People he was acquainted with' might be a better term. Men like my brother don't have real friends."

"Probably not."

"I know some of his hangouts. If anyone has seen him, they told me they hadn't. Honestly, none of them were happy to see me." She pouted, showing off her full, plump lips. Greg seriously doubted Sam was as ignorant as she liked to make him think.

Everything about Sam spelled out a very experienced cougar. He'd seen enough of them in his lifetime to know all the signs.

"My last stop was the Brazen Pony, a pool hall downtown. You might be familiar with it?"

"I know of it." He was more than familiar with the slimy hole-in-the-wall where more warlords cut deals than cops made busts. If Sam went there dressed as she was now and made it out of there unscathed, she probably had at least as many connections there as her brother.

"Greg," she said, her soft, alluring tone back in place. "I'm not a fool, regardless of what you think." She moved until she was close enough to touch him. "There were some men down there, and once I was able to get cozy and have some drinks, I learned a few things."

"I'm sure you did."

She ignored his insinuation and rested her warm, damp hand on his arm. "Los Angeles isn't as big of a city as many people like to think," she continued. "I was asked to give you a message."

"From whom?"

"The message is, The Bird has flown the coop."

Chapter 6

Haley pushed away from the counter as she finished off her beer. She was ready to find Greg. A few minutes ago she swore the beeping she heard meant the front door had opened.

"Want another one?" Jake asked.

Marc stepped to the refrigerator. "I'll get it for you."

"No, thank you," she said, watching both of them text although they barely looked at their phones. Neither had blinked when the door beeped but continued texting. "If I didn't know better I'd swear you two were trying to get me drunk."

"Just because you're the prettiest lady I've ever laid eyes on," Jake drawled, his crooked grin making him look just like his father, "that doesn't mean I'd try and get you drunk."

"You don't actually try to use that line on women, do you?" she asked, shaking her head. Jake was as much a player as Greg used to be back in high school.

"You'd be shocked how shameless he is." Marc rolled his eyes, still the levelheaded one of the two. "He's a damn slut."

"Hey! Watch it!" Jake punched his brother in the arm. "Don't talk like that around Mom."

Marc came back at him with a deadly blow of his own. Haley made a show of scolding both of them.

"Enough of that, both of you. No fighting. No biting." Memories of reprimanding them when they'd been younger flooded her thoughts, except now they were head and shoulders taller than she was.

"I remember when you used to say that," Marc said his expression sobering. "Mom, why didn't you tell us? I was nineteen. I would have understood if you were testifying. We would have protected you."

It was the only question they hadn't asked yet. After walking along the beach, listening to her sons, it was easier to believe there was no resentment. Marc and Jake needed to share all their concerns, their fears, and all the confusion they'd experienced after she left. After glancing at Jake, who stared at her, she returned her attention to Marc, sighing loudly before placing her hands on each of their shoulders. It was a stretch to reach them. Both men stood well over six feet, at least as tall as their father, if not taller. Their size was comforting, though, as was being between both of them.

"I wish there was a simple answer that would explain everything and satisfy you," she admitted. "I didn't plan any of it. Although truth be told, if I had it to do again, I would have done the same thing."

"Are you talking about testifying?" Jake asked.

She walked out from in between them. "Tell us the whole story, Mom," Marc said.

Haley ran her hand over the countertop, aware of how everything was in order but lacking a good deep cleaning.

"I'm sure you remember before I left I was working as a teacher's aide and sometimes a substitute teacher in the public school system. They always sent me to the rougher schools since I was willing to go. The schools were under-funded, and young kids were often on drugs and had teachers who didn't care."

"And you thought you could fix all those kids single-handedly?" Marc asked dryly, although his tone wasn't condescending.

Haley shook her head, remembering her dreams of grandeur and thinking she could make a difference. "You two were almost grown. We did a good job with both of you. And here were all of these children without anyone who gave a damn."

"It's always going to be like that," Jake told her, crossing his arms and looking so much like his father.

"And it will get worse if no one does anything." She studied both of her men for a moment. The two of them returned her brooding stare. "A year or so before you finished high school," she continued, nodding at Marc, "I started working with the after-school program through the inner city school district. The same man would always come around and he wasn't picking up kids, although several of the children would go to his car. It didn't take rocket science to see what was going on. The school administrators didn't give a damn. I tried complaining to the principal and was told if we pulled one drug dealer off the street another would replace him within minutes."

Repulsion filled her just as it had then. Maybe she was idealistic, but that didn't make it any less sickening when realization kicked in as to how few people would trouble themselves to right a wrong. "No one cared that those kids were buying drugs."

Jake and Marc didn't say anything, but then what was there to say? It was true. They all knew it. Her sons worked alongside their father doing what she'd done in Omaha, fighting the odds nonetheless in an effort to make their world a little more crime free.

"I kept watching this man and one day I followed him. I don't know what compelled me. I was angry. He was getting too cozy in the parking lot, apparently thinking no one would stop him."

"He thought he ruled the school," Jake muttered dryly.

Haley nodded. "I watched the man meet another man. I had no idea what I was seeing." She leaned against the counter, clasping her hands behind her head as the memories came back to her. "Let me rephrase. I knew what I was seeing. It was a drug deal. I didn't realize I was witnessing the largest drug dealer in LA and one who'd successfully eluded the cops for years. Over the next month or so I continued following the punk who was dumping drugs at the school until I couldn't stomach it any longer and called nine-one-one."

"Why didn't you tell Dad?" Jake asked, opening the refrigerator and pulling out a beer.

"Because he would have stopped me, or intervened, or forbidden me to keep working at the school. I knew what I was doing was dangerous and I was hooked. There was no way he was going to take me away from my first bust."

Neither of her sons commented, but they didn't have to. Haley knew they both understood what she meant. There was a high no drug could offer when hunting a criminal, closing in, and making the kill. She'd had a taste of it for years now and had no intention of giving it up.

"I met with a detective on the force, and since it wasn't the precinct where your father worked no one had a problem staying quiet. Perry Pierre knew every dirty cop and lawyer in the city, and the fewer people who knew what was going on the better." She remembered the day they'd wired her, how she'd felt violated when they had to lift her shirt to ensure the jellied pads stuck to her skin. She'd been scared to death and also anxious to see if she could act well enough to lure the drug dealer in. "I followed the drug dealer from the school, knowing an unmarked car was on my tail, and led them to the location where he met Perry Pierre. This time, though, I approached Perry and told him I was one of the teachers from the school and wanted in on the action. I couldn't believe how easily he agreed, but he did. I bought the drugs from him and they arrested him."

"What happened next?" Marc asked, looking hooked on her story.

Both Marc and Jake watched her attentively, all ears as they anticipated the good part of the story.

"He threatened me, as I'm sure you could guess," Haley told them. "Perry made all kinds of promises of torture and brutal pain for my mistake in messing with his life. He informed me he'd be back on the streets before I made it home to my husband. And he would have been right, too. But I didn't go home. I went down to the precinct and insisted on talking to whoever had the authority to keep him behind bars, promising to testify or do whatever they wanted to make sure he never as much as sold another joint."

"When did Dad find out?" Jake asked, glancing at the door leading into the rest of house, which was dark and quiet.

Haley looked that way, too, wondering where Greg was and what he was doing. More than likely he was listening to every word she said.

"A U.S. Marshal contacted me the next day. That's when I told your father. Needless to say, he was livid. I don't think we ever fought like we did that night. It got pretty ugly. I was determined to see it out and he was determined to yank me away from the entire scene. I think at one point he even threatened to handcuff me and ship me overseas so no one could find me."

Marc and Jake snorted, although their expressions remained serious. She didn't have to tell either of them how serious Greg had been when he'd threatened her.

"Things got ugly for a while," she told them. "I wouldn't back down. I'd seen what this guy did, and after helping bust him and researching him further, I learned how many times he'd been brought in and how many times charges had been dropped. Your dad and I quit talking to each other over the ordeal. It hurt. I loved your father so much." She dragged her fingers through her hair and squinted into the dark dining room but didn't see Greg. "I couldn't get your father to understand how important it was that Perry Pierre never walk again. Not to mention, as I pointed out to Greg, if he did, he would come after me."

"I can imagine Dad's response to that one," Marc sneered.

"And you would have been right. I tried every angle I could to get your dad to see how important it was that I testified." She'd managed to get past all their fighting. Thinking of it now put a nasty knot in her gut. "Your dad was a cop. He knew how many perps walked without the witness's testimony. When it became apparent that the only safe way to testify was if I entered the Witness Protection Program afterward, your dad thought that would end the matter."

"Man, where the hell were we through all of this?" Jake asked. "I don't remember you two fighting over this case, or any case for that matter."

Marc frowned. "Me, either."

"You two were seventeen and nineteen, both in your own worlds. Your father hadn't retired yet and both of you had jobs. It wasn't hard to discuss it only when the two of you weren't home."

"Obviously you testified, so it didn't end the matter," Marc pressed. His beautiful eyes were just like his father's.

Haley shook her head, her smile sad as she looked from him to Jake.

"No," she said quietly. "By the time the Witness Protection Program was brought up, the impact of that case went way past our family of four. My testimony would help protect schools, neighborhoods, our entire community from Perry Pierre." Haley watched their somber expressions and guessed their thinking. She added, "I didn't do it for the greater community. In the end my family always comes first."

"But, Mom." Jake looked confused.

Haley held her hand up and silenced her son. There was pain on Jake's face. Marc looked more serious than he had all evening. Haley's heart went out to both of them.

"The trial became very high profile," she told them, watching both her sons carefully. "We started getting death threats and I hadn't yet had my day on the stand."

"Death threats?" Marc frowned.

"I remember you had jury duty right before you left," Jake announced, snapping his fingers and looking at Marc.

"That was one of the few things we agreed on," Haley said. "We weren't going to tell either of you about the trial, or that I was testifying."

This time when she paused, neither of them said anything. They watched her, waiting. Haley started trembling and gripped the counter on either side of her, praying for strength. Marc and Jake were grown men. They would forgive her, or they wouldn't. She just hoped she could live with herself if they didn't.

"It became clear to me that whether I testified or not, I had put all of you in serious danger. It was no secret your father and I were fighting. When you're a cop, you're part of a very tight family. If I backed out on testifying, it wouldn't have mattered. The damage was done. One or more of you could have been hurt or worse. The only way I could make sure none of you got hurt was to testify, then enter the Witness Protection Program."

Haley slapped at a tear that slid down her face. She didn't look at her sons. She couldn't. If either of them resented or hated her for leaving, she would die inside. She waited for their understanding, their acceptance and forgiveness for leaving for so long without a word. She'd imagined this moment many times over the years and knew it would be tough. The pain constricting around her heart as she anticipated the worst made it hard to breathe.

"Your father agreed but made it clear he didn't like it. I knew he'd be stubborn about it. I had to go, though. I know it's easier to protect others than yourself. I left to protect you two but also to protect Greg. He hated me for it but I did the right thing. Although I swear I died day after day while I was gone. You don't know how glad I am to be back."

Another tear fell but then they came down in torrents when both of her sons buried her in a group hug.

"My men," she mused. Marc and Jake begged off after a moment, mumbling a reason she didn't hear. Left alone in her kitchen, she straightened up, then headed through the dark house to find Greg.

The light was on in the main office and her stomach twisted in anticipation. Greg was probably in there. She walked cautiously across the thick living room carpet, not making a sound.

It was the same carpet they'd chosen together years ago, hoping its plush durability would endure two lively boys. Haley froze when she reached the open doorway to the office and stared at the woman whose arms were wrapped around Greg's neck as she leaned into him.

Haley's mouth went dry and she couldn't swallow. The woman wore a dress that might as well have been painted on her, and her high-heeled sandals showed off long, tanned legs. She wore so much perfume Haley almost gagged on the stench as she gawked, pain and outrage hitting her hard enough she staggered.

She turned, racing to the nearest door, needing out of the house. Fresh air would help. Once she calmed down, Haley was sure she'd see the logical explanation. If not, she would give Greg two seconds to provide her with one.

The security alarm beeped the moment she yanked open the front door. Haley barely made it outside.

"Haley," Greg said from behind her.

She couldn't turn around. If she did she might start swinging before hearing the explanation she had just told herself she'd wait for.

"Where are you going?" he asked, and wrapped his arm around her shoulder, then pulled her against him.

"I thought I'd wait outside for the boys to take me back to the hotel," Haley lied, overly aware of all that roped muscle bulging against her back. "The fresh air sounded good."

"Wait inside for them," he said, turning her around and tilting her head back with his knuckles under her chin. "You're not standing outside alone," he whispered.

For a moment she thought he'd kiss her and she caught herself holding her breath, waiting. She didn't even have her explanation yet. Something caught her attention out of the corner of her eye.

When Haley looked away from Greg, he straightened, wrapped his arm around her possessively, and turned in the direction she looked.

"I'm Samantha Wilson, from high school. Remember?" The woman who'd been hanging on Greg stepped forward, extending her hand.

"I'm sorry. I don't." Haley didn't like the woman's smug smile.

"What a shame," she pouted, then shifted her attention to Greg and smiled. "Greg remembers me, don't you, darling?" she purred, sashaying across the room and placing her hand on Greg's chest.

Greg stepped away from her touch, being very subtle about it, as if he didn't want to offend either woman. He moved behind Haley and put his hand in the middle of her back. Greg guided her to the covered front porch they'd converted into KFA's office.

"Samantha wants us to find her brother," Greg explained as they entered the well-lit, professional office.

"So how long are you in town?" Samantha asked when Greg turned his back on Haley and moved to the large desk. "Are you just passing through?"

"I don't know how long I'll be here," she told Samantha, something about the woman, other than that she was mauling Greg, making her wary. "I'm not interrupting anything, am I?"

"Not at all," Sam crooned, returning to Greg's side as if claiming her spot when he leaned against the desk. "Greg and I were just chatting, weren't we, darling?" she asked, her back to Haley when she ran her red daggers over the top of Greg's head.

"You'll have to help me remember what classes we were in together," Haley suggested, walking into the middle of the office and making a show of looking around.

Several newspaper articles, framed and hanging on the wall, caught her eye. They were clippings she'd framed and hung in her and Greg's bedroom. He had hated them, which made her wonder why he'd moved them out here. God! He'd missed her enough to keep things about her he had hated.

Forcing her attention back to Samantha, she glared at her

perfectly round butt, and fought the urge to pounce on her and yank her away from Greg. "You were a couple grades ahead of us, right?"

Greg watched Haley over Samantha's shoulder, although his expression was masked.

"You're older than I am, darling," Samantha said, giggling as she shifted, facing Haley and damn near sitting on Greg's lap.

"Is that so?" Haley continued with her smile, finding herself walking across the room toward Samantha before giving it thought.

Greg jumped away from the desk, almost knocking Samantha over and forcing her to maintain her balance in her high heels.

"Sam showed up here tonight with information on her brother," he offered quickly, moving between both women and facing Haley. "She didn't understand a message she was given and asked me about it."

"Is this how you work with all female clients?" Haley asked, barely managing to sound calm.

"You know better," Greg growled, growing in size before her.

"What is she doing here?" Marc asked, appearing in the doorway to the office. He looked anything but pleased as he scowled at Samantha, then shifted an inquiring look at her and his father. "I thought I heard the alarm beep. What's up?" He sauntered into the office and paused when he stood next to Haley, crossing his arms and scanning the room before focusing on Haley.

"I heard some juicy gossip and came over to share it with your dad," Samantha offered, before anyone else could speak. She planted her round butt on the edge of the desk and looked at Marc as if he were fresh meat she couldn't wait to devour. "I did a bit of investigating on my own this evening."

"Oh yeah?" Marc cocked one eyebrow, barely sounding interested.

Haley started around Greg. She'd had enough. No one looked at her men as if they were prime meat in some stud market.

"If you'll excuse us a moment." Greg took Haley's arm and escorted her out of the office into the dark living room. His solid grip left little choice other than to let him almost drag her out of earshot of Marc and Samantha.

Haley ripped her arm free the moment they were shrouded by darkness. "Why was that woman—?" She swallowed her words when Marc appeared next to them. Haley gave silent thanks, realizing she might have made a complete ass out of herself if she'd torn into Greg when any of them might have overheard.

"Are you ready to take me back?" she asked Marc, shifting gears as she rubbed her damp palms down her sides. Her nerves were frazzled, and if she didn't have time to sort her emotions out soon she would make a fool out of herself, or worse.

Marc stiffened. "Mom, you're safer here."

"Good thinking." Greg's hand suddenly seared her back when he pressed it against her spine, guiding her forward before she could stop him. "I'll take her to gather her things. We'll be back shortly. Marc, you can see Sam out, can't you?"

The alarm beeped again when he unlocked the door and the cool night ocean air filled Haley's lungs as Greg continued pushing her along the walk toward his truck.

"I never agreed to stay here," she said, wishing he would quit touching her and that her head would clear. Thoughts of staying the might with Greg fogged her brain even more.

"You can chew me out on the way over to your hotel," Greg said coolly, pulling keys from his pocket and pushing the button to unlock the truck. He opened the passenger door and held it for her until she climbed in. "Although honestly, I didn't mind at all how jealous you got in there."

Haley tried glaring at him when he grinned, then closed her into the dark cab of the truck.

"Jealous, my ass," she muttered the moment he opened his

door and slid in next to her. "Is there something going on between you and that woman?"

"Absolutely not." Greg started the truck and slipped it into gear as cool air blew on Haley from the vents in the dash. "You need to learn to observe a situation a bit more carefully, sweetheart," he added. "If you had, you would have seen my arms weren't around her. And although you couldn't know this, I'll add that her arms weren't around me until she caught a glimpse of you in the living room. Sam tried to piss you off and did a pretty good job of it."

Haley stared at his solid profile, finding herself admiring his strong jawline and the way his closely trimmed hair had slight streaks of silver tracing through the brown that hadn't been there before. Although Greg was still holding on to his bad-boy roguish good looks, there was an air of dignity about him that she didn't remember being there six years ago.

"I don't even remember her," Haley said, turning her attention to her lap and her hands clasped over her legs. That's when it hit her she'd left her purse at the house. Damn it. Her keys were in her purse, along with the key to her room. *Crap!* "Why would she care if she pissed me off or not?"

"That's what I was wondering," he said, glancing at her although she refused to look at him. "My guess is she wanted to know exactly where our relationship stood. And you don't have your purse."

"I can get a key at the front desk." She shot a look his way and caught him studying her.

"Marty Byrd. Does that name mean anything to you?"

Haley ran her fingers through her hair. Greg had switched gears on purpose. It was the seriousness of his tone that had her deciding not to remind him how bad he'd always been about talking about his emotions.

"I'm not sure. I think I've heard his name before." She fought to remember what she'd heard about him. "Wait a minute. He's an assassin." She snapped her fingers and pointed at

Greg as it came back to her. "The Bird. Yes. He worked with the FBI on a case John had a couple years ago."

"He works both sides of the fence." Greg's brooding expression created a heat inside her as he studied her a moment before returning his attention to the road. "So John has worked with him before?"

"Not directly. Not that I know of. And he definitely was never a client. I would have known if he was."

"Sounds like you and John worked pretty closely with each other."

"It got to that point." She turned her thoughts to John, wondering where he was at the moment.

John wasn't a young man anymore. Although in his early sixties, he'd already given up on cases that caused him to run around hell and back or do stakeouts that lasted for hours on end. For most of their cases, Haley worked up the profiles, did the fieldwork, and provided him with his proof, leaving John to simply drive where he needed to be at the right time to make his bust.

"There were parts of the job I enjoyed more than he did," she added, sending up a silent prayer that John was okay. She doubted he'd be able to handle too much torture or abuse. Even though he'd slowed down when it came to chasing criminals, Haley had still chewed his ass daily about his salt intake and fought to get him to watch his diet. She knew his blood pressure would do him in before any torture would.

"We'll find him, sweetheart," Greg told her, reaching over and placing his large hand over both of hers and squeezing. "I swear it."

"You're right. We will." Haley wondered when Greg said we, if he meant him and her, or him, Marc, and Jake. "So how well do you know Sam?"

"I don't know her at all." His jaw was set hard as he let go of her hands and gripped the wheel at ten and two.

"Really? How many women clients grope you on a regular basis?"

"She's the first," he said, his fingers tightening on the steering wheel. "She's after something."

"She sure is," Haley drawled, staring at him as she lowered her lashes, letting her vision blur slightly, although it didn't do a damn bit of good in making him appear any less sexy. The longer they drove together, sitting so close, made it harder to focus on anything other than it had been six years and her body was screaming for him now. "Now I wonder what that might be."

"You're being obvious, Haley."

Her emotions were wound too tight. The last thing she'd be able to handle was mind games with Greg. She twisted in the seat and faced him.

"What's wrong with obvious?" She crossed her arms and glared at him. The brief look he gave her before returning his attention to the road made it damn hard to be mad at him. God! He was sexy as hell. She sucked in a breath. "Obvious is what allowed us to see your Samantha wants something."

"I see."

"If you could see past your male ego, you might see she's after something other than you."

"Marc? Jake?"

She growled before she could stop herself. Greg's grin could only be described as wicked. Greg pulled up in front of the hotel a few minutes later. Haley jumped out when he put the truck in park.

"How much stuff do you have?" he asked, meeting her on the passenger side of his truck and closing her door for her. "You used to wait for me to open your door for you," he said quietly, speaking over her shoulder when she led the way into the hotel.

"Sounds like it's about time I returned the favor." She ignored the rotating doors and pulled open the door next to them. "After you." She stood to the side, holding the door for him.

Haley grinned when Greg scowled, then followed him

inside. After getting a new key card, Haley joined Greg at the elevator.

"Why did you ask how much stuff I have?" she asked. The doors opened and Greg gestured for her to enter. Haley walked in first and faced him. "And who is Marty Byrd?"

"I might have to rearrange a few things in the back of the truck."

The doors opened and Greg placed his hand over them, preventing them from closing. He stepped out as Haley did, glancing up and down the hallway. She was once again at the side of her giant protector.

Haley held her card as she led the way to her room and slid it alongside the door handle.

"I just have a couple suitcases."

"Do you have stuff in storage?"

"No." She shook her head as she pushed open the door. "Everything is still at my place in Omaha."

Greg reached over her head, pushing the door open further. "Why wouldn't you bring everything with you? Were you not sure if you were staying?"

"Oh my God," she whispered as she stepped into her room. Her purse was back at the house, which meant she didn't have her gun.

"Don't touch anything," Greg said, when he saw the room. His arms snaked around her waist as he pulled her back against his virile body.

"They're feathers," she muttered, staring at feathers that were everywhere. "It looks as if birds were fighting in here."

"Bird," Greg muttered, pulling her to his side and closing the hotel room door at the same time. "Stand right here and don't move." He pushed her behind him and up against the door as he moved farther into her room.

She ignored him. "Do you see the bird?" she asked, staying behind him as she walked toward her large bed and all of the feathers scattered across the comforter. "We don't have gloves. Be careful what you touch."

There were feathers all over her suitcase and her overnight bag, which were on the counter next to the bathroom. Feathers were on top of the TV and all over the floor.

"I don't think there was an actual bird in here," Greg mused, pushing past her and entering her bathroom. He reappeared in a moment. "Just feathers."

"I don't get it." She studied a group of feathers in a pile on the table next to the TV. "They almost look fake, but damn, they're everywhere."

"I think I get it," he said, his expression grim. "Someone has sent either you or me a message."

"A message from who?"

"Isn't it obvious?" Greg asked, looking around the room again. "It's from The Bird."

Chapter 7

Haley sipped the strong coffee, absently twisting a strand of damp hair as she stared at nothing. The Avalanche was amazingly well-stocked for a crime scene. They'd gone back to it with gloves, a camera, and a finger-printing kit. The two of them worked alongside each other as if they always had.

Her hotel room had tons of artificial feathers dumped in it, but otherwise there wasn't any damage. Nor did anyone at the front desk have any knowledge of anyone asking about her or her room number. The door hadn't been damaged.

"Someone had a master key card," Haley mused, after gathering all her personal belongings, confirming nothing had been messed with, and snapping her suitcases closed.

Greg grunted, took them from her, and led the way to the truck. He'd been noticeably quiet as they returned to the house. Haley had been wired, ready to analyze everything they'd seen.

"Oftentimes great ideas come out of brainstorming," she'd argued when Greg had refused to respond to her comments.

"Haley, you're in danger." He'd given her a hard stare before returning his attention to the road.

She'd been convinced there was no way she would be able to sleep in the clean but unadorned guest bedroom that she'd never had time to do anything with before getting involved with Pierre's trial. It was across the hall from her and Greg's old bedroom, and just down the hall from Marc's and Jake's rooms. But Greg had muttered something about being tired, disappeared in to their old bedroom and had closed the door.

Haley downed coffee, listening to birds chirp outside, otherwise aware of how alone she was in this large house. Greg, Marc, and Jake were gone. She'd figured that much out after showering, nervously coming downstairs, and anticipating seeing Greg. She walked out to the back screened-in porch and stared at the ocean past the privacy fence.

Waves rippled gently against the satiny-looking beach. It was a view she had never missed when she rushed out of this life. Back then she'd left dead inside, knowing she was losing her family but focused on putting a deadly criminal behind bars and knowing he would stay there because of her. Now she had raced back, more alive than she had ever been.

John, what do you have to do with The Bird? There had to be a connection. She continued watching waves chase one another across the sand, staring out the screened porch, beyond the privacy fence Greg had put up sometime after she left. It stole some of the view but offered a strong sense of security.

There was a connection between her boss and the assassin or he wouldn't have trashed her hotel room. She didn't have any association with The Bird. "Did you tell me to go home so I could find the connection between you and Marty Byrd?" she whispered, holding her cup to her lips.

Haley thought she heard something around the side of the house. Stepping inside, she swapped her coffee for her gun, which was in the purse that she'd brought downstairs with her. Then stepping back onto the back porch, she shoved her gun into the back of her shorts and stepped into the yard.

The sounds she heard were coming from the side of the house. Haley paused when she rounded the house.

"That didn't used to be there," she muttered, staring at a

detached garage, set back from the front of the house. Its secluded location would make it hard for anyone to see from the street. Haley tugged down her shirt, making sure her gun was concealed. She walked around the garage and paused at the open garage door.

Greg looked up as Haley stood facing him. She swore she saw something similar to regret on his face before he looked back down. She approached slowly, studying the large motorcycle he was meticulously cleaning.

"You finally got your bike." She ran her fingertip across the leather handle, noting how the large bike seemed incredibly appropriate for Greg.

"You weren't here to tell me no." His tone almost sounded accusatory.

She wouldn't let him get under her skin. "Then I guess some good came out of all of this after all."

He responded to her with a scathing look before returning to firm, long strokes over the chrome as he buffed it to a radiant shine. Haley watched him for another second and found herself focusing more on how his muscles rippled under his skin as he stroked. Every inch of Greg was so perfectly toned. She forced herself to look away before she pushed him back and made him forget about his bike.

"Well, this explains a lot," she said when she'd stepped around Greg and his bike and stared at a rather extensive workout area. Gym equipment filled the back half of the large garage. Greg didn't say anything and she explored some more, slowly turning as she took in all of the contents. Tools hung on a peg board on the wall. There were garden and yard equipment. The garage was a man's paradise.

Haley continued turning until she stared at Greg's backside. She wondered how much time he spent out here. "This is impressive."

"Thank you."

Haley wasn't sure what she'd done to deserve such a cold shoulder but she was getting really tired of it. Coming up behind him, she reached to touch his shoulder and stared as roped muscle flexed under his shirt while he worked. She balled her hand, preventing herself from putting it on his shoulder.

"Greg," she said.

He grunted.

"What did I do?"

He stopped cleaning his bike but held his position, squatting next to it. For a moment she worried he wouldn't tell her and she'd have to start a fight just to get him to talk.

"You didn't do anything." Greg sounded resolved as he stood slowly, dropping his cloth on the garage floor next to the bike. "Not a damn thing, Haley."

"Damn. I'd love to see how you'd react if I did do something." She didn't try hiding the sarcasm in her voice.

When Greg turned around and she saw how tortured his expression looked, she almost regretted her words, almost. Instead of saying something reassuring without knowing what was wrong, which was what she probably would have done six years ago, she continued standing there. If anything, she agreed with him. She hadn't done anything. Haley wouldn't tolerate more arguments about her leaving for the program. That was over and they were going to put it behind them, one way or another. Since her arrival home and this moment, which wasn't quite forty-eight hours, she couldn't think of anything to apologize for, or when Greg's feelings might have been bruised.

It would probably take a stepstool for her to climb onto the bike. The bike was the perfect fit for Greg. He touched the seat, and with him standing next to it she could see him sitting on it, his legs stretched over the large motorcycle. The two would be an invincible pair and would probably be the sexiest team on the road.

Greg sighed and she held her tongue, watching him and the turmoil crossing his face.

"You knew how I'd react," he said, disgruntled.

"Not how you're acting now," she said, tilting her head and studying him. "You've been weird since we left my hotel last night when I was all wound up and eager to brainstorm the scene."

"I know. I'm a regular asshole." He reached down and scooped up the cloth he'd been using and tossed it on the work counter along the wall.

"Okay," she said slowly. "I know there are times I might agree with you," she added, ignoring the scowl he gave her and grinning at him. "But this time you're going to have to clarify a bit."

"Haley, you're a good investigator."

She tried not to smile. He had no clue how much his praise meant to her. "I know," she said, unable to hide her happiness. "And thank you."

"You're welcome. I don't say things like that if I don't mean them."

He was right. Greg had never been big on praise, but when it came to his line of work, he was incredibly hard on anyone in the field.

"You're even better at making the praise not sound like a compliment." She made a face at him although her irritation was growing. She hadn't come here to fight with him. It was the last thing she wanted to do.

"You're right. Which is why I've been avoiding you."

"You've been avoiding me?"

"You couldn't tell?"

Haley could tell. It had been so obvious it had driven her nuts. "I could tell and it's why I sought you out. Why does it bug you that I'm good at what I do?"

Greg blew out a breath and dragged his hand over his short hair. He turned away from her and walked around his bike, picking up the cloth he'd tossed on his work bench and folded it, then placed it on the corner near the door.

"Last night when Samantha showed up, she told me one of her buddies at the Brazen Pony had a message for me. The message was, 'the bird has flown the coop'." He turned around and faced her. His face was now devoid of emotion, chiseled in stone. It made him appear hard, heartless, and cruel. "Then I took you to your hotel and there were feathers all over the place. No one had a key to your room but you. The hotel couldn't help us and the room didn't show any signs of being broken into."

Now apparently he was ready to brainstorm. Yet he'd thrown some curve balls that left her unsettled enough that she wasn't able to twist her brain around things as well as she probably could have last night.

"You didn't tell me Samantha said that."

"You weren't in the right frame of mind to discuss her."

"No matter what frame of mind I'm in," she snapped, unable to stop herself. "I should always be told clues whether they appear important or not."

Greg raised one eyebrow and moved in on her slowly. She didn't budge, in spite of thinking he was trying to bully her. He'd never scared her and he didn't now. But he was pissing her off, which was annoying her. He was trying to tell her something but what he was really doing was insulting her every time he opened his mouth. She didn't know why.

"So are you in charge now?" he whispered, when he stood inches from her.

"I'd like to be a team now." She held her pose, not blinking, staring into his hard gaze.

Greg looked away first, growling.

"What crawled up your ass?" she demanded, leaping after him. He wasn't going to grunt at her after she suggested they were a team, because she sure as hell wasn't going to take orders from him.

"Haley, you don't see, do you?" He spun around, grabbing her by her arms and squeezing. He wasn't hurting her but he held her with enough strength she couldn't move. He leaned forward, his face close enough he could kiss her, except his hostile look was anything but a turn-on. "You tell me your boss calls you and tells you to go home. I get a message telling me the bird has flown the coop. Then we find feathers all over your hotel room. Someone is after you." He gave her a quick shake but then put her down fast enough that she almost teetered when he let go of her.

Haley stared at him, taking a minute to digest what he'd just said. She knew all the facts but hadn't put them together the way he just had. Greg stalked away from her, looking larger than usual. When he spun around to face her, she straightened instinctively, positive her expression remained serious. Greg wouldn't scare her, no matter what he said. She was a professional, and although she had never had a case surrounding her, she'd worked through some doozies before. All she needed was a few minutes to let all this digest and she could handle it.

"I'm not completely incapable of taking care of myself," she informed him, staring him down when he stalked back toward her.

Haley wasn't ready for it when he suddenly grabbed her, tossed her over his shoulder, yanked her gun out of the back of her shorts, then tossed her to the ground. Haley fell backward, flinging her arms out on either side of her. When she backed into Greg's bike, he stepped forward, moving too easily, his expression not changing when he grabbed her by her shirt collar and pulled her to him.

She grabbed his wrists, which she couldn't wrap her fingers around, and held on when he wouldn't let go. "Greg!" she complained. "You're not playing fair."

"And you think some psychopath is going to play fair?" He tightened his grip on her shirt until she heard threads break.

"Enough, Greg," she said, relaxing in his grip and staring into his eyes. "Let me go, now."

He did, then adjusted her shirt for her. "Now you know why I was avoiding you."

"Because you were in asshole mode?" she complained, making a show of straightening her clothes. "And give me back my gun."

Greg checked to see if it was loaded, looked even more

upset when he learned it was, secured the safety, and handed it over. Haley took it, sliding it into the back of her shorts, and faced him.

"Here's what I think," she began, aware they were going to fight and not seeing any way out of it. If Greg couldn't handle her investigating her missing boss, and any other clues appearing to be associated with John, they were going to have serious problems.

"You're right." He held up his hand, but dropped his gaze to the floor. "You think I'm going to have a problem with you investigating this case. You think that although I am capable of acknowledging how good you are, that apparently I'm incapable of separating my ingrained need to protect you so I can view you as a partner."

She stared at him, seeing now why he'd been out here alone. He was working through demons. She wondered how many days he'd spent out here since she'd been gone, dealing with demons that were attacking him ruthlessly. A weaker man might not have made it through the stress.

Haley wasn't sure if it was her maternal side, or her deep, unwavering love for him, but she was hit with the overwhelming urge to run into his arms. She almost dug her heels into the cement garage floor to keep herself from moving. Greg had started the process of accepting her as an investigator. Cuddling with him would only set him back. He preferred seeing her as his beautiful lady who would always need to be protected.

"I might not be invincible," she began and knew she was right when he shot his gaze to hers. The pain in his eyes cut her to the quick. Haley blew out a breath, taking the long way around his bike to the garage doors. She needed space. "You aren't invincible either, Greg King," she shot over her shoulder. "You might be incredibly large, very strong, and look intimidating as hell, but my looks have their advantages, too." She hurried out of the garage but not fast enough to not hear him growl and hit something, hard.

Haley hated not understanding the facts. But there were

names popping up she didn't know, her boss calling her and telling her to go home. There were still feathers in some of her clothes. She slipped the latch up on the gate at the end of the yard and let herself out, then turned to make sure the gate was closed before turning toward the beach.

"What are you doing?" Greg's deep baritone startled her when he appeared at the end of fence and pushed against the gate, preventing her from putting the latch in place.

"Nothing." Haley shrugged, dropping her hand and turning from the gate. "I thought I'd take a walk along the beach."

"Oh?" He glanced past her toward the ocean as he closed the gate. "Sounds good. Let's go."

"Really?" She wished they hadn't just argued. All she'd wanted since she woke up was to find Greg and be alone with him.

Greg dragged his hand down her back, resting it just above her rear end.

"Did you think I'd say no?" Greg asked.

"I wasn't asking for permission." She crossed her arms over her chest.

"There's a difference between asking permission and letting someone know where you are. You can't take off alone, sweetheart, not until we figure out this mess."

"I understand everyone checking in." She wouldn't let this be just about her. If someone had targeted her, and she wasn't sure that was the case yet, her family could be targeted, too. "We've got to work together on this, Greg."

He glanced down at her. "You know as well as I do something is seriously wrong. And I admit it's making me nuts that I don't know yet how or why you're involved."

"I don't, either." She focused ahead of them, squinting at the secluded beach stretching out and fading into the ocean. The smell of salt water hanging heavy in the air filled her lungs when she sucked in a frustrated breath. "This might have started in Omaha with John disappearing, but it's moved out here to California with my hotel room being trashed. I went through everything again this morning. Nothing is missing. They weren't trying to steal anything from me, just scare me."

"I'm going to find out why." He gave her shoulder an affectionate squeeze.

Haley looked up at her husband thoughtfully. Greg would always be the protector. It was in his nature. "*We're* going to find out why," she corrected him.

Greg squinted ahead of him, his expression pinched.

"Greg." She whispered his name and didn't continue until he looked down at her. "You've already acknowledged I'm good at what I do."

"Don't patronize me, Haley." He let his hand fall from her back, keeping pace but no longer touching her. "I already know I'm being a dick. You don't have to hold my hand until I start acting reasonable."

"I guess I'm as protective of you as you are of me."

He looked ahead of them again. Greg walked tall and proud, his relaxed, confident stroll not having changed over the years. Haley had often looked at him as her dark warrior. He was a dangerous predator who would sometimes show how strongly and deeply his emotions ran.

"This is going to take me some time," he said after a minute. "Yes, you showed me last night you know your way around a crime scene. But I haven't trained you how to apprehend a fugitive, or what to do when they come at you."

"I don't get it," she said. "I know you love your sons at least as much as you do me, and I've never thought of you as sexist."

Greg grunted, or maybe it was a laugh. "You know I've never had a problem with women in law enforcement. Some of my partners were women."

"You could work with them and not me."

"I didn't love them," Greg muttered.

"Damn good thing." Haley was starting to understand. She didn't like it and Greg admitted he was being an idiot. The only woman he didn't want chasing criminals was her.

Greg slowed his pace, finally stopping, and took his time searching her face. He looked as if he'd say something else but didn't.

"I'm going to find John."

"I know," he whispered. "I'm going to help you."

"Good."

Greg stroked a strand of hair behind her ear. "Your skin isn't accustomed to this sun anymore. We're going to have to buy you some sunscreen."

To prove his statement, he pressed his thumb over her bare shoulder, and immediately she felt the tightness in her skin. She wasn't ready to turn back and doubted she'd burn that fast.

"It's been a while since I've seen the ocean. We'll go back soon." She turned her face into the breeze and enjoyed the salty, moist air on her face. "I didn't realize how much I missed the ocean."

Greg didn't answer and instead started walking again. He kept his pace slow the way he usually did, so she could keep up, but didn't say anything. Greg had opened up and shared how his line of thinking was torturing him. He was definitely making a show of understanding that she was an investigator, too. Or she would be once she was licensed. Her heart swelled and suddenly it was a lot hotter outside than it was a minute before. She shielded her eyes, making a show of staring ahead of them, partially so he wouldn't see the tears welling in her eyes.

"Marc and Jake went to check out your hotel room," he said, breaking the silence between them.

"How did they get in?" Haley had taken her purse, which had her hotel card in it, to her room when she'd crashed last night. Not that either of her sons would go into her purse no matter where she left it.

For the first time that morning Greg gave her a crooked grin. "Your sons informed me not to worry, that they'd be able to get in."

"I'll be curious to learn how they do it," she said seriously.

"Whoever blessed me with all those feathers might have gotten in the same way."

Greg cupped the back of her head and began toying with her hair. "They'll check in when they're done." His large body shielded her from the sun as they walked.

"Why did Roberto Torres hire your boss? What was John doing for him?"

"I don't know." Her skin did feel tight. They would have to turn around soon or she'd be sunburnt. That was the last thing she needed.

But when she inhaled, the salt air was mixed with the smell of Greg's aftershave and something stronger, richer, his own unique scent. Their arms brushed together and she ached for him to touch her more. It was almost too much, trying to figure out the connection between her and men she knew nothing about and at the same time contemplating the thought of making love to Greg right now.

She let out her breath, sounding as exasperated as she felt. "I've always been up on every one of John's cases as long as I've worked for him. I wasn't there a year before I started working in the field. But he was very closemouthed about Roberto, to the point where he actually snapped at me last week when I pressed him about it."

"More than likely he was simply trying to remind you not to overstep your boundaries as his assistant."

"John wasn't like that. He knew I was on top of those cases sometimes more than he was. That place couldn't operate without me. John knew I was just as capable of solving his cases as he was."

"Could his opinion of you been a bit too biased?"

She glared at Greg, but he stared straight ahead, his expression pinched into a determined scowl. Maybe years ago she wouldn't have argued with him when he entered into his stubborn mode. Haley still recognized it for what it was today but would be damned if she didn't make him see the truth of the matter.

"His opinion of me was not influenced by anything other than that he saw, and appreciated, how intelligent I am."

"Then he was a smart man. I just hope he knew how lucky he was."

Haley nudged her arm against his again. He was warm and strong and felt too damn good. "Why did you ask about Roberto?"

Greg's eyes dulled, turning a milky blue when he quit walking and stared down at her. "Maybe he knew how much you cared for your boss," he said.

"What?" she asked, not following his line of thinking. "I didn't treat John any differently than I would have any co-worker who cared about the job."

"Possibly he took your boss because he knew you would come here."

"That doesn't make sense. They knew me only as Hannah McDowell. You're suggesting this might have something to do with you?" She shook her head, not buying that theory. "If they're after me, it isn't because I'm a King."

"It would be one hell of a motive."

"There's another reason. Do you know anything about Roberto Torres?"

"Only what I learned about him after you brought up his name," he said. "The most interesting fact being Torres has done business with Byrd in the past." He pressed his lips into a thin line. "Byrd is an assassin, sweetheart. There aren't many men more dangerous than him."

"I think you'd be happier if you could lock me away somewhere instead of working this case with me."

"Your boss is missing and your hotel room gets trashed. I need to protect you," he said, reaching for her.

"I can protect myself." She willed herself to back up.

Greg dropped his arm. "If that's the case, then why would you need me?"

Haley sighed, looking away from him first. She'd wanted his hands on her. When he didn't touch her, she started down the beach, not running, but resuming their walk, knowing if they continued it would turn into a shouting match that wouldn't get either of them anywhere. But she wouldn't be smothered or stashed away somewhere so she couldn't breathe either. Would Greg ever be able to have a woman who wanted to live on the dangerous side along with him?

"We need to know what he hired John Payton to do. If he wanted John to find someone for him, than who was it?"

"What makes you think it was a missing-persons case?"

"I don't. But its our only similarity right now. People are coming up missing, breaking out of prison, disappearing, and we need to find out why."

"Were these people missing when Roberto hired John?" she pointed out. "Do we know if Roberto is connected with Jason, or whoever else you've been told is missing?"

"I'm going to find out."

Haley studied his hard, strong features until he looked down at her. "We'll find out," she reminded him. Her heart started pounding the longer she studied him, but she needed him to understand.

"I came here to be with you." A lump lodged in her throat when his eyes grew as bright as sapphires. She wanted nothing more than to walk into his arms. Instead, Haley sucked in a breath and said, "But I've been looking forward to working at your side for years now."

Greg reached for her face, cupping her cheek with his large hand. "I want you to be happy."

It was a start. Her dark warrior was trying. She would have to show him how good, and capable, she was.

Chapter 8

Houses lined the edge of the beach, spread apart, with well-maintained yards and expensive security systems. Greg knew everyone in the area, although he wouldn't consider any of his neighbors close friends. It was a pricey neighborhood and those who lived here paid out the ass for their privacy. Having a screaming match with his estranged wife would be enough to hit the local gossip column, which wouldn't do either of them any good.

Haley hadn't let him protect her after testifying for Pierre, but now that she was here Greg would protect her no matter how much she screamed and yelled about it. He *wanted* to protect her.

The men's names that were popping up weren't the kind of guys who were small time. Haley was sharp as a tack and worked like a pro by his side in her hotel room. She was right about him using his size and strength when needed. When she told him she did the same, it had scared him to death. Haley was sexy as hell. Any way she would use her good looks would only put her in more danger.

"How well do you know Roberto Torres?" he asked, watching how the sun accentuated different shades in her hair. Her natural brown hair color gave her a regal, sultry look, and definitely added to her sex appeal, making him want to protect her all the more.

"Roberto runs several different businesses, none of which are in Omaha. He sought out John because he was a private investigator off the beaten path, or at least the path Roberto was accustomed to using."

"How did you find this out?"

"I figured it out. It makes sense. He has offices in Detroit and in Chicago. It's a family business, Mafia operations that he took charge of after his uncle retired. Do you know how many private investigators there are in Chicago and Detroit?"

"Point taken," Greg said. "So Roberto came to John to have him help with a business problem?" That would shoot Greg's missing-person theory out of the water.

"No. Roberto has several lawyers on retainer that I know of. Two of them contacted the office over the past month, both times wanting answers and growing irate when I wouldn't tell them anything."

"What did they want to know?"

"A couple weeks ago one lawyer called telling me he was simply the family lawyer and wanted to know if Roberto had been in the office that day. When I wouldn't tell him he called me a few choice names and hung up on me."

Greg could easily see Haley handling herself when it came to anyone pushing for information she wouldn't give out. All client matters were completely confidential. Any lawyer would know that.

"Also, John was handling Roberto's case differently than we usually handled cases but I couldn't figure out why. The main difference being he wouldn't discuss Roberto with me. At first he just avoided answering my questions, but toward the end he was rather blunt about it."

"What did he say when you asked?"

"He told me not to ask." She let out a frustrated sigh as she stared ahead of her, pursing her lips and shaking her head.

"Something was seriously wrong and I should have pressed him harder to learn what it was."

"Is there any way you could find out for certain what John was doing for Roberto?" he asked.

Haley stopped walking and took a moment to look up at him. Her gaze burned his chest, his neck, until finally she searched his eyes, her expression wary. "Possibly," she said slowly.

"You have access to everything in his office?"

"Yes because we worked together. But the Roberto Torres file disappeared."

"What about his house?"

"I could possibly get in."

"Good." He placed his arm on her shoulder carefully, aware of how pink her skin was turning. "We're going to Omaha."

The airport in Omaha, Nebraska, was no more than the size of a large bus station. Greg grabbed their suitcases off the ramp where all luggage from the plane had been dumped and nodded to Haley. His cell buzzed against his hip, but he ignored it. Marc and Jake had gotten pissed as hell when Greg told them he and Haley were heading to Nebraska alone. He needed men on the home front, carrying out business as usual and keeping him posted on any new developments at that end.

Haley hurried ahead of him, reaching the counter where they would rent a car before he fell in alongside her. He placed their luggage on either side of him and watched her complete the paperwork, noting that she filled out the paperwork as Hannah McDowell and paid for the car with Hannah's credit card.

"Why did you use that name?" he asked when they walked through the automatic glass doors into suffocating heat. Immediately sweat broke out on his chest and down his spine, causing his T-shirt to stick to him.

"It's the only name I have credit cards in," she explained,

and fanned herself with her hand. "I don't know which is worse, the glaring California sun or this god-awful humidity."

"They can have their humidity," he said. "Which one is our car?"

Haley squinted at the parking lot and then pointed. "The new Kia along the fence."

A short time later they headed out of the airport parking lot in a brand-new green Kia with less than a thousand miles on it that barely offered enough leg room to get comfortable. Haley messed with the air-conditioning controls on the dash while he watched signs that took him out of the airport.

"How do we get to your place?" he asked.

"We're going straight to the office," she informed him, pointing to the exit sign. "That's your exit. I want to check there first."

They would need to discuss a game plan once they got to her office.

"Okay, slow down and park here on the street." Haley had given directions without any other conversation as they drove through Omaha. She gestured to metered parking and waited until he'd put the car in park before getting out on her side.

Greg worked his way out of the cramped car and came around the front as Haley fed the meter. The humidity hanging heavily in the air made him ache for the one-hundred-degree temperatures of dry desert heat they'd left behind. Just getting out of the air-conditioned car made him want to climb right back inside, in spite of being cramped. He swore his shirt was melted to his torso.

"Lovely weather," he grunted, glaring up at the gray brick buildings towering on each side of the street.

Haley almost glowed as she smiled. She really looked happy to be back here. "I guess I grew accustomed to it. It feels great."

"If you say so." He tugged at his T-shirt and ignored her content expression as she headed toward the building in front of them. The tank top she'd chosen to wear clung to her back and waist and her light blue cotton shorts showed off her firm, round ass and long, slender legs. Maybe it was the only good thing about this blasted humidity. Watching Haley move when she climbed the few stone steps to the office building, he got one hell of a view of her perfect body. God, he wanted to sink deep inside her. It would feel like the first time after all these years. It would feel like coming home.

In spite of the waves of heat surrounding him and soaking his flesh, Greg's cock surged to life, eager to make his thoughts become reality. He reached over her head, pulling open the large metal door. A rush of cold air-conditioning attacked his senses so quickly he could hardly breathe. The contrast from hot to cold was more intense than day to night.

"I need to check mail," Haley said, pulling keys out of her purse and unlocking a small compartment in a row of mailboxes for all of the businesses in the building. "This is my morning routine," she explained, tucking the stack of envelopes under her arm, then heading across the foyer to the elevators. "I always got the mail when I checked in. John and I usually shared a cup of coffee, talked about any local gossip, then hit the field." She sounded excited to share her daily activities with him. The elevator beeped as it neared the first floor, and Haley stared at the numbers over the doors until they slid open.

Stepping inside, she faced him. "I'm usually here by seven thirty or so every morning. I really love not sitting behind a desk all day, although I became a regular in several diners and neighborhood bars."

The doors slid closed behind Greg and she reached to push the button for the second floor.

"When I came to work last time I was here," she continued, stepping back and leaning against the wall, her eyes bright as she stared into his and continued explaining her routine. "I picked up the mail as I always did, then unlocked the office. It was the third day John hadn't shown up so I wasn't staying here as long. We'd wrapped up several cases recently so I hung around the office, taking care of some paperwork that I always put off until there was nothing else to do. It was after nine when Roberto Torres showed up."

"And John hadn't been here in several days?" Greg stepped out of the elevator first, glancing up and down the quiet hallway.

Haley focused ahead as she walked with a fast clip to the office door that said "Payton Investigative Services" on it. She juggled the mail as she played with her keys until finding the right one.

Greg took the stack of mail from her. She looked up at him quickly, sucking in a sharp breath when they touched. Sticking the key in the keyhole, she didn't say anything, although she pressed her lips into a thin line. Her fingers shook slightly as she jiggled the lock until it opened. She wanted him. Her aggravation she couldn't hide fast enough when his hands brushed over hers proved that. Haley wore a strapless bra under her sleeveless shirt, and in spite of the full, round cups, he saw her nipples harden.

It was one hell of a mouthwatering view, one he hated pulling his attention from when she pushed open the door to the office. No one had been here in a few days. Greg wouldn't allow his sexy wife to distract him from protecting her and ensuring both their safety. He stepped in front of her, clasping the mail in one hand and holding his other out, blocking her, as he entered the quiet, musty-smelling office. It was obvious the AC hadn't been turned on in a couple days.

"John was a creature of habit, always coming and going at the same time. He was also one of the nicest men you could meet. Everyone said so. At first I couldn't see him as a detective but his likeable, laid-back nature helped people open up and answer his questions. He was over fifty, had been investigating crimes for over twenty years, and was beginning to slow down."

"You think life ends at fifty?" Greg ran his finger along the length of the wooden desk in the outer office, noting the computer, which was shut off, and an in-basket with a few papers lying in it. He picked up the papers, glancing over them.

Haley dropped the mail on the desk and walked around him to the only other door in the room and unlocked it. "I think John was getting tired of some of the more tedious cases. He called in younger detectives to chase around cheating spouses, things like that."

"Saved the good stuff for himself?" Greg dropped the papers, which appeared to be receipts, back in the in-basket and was by her side before she could open the door. "Let me," he told her.

Haley grunted. "I can do it."

"Humor me."

"Fine."

She nodded at the door, making a swooping gesture with her hand, as she left her keys hanging in the doorknob and stepped out of his way. Greg pushed the door open and entered another office. The desk in there was much larger and cluttered with enough papers that it was impossible to see the wooden surface.

"Where does he keep records of what he's doing every day?" Greg asked, shifting his attention to Haley when she entered behind him and moved around him. "We need to find out what he planned on doing the day he disappeared. And I want to know what his involvement with Roberto Torres was."

Haley walked around John's desk and sat in his seat, moving papers and finding a small, black schedule book that she flipped through until she reached the right month. Greg walked around and stood next to her, looking over her shoulder and focusing on the few days of the month that had something written on them.

"There's nothing written on the day he disappeared."

"Which means something came up that he didn't have scheduled."

"Or someone detained him on his way to the office." Haley glanced up at Greg, stating the obvious, then pursed her lips. They looked perfect for kissing.

Greg stared at her a moment, briefly lost in thought imagining himself leaning over the chair, capturing her mouth, and kissing her until she came. His focus dropped to the top of her shirt. As if she knew where his attention focused, Haley straightened, creating an incredible show of cleavage that made it damn hard to force his thoughts back on topic. He swore she arched her back, taunting him intentionally. "There's nothing here." Haley looked up at him and moistened her lips.

"And you have access to his house?" he asked, diverting his attention across the room to the white, unadorned wall.

Haley shifted in the office chair, pulling his attention back to her like a magnet. That damn strapless bra didn't do a thing to prevent her breasts from bouncing when she almost hopped around the desk to the filing cabinet.

"John always kept a spare set of all his keys," she told Greg, speaking as she found yet another key on her key chain and unlocked the filing cabinet. "They were backups, just in case."

"He kept them in a locked filing cabinet?" Greg questioned the wisdom there but didn't push it.

"Yup and had all the years I worked here. You'll like him once you meet him, I promise."

If he ever met him. Greg didn't stress that point. Already they were on day five since the man had disappeared and had nothing more than one phone call telling Haley to go home.

"We're going to figure out why he disappeared, even if we can't locate him today. I'm starting to wonder if Roberto has disappeared, too."

"What makes you think that?"

Haley didn't answer as she combed through files and searched each drawer in the cabinet. She grinned triumphantly when she pulled out a large, round key chain with a group of keys on it. She also pulled out a Glock, dug deeper, and found bullets.

"Roberto Torres is a creep. He has a MySpace page where he finds women. And he's a married man."

"Checking him out, are you?"

Haley made a face, wrinkling her nose in disgust, which

made her look adorable as hell. "You know it," she said. "I'd been keeping an eye on it since I discovered it, and it always showed he'd logged in every day. When I looked at the page the other day, he hadn't been online for almost a week. It's not the norm for him."

"Maybe his wife busted him."

"I'm just speculating here. I don't know Roberto's story, and don't care unless he's tied into John's disappearance for some reason." Haley's deep green eyes darkened and she brushed brown strands of hair behind her ear. "But if he did disappear, and wasn't kidnapped, he went into hiding for a reason, not simply just to run away."

"Is there anything else you want to look at here?" she asked, glancing around the office.

"Not right now. But at least now we're both armed."

Again she nodded. Greg took the Glock, loaded it, and checked the safety before shoving it in his back pocket. He half expected Haley to insist she carry the larger weapon. This time he went into the outer office before she did, allowing her to lock up. Greg missed the AC when they left the building and were back out on the street. The car was even hotter and he swore if his shirt didn't melt into his flesh, the leather seat would sear his skin clean off his bones. Haley climbed in next to him, appearing indifferent to the temperature in the car and instead focusing on a few pieces of mail she'd brought with her. He wouldn't bitch further about the heat and appear a wimp when she wasn't complaining.

"What do you have there?" he asked, hurrying to crank on the AC once he had the car running. Thank God for it being a new model. At least the air blew out cold without having to wait for the car to warm up.

"Utility bills," she said, holding up two unopened envelopes. "I don't have access to John's personal checking accounts, but I do have his debit card. I figured I would pay these and find out if there is money in his account. They won't go through if there's no cash."

"And what will that tell you?"

"John always has at least a few thousand dollars in his bank account. He always has. There isn't a lot he spends his money on and he's been paid pretty well for some of the cases he's handled over the years. I've seen his bank statements. I'm curious to see if the accounts have been drained."

"Good thinking." Then, because he wanted to, Greg ran his fingers down the side of her hair, stroking her soft brown strands. "Which way to John's house?" he asked.

Haley shivered and he knew she wasn't cold. Greg couldn't wait for them to call it a night.

"Head up to the second light and then turn right," she instructed, pressing her legs together and sitting straight as a board in her seat while gripping the bills and her purse in her lap. "If we can't turn off his security system, be ready to be friendly to the Omaha police."

"I'm always good with cops," Greg reminded her, intentionally lowering his voice as he shot her an assessing once over.

Haley flashed him a quick look, batting her thick lashes over deep green eyes, before returning her attention to the road ahead of them. "I remember a time or two—," she began, but then broke off her sentence.

"Oh yeah? And what times would those be?"

"Turn right here," she instructed. "And it seems to me one Mr. Gregory King got a bit mouthy with a few police officers one night after a football game."

Greg couldn't help laughing. "And they had their way with me when I entered the force a few years later."

"They were just as bad in high school," Haley defended him, although if that were pointed out she'd deny it. "Even after you were a cop and got pulled over for speeding when we went to see your parents one summer when the boys were babies."

"Hey! That officer hadn't sat in a car with screaming toddlers for the past couple of hours. He got what he deserved pulling me over."

Haley smiled, then tilted her head back and laughed. "He did rush through giving you that speeding ticket."

"He couldn't hear me and I couldn't hear him." Looking back on it, Greg felt for the older cop who'd pulled them over and then tried to talk to Greg while Marc and Jake screamed in their car seats in the back. "And you didn't do a thing to help."

"I hadn't been speeding," she said, giving him an innocent smile. "Oh crap, you missed your turn. Turn left here and go back around."

Haley played navigator until they pulled into a narrow driveway with a tall, unkempt shrub on one side. "We're here," she told him, and pulled her gun from her purse, checking the safety before sliding it into the back of her shorts.

Greg decided to leave the car running this time and put it in park, then struggled out the driver's side door, managing not to bang his knee. Haley was fiddling with the key when he joined her on the cement slab.

"He's got a security system?" Greg asked, glancing up and down the street, which was crammed full of small brick homes, mostly A-frames, with little yards and a broken sidewalk working its way to the corner.

"Yes. I think I know the code. We'll find out in any event." Haley unlocked the door but then froze. "That's weird. It's not set."

Greg grabbed her arms and pulled her back against him. She was relaxed, but then stiffened, every inch of her alert. The cool, hard gun pressing between them reminded him of how smoothly she'd armed herself before jumping out of the car, as if she'd done it a hundred times. Holding her against him, he stepped inside, methodically looking over the contents in the living room. It was cluttered, with newspapers strewn over a coffee table and a plate with something on it that looked like a partially eaten piece of toast. There was a coffee cup next to the plate. Those items didn't catch Greg's attention as much as the fact that the TV was on and there was a pair of shoes in the middle of the room.

Haley twisted in his arms, looking up at him, her green eyes wide with concern as she pressed her finger against her lips, indicating they should be quiet. Then pointing at the shoes she mouthed that they belonged to John. Her full, round breasts brushed against his chest. Although acutely aware of her nipples hardening, now wasn't the time to remind himself how sexy his wife was. He needed to secure the house.

Greg considered telling her to go to the car and call for backup if she heard anything strange coming from the house. Although he hated being in a situation like this and not being in his own town, knowing the cops on the force, and having the comfort of home turf, it wasn't the first time he'd handled a crime scene under such circumstances. He would keep his cool no matter where he was. Clues were clues and criminals were criminals.

Greg patted the Glock, grateful to have it. Years on the force made the gun feel natural there, a part of him, and brushing his fingers over the cold metal assured him he had what it took to protect Haley.

She looked up at him and pointed toward the kitchen. Haley had pulled her gun and backed out his arms.

Haley headed out of the living room, her gun held low, when Greg started toward the kitchen. As he moved through the house, Haley called out that it was clear. There wasn't anything in the sink and it was a damn good thing. Water ran full force although it hadn't overflowed. The plumbing must be good in the house. John Payton might end up with one hell of a water bill, but at least any evidence lying around hadn't been washed away.

There was a small hallway and a bathroom and bedroom, then a screened-in porch outside the back door. The backyard was overgrown and small. All indications showed someone lived here who didn't take a lot of time making the place homey. It also appeared John had left quickly, so fast, in fact, that he was in the middle of doing something, or a few things, when he was interrupted and taken from the house.

"I think we can rule out him leaving of his own accord," Greg said once Haley had joined him and they knew they were alone in the house.

Haley returned to the living room, and closed the front door, then locked it. "I'm going to call the police," she told him.

"What's your take on your local law enforcement?" he asked.

"There are a few men on the force John usually sought out when he needed a badge."

"You have their direct lines?"

"At the office." She turned, dragging her fingers through her hair, and pushing it behind her shoulder while she took in her surroundings. "I'd say he was waking up, starting his day, probably getting ready to come to work when he was interrupted."

"I don't see any sign of a break-in." Greg finished checking out the back door, which had been locked from the inside, and once again inspected the front door. "It wouldn't hurt to dust the place."

Haley walked over to the coffee table, standing between it and the couch as if she planned on sitting. "John was right here, eating breakfast and watching TV. Those are his shoes. He probably was in the process of getting dressed. I don't get the running water, though."

She returned to the kitchen and Greg followed her, staring over her at the items on the counter. It was a small kitchen, too small for a table. The floor was a worn pale green vinyl that looked as if it hadn't seen a mop in years. Although there wasn't trash anywhere, John wasn't a housekeeper by any means.

"He came in here to start coffee," Greg said, pointing to the coffeemaker pushed up against the wall on the counter underneath the two cabinets. "He turned on the water, reached for the coffee pot." Greg moved around Haley, positioning himself in front of the sink, and reached for the glass pot that was still sitting on the burner in the coffeemaker. "Look," he said.

Haley stepped around him with a ballpoint pen in her hand. She used it to slide out the basket where the coffee went. "He'd already poured the coffee into the filter."

Haley moved in next to Greg, taking a closer look at the coffee. "It definitely never got started. This coffee is dry and still fresh."

"John drank a lot of coffee?" Greg noticed there was enough coffee in the filter to make a full pot. "Either that or he expected company and was making a full pot that he expected to share with someone else."

"If he was expecting someone, then he would just holler for them to come in, possibly turning from the running water, but not leaving the kitchen."

"Did he do that? When you came over here did he yell at you to come in or did he go to the door and open it for you?"

Greg watched her consider his question, frowning as she stared across the room. "I think maybe I've been over here twice while John was here. And yes." She snapped her fingers and looked up at him. "The last time I came over I knocked and he yelled for me to come inside."

"You've been here twice while John was here? Did you ever come over here when he wasn't here?"

"Several times. The last time was just over a month ago. He'd forgotten a file and couldn't make it back home, so I came by to pick it up since I was on this side of town."

"Where was the file?"

Haley pointed, turning as she did, and led the way into John's bedroom. The bed wasn't made and two pillows were scrunched together showing the imprint of where John's head had been last. Greg would need the pillowcases and sheets checked for body hair, anything they could use to help authorities identify John's current whereabouts. Greg studied the twisted sheet and single bedspread that was tangled around the sheet. It appeared John did a lot of tossing and turning at night, as if something was keeping him from getting a good night's sleep.

"On his desk here." Haley reached for a stack of manilla folders.

Greg grabbed her wrist. "We need gloves."

"I'm not an amateur. I wasn't going to touch anything." There wasn't a bite in her tone. Haley sounded more as if she was explaining something to him. He couldn't argue with her. She was definitely no amateur. "There are some back at the office, but as far as I know this is where he kept his work." She used her pen to push the files.

"We're locking this place up and heading back to your office for any supplies you might have. I want prints, pictures, and I want to go over every inch of this place with a fine-tooth comb."

Haley was already heading to the front door. "Agreed. I'll call OPD after we discover any evidence we can. Let's go."

Chapter 9

There was one hell of a magnificent sunset Greg hadn't noticed until that moment. His shirt clung to his body and he tugged on it. There was so much dried sweat on him he'd have to stand in the shower for a good hour before he felt himself again. He remained in front of the rental car they'd driven there, taking in the dark shadows surrounding them. The air was thick enough to cut with a knife.

"Hannah, we have a detective on the case and a missing person's file started." Seth Gere, a young punk introduced to Greg as a local bounty hunter who handled John Payton's missing-person cases, smiled down at Haley.

It seemed Seth gave Haley too much attention since he'd first arrived at Payton's house well over an hour ago. The young stud struck a pose, his short-sleeved white T-shirt, faded jeans, and black boots giving him somewhat of a James Dean look. Not that the kid probably had a clue who James Dean was.

"I wish you would have called me sooner, Hannah. I would have been on this immediately."

"I went out to California right after he disappeared." Haley didn't tell the kid about the threatening letter she'd found on her desk.

Which was just fine with Greg. Seth didn't need to be filled in on all of the details. This wasn't his case.

"You've got my number, right?" Seth pushed, shooting Greg a quick glance that might be construed as that of one predator sizing up another. "I want you to call me if anything happens, Hannah. Okay? I don't care what time of day or night it is. I'll be there within minutes. You need me, you've got me. I don't like any of this."

"You're a sweetheart, Seth." She stood facing the young punk as he pulled his wallet out of his back pocket, flipped through it revealing a few large bills, and finally pulled out a card, which Haley accepted and dropped into her purse. "Thanks again. I promise I'll call if I need you."

Greg wanted to inform him that Haley would not need his help, for any reason. He stared the kid in the face, silently daring him to make eye contact again. Seth didn't look at him but had the nerve to pull Haley into a hug, keeping her in his arms a bit too long for Greg's tastes, before putting her at arm's reach and smiling down at her. He had fucking dimples and was probably still trying to control wet dreams at night. When he left them, he headed to a motorcycle parked in the street and gunned it to life. The bike didn't hold a flame to Greg's.

"He's probably not much older than Marc," Greg whispered into her ear.

Haley glanced over her shoulder at him, grinning. "I think by a couple years. And from what I've seen Seth is about as good a bounty hunter as Marc is."

She walked around Greg before he could say anything else that would remove all doubt he was jealous and joined the detectives who were coming around from the back of the house.

"Are you staying in town, Hannah?" Detective Frank Roster glanced past Haley at Greg before giving her his attention. "And do I have a contact number for you?"

Haley pulled out a business card. "This is my cell phone. I have it on me always. Call right away if you hear anything, please."

"Will do. You're staying in town, right?"

"Yes," she said, sounding for a moment as if she would say more, but she didn't.

Roster started toward his car, the other detective lingering while making a show of taking notes. Haley fell in alongside Roster.

"John is a good man," she began.

Greg was behind her when Roster paused at his car. The detective gave him an appraising once-over.

"I've known Payton for years." Roster shifted his attention to his partner as the guy walked into the street and opened the driver's side door. Roster opened his passenger door but then leaned on top of it. "Hannah, you already know this doesn't look good. He's been gone several days now."

"I know," she said, sounding as if she choked the words out.

"We'll be in touch." Roster slid into the car and gave them a salute as he pulled the door closed.

"I want to take one more look around the place," she told Greg after the detectives had left.

Greg followed her into the house, trying to focus on his surroundings instead of the scene into Halcy's life he'd just witnessed. She had an established life here. Six years of an established life. The detectives addressed her by her first name. And Seth Gere. Had she gone out with him? The overgrown punk sure acted a bit too comfortable around her.

"I know. We've been through all of this," Haley said as Greg leaned against the doorway to John's bedroom and stared inside.

Greg put his hands on Haley's shoulders, understanding what she was doing, and it wasn't something taught in a textbook. She was looking at the scene with her gut, searching for that one clue that would piece all of this together. His wife had turned into one hell of a detective.

"What do you think?" he asked.

"I'm not sure. I just wanted to take another look. She

entered the bedroom and stood over his desk. "Two of these are old cases."

She pointed to the files, which he slid apart from the others. "Then this file that isn't labeled contains information on Roberto Torres, just not enough information. I went through it already and there isn't anything in it that indicates why John would just disappear."

Greg stacked the files on top of one another and tucked them under his arm.

"They asked us not to take anything from the house." She frowned, straightening as if she could stop him from leaving the room if she tried. "There will be more cops here in the morning to document and tag everything into evidence."

"We'll bring it back." He turned her around and kept his hand on her shoulder as he guided her to the front door. "I know you want a shower, and a steak sounds really good right about now."

"Yeah, but coming back later tonight doesn't sound good," she complained, and paused at the front door. "I'm going to set the alarm. I'll call Frank Roster and let him know that it's set."

"Good. That way if they want in we'll have to come back over and will be here if they go over anything." He left her side long enough to double-check the back door. "You sure you know the combination to set the alarm?"

"It's my birth date."

He stared at her. A funny tightening in his gut made it hard to catch his breath for a moment. She hadn't been involved with her boss, had she? Any man who thought Haley was single would put the moves on her.

He wouldn't humiliate himself by asking. Haley was back and she would never leave him again.

Haley typed her birth date into the keypad on the wall and the alarm started beeping. Greg checked the door after she'd closed it and then reached her car door in time to open it for her. The inside of the car wasn't an oven anymore, but it was still damn hot.

"How do we get to your house from here?" He watched her when she looked at him.

"My couch isn't big enough for you. And Greg, you aren't sleeping with me." She sounded tired. "We wouldn't fit. I hate saying it but you'd be a lot better off in a motel room."

"You're going to make me drive around until I figure out where you live? I probably could."

Haley rolled her eyes and looked like she hid a smile. She gestured with her hand, giving directions until they pulled up behind a small, silver Toyota, the car Hannah McDowell had bought and financed and finally paid off over a year ago. Greg stared at the car, it hitting him once again how much of a life Haley had created for herself here in Omaha. While he'd been building his business, his garage and turning the front screened-in porch into the KFA office, Haley was out in the Midwest, creating a new life for herself. If her boss hadn't disappeared, and if Pierre hadn't died in prison, Greg wondered how long he and Haley would have continued with their own lives. The thought soured his mood even after he tried pushing the depressing thoughts away.

Greg cut the engine and climbed out. Popping the trunk, he hauled their luggage to the front door.

"Greg, I'm tired and getting grouchy and I don't have the energy to fight you. I honestly don't know where you can sleep," she stressed, looking pointedly at his suitcase he held in one hand, with her suitcase in his other.

"Sweetheart, I'm not a rapist. I've never forced you into anything sexual that you didn't want. So why are you worried?" He knew damn good and well she wanted him as badly as he did her, and maybe his look told her as much.

"Go to hell, Greg," she grumbled under her breath, and unlocked her door. Then stepping inside, she pushed a small panel on the wall next to her door that looked identical to the one at John's house.

Greg imagined them being installed at the same time and wondered who had instigated buying them and what had happened to make John and Haley install home security. She turned off the alarm and moved through her dark house to her kitchen, leaving Greg to close and lock the door. He heard her open her refrigerator and then water running as he put their luggage down and took in the contents of her living room.

Greg picked up and aimed the remote at her TV and turned it on, then started flipping channels, impressed that she had a pretty elaborate channel lineup. Haley was never one to watch a lot of TV. Maybe too many nights sitting at home alone had made her pick up the habit of being a couch potato. He couldn't picture it but didn't question the small discovery. He checked out her couch, agreeing it was definitely not long enough for him to sleep on, but managed to get comfortable by stretching his legs across her coffee table and reclining in the corner as he continued checking out the prime-time lineup.

Greg closed his eyes, balancing the remote on his thigh, and listened when a shower turned on somewhere in Haley's house. The sound of the water relaxed him, or most of him. Imagining Haley naked in the shower, running her bar of soap over all those perfect curves, and suds streaming down her body, made it impossible to fall asleep. His cock grew harder than steel, and he placed one hand over the bulge in his jeans, part of him demanding that he strip and go join his wife in the shower.

A marriage certificate was just a piece of paper and had nothing to do with what made up a marriage. It took trust, not only loving each other but also really liking each other. Haley had always supported and defended Greg and he tried remembering when he'd done the same for her. Greg was being given a chance to start over with everything he'd learned over the years intact in his brain. He would be the best husband for Haley.

The sound of the shower continued torturing his thoughts. And a newscaster on the TV became a droning background noise as Greg let his thoughts wander, visualizing Haley's body naked and dripping wet. He already knew she was in great shape, but he wondered in what ways her body might have changed over the years. He knew that her nipples would turn to hardened peaks if he so much as blew on them. He wanted to take them in his mouth, suck on them and hear her make that breathy sound she always made.

He moved his hand off his cock, but his raging hard-on wasn't going away any time soon. It might get a little awkward if Haley walked into her living room and caught him sprawled out on her couch sporting a cock fit to be ridden. Once, Haley would have done just that—used him for her own satisfaction without saying a word or batting an eye. Her mischievous grin as she would undress him, slapping his hands out of her way if he tried helping, or copping a feel, would be as much torture as the pleasure she would then offer.

All his blood drained to his dick. He imagined her touching him, making his balls tighten with the urge to come. It was as if she were really there, her fingers brushing the length of his shaft. He almost opened his mouth and told her that he liked it just like that, but caught himself just in time. It would be his luck Haley would walk in just as he was stroking himself and telling her how good she was at doing it.

If she was still anything close to as good in real life as she was in his dreams, he would be in serious trouble. The fire burning out of control inside him, and the pressure torturing his balls, would do him in before he even got close to her. He needed to get a grip. And not the grip he wanted on his too-hard Johnson.

But then he heard a yelp. Reality hit hard, sinking in his gut like a brick. Greg knew it was too late.

He opened his eyes and saw Haley standing over him. She had a terry-cloth bathrobe wrapped securely around her, barely showing any skin below her neck. It ended before her knees, which were pressed together firmly. Her mouth was opened in shock.

Greg glanced down his body, staring at his cock fighting

against the restraints of his jeans, then returned his attention to her face.

"Was there something you wanted?" he drawled, fighting a grin when her mouth snapped shut and her cheeks burned a brilliant rosy red.

"Your cell phone kept ringing," she said finally, nervously tightening the tie to her bathrobe around her waist.

He moved to sit up straight and that's when he felt his phone, halfway out of his front pocket. She'd been trying to pull his phone free and her fingers got a bit too close to something else. He must have been really out of it if he hadn't noticed the leading lady of his fantasy leaning over him. He was really going to have to do something about this situation soon. Greg grinned, letting his legs drop off the coffee table, enjoying how she paced off her embarrassment.

"Someone keeps calling you." She waved her hand at his phone that he now held in his hand. "It wasn't waking you up and since you were so far gone I tried answering it for you."

Haley quit pacing and tried very hard for a placid look as she stood facing him on the other side of the coffee table. He wasn't through enjoying how she'd made him hard as a rock. Not to mention, he was positive she was burning alive with desire. The way she shifted back and forth, rubbing her legs together, and rubbed her belt showed how restless and affected she was. Haley was saved by the bell, or buzz, when the phone vibrated again.

"It's Marc," he told her.

"I thought it might be one of the boys." She licked her lips, nodding and holding on to her matter-of-fact expression.

Greg handed the phone to her for her to answer. "You worked so hard for it, darling," he drawled, and didn't fight a smirk this time when she scowled at him and the flush in her checks returned.

When it rang a fourth time and he continued to hold it out to her, Haley finally snatched it from his hand, pressed the button, and answered it.

"Hello," she said, her voice tight as she shot him a condemning look.

Greg stretched back on the couch, his cock still semi-hard. If Haley thought getting grouchy with him for getting turned on when she was around would turn him off, she needed a reminder of how much she turned him on. He laced his fingers behind his head, relaxing against the back of her couch, which wasn't that uncomfortable, and watched her talk to their son.

"No. He's right here. He's being an ass and made me answer his phone."

Greg heard his son laugh through the phone and watched her pretty green eyes flash although she didn't look mad.

"Okay, hold on. I don't know how to do it." She held the phone out to Greg. "He wants to be on speakerphone."

Greg extended his hand for the phone but didn't lean forward, forcing her to bring it to him. Haley moved to the edge of the coffee table and he took the phone. The urge to grab her and force her down on his lap caused every muscle in his body to harden. Haley must have seen he was ready to pounce, because she almost tripped over her own furniture hurrying to get out of his reach.

"What's up, son?" Greg asked, flipping the phone to speaker and then holding it in his hand.

"Just checking in. I take it you two made it to Omaha okay."

"Yup. Your mother is entertaining me at her home," Greg told him, and grinned when Haley growled.

"I can imagine," his son drawled.

Greg wouldn't torture Haley in front of their boys, in spite of what she might think. "Are you holding down the fort?" he asked, moving the subject to safer grounds. They had a few open cases at the moment and he needed to make sure the boys were handling them properly. Although he'd never left them in charge before, he believed both of them were capable. Either way, it didn't surprise him that Marc would want to touch base, run everything he did past his old man, and make sure it met with approval.

"We brought in Bob Easley this afternoon," Marc offered. "Margaret was surprised you'd left town."

"I left the business in competent hands. Good work on Easley."

"You did, and thanks," Marc said matter-of-factly. "Sam Wilson stopped by today. She was pissed off when she learned you'd left town," he added, laughing. There was a comment in the background Greg didn't catch, and he guessed Jake had thrown in his two cents.

"I'm sure she was," Haley muttered.

Greg glanced up at her pinched expression and decided he didn't mind her jealousy although she'd learn soon she had no reason to be. "Did she say why she stopped by?"

Haley crossed her arms against her waist. He looked down so she wouldn't see how much he loved seeing how she could so easily be turned into a possessive female.

"That's part of the reason why I called. She received a threatening letter this morning. It was slipped under her windshield wiper. She brought it over to us and I checked it for prints, but there weren't any on it."

Another comment in the background.

"Fine. We checked it for prints," Marc stressed.

"What did it say?" Greg asked.

"It said: 'You can run but there is nowhere to hide.'"

"What?" Haley squealed.

"Are you okay, Mom?" Marc asked through the phone.

"Do you have a way to fax it to us?" Haley moved closer to the phone, obviously no longer dwelling on Greg grabbing her.

"Sure, if you want. Just give me a fax number."

She repeated her fax number to him several times until Marc had it. Haley hurried out of the living room. Greg pushed himself off the couch, following her down a narrow hallway and past a closed door to the room at the end of the hall. It was her bedroom. The first thing he noticed was her single bed pushed against the far wall, definitely not suitable for entertaining a date she might want to bring home. The knowledge that Haley wasn't sleeping around, and by her choice of furniture never intended to, made his heart swell to the point where for a moment he could hardly speak.

"We're faxing it now. Why do you want to see it?" Marc asked.

"I received the exact same message the day I left work. I want to compare the two and see if they look the same," Haley explained as she leaned over the small desk that was just inside her bedroom and housed her computer, and made sure there was paper in her printer. "If they do, whoever left the threatening letter on my desk is now in Southern California."

"The fax machine is ringing," Greg told Marc, staring at the machine as he wondered if whoever had left the message had gone to California when he came here, knowing he'd be out of town. "Marc, Sam is going to need protection. I want full surveillance on her until we can nail whoever sent these letters."

"Agreed." Marc was all business on his end of the line. "And I've already taken the initiative. She was pretty upset when she brought over the letter and I didn't want her driving. We have her in the guest room right now. I think she took a Valium, or something. She's out like a light."

"I bet she wouldn't be if you were there," Haley muttered.

"What was that?" Marc asked.

Greg tapped Haley on the nose, grinning when she swatted at his hand. "Nothing, son," Greg told him, but then leaned over the fax when it began printing.

Haley moved around him, hurrying out of her bedroom, but returning a moment later with her purse, which she placed on her bed. Even with the knee-length cloth robe wrapped around her, her round ass looked damn tempting as she kept her back to him, digging through her purse. She turned around with the letter she'd shown him earlier that week and held it out as the fax finished printing. Greg pulled the fax out of the tray and held it up to Haley's letter.

"They're a match," Greg announced. "The font is even the same."

"Don't hold me to this, but the font looks new, like one of those offered on Windows Vista and not on XP."

"Mom the computer buff," Marc teased. "Who would have guessed?"

Greg smiled and shot Haley a quick glance. He wasn't too thrilled, though. The threatening messages did appear identical. Either someone was jumping across country just as they were or there was more than one person involved here.

"When will you be heading back?" Marc asked.

"Not sure yet," Greg said, and offered a brief summary of visiting John Payton's house. "We need something to tie all of this together."

"We have it," Haley mumbled, letting the letter she held drop onto the desk, then hugging herself. "John said the same thing on the phone that these messages say."

"What's that?" Marc asked.

"There's nowhere to hide."

"Marc, I'll give you a call back in a bit." Greg would be the first to argue Haley could hold herself strong in a crisis situation, but someone she cared about had disappeared, and now the letter she'd received had just appeared across the country. They were both exhausted and this was a bit overwhelming. "And we'll be home soon. Keep in touch and we'll do the same."

Greg hung up the phone and placed it on Haley's desk. He pulled her into his arms and began massaging her back when her body started shaking. She began sobbing, the soft, whimpering sounds hardening every inch of his body as he tightened his grip on her, pulling her closer and stroking her silky hair. So far he'd seen the perfect woman who was good at everything. She didn't need him anymore and that terrified him. Greg prayed he could always keep her wanting him.

A few minutes passed before Haley pushed away from Greg. "This doesn't make sense," she complained, wiping her eyes. "I drove out to California, told no one I was leaving. I was so damn careful to make sure it wasn't obvious I left. I paid cash for everything. How could someone have followed me?"

"Maybe they didn't." Greg watched her as she began pacing in the small amount of space between him and her bedroom door and the opposite wall on the other side of her bed.

"All I thought was I could return to you. If I'd stayed here, gone to John's house, maybe someone would have found him by now." Haley dragged her fingers through her damp hair, leaving it tousled around her flushed face when she stared up at Greg with moist green eyes. "What do you mean?"

"It's normal to shoulder the pain, sweetheart, but it's not your fault. I'm starting to think there is a connection here that has nothing to do with you at all. You were left a warning so that you wouldn't interfere with a much bigger picture."

"And what is that bigger picture?" Haley was obviously distracted enough not to worry about her bathrobe as she faced him. She didn't fix it when it parted, creating a V that showed off the swell of her breasts.

Greg forced himself to stare into her eyes, fighting with the sudden knowledge that she wasn't wearing anything under that bathrobe.

"John Payton has disappeared. Feathers show up in your hotel room and I'm sent a message from a seedy bar and a supposed client telling me The Bird has flown the coop. That would mean The Bird has taken off, also gone. I can't verify the connection yet, but Samantha Wilson's brother, Jason, didn't show up for court and we can't find him. Not to toot our own horn, but we've got a pretty good track record of bringing in delinquents. Jason Wilson seems to have disappeared into thin air."

"So," she said slowly, blinking and rubbing her eyes, offering even more of a view as she moved and her bathrobe shifted over the front of her body. "And now you're going to tell me how all of this ties in together?"

A ready answer wasn't there for him, either. "I wish I could, sweetheart," he said, lowering his voice and aching to pull her back into his arms. "What I can say, what I believe, is that all of these things didn't happen randomly. There is a connection."

Haley pulled out the chair pushed under her desk and plopped down in it, picking up the letter left on her desk and the fax Marc had just sent over. She held one in each hand, staring at them and not saying anything for a moment. Then dropping the papers, she moved her mouse, clearing her screen so her desktop became visible. The backdrop was a picture of a beach with a magnificent sunset. Maybe she'd stuck it out in the Midwest out of sheer stubbornness, but Haley hadn't let go of her roots, her home, which was back in California with Greg and the boys.

"What are you doing?" he asked, resting his hands on the back of her chair. A picture of Marc and Jake, when they were probably around twelve and fourteen, hung on the wall over her desk. Another sign of her stubborn streak since he knew WP didn't allow anyone in the program to hold on to their past.

"I'm going to check John's e-mail."

"You have his log-in information?" Greg ignored the look she shot him over her shoulder. "You should have told me that. We might learn something from the mail he's received or sent."

"I checked it a few days ago." Her fingers moved over the keyboard as she kept her eyes on the screen. "He hasn't sent any e-mails out and I haven't answered any of them, since I didn't know when he'd be back."

Her ring finger had an indentation on it, the skin a slighter paler shade where a ring recently was. Had she worn her wedding ring up until recently? Or was another ring on her finger and she'd taken it off before seeking him out, so he wouldn't notice it?

"You don't have to answer anything, but it wouldn't hurt to keep an eye on his mail. Did you usually answer John's e-mails for him?"

"Always. Most of the mail was more for me anyway. John

didn't like computers. He claimed they provide an ambiguity and prevent people from really knowing each other."

A man after his own heart. Apparently his not answering showed Haley exactly what he thought. She glanced up at him, twisting her torso and showing off enough breast that his cock got hard as a rock all over again.

"He really was a lot like you," she murmured, looking away, but not fast enough that Greg didn't notice the sadness in her eyes.

"We'll find him," he promised, gripping her shoulders and massaging them through her bathrobe.

"I just hope before it's too late," she whispered, but then moaned. "You need to quit doing that," she added, her voice a bit huskier than it was a moment before.

"You used to love it when I rubbed your shoulders."

"Umm," she said, her fingers no longer moving over the keys.

He spread his fingers over her slender shoulders, pushing her bathrobe out of his way. Haley made another sound in her throat but didn't stop him. He remembered how giving her massages turned her into putty in his hands. It amazed him how much he knew about Haley and yet there were times when he was getting to know her all over again. It created an excitement inside him. It was a need to learn and relearn every little detail about her.

"We're not going to worry about the case any more tonight," he told her, and cleared his throat when his voice sounded too gravelly. "Tomorrow morning we'll catch a flight back to LA and compare notes further on the two messages left for you and Sam."

"Hm," Haley said, letting her head fall forward when he worked his thumbs into the nape of her neck.

Her skin was smooth, soft, and slightly tanned. Strands of light brown hair brushed over his knuckles and fanned across her shoulders. He itched to get her bulky bathrobe out of the way, carry her to her bed, and lay her facedown, then massage all her worries away. Running his fingers over every inch of her, taking his time getting familiar once again with every curve, every hair on her body, sounded like one hell of a good idea.

Greg ran his fingers over the length of her shoulders to her arms, pushing her bathrobe farther out of his way as he did. It fell to the top of her arms, still covering her but giving him full reign over her neck and the top of her back. He ran his thumb over a few freckles, thinking it would be a damn good idea to kiss each one.

Haley jumped and squealed when her cell phone rang in her purse, and almost fell out of her chair.

Chapter 10

Haley straightened quickly then grabbed her bathrobe. She yanked it up around her neck, as if she'd just now noticed how he'd almost slid it off her.

She dug into her purse, pulling out her phone, then stared at it, not answering.

"Who is it?" Greg leaned so he could see the screen.

"It's the same number that called me the other day," she told him, continuing to stare at the phone as it rang a fourth time. "It's John," she added, her voice cracking.

Haley pushed away from the desk, grabbing the belt of her robe and trying to answer the phone at the same time. "Hello," she said, staring at the floor and allowing her hair to fall around her face.

"Speaker phone," he whispered, trying to make as little noise as possible.

Haley didn't look at him but pulled the phone from her ear and pushed the button to set it to speaker.

"Hannah," a scratchy male voice said through the small speaker. He broke up as he spoke her name, which meant either he was weak or there was a piss-poor connection.

"John?" Haley asked, holding her phone in front of her face and straightening, using her free hand to pull her hair away from her face. "Where are you?" she demanded.

"I'm not sure." There was silence for a moment, possibly as he received instruction as to what to say next. "You need to go to work tomorrow," he said.

Greg gestured for her to agree.

"Okay," she said slowly. "What do you want me to do?" she added on her own, meeting Greg's gaze with dark green eyes that were milky with concern and worry.

"Stay at work all day." John's voice broke up as he spoke. "If someone comes in to see me, tell them I'm out of the office at the moment, but set up an appointment for me to meet with them."

"When should I set up the appointment? And who is coming to see you?" she asked, speaking quickly so one question rolled over onto the other.

"It doesn't matter what time the appointment is set," John said, his voice fading as static replaced it.

"I can't hear you," she complained without being prompted. "Where are you, John? Are you hurt? You need to come home. The police know you're gone now."

The silence that followed lasted so long Haley glanced at her screen to make sure they were still connected. "John?" she asked, her tone rising as she sounded panicky. "John, answer me!"

"Don't involve the police," he said finally. "It will complicate things," he added slowly.

"Complicate what things? John, you aren't making sense. I don't understand. Where are you?"

"Make an appointment with anyone who comes in to see me."

There was a loud pop of static and Haley frowned at her phone. "He hung up," she announced, continuing to stare at it. "God, he sounded really bad."

"He sounded alive," Greg pointed out, and took the phone from her, then pushed buttons to learn the number and wrote it down along with the call time. "It sounds as if whoever has your boss thinks someone is going to come looking for him. They don't want them knowing John isn't there."

"None of that changes the facts here," Haley pointed out. "This is personal. These messages are personal. My hotel room was trashed. I'm good at what I do, Greg. My track record is outstanding, but honestly I don't know what to think about all of this."

"Haley, only the very best of detectives admit when they don't have a clue."

"The very best?" Haley looked up at him in awe before a small smile appeared. "Oh, Greg."

She cried out when he lifted her, wrapping his arms around her and holding her against him as he captured her mouth. Any other words were lost as he impaled her, drowning in her heat. She tasted better than the last time he'd kissed her. Haley was irresistible, an addiction he never wanted to overcome.

"You are the best, sweetheart," he whispered into her mouth, moving to the bed with her in his arms.

"I don't think—my bed," she began, but then let her head fall back when he ravished her neck.

"Don't think," he told her. "Let go tonight, sweetheart. We want each other. This looks like the perfect place to me."

He laid her down on her single bed and she stared up at him, her eyes opened wide, pools of deep, sensual green. "My bed isn't made for this," she said, the scratchiness in her tone as raw as his emotions were.

"Your bed is perfect," he told her. "But that bathrobe has to go."

Haley didn't take her gaze off his when she reached for the tie secured around her waist. As many times as they'd made love over the years, done sexual things he never would have dreamed of doing with another woman, the way Haley watched him at this moment tightened his insides as if it were their first time.

Hell, she'd carried his children. He'd stood there and watched her give birth to them. She and Greg had paraded around each other naked over the years. But when he tugged his shirt over his head, letting it drop to her floor next to him, Haley sucked in a breath, her gaze dropping to his bare chest.

"You don't look like you're forty-five," she whispered, offering a small smile as she loosened her belt.

He wasn't sure he could handle her praise. Already he was too close to the edge. Not to mention, the longer they stared at each other, undressing, exposing themselves, the more raw his emotions grew.

"And you don't look like you're undressing," he said, pressing his lips together so he wouldn't smile when she made a face.

Haley pushed herself to a sitting position and shoved out of her robe, letting it pool around her hips. Anything else he might have said escaped his thoughts. In fact, he wasn't sure he could form a thought at that moment.

Her breasts were full, round, and her nipples large and erect, puckering into light brown beacons that made his mouth water. The rest of her was slender, firm, and in shape.

"God damn," he muttered.

Haley turned over and got on her hands and knees, giving him a view that damn near brought Greg to his knees. Haley glanced over her shoulder at him and pushed her hair out of the way. A purely wicked smile graced her lips.

"Forget what to do, cowboy?" she purred.

How many years had it been since she'd called him cowboy?

"Oh, hell no," he rumbled, his voice rough although he no longer cared.

Greg grabbed her hips, pulled her back to him, and slid his cock between the soft curves of her ass. If she wanted it quick and fast Haley would be disappointed. He wasn't going to just fuck her. Years of need for her were coming to a head and he had every intention of making passionate love to her.

"I've dreamed of this," she whispered, shifting her weight

so he couldn't slide in and looking over her shoulder at him. Haley batted her lashes, licked her lips, and let her gaze travel up him slowly until she stared into his eyes.

"Tell me what you want, sweetheart."

"I was about to do just that."

Haley flipped to her back and spread her legs on either side of him. Her hair fanned around her head, falling in soft waves on the bedspread around her. She held Greg's gaze as she dragged her hands up her body before cupping her breasts and pinching her nipples. Haley moaned at the same time Greg dragged in a ragged breath.

"Get me off, darlin'," she whispered.

Greg was only too happy to oblige. He went to his knees before running his fingers up the inside of her thighs. She gasped, caressing her breasts and flicking her nipples with her fingernails as her lashes fluttered over her eyes. "I want you to come for me like you've never come before," he growled.

Haley reached for him, running her fingers through his hair, encouraging him closer to her pussy. And God. It was shaved.

Every ounce of blood drained from his brain to his cock and Greg breathed in deeply, taking her rich, intoxicating scent into his lungs. He stared up her body, over the swell of her perfectly round breasts, and focused on her face.

She bit her lower lip as he dragged his tongue down the length of her entrance, parting her slender folds as he did. Haley tasted good, rich, her smooth cream instantly filling his mouth and making him crave more. He moved to her clit, teasing the small nub, and Haley damn near jumped off the bed. He held her still, controlling her.

"Don't fight me, darling," he ordered, aware of how fast her breath was coming.

Haley moaned and closed her eyes, giving herself over to him completely. Greg continued watching her while he feasted on her pussy. It was a hell of a lot of work staying put, pushing her over the edge, when his balls constricted and his dick weighed half a ton between his legs. More than anything he wanted to bury himself in her heat, feel the moisture that he drank into his mouth soak his balls. It would be worth it to watch her climax, though, to see her finally let go.

Haley still loved him. It was obvious when they kissed each other outside the football field. He saw it when she stared at him and even when they sparred. There were a lot of changes in her, although from what he'd seen so far, they were changes for the better. He'd always loved the old Haley, but the new Haley challenged him a lot more. And he had to admit, he loved how strong and independent she'd become.

Greg didn't have a problem taking on her stubbornness. The easiest way to break through it would happen here any minute. He sucked her clit into his mouth, wrapping his lips around her smooth, round, swollen flesh, and used his arm to keep her from flying off the bed again. Gripping her breast and rolling her nipple between his fingers, he gave the puckered flesh a good, hard squeeze and at the same time impaled her soaked pussy with his tongue.

"Oh my God!" Haley wailed, letting go of his wrist and tangling her fingers in her hair as she thrashed her head from side to side.

Rich, moist cream soaked his face as she came. She cried out again, arching her back, then reached for him. Haley grabbed his shoulders, her fingernails pinching his flesh when she dug in, moaning as her orgasm continued spasming through her.

"I can't believe—," she gasped, but didn't finish her sentence.

It wasn't the first time Greg got her off this way. As a cop he had often worked late hours and too many times came home to his family already sound asleep. Over the years he'd learned letting Haley sleep at night made it easier for her to keep up with their active boys while they were growing up. But that didn't mean there weren't the occasional times when he and Haley had enjoyed each other during the night, or sometimes while Marc and Jake were in school. Those moments had been treasured and never happened enough. Possibly now, at this stage in her and Greg's lives, moments like this could happen more often.

Now wasn't the time to ask what she couldn't believe.

"Breathe, darling," he coaxed, stroking her stomach and breast with his palm. "You aren't done yet."

"Nor are you." She surprised him when she sat, appearing more invigorated than he thought she'd be after coming so hard. "I want you to take me doggy-style."

"Still giving the orders, are you?" He laughed, finding her determined expression rather enlightening. "If the lady wants to be on her knees, then that is where the lady shall be," he said, grabbing her before she could move and flipping her around.

He placed her on her knees, situating her so she was sideways on her bed, her ass facing him as he slowly stood. The throbbing in his cock pulsed throughout his body, the hard, demanding beat increasing in moderation as he held on to her with one hand and gripped his cock with the other.

Haley shook her ass, not looking over her shoulder this time. Her hair streamed down her back, soft waves fanning over her shoulder blades. He would do whatever it took to make sure Haley was always happy and satisfied. And not just sexually.

Greg made that promise to himself as he pressed the tip of his cock against the entrance of her pussy, feeling her incredible heat and the moisture clinging to her skin draw him in.

"This is it, baby. Oh crap!" he hissed, wrapping his arms around her and grabbing her breasts while burying himself deeper inside her.

"Greg!" she yelled, tensing and trying to collapse on her bed. "God, Greg," she cried out again.

A mixture of pride and wonder filled him, knowing he was large enough that she couldn't handle him all at once and amazed at how incredibly tight she felt. He wanted to know how often she had gotten laid over the past six years. Even if he asked, she might tell him to go to hell and not answer. His new Haley was fiery tempered, spunky, and going to challenge him every minute they were together.

"Don't go slow," she gasped, pushing herself back to all fours as she straightened her arms. "Fuck me. Fuck me hard. Now!"

"I don't want to hurt you," he told her.

Haley laughed. "Your ego sure as hell hasn't changed. Now fuck me. You've never hurt me before and you aren't going to do so now. So unless you don't have what it takes, cowboy, give it to me."

Greg growled, her sassy nature adding to the fever already raging out of control inside him. "You asked for it, my dear."

And he let her have it. Letting go, thrusting deep inside her incredibly tight pussy and feeling her wrap around him like a glove, Greg gave her all she asked for. She cried out and gasped, her breathing coming hard and quick as she took all of him.

There wasn't any stopping now. No more orders. Nothing granted or requests fulfilled. This was it. What both of them had needed for so long. Greg impaled her, building momentum and drowning in her heat until the pressure was too much to endure any longer.

"Sweetheart." His voice was so raw from need finally reaching its climax he sounded foreign even to himself. "It's my turn."

"Yes," she agreed, and her pussy clamped around him, holding on tight when he exploded, as if she planned never to let him go.

Chapter 11

Haley blinked and sat up in bed, frantic that she'd overslept. She searched for her cell phone, praying she hadn't forgotten to set her alarm. Then it hit her. Like a ton of bricks upside the head, everything from last night came sliding into her memory with a rush too strong to endure.

"Greg" she whispered, and realized how hoarse she sounded. "Of course he couldn't sleep with me."

As she continued sitting in her bed with her blankets wrapped around her waist, replaying the events from the night before, one thing was clear. There were no regrets. She felt better than she had in years, had slept better than she could remember. A twinge of excitement created a burning pressure deep inside her womb. She could have Greg again. Right now if she wanted.

She shifted her attention to her opened bedroom door, listening for sounds of Greg moving around her house. The central air kicked on, its humming making it hard to hear anything else. That's when she realized she was naked. Haley didn't sleep naked. Had she fallen asleep after making love to Greg and he'd tucked her in?

Cold air blew out of the vent by her closet, causing the shirt she'd worn the night before to flutter slightly as it lay on her floor near the vent. Haley tucked the blankets around her body, continuing to sit in the middle of her bed, and replayed the events from last night.

Her body still tingled from being with Greg. She'd been so daring, demanding, telling him what to do. That wasn't how it had ever been between the two of them. Granted, she'd enabled his dominating her. In their early years she'd adored the ground he walked on, put him on a pedestal, and done whatever he said. It turned her on, got her hot, when he controlled her. Their sex would get rough, wild, and she'd loved it. She'd missed being with Greg.

Now both of them had changed.

Haley scrubbed her tangled hair with her fingernails, surprised at how incredibly messed up it was. She had to look like shit, even though she felt incredibly good at the moment.

Once she'd loved the macho he-man. Today she wouldn't be able to take a man like that. Greg would dominate her if she let him. He'd grown and matured and could admit how good Haley was at what she did.

Today Haley needed a best friend, an equal. Someone who would acknowledge when she was right, but accept that she would admit it if she didn't know what she was doing. She needed mutual respect, that bond that made her best friends with her lover. And of course, she needed to be loved, too. Haley needed to get exactly what she would give.

Haley could sit here and ponder how their relationship would work all day and not have any more answers than she did right now.

"Oh crap," she hissed, untangling the sheets from around her waist when she remembered she was supposed to go into work today.

Haley opted for a shower first, all too aware of the heavy breathing coming from her living room when she traipsed to her bathroom with clean clothes in hand. As the water hit her, images of Greg between her legs came to mind, his blue eyes staring up at her as he feasted and got her off better than she'd ever gotten off in years. Her emotions had been so frazzled after seeing John's house. Brainstorming the case with Greg was like a glimpse into how their future could be. Haley needed to know he wanted her working alongside him as much as she wanted to work alongside him. And not because she needed his help. Haley wanted a partner in investigation and the hunt who loved what he did as much as she did: Her answers would only come with time.

Haley finished her shower, dressed, and messed with her hair until it appeared she might have a decent hair day. She wiped the steam from her mirror and posed in front of it, remembering Greg commenting on her breasts. The shirt she chose for today showed off just enough cleavage to distract a man. Not that she wanted Greg distracted from the case. She liked the way he looked at her, though. Thoughts of seducing him into submission, the way he used to do her, had her hot and bothered before she was out of the bathroom.

When her kitchen was clean and the coffee not yet started, Haley knew Greg remained on the couch intentionally. He wasn't the kind of man who would avoid her the next morning, but she hated thinking he gave her space believing she would feel weird after last night.

Making quick time getting coffee going, she glanced at the clock, then marched into the living room. Greg lay sprawled on her couch with his long legs draped over the coffee table. He held a bottle of water in his hand, resting it against his chest, and the remote in his other hand. The TV was on, but the volume was so low she hadn't heard it from the other room.

"Good morning," she said, planting herself firmly in the single upright chair that was the only other place to sit in her living room. "I go into work at eight."

Greg studied her a moment, his sky blue eyes exceptionally bright this morning in spite of them being in her dimly lit living room. "Is that what you're wearing to work?"

"Yes." She bit back the urge to ask him what was wrong with what she wore. No way would he dress her. "We've a casual atmosphere, but neat." When his gaze dropped to her cleavage, Haley felt the heat pooling between her legs. She refused to let his hungry stare distract her. They would make love when she decided it was time. "Do you want coffee?" she asked, standing.

Greg stood as well, letting the single blanket he must have found in her linen closet fall to the floor. He wore boxers and showed off way too much muscle and brawn.

"Sounds good."

God. He looked good, too.

Haley returned to the kitchen, forcing her thoughts on John as she took two mugs out of her cabinet and poured coffee. "What are your speculations on why I'm supposed to be at work today?" She needed to think about the case and not how to turn Greg into putty in her hands.

"Do you regret last night?" he asked, and sipped his coffee, staring at her over the rim.

"Not at all," she admitted, but then turned to face him. "Is there something wrong?" It hadn't occurred to her he might have lain on the couch brooding about something.

"No," he said, studying her. "How could there be? Haley, you're absolutely perfect. Beautiful. Sexy. You're good at your job."

"Last night I was the best," she drawled.

Greg grinned and moved into her space with enough comfort and ease as if he did it every day. He pressed his finger under her chin, urging her to tilt her head and focus on his face. Then pressing his lips to hers, she tasted the fire raging through him, which matched the intensity that was eating her alive.

"Everything about last night was the best," he whispered, moving his mouth over hers. He backed up just a bit, barely enough to allow her to focus on his compelling blue eyes. "I woke up this morning fighting the urge to return to your room and make love to you again. And although last night I was thrilled to see that single bed, which would make it damn hard to have a guy stay the night, this morning I cursed it because there was no room for me."

"When I bought it, I never thought you'd be here." She went up on her tip-toes, leaned into him and kissed his cheek.

"We should get going." He made a show of looking at the clock on her wall. "We need to get to work, sweetheart."

That dominating, possessive stance he made was so damned hot. Taming her giant, muscular husband, so he would come at her beck and call, sounded even hotter.

"Give me a minute to get dressed."

"Do you eat breakfast?" he called out, padding barefoot back into the other room.

"Not usually. I don't often get hungry before lunch."

"I'd forgotten that about you," he mused, returning to the kitchen as he pulled the same T-shirt he'd worn yesterday over his head and down his torso. "It's rather interesting how I thought I'd held on to every little memory, but now that we're together I'm learning how many things I'd forgotten. As well, how much you've changed," he added, giving her a knowing look as he took in her body. "And not just physically," he drawled, his brooding stare creating a quickening in Haley's gut.

"Greg," she said, turning her back to him and downing more coffee. It was hot and burned her esophagus, but she used the discomfort to help focus. "I think we should lay some ground rules."

"Oh yeah?"

"Once we're on the clock we should agree to only discuss work."

Haley squealed when powerful arms wrapped around her and dragged her backward against so much roped muscle.

"Then with the few minutes we have left before we clock in, I need to make sure you know how incredible you are," he whispered in her ear.

Her heart damn near exploded in her chest as a rush of happiness almost made her light-headed. "I've always known how amazing you are." She twisted in his arms. "But do you really mean what you're saying? I know I've changed."

"Sometimes change is for the good. It keeps the sparks flying." He sounded amused.

"Are you willing to take orders? If we get a case that I happen to know the details about, will you follow my lead?" she challenged.

Greg didn't answer right away. His expression relaxed, but was completely unreadable.

Helping her husband see he would enjoy life if he let go and trusted her at the helm would be a challenge. Not that she didn't know that already.

"Do you want to be in charge simply to have control?" There were probably many who would be intimidated by Greg's size and powerful, deadly appearance, especially when he spoke in a grumbling whisper as he did now.

"I just told you," she pointed out, glancing at the clock then heading for her bedroom and grabbing her purse before joining Greg in the living room. "Whoever had all the info would take the lead and sometimes that would be me. Can you live with that, Greg?"

She opened her front door and leaned on the doorknob.

Greg headed out of the house without saying anything and unlocked the rental, climbing in on his side and starting it. She took her time setting the alarm, her insides twisting. Had she been so blinded by wonderful sex and a flood of happiness that she'd pushed too far?

Haley stared at Greg when she slid in to the car next to him. "Please answer me, Greg."

"I thought we only talked shop on the clock."

Her sigh must have sounded too exasperated.

"Okay, sweetheart," he said, putting his hand on her leg. "You deserve a hard yes to that question, Haley. You're good, very good." He paused, searching her face and looking very serious. "Haley, I'll try. Just be patient with me, darling. I've always been in command."

"I've had a taste of it, Greg. I've tasted the craving for the hunt and the satisfaction of leading a team to a bust. I love it, Greg. I really do. But I'll never be truly happy without you by my side."

"We'll make this work," he assured her, patted her leg, then started out of her driveway.

They pulled in front of the building where she worked just ten minutes later and Greg cut the engine. He got out of the car and she got out on her side slowly, checking him out as he gazed up and down the street. He was always on the watch, always making sure his surroundings were secure. She glanced up and down the street as well, didn't see anything out of the ordinary, and headed into the building. Greg reached around her, pushing the button to open the elevator before she even knew he was there.

The elevator beeped when it hit the lobby floor. "I don't know if you remember every detail about me," Greg said, holding the door while Haley entered the elevator.

"What?" She frowned, watching as he pushed the button, then stepped in closer as the doors closed behind him.

"I've often had a problem with not always following the rules." He rested his hands on her shoulders and stared down at her with sky-blue eyes so bright, yet clear, that she swore she saw straight into his soul. "I need to know, Haley. Did I upset you? I thought about lying."

"Don't lie to me."

"I didn't. I can't handle seeing you glow with happiness and knowing you're going to be disappointed."

Haley turned when the elevator doors opened and stepped into the hall. "Do you think you're going to disappoint me?"

Seth Gere stood outside the doors to Payton Investigative Services and turned to face them, cocking one eyebrow as he stuck his thumbs through his belt loops.

"Good morning, Seth," Haley said cheerfully, praying Seth hadn't overheard her and Greg's conversation.

"Morning," Seth grunted, eyeing Greg warily.

"I hope you haven't been waiting here too long." She struggled with her keys, then unlocked the office door.

"Nope," Seth said, still in grunt mode. "I've been up for a while, though, and thought I'd stop by."

"Any word on the streets?" she asked, catching Greg's brooding expression when he stepped around her and entered the dark office before she did.

Flipping on the light in the outer office, Haley walked over and unlocked John's office. She got the sensation a testosterone showdown was about to take place and really didn't want to be stuck in the outer office with both of them when it did. She made her way around both men to the coffeepot. With the two of them in her office, the space seemed suddenly very cramped.

"Anyone else want coffee?" she asked, not turning around but instead grabbing the can of coffee and filters, then taking the pot to the small sink to fill it with water.

Two men grunted behind her. It was going to be a long day. Someone wanted her to be here, though. And that someone very likely knew where John was. Seth Gere had worked with John for quite a few years now. He took the high-maintenance cases that John no longer dealt with, and truth be told, Seth had a damn good track record. He was young and cocky and built like a lumberjack. Haley knew his good looks and roguish charm helped in getting information from the ladies. His intimidating size worked well on the men. None of Seth's attributes impressed Greg.

Had Seth Gere impressed someone else? Was he the reason they were supposed to be here today?

"Can I talk to you for a moment, Hannah?" Seth asked, focusing on her when Greg pierced him with a hard stare.

"Sure," she said, managing to work her way around both of them to her desk. "What's up?"

"Alone," Seth added, this time returning Greg's stare.

Haley watched Greg tense. "Of course, Seth." She nodded to John's office. "I'm afraid in here is the best I can offer."

Greg leaned against the edge of her desk, crossing his arms

over his massive chest, and watched the two of them walk into John's office. She met Greg's disapproving scowl for only a second before closing the door. Then facing Seth, she hoped her smile appeared relaxed.

"What's up?" she asked again.

"Are you okay, Hannah?" Seth asked the moment she turned her back on the door, keeping her hands on the doorknob behind her. "I noticed him hovering around you at Payton's house last night, too. How well do you know him?" Seth's face was lined with concern. "Just say the word and I can get rid of him for you."

Haley managed not to laugh. In the years Seth had been coming around, picking up the more gruesome cases for John and doing a damn efficient job of tracking down some nasty criminals, he'd always been quite the gentleman in spite of his rather rough appearance. Rumor had it he'd recently moved in with his girlfriend and was keeping regular hours.

"You're a sweetheart, Seth," she said, walking around and sitting behind John's desk. "You don't need to get rid of him, though. He's a bounty hunter who knew John and is worried about him as we are."

Seth stood in the middle of John's office, his legs spread and his black boots adding to the bad-boy image he worked hard on. He crossed his arms across his chest and for a moment reminded her of her sons. Marc was a bit cleaner cut and Jake was still too much of a pup. None of them had the hard-ass look Greg could master.

"Do you have any idea why John disappeared?" Seth asked, keeping his voice low.

If it weren't for John telling her to do so on the phone last night, she wouldn't have come in today. Seth was here waiting for her, as if he knew she would be here. Maybe he didn't know she was supposedly out of town. Haley wouldn't turn paranoid and start worrying everyone she'd known for years might be someone other than who they appeared to be. But she would be cautious until she had more answers.

"Disappeared? Do you think he's taken off on his own, or someone took him?" she asked, curious if Seth knew the office had been closed. She hadn't put the On Vacation sign back up when she and Greg had left last night, but if Seth had been around recently he would have seen it.

"Come on, Hannah," Seth complained, throwing his arms up in the air, then slapping them against his thighs. He moved in on her, leaning and planting his fists firmly on the desk. "I don't know what the hell is going on, but I can find out. Give this one to me. Give me a name, anything. John Payton has given me work when others wouldn't. I owe him this. And you're the boss here now. Give me this one and I'll track John down for you. I promise. He didn't just take off and you know it. Something happened to the old guy and he deserves the best there is trailing him."

Haley leaned back in John's chair, pressing her hands together and resting her elbows on the armrests as she pondered Seth's offer. She already knew he was one hell of a good bounty hunter. Maybe asking him to track down Torres would allow her and Greg to focus on where John was, or who sent the letters. There were too many angles to this case right now and possibly a bit of delegating would help bring it all into perspective sooner.

"Fine." Haley noticed immediate relief on Seth's face. "Here's what I'm going to do."

Greg was still sitting on the edge of her desk, his arms crossed, and scowling at the floor when Haley walked into the outer office. He looked up slowly, his blue eyes the shade of a turbulent thunderhead ready to explode right before a storm.

"What are you going to do?" Seth asked, following her.

"Greg King, I'd like you to meet Seth Gere." Haley made introductions instead of answering Seth's question.

"Greg King? The bounty hunter out of California?" Seth asked, giving Greg an appraising once-over. Seth frowned at Haley as if something didn't make sense to him. "Greg King is one of the most successful bounty hunters in the nation."

"I'm afraid I can't return the compliment." Greg sounded guarded when he accepted Seth's extended hand and shook it. "I can't say I've heard of you."

"No, you wouldn't," Seth said easily. "I've been a bounty hunter for going on five years now and most of my work comes from this office, although I pick up a few jobs from bondsmen, too. John doesn't go for a lot of the down-and-dirty cases anymore. I guess you could say I do his dirty work."

"Someone's got to do it." Greg wasn't smiling, but some of his hostility faded from his face. "What were you two discussing in there?" he asked, not hesitating in demanding to be filled in.

Haley opened her mouth to explain, but Seth spoke before she could. "I was begging for work from the boss. Payton's name might be on the door, but anyone will tell you this lady cracks the crimes. But you, what are you doing here? What brings a California bounty hunter to Omaha, Nebraska?"

"Hannah and I go way back," Greg said. "I'm here to do whatever the boss tells me to do," he added, his blue eyes flashing in her direction.

"I see," Seth said. Whether he did or not wasn't clear.

Haley wouldn't worry about what either man truly thought of the other.

"I'm sending him out to find Roberto Torres," Haley informed Greg. She shifted her attention to Seth. "I want you to go through this town with a fine-tooth comb, learn everything you can. Find Torres for me, if he's in town. He might know where John is, or have some knowledge about his disappearance. I want to know everything he knows."

Haley lifted a file off her desk next to where Greg sat. She skimmed over the few papers that were inside. The standard form all clients completed with general contact information and a disclosure form were stapled inside the folder. The section where the client was to write out his reason for hiring Payton Investigative Services was blank.

"I don't have much on Torres right now," Haley said,

handing the file to Seth. "All I know is he hired John and right after that John turned real secretive."

Greg took the file before Seth could and looked over the papers before handing it to Seth. "So what's your plan?"

"I've got some really good contacts in the area. If he is anywhere nearby, I'll track him down and bring him in."

Greg nodded, apparently satisfied with the answer.

"I'll be in touch with you before the day is out," Seth said, nodded to Greg, then left, closing the door behind him quietly.

Haley didn't hear him walk down the hall and decided it must be a trait unique to bounty hunters to be so large yet able to move without being noticed.

"He respects you."

Greg's comment surprised her and she faced him, impressed even more at his relaxed expression. The worry lining his face earlier seemed completely gone.

"I admit at first I thought he wanted to fuck you," Greg continued, remaining perched on the edge of her desk with one leg crossed over the other. "And he might fantasize about it from time to time, but he admires you and views you as a colleague."

"And that surprises you?"

Greg exhaled slowly, keeping his attention on her face. "I think my ego wanted to find you a bit more helpless after all these years. It would have been a lot more satisfying to learn you had struggled and had a hard time making it. But instead I learn you don't need me at all."

"Could you handle it if I didn't?"

Greg raised his hand and crooked his finger, gesturing for her to come to him. Haley cleared the short distance between them without hesitating. Greg straightened his legs so she was able to stand between them and draped his arms around her waist, his large body slowly enclosing her against him. Haley rested her hands on his shoulders, admiring his perfectly chiseled features and how his blue eyes glowed with more emotions than he would ever admit having.

"I could handle you not needing me on one condition."

"What's that?" she asked.

"As long as I know you want me."

Chapter 12

Greg remained on the edge of Haley's desk, watching her chew her lower lip as she studied him. "We're not doing a good job at all of only talking shop at work."

"Probably once we know where we stand at home and work it will all be easier."

"Why can't we just say we stand together no matter where we are?" Haley scowled when he shook his head. "You know, this isn't fair," she snapped, tightening her arms on either side of his neck. "You're upset thinking our relationship won't work if I don't need you, but we were married twenty years and you didn't need me—you wanted me."

Greg stood, holding Haley by her waist, when someone turned the door handle and entered the office. Haley stepped away from him, not making eye contact as she moved around her desk.

"Hi there, Slap." She sounded unbelievably cheerful, as if she'd just laughed at something Greg had said. She sat at her desk, sliding the papers into Roberto Torres's file as she focused on Slap. "What can I do for you today?" she asked.

"I need to talk to John." The odd-looking man, who possibly stood five and a half feet at the most, looked incredibly nervous. "I've got an emergency."

"He's not here, Slap." Haley's expression looked pained. "What's your emergency?"

Slap moved cautiously around Greg, eyeing him as if he thought Greg might pounce and attack with less than a moment's notice. The small man moved with a limp. One leg appeared shorter than the other. Greg took in the bushy red hair on the man's head, the long-sleeved flannel shirt that was untucked and hung past his rear. He was about the most unique-looking man Greg had ever seen, yet Haley smiled at Slap as if she believed him a very special person.

Slap fisted his hands on the opposite end of the desk from where Greg had sat and leaned into Haley. His gaze dropped to her cleavage, but Haley didn't seem to notice. Instead, she remained relaxed, approachable looking, and waited for Slap to speak.

"I need to talk to you."

"It's okay, Slap. Greg is a colleague of ours. You can say what you want."

His watery pale eyes looked tired as Slap sized Greg up. When Slap returned his attention to Haley, he leaned in farther.

"I'm hearing things," he whispered.

"What are you hearing?" Haley didn't whisper back but lowered her voice, giving Slap all of her attention.

"Things I don't like. I really need John."

This would be where Haley insisted this odd-looking man set up an appointment. Greg wondered when John would call Haley to find out what appointments were set. It would make sense that call would take place at the end of the day if they, in fact, wanted them set. But if John had been told to have Haley make appointments so whoever his abductors were would know who was coming around looking for him, then Haley would put every person entering this office into danger.

"John is missing," Greg announced.

Haley looked at him, surprised, but regained her composure quickly, snapping her mouth shut and looking down as she tugged on her shirt. When she shot Slap a side-glance, the odd man didn't notice the even better view of cleavage she just offered but instead gawked at Greg.

"What I'm hearing is worse than I thought," Slap said, and began wringing his hands as he moved away from Haley. When he stood in the middle of the office, he continued shooting Greg wary glances as he tried focusing on Haley. "People are disappearing. No one who wouldn't improve the streets by being gone," he added quickly, but then held out his small, almost deformed hands. "Except John. He's a good dick. Always has been, and I'd tell anyone that."

"We know he is," Haley soothed, her calm, mothering tone having one hell of an impact on Slap. "Help yourself to coffee and I'll get chairs. We're going to sit down and you're going to tell us everything you've heard."

Greg watched Slap pull a cup with a lid out of the pocket of his flannel shirt. It was the type picked up at convenience stores, except the name of the store had long since worn off this cup. Slap turned to the coffeemaker, mumbling something under his breath. He appeared to carry on a conversation with himself, suddenly oblivious to the two of them being in the room with him.

Haley hurried around her desk and into John's office and reached for the chairs in front of his desk. Greg placed his hands on her shoulders, feeling her tense under his touch for just a moment before relaxing and glancing curiously over her shoulder at him. He should have given her rule more consideration, then they wouldn't have started something they couldn't finish. Haley wouldn't have distanced herself because he was a big oaf when it came to expressing himself.

"We're sitting in here," she said. "That way we aren't interrupted if anyone comes in."

"Go back out there. Make sure we have enough coffee and talk to him for a minute. I'll arrange the chairs and make sure we don't have any bugs floating around."

Haley glanced around the office, and when she looked at

him, her eyes were still troubled. "That's fine." She tugged at her shirt, a nervous action and not one intended to give him a better view of her soft, full, round breasts.

Greg watched Haley leave the office and pull the door three quarters of the way closed. They were breaking ground and possibly would come out stronger than ever if he could just learn how to properly express himself.

Greg inspected the office, searching for all standard bugs and anything off the market. Although a few existed that were nearly impossible to detect without special equipment to narrow in on them, he was pretty damn sure a short time later that the room was secure.

If only he could say the same about him and Haley. When she'd come home, Greg had had no doubts she'd stay with him. His wife was back. There would be some issues to iron out, which they would, and life would move forward finally. Now he saw it would take a bit more work than he'd originally thought. Because of him. Haley had evolved, grown, become even more incredible than when she'd left. Greg needed to show his wife he was worthy of her. He paused in the middle of the office, glancing around at the dingy-at-best surroundings. They didn't bring him down but instead offered hope. Whatever it took, he would show Haley he was still her partner in life, that they were soul mates and always would be.

"Are we ready?" Haley asked when he opened the door and saw her sitting on the edge of her desk where he'd been sitting.

"I think so." He looked at Slap, who furrowed his bushy eyebrows, giving him a scowl as if he didn't approve of Greg being here. It shouldn't surprise him that Haley's alternate world wouldn't want her to leave. "Shall we?" he asked, and gestured to the open office door.

Slap entered first and Greg guided Haley in behind the short man, noticing she stood taller than Slap. Haley moved around the desk, sitting in John's seat and taking the helm.

"Is the coffee good?" Haley asked Slap as he sipped from his plastic cup.

"Hm. Yes. Thanks."

"Good. You started telling me what you heard, but please, start over," Haley instructed, giving Slap that motherly smile of hers.

Greg imagined it probably worked well on many people who entered this office. Haley was a natural. When someone had uncomfortable information, or knowledge of something that bothered them, being put at ease helped them share what they knew so much better. Greg leaned against the door, remaining behind Slap so the odd little man could focus only on Haley.

"I was down at The Dog House the other night, you know, just making my rounds as I always do after work. Things have been quiet lately, which is a good thing, although I guess you don't make as much money when it is," he said, then cleared his throat, grunting and mumbling something to himself. "And don't get me wrong; I'm not one to try and drum up trouble just to get an extra dime," he added, suddenly speaking too loudly.

"Of course not," Haley assured him.

"I didn't come down here thinking I could exchange information," Slap persisted, speaking in a normal tone again.

"No one thinks you're doing that." Haley leaned back and crossed her arms. When she did, her breasts pressed together and the cut of her shirt showed off their full roundness to Greg's distraction.

"Good. Good," Slap repeated himself, looking at her but then focusing on his coffee and taking a long gulp. "So I'm at The Dog House and there is a guy in there I don't know. And I know everyone. You know that. Slap Happy knows everyone and is welcome everywhere. That is how it is."

"Yes," Haley agreed.

"This man is at the bar, drinking with a couple guys I do know. So I take my spot at the end of the bar and get my draw like I always do. They leave me alone and I do the same, focusing on my beer and listening. And that is how I found out."

"What did you find out?" Haley asked.

Slap looked over his shoulder at Greg, as if Greg had asked the question. He stared at him a moment and looked as if he'd lost his train of thought. When he finally continued, he'd shifted so he could keep an eye on both of them.

"There are certain men in town who do what they want. The cops leave them alone and the criminals do the same. They run their business and do what they do. It's how it is. No one messes with that."

Greg nodded, willing Slap to get to what he knew but understanding the type of man Slap Happy was now. He was an informant, a fairly simple man, possibly living on the streets. He probably worked both sides of the street, doing whatever it took to ensure his next meal and a dry bed.

"When something happens to one of these men, it messes up the natural flow of things. Like if all the dogs disappeared, then we'd have way too many cats."

"Who has disappeared?" Haley asked.

"Right." Slap nodded, spinning around and snapping his stubby fingers at Haley. "Now when small men disappear, we worry but keep our noses clean and pray we aren't next. But this man at the bar. His man in Nebraska, who apparently worked the Kansas, Missouri circuit, too, is gone. I didn't catch his name, but I'll find it out for you. I promise. And you know I'm good for my word."

"Who disappeared, Slap?" Haley asked calmly. "Do you know who the man was at the bar? Did anyone call him by name?"

Slap shook his head. "They don't use names at The Dog House. No one uses names. That would cost you more than a warm meal. But he's gone for a reason. And the man talking to the other men sitting with him at the bar made one thing clear to them."

"What's that?" Greg asked, knowing Haley would have a good reason for using an informant who appeared not to have all his oars in the water.

"The Bird says who is in the birdcage and that is how it is."

Slap looked confused and turned to Haley. "That is what the man said that I didn't know. He said anyone who matters will disappear now that The Bird has flown the coop."

Greg waited while Haley locked up the office, his stomach growling after having spent the day living off candy bars from the vending machine. They had closed the office over the lunch hour, but only to meet the cops over at John Payton's house. Haley changed the pass code for John's home security, letting the detectives know the new code, which tied up an end for her here. No one mentioned her not leaving town this time.

"I'm booking us a flight out of here tonight," Greg said, once they were headed back to her house.

Haley glanced at him, her expression neutral as it had been since their conversation this morning.

"Haley," he said, focusing on traffic, if that's what this town could call the several cars in front of him waiting on a red light. "We should talk about this morning."

"Do you think what Slap Happy overheard meant this assassin, Marty Byrd, has disappeared?" she asked.

Greg looked at her and Haley returned his stare, slowly arching one eyebrow and looking more defiant than he'd ever remembered seeing her. At least it was an emotion, which was more than he'd read on her face all day.

"It sounds like it," he said slowly, cautiously, still watching her.

"What I thought, too," she mumbled.

"He's either disappeared or is the reason others are disappearing. We don't have a confirmed list of those who are missing, but someone left those feathers all over your room, which I believe was another message pertaining to The Bird. We can search for answers better once we're home."

Greg didn't break the silence that grew between them as he drove back to her house. Greg wasn't the same man he was when they first met, either. He'd never given much thought about what qualities would make up the perfect woman, but if anyone suggested the ideal lady for him today would be dominating and pushy, he would have laughed in their face. Yet they would have been right.

"I don't think we should leave for LA tonight." Haley paused in the kitchen doorway after showering. She wore a tank top with no bra and a pair of matching shorts that showed off her slender, trim legs. "Possibly we can leave in the morning."

He didn't want to fight with her. He wanted to sit down and have a nice meal with her. Hell, he'd even fix it, if there was food in her house. He'd love to cuddle, brainstorm the case with her, and experience more how his beautiful wife had turned into a talented detective. It was what she wanted; for him to acknowledge her investigative skills. The more time he spent with her, the more he wanted it, too.

"Hear me out," she continued, holding up her hand as if she could hear the argument he was preparing in his mind. "John, or whoever took him, wanted me in that office today. You confirmed the place wasn't bugged. So unless someone was camped outside, and I never noticed anyone parked and in their car on the street throughout the day, they're going to make John call back and want to know when those appointments are. I'm going to give him times for tomorrow; then we're going to watch the place, see who shows up."

"Good idea. I like it," he told her. "I say we go early so we can head to the airport after."

Something softened in Haley's expression. His praise of her suggestion affected her more than she wanted Greg to know.

"Then it's settled. "I'll order pizza. You still like pepperoni, right?"

He followed her into the living room, where she planted herself in the upright chair across from the couch and pulled out her cell phone. She brushed her light-brown hair over her shoulders, and the damp strands contrasted perfectly with her tan skin. Although his memories of his wife were of a platinum blonde, he was falling in love all over again with this stimulating, more natural-looking, sexy lady who challenged him with every breath she took.

"Marc called me today while you were on the phone at the office," he told her, taking his place on the couch across from her. "He ran that number that your boss has called you on through our system. It's a pre-pay phone which I'd anticipated since the number wasn't blocked."

Haley nodded. "I looked it up on the Internet. There's no way to trace them. I figured their using it was meant to be a personal stab. They are that convinced we'll never find them."

"You're right." Greg tried grinning but got nothing in return for it. "This tells us the abductors are cocky, arrogant, and have done something like this before."

Haley snapped her fingers. "Which means a possible rap sheet." She didn't wait for Greg to respond, but called and ordered food.

"They aren't blocking the number on purpose just to torment me," Haley said after placing the order. She stretched one bare leg over the armrest and stared at him for a moment. It looked like she might finally talk to him about this morning, but then she didn't. "You do think John will call again tonight, don't you?"

It was the first time all day she'd asked his opinion on anything. Haley had been full of telling him how things would be, doing her best to run the show. After their discussion this morning about wanting and needing each other, he wasn't sure if she behaved like that around him because she was trying to impress him or because it was simply who she was now. It might be a bit of both, but either way, he liked knowing his opinions still mattered to her.

"They're going to make contact with you somehow. I'd bet money on it," he said, leaning forward and grabbing the remote off the coffee table. He stretched out, crossing one boot over the other as he reclined into the corner of the couch. "The question is, though, do they want to keep you guessing? Or do they care that you would anticipate a call and receive it?"

"That might have something to do with the type of personality we're dealing with. John is placing the calls, but he's being instructed. Otherwise he would explain to me what's going on. He's never been one to keep me in the dark."

"Does he have any kind of surveillance equipment?"

Haley blinked, studying his face before frowning. "What kind? And what for?" she asked.

"To put around the office. That way we would know who is coming and going."

Haley turned her attention to the TV when he flipped it on, the volume still down from this morning. She tapped her finger against her lips, pursing them into an incredibly enticing pout.

"We discussed it a time or two, but he never installed a camera at the office. Any equipment he might have would probably be in his house," she mused, staring at the TV. "Since I've changed the password on his home security and turned that information over to the police, going over there now would be breaking and entering, or at the least obstructing an investigation."

"It wouldn't look good," Greg agreed. "After supper we're going to do some shopping. We can get most everything I want at Wal-Mart."

Haley continued speculating over the case after their pizza arrived and comparing it to other cases she'd worked over the years. He enjoyed watching her enthusiasm discussing it. Even at Wal-Mart, while keeping an eye on shoppers around them to make sure no one appeared suspicious, or to be watching them a bit too closely as they shopped, he felt a comfortable companionship developing with Haley.

He wouldn't say "old habits." Once, Haley had agreed with anything he said. She never questioned him, and even when he used to ask for her opinion she always told him whatever he wanted was fine. There were times when that annoyed the crap out of him. At some point in time as the years went by, Greg quit asking what she wanted and instead told her what she would do. It hadn't been a conscious decision to control his wife. It was just how they'd ended up. Greg had never thought of Haley as stupid. He'd always known she was incredibly intelligent.

The pizza arrived and not much was said as they ate. It was an amiable silence, though, followed by showers, which were taken separately. It crossed Greg's mind to ask Haley about that morning, but their ride to Wal-Mart turned into a discussion of surveillance equipment.

Haley had changed so much. She'd always been energetic, driven, willing to take on any situation. But it had always been at his side. They'd been a team, inseparable. Or so he'd thought. This woman sitting next to him, so charged with energy he swore it made the air between them spark with electricity, was full of ideas, eager to explain how something worked, and therefore should work that way again, and at the same time speculative as to who might show up at her office.

Greg was proud of himself when he found the street he needed that led downtown after leaving Wal-Mart. He kept an eye on what little traffic was out as he turned on the street where her office building was. When he parked out front, Haley didn't move from where she sat as he climbed out the driver's side and pulled the bags from the backseat.

"What's wrong?" he asked, leaning in and looking at her as she stared at her lap. All of her enthusiasm over setting up their brand new spy equipment had vanished in the time it took him to grab everything out of the backseat.

Even in the dark he noticed how pinched her expression was. Whether it was from his comment or something else he wasn't sure.

"I just got a text message," she said.

He noticed the phone gripped between her legs. "Who's it from?"

She shook her head. "It's not the same number John was calling me from. All it says is: 'What time are the appointments?'"

Greg glanced up and down the street again, an unnerving chill rushing down his spine. "Let's go inside. We'll figure out how to answer once we're in the office."

He waited for Haley to get out on her side, then locked the car. Hauling the two plastic bags of supplies they'd purchased, he stood behind Haley as she unlocked the main doors to the building. Again he glanced into the dark shadows surrounding them, a sensation he didn't like making his skin crawl. He'd been a cop for years and a bounty hunter for quite a while now. Long enough to know to pay attention when his gut sensed trouble.

"Maybe I'll just text back that there is one appointment time." She held the door until Greg entered, then locked it behind them. Her tennis shoes squeaked over the tiled floor when they walked to the elevators. "That way we'll have one time when we need to be focused on the office. The earlier in the day, the better."

It was sound thinking. "Let's set up this equipment and then text them."

"If we wait too long to answer they might think we're plotting the best answer to give them."

"Good point."

"Thank you." She didn't smile at the praise this time. Haley was concerned and focused on her thoughts.

They entered the elevator and he pushed the button for the second floor. "Haley," he began.

She held up her hand, her expression serious when she shook her head. "Don't, Greg. We have a job to do. Let's just focus on that right now."

"Alright. But later we're talking about how we feel."

Greg couldn't believe he'd just insisted they talk about their feelings. Shifting the bags so he held them in one hand, he cupped her chin with the other. "Not a minute goes by when I don't worry about you," he whispered, and brushed his lips over hers. "I know we've got things to work through."

"I worry about you, too," Haley said, moving her lips against his as her lashes fluttered, hooding her gaze. "And we'll work through them as long as we can both accept who each of us is today."

The elevator reached their floor and he straightened, stroking her cheeks with his knuckles and brushing hair away from her face. Was he a much different man than he'd been six years ago? He wasn't going to ask right now.

"We'll take the stairs down. I haven't taken them yet and want to be as comfortable using them as the elevator," he said, digging through one of the bags as they headed to Haley's office.

"The stairs are on the back side of the building and don't enter as close to the office as the elevator. That's the only reason I always come up this way."

"Makes sense."

Haley slid the key into the lock and opened the office door. She didn't turn on the light but held on to the door when Greg entered the office. They didn't say anything as Haley closed the door and leaned against it as he pulled the contents out of the bags and placed them on her desk. Light glowed through the opaque glass in the door from the hallway, creating a ribbon of visibility through the otherwise very dark office.

Greg wondered how often she'd played part in setting up traps to catch a criminal. She had a gift for talking to people, putting them at ease, and even keeping her cool in crisis situations. Placing surveillance equipment in strategic spots in public places was a hell of a lot more nerve-racking than many guessed. It appeared fun and exciting in movies and on TV shows, but that was fiction. In real life, it often proved a heart-pounding, brow-sweating, and adrenaline-overloading experience. Experience all those sensations at once and the highest trained investigators might have a problem thinking clearly.

"I'm honestly surprised your boss didn't already have surveillance equipment installed in here." Greg pulled the small camcorder out of its box and freed it from the packaging. "This little beauty can be placed almost anywhere and it won't be noticed."

"Very little action ever happened here. If we recorded something, it was always with the client's consent."

"This time we're going to pray for a bit of action." He glanced at her as he set up the camcorder. "You better send that text."

"I already did." She stepped forward, grabbing the packaging he'd pulled out of the box when it almost fell to the floor. "I told them ten A.M."

"That sounds good. Have they responded?" He placed the small recorder on the top of a filing cabinet behind Haley's desk, adjusting a pencil sharpener and three-hole puncher so they didn't block the lens but helped hide the small camcorder from view.

After turning on the recorder, checking its battery life, and testing it, he was satisfied it would record anyone coming into the office. It sucked that he couldn't install a few other toys he loved using, but they were all back home and not easily obtained on a moment's notice. For now, the camcorder would have to do.

"I want to dust down all the furniture," he told her, unwrapping a bag of washcloths he'd picked up. He took a cloth and handed one to Haley. "Wipe down everything, every inch. We're going to make this place one hundred percent fingerprint free. If our friends show up and touch anything, our prints or the prints of anyone else who has been in here won't mix with theirs."

"Okay," she said, wiping the cloth over her desk.

"Don't pick anything up. Don't touch anything. Just wipe with the cloth," he instructed, taking on the filing cabinet and even the camera.

As he ran the cloth over the door to John's office, wiping down the doorknobs and even the walls alongside the doors,

Greg realized Haley did as he said without question. She didn't tell him not to boss her around, or refuse to listen to him. Haley dished out orders just as well as she took them, which wasn't how she'd acted when she first arrived in LA. Was she slowly converting back to the old Haley now that they were together again?

"Alright, we're ready for company," he told her, putting the thoughts out of his head and at the same time wondering why they bothered him. "Head on out and I'll turn on the camcorder. It will record for twenty hours, which will take us well past ten in the morning tomorrow."

"If they show up. They might just wait outside and see who enters the building."

"I've already thought of that." He waited until she'd opened the door to leave the office before turning on the camcorder and following her out into the hallway.

Something sharp zapped him in the side of his neck when he tried walking around Haley.

"Greg!" Haley wailed, trying to grab him.

He couldn't get his thoughts to cooperate. And it didn't make sense why Haley grabbed him, but then it seemed her hands scraped over his flesh, as if she was being pulled away from him.

Again he tried saying her name. This time his muddled brain managed to wrap around what was going on around him. He turned in time to stare into cold, demonic eyes, realizing he'd been shot. A raging fury shot through him, helping to sober him further.

He'd been second-guessed. All along he'd assumed their perp would show up at the time they set the appointment for. Which was exactly what their guy assumed Greg would think. Obviously they'd also guessed he would come down here and lay traps.

Greg hated fucking up. It pissed him off more than anything. He fought to focus. It was so damn dark. He needed to find Haley. The pain continued riveting through his head, but he was pretty sure he hadn't been shot. At least not with a bullet. It wasn't the same kind of pain. Maybe he'd been tranquilized, which would be bad. Real fucking bad.

Haley! He tried screaming for her, forcing his body to cooperate. Insisting his body listen to him only intensified the pain. Then there were those glaring eyes again. He felt hands on him, and they weren't Haley's. Hot, foul breath burned the side of his face.

Someone said something to him: "The Bird has flown the coop. He says who is part of the game and you're next."

Chapter 13

Haley ran down the hallway. She hauled ass to the stairwell. Her heart pounded so loudly that between the beating in her head and the repetative squeak of her shoes hitting the floor, her entire world sounded like a fucking drum line. The image of Greg falling and those men appearing out of nowhere tortured her brain.

Just keep running. Run!

Whoever took Greg wouldn't capture her, too.

"God damn it," she hissed, hearing footsteps behind her. "No. No, no!" she whispered frantically under her breath, somehow needing to find a place to hide, somewhere, anywhere. God, they were going to capture her, too.

How would she get Greg back if they took her?

But if she ran too far, or hid too well, she wouldn't know who took him, or where they took him. Her brain seemed to ring with too much clarity, all these thoughts hitting her at once, as she almost slid down the first flight of stairs. She hurried down the second flight. Panic suddenly hit her harder than if she'd run into a brick wall. She might be trapped in the stairwell if they were right behind her and also downstairs.

Haley slowed at the bottom of the stairs, hesitating in opening the door leading to the first-floor foyer. She strained to listen, waiting to hear them coming down the stairs. Pressing her palm against the cool metal door, she struggled with her purse, unable to see a thing and dragging her phone out but then dropping it. It made a loud clattering noise and bile raced to her throat. The sound was louder than an explosion.

"Crap," she hissed, squatting and running her hand over the floor until she found her phone. She needed to get a grip. Panicking wouldn't help Greg any. If she had a clear head she could figure this out. "Focus on what you know," she whispered.

Greg had the keys to the rental. She was stuck. Seriously and dangerously stuck. Greg was upstairs and their car was out front. She needed to get Greg and get out of the building without getting shot. She needed back-up. Haley pushed the buttons on her cell phone, scrolling through her address book. The light from the small screen was blinding.

But who would she call?

Everyone dialed 911 in a crisis. But this wasn't your average crisis. If these people were good enough to capture Greg, they might be good enough to manipulate the cops. She wouldn't call 911 until she knew more. Her sons were on the other side of the fucking country. There wasn't a thing they could do to help.

"Oh Lord," she moaned, pressing her back against the door to the foyer as she stared up the stairs and felt her legs go weak underneath her. She needed to figure out what to do. "Think. Think," she hissed under her breath.

It was too quiet. Moving Greg anywhere would make noise. If anyone entered or left the building, she'd hear the door.

Haley grabbed the handle on the door, deciding outside was her best bet. She pulled the handle and her phone rang. Bile raced into her throat and her heart began pounding painfully. She stared in horror at her phone as it lit up and she recognized the number John had called her from. Whoever shot Greg would hear her phone!

They were calling to learn where she was. Haley sent the call to voice mail as her world seemed to teeter and sway around her.

Haley stuffed her phone in her purse and prayed she could find another hiding place before they called her again. It would be smart to put her phone on silent. But what if Greg came to and tried calling her? It was insane thinking. Usually she was more level-headed. She'd never worked a crime scene involving someone she knew.

"I can do this," she said with conviction, searching for strength to make her next move. Then, licking her lips but unable to moisten them, she reached for the door handle again, her palms too damp and her entire body shaking.

Her eyes had adjusted to the darkness a bit and she glanced around her, as if someone might jump out of the corners and pounce at any moment. That's when she spotted the door. It led to a storage room. She'd been back there, behind the stairwell, once when she'd searched for a stepladder to change the fluorescent light in their office. And she had a key to it.

Daring to reach into her purse for her keys, Haley fought to find the right key in the dark and not make a single noise. She tried two keys before the right one slid into the lock on the door handle. The lock clicked, unlocking, as someone opened a door above her in the stairwell.

"Haley King," a male voice bellowed, causing her name to echo in the stairwell. "You don't want us to leave with your husband without you, do you?"

Haley disappeared into the storage room, closing the door silently and shutting herself into complete darkness. Lord, they knew who she was, her true identity. And they were searching for her.

They were searching for her! They didn't want to leave without her. That meant she had a bit of time.

She turned her back to the door, forcing several deep breaths into her lungs and ordering herself to remain calm and think clearly. Running her hand along the wall, she found the light switch and flipped it on. The door was heavy, and there wasn't a crack underneath it. No one would know if the light was on or off. She needed to get her bearings, or trying to run from these monsters would be useless.

There were the usual janitorial items: buckets, mops, brooms, and cleaning supplies on the shelves lining the wall. Haley glanced around, then focused on the door facing her on the other side of the small room. She was hit with an incredible urge to grab the door handle and turn it to make sure it was locked, but didn't dare offer any indication of her whereabouts.

"Haley!" a man yelled, sounding as if he were right behind her.

Haley slapped her hand over her mouth, determined not to make a sound. She worked her way around the objects in the small room until she stood at the door on the other side. She ordered her brain to work so she could remember where the other door opened in the building. Maybe she was better off staying right where she was. Reaching for the door handle on the door in front of her, she touched the cool metal, her fingers trembling.

"Think, Haley. Think." she whispered, glancing around her.

Her phone rang again and Haley shot her attention to her purse. Her chirpring ring tone was a muffled sound at the bottom of her purse.

She pulled it out and put her finger over the button to end the call when she stared at the name of the caller. It was Greg.

She'd seen him collapse to the floor, lifeless. That couldn't have been more than ten minutes ago. Someone was using his phone.

"Hello?" she said, whispering.

"If you come out now, your husband won't die."

Haley gritted her teeth as the fear she'd initially experienced was being overtaken by anger. "If there is as much as a bruise," she whispered, knowing they wouldn't overhear her if she kept her voice down.

"Damn it," she cursed under her breath when they hung up

on her. There were two choices: stay where she was, or make a break for it.

Or there was a third choice. She could call for help. The best investigators knew when to call for backup. Haley started scrolling down her phone list again, this time knowing who to call.

"Please answer," she whispered, pushing Seth's Gere's number, the bounty hunter John always said could get any job done. That was the man she needed.

"Seth Gere," a calm baritone said, his lazy drawl possibly meaning he'd been asleep.

"Seth, this is—" Haley almost said her real name. She adjusted her legs, stretching them out in front of her and pinching the bridge of her nose as she fought for a calming breath. "Hannah McDowell. This is Hannah McDowell."

"What's wrong?" he asked, his deep voice still calm and sounding very much in control.

"I'm on the first floor of the office building where Payton Investigative Services is," she began. "I was in the office with Greg King when we were attacked. Greg was shot, although I don't think it was a regular gun. I got away, at least for now, and am hiding in a supply closet. I need your help, Seth."

"I'm out the door right now," he informed her, speaking faster than he had a moment before but still sounding calm. "Are you hurt?"

"No. But they're searching for me. They keep calling my cell phone and just called me on Greg's cell and told me if I came out of hiding they wouldn't kill him."

"So they're still in the building?"

"Yes. I'm pretty sure."

"Stay right where you are. Have you called the police?"

"No. Not yet."

"Hold off on that. I'll be there in a few minutes with backup. How many are there? Do you know? Do you know who they are? How was the gun they used different?"

His questions spun around in her brain and she shook her

head before speaking. "The gun was longer, larger, I think it was a tranquilizer gun. Whatever it was, Seth, it was strong. Greg hit the ground in seconds. And I don't know who they are. But Seth, I think I know why they took Greg."

"We'll discuss that after I get you out of there."

The more Seth knew the better job he would do. There were a few things Seth would never know but Haley would give him enough to make him hunt to kill.

"We can't let them take Greg. They already took John."

Haley could hear the rumble of Seth's motorcycle and a rushing sound through the phone that she guessed was wind as Seth stayed on the line with her while driving.

"We'll get both of them back, I promise you, Hannah."

"Yes, we will. And I really appreciate your help." Forcing herself to sound calm and keep her voice quiet, she hoped Seth could hear her. "I've talked to John."

"Hannah?" Seth asked, interrupting her.

"What?"

"There's a cop car out here. You didn't call the police? Is there an alarm anywhere you might have triggered?"

"No. I haven't called the cops."

"Okay. Hang tight. I'm coming in."

Haley held her breath, glancing from one door to the other. As she studied the back door to the storage closet, a loud explosion echoed off the walls, piercing her eardrums and ripping a scream from her throat.

"Scth!" she hissed into the phone. "Seth!"

Haley repeated his name several more times when she realized the line had gone dead.

"Crap, crap, crap," she hissed, suddenly feeling like a caged animal. If she'd just pulled yet another bounty hunter into this nightmare and brought harm to him in any way, she'd never forgive herself. Maybe she should call the police and let Dispatch know where she was.

Haley glanced from one door to the other before acting on impulse and hurrying to the back door. She grabbed the door handle, turned, and pulled. It opened silently and she peered at the hallway, not seeing anyone or hearing a thing. She did spot a service elevator. Hurrying to it, she pushed the button, and the door opened immediately.

Thankfully, the elevator didn't crawl to the second floor. Haley raced down the hallway, skidding to a stop at the door to their office. She fumbled for her keys and then remembered she hadn't locked the office. As she entered, she stared at the small camera, which remained where Greg had put it, undisturbed. Well, it would just have to record her running in and out of the office.

There was another gunshot and men yelling somewhere in the building. Her fingers shook and her palms were way too damp, but she unlocked John's door then the bottom drawer to his desk. She grinned when she found his personal gun and the bullets that were kept next to it.

The gun built her confidence. She was a damn good shot. Gripping the cold metal helped clear her head, allowing her plan of action to form. She checked the safety then held the gun firmly at her side as she headed back out of the office.

"Did you forget something?"

Haley spun around, aiming her gun, and stared into Roberto Torres's cocky grin.

"Where is my husband?" she asked coolly, holding her finger against the trigger and knowing the slightest effort on her part would allow her to kill him. "And don't lie because I don't like you very much anyway."

"Put that down before you hurt yourself."

"I promise I won't get hurt," she hissed, clutching her purse to her side and lowering the gun slightly so she aimed it at his stomach. "Tell me where he is right now."

"He is where everyone will be until The Bird says otherwise."

Haley lowered the gun just a bit more and was truly surprised when she pulled the trigger how easy it was to bring a man to his knees. Roberto's look of surprise was comical.

"You misjudged me," she told him calmly. "I don't answer to a bird."

Blood soaked through his pants, filling the hallway with a disgusting metallic odor. Haley doubted she'd ever be able to stomach the smell.

"Tell me where the fuck he is," she snarled, locking her arm at the elbow and raising the gun to fire again.

"My God! You've shot me." Roberto leaned over, clenching his pant leg where she'd shot him as blood started pooling around him on the floor.

"Where is he?" Haley whispered, her voice sounding demonic.

"I don't know!" Roberto screamed at her, leaning over farther and then falling to the ground. There was blood everywhere. "You don't get it. You don't have a clue!" he continued to yell. "In this world you do what the hell you're told to do. Especially now. If I were you I wouldn't worry about him but go home and pray they don't come after you, too."

"Too late. They already are. And I think you know that." She lowered her gun and pointed it at the floor, aware of how pathetic Roberto looked. "You aren't going to die," she said, hearing the cold whisper that left her mouth and noting how it didn't sound like her at all. "The police are here, and if I let them know you're up here, you'll be in a hospital, sedated and mending in no time. Or I could not mention you and you'll lie there in pain until you pass out. The choice is yours. Where did they take Greg King and John Payton?"

"You stupid little bitch," Roberto snarled, curling his lip at her as he stared up at her with icy cold eyes. "There are no cops here that will help me, or you. You just don't get it. If you want to know where they are, go find them yourself. No one here will help you. And a bit of advice," he added, his accent thickening. "Don't believe everything you see. A uniform doesn't make a person good."

Haley stared at him, his meaning slowly sinking in. When she ran down the hallway, Roberto was laughing at her.

Haley wasn't sure why he suggested the cops who were here were bad cops. Maybe being shot helped him believe he was now removed from the situation. She had seen it before. An injured criminal often talked a lot faster than if he, or she, wasn't hurt, often spilling all their secrets. Whether it was his intention or not, Roberto had just helped her. Although even if he hadn't, there was no way she would allow him to bleed to death. The cops who were supposed to be here might not call for an ambulance. Hell, maybe they weren't really cops. Regardless of who, or what, they were, Haley would call 911. She knew there were good cops in this town.

Haley flew down the stairs so quickly she almost fell over her own feet. She slid into the door on the first floor, gun in hand and knowing she needed to find Greg now.

Adjusting her purse under her arm, she clutched it against her side, gripped the gun, and pulled on the door. It opened into the foyer, which was dark, with long windows along the street-side glaring a shiny black, like soulless eyes. Her heart swelled into her throat when she stepped out of the stairwell. The doors leading outside were within reach. She could make a break for it, call for more help, and then figure out where Seth and Greg were.

Haley ran to the main door leading to the street.

"Hold it right there," a menacing-sounding growl hissed from behind her.

Haley reached the door, grabbing the door handle, as her purse slipped and fell to the floor.

"Turn around slowly," he ordered.

Tears burned Haley's eyes, but she wouldn't let this asshole see her fear. Instead, focusing on the fact that he had drugged and possibly killed Greg, she turned, almost tripping over her purse, and stared into the cold, black eyes of the man she'd seen appear behind Greg upstairs.

"Where is my husband?" she demanded, noticing a second man standing near the elevator. She shifted her gun from the man glaring at her to the other man standing behind him.

"Don't even think about it," Seth growled, appearing out of the shadows and aiming a bigger gun at the man's head than she or the man had.

The man wasn't ready for Seth to be there. He turned, his expression changing to shock at the sight of the large gun so close to his face. Haley didn't care what happened next. Greg was still here. Darting outside, letting the door slam shut behind her, she embraced the still, muggy night air as she searched frantically up and down the street.

Seth's motorcycle was behind the rental car. Another car was parked in front of the rental. And it was running. It might not have been her smartest move, but Haley hurried to the car, yanked open the passenger side door, and pointed her gun at the surprised-looking man sitting behind the driver's wheel.

"Give me back my husband, now!" she demanded.

Chapter 14

"What the fuck!" The man twisted in the seat, taking his hands off the steering wheel and looking for a moment as if he'd climb over the seat and come after her.

Haley didn't take time to register what he might be doing. Greg lay slumped over in the backseat, his body barely fitting in the confined space. She pointed her gun at the driver, aiming to kill. It must have shown on her face. The driver froze.

"Good boy," she said. "Now it's going to take a few minutes to get him out of this car and into mine. What did you shoot him up with?"

"Go to hell," the man snarled at her.

Haley shook her head. "I really plan on going to the other place."

Resting her hand on Greg's leg, she leaned into the car, keeping the gun pointed at the driver's head, and ran her hand up Greg's body to his chest. His solid heartbeat under his shirt was the best thing she'd felt all evening. She almost banged her head on the side of the back door of the car when someone approached behind her.

Seth had his gun aimed at the driver. "Need some help?"

"Thank you," Haley said, glancing at the dark building behind Seth and praying there were only the three men and not more they'd have to deal with before taking care of Greg.

She returned her attention to the driver, who now had his hands in the air, looking wide-eyed from her to Seth. "I think it would be better if you got out of the car," she told the man.

He nodded so quickly his jaw snapped open and closed. The man almost fell out of the driver's side and scrambled to his feet, but not quickly enough to keep Seth from closing in on him and lifting him off the ground by his shirt.

Haley would sing Seth's praises later. She raced around the car and slid into the driver's seat. "Sorry about this. I need your car. I'm sure you can catch a ride when the cops show up."

"I got it covered here," Seth told her, pushing the man to the curb.

"I'll call nine-one-one on my way to the hospital." She placed her loaded gun on the seat next to her and shifted the car into drive. "Hang in there, sweetheart," she told Greg, not sure if he could hear her or not. "I love you and you're not leaving me now that were back together."

Haley hated hospitals. They were fine when her only memories were of birthing babies. But in her line of work, gunshot wounds, even flesh wounds, meant pacing and waiting.

"How's he doing?" Seth Gere appeared in the doorway of the small waiting room where she'd come after getting coffee. A very pretty woman stood by his side, her thick long brown hair falling well past her waist.

"He's asleep. Thanks again for showing up so quickly last night," Haley said, reminding herself as she spoke that it had been just last night. It seemed she'd lived through a forty-eight-hour day so far, and it wasn't over yet. "I'm not sure I would have made it out of there without you."

Seth shrugged off the gratitude, entering the small room with the woman sticking to his side. Haley guessed her to be the girlfriend she'd heard he'd moved in with. She was too tired to push for introductions, though.

"What happens now?" he asked, dropping his voice to a low whisper even though they were alone in the waiting room.

"Roberto Torres and his buddies were all taken into custody. One of them, Arnold, was a cop with Omaha PD," she explained. Since Seth took away her pacing space by standing in the middle of the room, Haley moved to a nearby chair. Seth took the seat next to her, his girlfriend sitting behind him, almost hidden by his large frame.

"His name doesn't ring a bell. Probably a new guy on the force."

"He's not on the force anymore," Haley pointed out. "There's something else."

"What's that?"

She glanced at the glass walls and the hallway outside the room. There was a nurses' station not too far down, but she didn't see anyone. Turning to face Seth, she shared with him how she and Greg had bugged the office right before being attacked. "I watched the tape on the camcorder after Greg was admitted here last night."

"The cops didn't take everything?" Seth sounded surprised.

"I was pretty tired last night. I forgot to tell them about the equipment we'd set up and managed to get it out of the office before they noticed and confiscated it."

"You're impressive as hell, Hannah." He frowned at her then, searching her face as if there was something he wanted to say, or ask.

Haley guessed what it was and wondered how much information she wanted to share with him. "What do you know about Marty Byrd?" she asked instead of entering into the conversation about her true identity.

Seth's girlfriend peered around his large body, glancing at Haley with an appraising once-over before sliding her hand on Seth's thigh. Seth didn't look down when he placed his hand on top of hers.

"We know the name," he said without elaborating.

That was fine. This was a need-to-know conversation, Haley decided. Seth didn't know everything about her and she didn't know all there was to know about him. She did know John trusted Seth with his life, and his reputation. Seth had proven his worth to her last night.

"I'm almost positive he took John, and there is information we recorded last night that confirms that."

"Where did they take him?" Seth asked.

"Tijuana."

"Where in Tijuana?"

"That's just it. I don't know where and it's a big city."

"Not so big we can't go down there and sniff him out. Get me all the information you can and we'll go get him," Seth decided.

Greg would need time to recoup and they didn't have time to lose. Haley nodded. "Sounds like a plan," she decided.

"We thought we'd go say hi to Greg. Is that okay?"

Haley stood when they did. "Yes. I'll go up with you. Do me a favor, though. Let's not tell Greg yet that you're going to Tijuana. He'll be upset he can't go, and he needs a few more days to rest."

"Understood." Seth walked out of the waiting room with his girlfriend at his side.

Haley followed, knowing Greg would be pissed as hell when he learned Haley allowed Seth to remain involved with the case. But she wasn't worried. Greg was alive and would be fine. That was all that mattered. But even still . . . she'd wait a few days to tell him.

Chapter 15

Greg hated sitting shotgun. Marc merged onto the interstate, finally out of the zoo of traffic around the airport, and glanced over his shoulder at Haley instead of watching oncoming traffic.

"We still don't have anything from the hospital," Marc told her, avoiding a car coming up behind them as he shot over to the far lane. "Are they faxing your prescriptions to our pharmacy?"

Greg glared at Marc, who appeared oblivious to how close he came to smashing Greg's Avalanche.

"I'll call them again when we get to the house," Haley said, sitting behind Greg and next to Jake.

"I want to hear again how you pulled open the getaway car and took the driver on at gunpoint to rescue Dad," Jake said, offering a toothy grin.

"She's damn lucky she didn't get shot," Greg informed all of them. It had taken a day of recovery in the hospital and time to let the tranquilizer he'd been shot with wear off, but he'd been grumpy ever since she'd filled him in on what he'd missed.

"I am lucky I didn't get shot," Haley agreed, her soft tone sounding too consoling, as it had ever since he'd woken up in that hospital bed. "But you would have done the same for me."

"Yup. He sure would have," Marc agreed quickly, grinning at his mom over his shoulder.

"Keep your eyes on the road," Haley told him, saving Greg

the trouble. "And it's still rather a blur as to what happened after that. I remember pointing the gun at the driver and seeing your father slumped over in the backseat."

"So how did you get Dad out?" Jake asked.

"He was pure deadweight. I think I had enough adrenaline pumping through me at that point to have hauled an elephant out of a car." Haley smiled, and looked tired. "I would have tried if Seth hadn't shown up and removed the driver so I could take the car and your dad to the hospital."

"You are not comparing me to an elephant," Greg complained.

Marc and Jake burst into laughter. Greg had been taken out of the action by his own inattentiveness. If he'd noticed that guy coming down the hallway, the entire story they were rehashing right now would have been completely different. Just thinking how Haley hid in that storage closet, shot a man, and took on another man at gunpoint so she could rescue him, while dialing 911, amazed the hell out of him.

"There were three men," Haley told her sons. "Two were in the building and one was waiting in the car. Roberto Torres was one of the men, and he admitted leaving the note for me the day I closed the office and came out here. But he denies leaving the note on Sam Wilson's car. His story is the note was e-mailed as an attachment and he downloaded and printed it, then followed instructions to deliver it. I'm still waiting to hear the results once they seize his computer and try tracing the ISP to the sender of the e-mail."

"He won't say who sent the e-mail?" Marc asked.

"Nope," Haley said.

"I'd get him to talk," Jake growled.

"How would you do that?" Marc countered. "Take him out and get him drunk?"

"Whatever works, man," Jake snapped.

"We have a few more established clues," Greg began, ready for his sons to quit jabbing at each other. "But we're still too far away from knowing the truth for my comfort."

"I think we know quite a bit more now, although I admit I'm not too sure where to take it from here," Haley mused. "We know someone is abducting bounty hunters and known criminals who apparently have had involvement with this assassin, Marty Byrd. But we don't know why. And we don't know where Marty Byrd is."

"That's what I'm focusing on as soon as I get home. It's been many years, but I'm going to try contacting The Bird." Greg ignored Marc when he shot him a concerned look. His son must have done some research on the Bird. "But I already have my fears there."

"What's that?" Marc asked.

"I think The Bird has disappeared, too. We've received messages telling us The Bird has flown the coop. That tells me that Marty Byrd is missing. I want confirmation, though."

"How do you confirm one of the best assassins in the world is missing?" Jake asked, serious now.

"Watch and learn from the expert, my son."

"In other words," Marc shot out, "he doesn't know how he's going to do it yet."

"Don't think I can't still take you down," Greg snapped, but crossed his arms over his chest, hating to admit he still felt a bit too tired for his own good. His assailant had hit him with one hell of a large dose of a horse tranquilizer. The doctors had told him if he'd been shot with just a bit more, it would have killed him. Greg believed his assailants knew that and gave him just enough to render his ass useless.

"At least Seth Gere wasn't hurt. I never would have forgiven myself if the two of you disappeared that night."

Greg remembered Seth coming to see him in the hospital with a pretty young woman at his side. Gere was a cocky, arrogant ass, probably a lot like Greg was at that age.

"You're a hero, Mom," Marc said proudly. "And that rates a hero's dinner."

"It's a King tradition, one we started after going into business together," Jake told her.

His sons began speaking over each other, announcing the meal they had lined up for Greg and Haley to welcome them home, and to honor Haley in saving his life.

"Aw, shucks, guys. I was just doing my job."

Greg felt Haley's fingertips when she began massaging his scalp. He leaned back, closed his eyes, and let the three of them talk. He was so damn glad Haley hadn't been hurt. A swell of pride mixed with the love he felt for Haley. Not many would have pulled off what Haley had in that office building. She was more than a hero—she was one hell of a good investigator.

"I'm good," Greg told his niece when Natasha offered him a beer after dinner. He hadn't had much of an appetite, but Marc, Jake, and Natasha had gone to some effort to prepare a steak dinner with fresh lobster. "Where did Haley go?"

"She headed upstairs after taking her plate to the kitchen," Jake offered, taking one of the beers Natasha had in her hand and then popping the lid into the trash. "She says she's worn-out."

Greg nodded. It had been all he could do to stay with his sons and enjoy the meal they'd prepared. Between his stay in the hospital recovering and then the flight home, he felt as if he could sleep for a week. Which wasn't an option. Haley was even more worried about her boss after the ordeal she and Greg had gone through. It showed in her eyes every time anyone discussed the case.

"Sam was looking for you," Marc said, a glint of amusement in his gaze as he sipped his beer and watched his dad over the bottle. "She was so concerned you were okay."

He'd been dodging Sam all evening and was too worn out to continue avoiding her. "Be sure and let her know I'm fine." Greg headed out of the kitchen and to the stairs.

"She's upstairs. I'm sure she'd love to see you," Jake teased.

Greg ignored the shit-eating grin on his son's face. They'd put Haley and Sam in rooms upstairs and Greg and his sons had moved downstairs while they had company. He didn't have to explain his actions to his sons if he wanted to see Haley before calling it a night.

"I'm sure," he growled.

Haley's bedroom door was closed and he rapped on it, then stood facing it as he listened for noise inside. Haley opened the door as quickly as if she'd stood just on the other side.

"What are you doing?"

She opened the door farther, stepping to the side, and looking incredibly sexy and sleepy in her robe.

Haley must have changed the moment she got up there, because she wore the bathrobe he'd seen her in at her house. She sat down at the desk, tucking one bare leg under the other. There was pink polish on her toenails he didn't remember being there before.

"I've been charting out everything we've learned since John disappeared," she explained, pointing to the screen on the laptop in front of her. Haley's fingernails were the same color as her toes. The dark pink shade looked good on her. "I received the threatening letter and headed out here," she began, pointing to the screen at the flowchart she'd created. "All the feathers were left in the hotel room."

"Sam Wilson received the same threatening letter you received," Greg pointed out, reaching over her shoulder and pointing at the screen to where that incident would have occurred.

"Right," she mumbled, leaning forward and adding it to her flowchart. "John called me the day I first saw you here in LA and then he called me again here." She pointed, dragging her finger in front of the monitor. "Then we're attacked in the office building."

"That entire matter was rather interesting. The camcorder worked, and recorded the men entering the office, but they were arrested, so recording their identity proved futile."

"Yeah, that's a shame," she said, and slid out of her chair, grabbed her purse, and fished through it. She pulled out something and flipped it between her fingers, watching him as a small smile played at her lips.

"What do you have?" he asked, coming closer until he recognized it. "You have the tape that was in the camcorder?"

"The police never really paid a lot of attention to it, so yes, I took it." The small cassette rested in her palm and she held it up to him, grinning as if she showed off some rare jewel. "Would you like to watch it?"

"What?" he asked, frowning. "Why are you grinning like that?"

"You'll see." Haley hurried over to her suitcases, which were pushed against the wall by the walk-in closet, and knelt down before them. She pulled out the camcorder and turned around, standing. "You paid for this with KFA money. There was no point in leaving it in Omaha," she told him, still smiling as she held it up as if it were a prize.

He didn't see any point in telling her he already owned one very similar to that one. "Good point," he agreed, fighting not to let his gaze travel down her body.

The silk nightgown she wore underneath her bathrobe showed off her large breasts to distraction. It was short, black, and hugged her slender waist without looking tight. The silky black material was edged with lace and ended above her knees, offering one hell of a view of her soft, slender legs. Haley didn't try securing her robe around her when she walked to him, camcorder in one hand and cassette in the other.

She plopped down on the edge of the bed and slid the cassette into the recorder, then pushed the button to make it play back. Greg joined her, moving in close enough to view the images on the small screen as Haley held it up so both of them could see.

"It's not so much what you're going to see, but what you're going to hear," she said, adjusting the volume on the side. "You're going to shit when you hear this."

"What?" he asked, all too aware of how her green eyes

glowed and contrasted beautifully with her light brown hair. He shifted his attention to the small screen, though, when shadowed figures appeared, two men who would be damn hard to pick out in a lineup if they hadn't already been caught, and if it weren't for the fact they were speaking and calling each other by name.

"Where the fuck did she go?" the stocky man, whose name was Arnold, complained. "That little bitch couldn't have just disappeared."

"She's here somewhere. No worries. We'll catch her." Roberto Torres spoke with a smooth voice of annoying confidence. "We're not wasting time with her. If you see her and can't catch her, shoot her. We've already got King."

"If she isn't on the list then why the fuck are we bothering with her?"

"She'll be a royal pain in the ass if we don't bring her in or kill her. Trust me on this one."

"I don't trust anyone," Arnold sneered, walking past the camera, and the sound of him trying to get into the back office came through on the tape. "This scene is too fucking big to do anything other than what I'm told, but that doesn't mean I'm getting buddy-buddy with anyone."

"No one asked you to," Torres said, still sounding calm, as if they were discussing the weather. "Don't underestimate her, though. She's not licensed as an investigator or bounty hunter, but that hot little piece of ass can hold her own. We take her with us or take her down. Then we head out."

"And then that is it. Our neighborhood is clean."

"It was clean until King sauntered into town."

"He's her husband."

"So I heard." Torres didn't sound too thrilled with this piece of information. "Her loss. She'll be a widow at this rate."

"King is to be turned over alive."

"They are all turned over alive to be part of the game. But I'm here to tell you, friend or not, you take my advice on this.

I've been in the business way too long and I've never seen a sting this big. The Bird is gathering his flock to win. I wouldn't want to play against him, not with the army he has on his side. You don't fill a coop with this many dangerous people and not expect fireworks."

"You think I don't already know that? The Bird is going to turn the entire world upside down. No one knows where he is, and we gather whoever is on our list and take them to a drop point. You know as well as I do the men we take King to will probably take him to another drop point. This game is too intricate, which means too many people involved, which means trouble."

There were some shuffling sounds and it appeared Torres glanced over the papers on Haley's desk. He turned and looked at the camera when there was a banging sound.

"She's not in here," Arnold announced.

"Then we check every office in this building until we find her. She's in here somewhere."

"We're running out of time. Do we have to take her? She's not on the list."

"Quit your whining. We'll have them to the airport in time. Sometimes in this business, my friend, you need to learn to think beyond instructions given to you. It helps you stay alive longer. She's stuck her cute little ass where it doesn't belong and will cause us trouble if we don't find her. The sooner Greg King and his hot little wife are out of the state the better off for both of us. Now let's get moving."

"I know why you want to find her." Arnold stopped in the doorway, preventing Torres from leaving. "You're flying with them to San Diego, and delivering them personally in Tijuana. I heard you on the phone, *my friend*." Arnold stressed the last two words, making them sound insulting.

"You'd be smart to focus only on your part in this," Torres hissed. The shadows were hazy, but it looked as if he pushed Arnold into the hallway.

"And you'd be smart to think with your brain and not your dick," Arnold snapped, his tone turning menacing.

The images playing over the small screen were hard to see with the lights off in the room. But the grunt and sound of a body hitting a wall were unmistakable.

"Search the building and find her," Torres demanded. "You're getting paid to deliver, not think. And obviously you don't think too well."

"I know more than you believe. She's one hot lady. That one is rather obvious. And we're wasting precious time just so you can fuck her while her husband is out cold."

Greg stared at the screen, his eyes burning when he didn't blink but tried his damndest to make out images in poor lighting.

"That's all there is." Haley's face was inches from his when he finally turned and looked at her.

Her grin was so triumphant it took a moment to switch gears and lose the outrage that had filled him when he heard the two men talking about her the way they had. Haley outmaneuvered them and rescued him. His anger dissipated just staring at her. Haley had always been wonderful. The way she looked at him, excited and happy, eager to show him a new lead, warmed his heart.

"This is incredible, sweetheart," he said, standing and moving away from the bed, his mind already churning with a plan. "We have a location now."

"I've sent Seth Gere to Tijuana," Haley said quickly, then watched, waiting for his reaction.

Greg looked at her. "What?" he asked, feeling every muscle in his body tighten as he stared at her. "When did you do this?" The warmth that had just surrounded his heart began cooling. He remembered their conversation in Omaha about taking turns being in command. She was testing him.

Haley turned off the camera and placed it on the desk next to the laptop. Then, wrapping her bathrobe around her, she approached him carefully, studying his face.

"Greg, you took in quite a large dose of tranquilizer and needed time to recoup. I needed to act immediately on this. Trust me, I was tempted to go myself."

"It's a damn good thing—" He stopped talking when she placed her hand on his chest.

"I'm not an idiot and I've been handling investigations now for quite a few years."

"I never said you were an idiot," he reminded her, exasperated.

"I know. But you're still struggling to see me as a legitimate investigator. I've been out in the field and I'm not bragging, but there were quite a few cases where I can justifiably take credit for solving them."

"How often did John tell you he was proud of you?"

She frowned at Greg, her expression quickly turning into a scowl. Haley waved her hand in the air, turning away from him. "You just don't get it, do you?"

Greg grabbed her, flipping her around. He did get it. "I think you've gone too many years without anyone telling you how incredible you are."

Haley stared up at him. His eyes held hers captive as he watched her large green eyes. They started smoldering. "Do you mean that?" she whispered.

"You saved my life." His voice dropped to a rough whisper. "You took on a deadly situation as a professional would."

"Thank you." She didn't look away when he brushed his knuckles down her cheek. "We'll leave for Tijuana when you've had another day or so to rest. Seth wanted to go and I needed someone on the trail while it was hot."

"You did the right thing." The words came out so easily. He understood the glow in her eyes. There was passion, but not just for him. Haley thrived on the hunt just as he did. Greg saw now that the unbridled need to sniff out a criminal, which ran strong in his sons, didn't just come from him. It also came from their mother. "That's probably what I would have done."

"I know how hard that is for you to say," she said, resting

her hands on his arms. "It means a lot to me to hear it." She smiled. "It's not what you would have done."

"Acknowledging how good you are isn't hard to say."

"Oh really?"

"You are good at many things, Haley," he told her truthfully, knowing she was hanging on to his every word. "That doesn't mean it will ever be easy to relax when you're in a dangerous situation." Greg brushed his lips over hers. "I don't want you hurt."

"As long as we've been married you've gone to work with a gun at your hip. Don't you think I worried about you?"

"That's always been different," he said, and then he kissed her.

Greg would never quit worrying about her. He would always protect her. That wouldn't ever change. And he would always be incredibly proud of her.

"Maybe it is in your eyes," she said quietly, her sober expression not accusatory, but he didn't see complete acceptance either.

"Why do you think I would have handled it differently when you learned about Tijuana?" he asked, knowing they wouldn't always see eye to eye and wouldn't do things the same. He'd had many partners in his life as a cop, some a good match and others not.

She didn't look at him when she answered. "If I had been the one injured and unable to continue with the hunt, you would have made sure I was one hundred percent safe, very well provided for, then you would have left me and gone to Tijuana to finish the case."

Greg stared at her soft hair as it fell around her face. She seemed content to stare at his chest. Apparently she understood the truth would cut him to the core. She was right. He wouldn't have hesitated or given thought to his actions being wrong or offensive. There was a perp to catch and his wife to protect.

"You know me pretty well," he grumbled.

She shot him a furtive glance. "If it had turned out that way, I would have been so pissed," she whispered.

He believed her. But promising her he would never piss her off would be a stupid move. He combed her hair from her face with his fingers. "It's going to take some time for us to get used to how we both are now."

"True. And I've got the easy end of it."

"How do you figure that?" he asked, trying not to grin when she looked so serious.

"You aren't asking me to change anything about me. I'm asking you to accept something you've never had to accept before."

"I've had to submit to others before. Don't tell me you've forgotten how many years I put in with the LAPD?"

She did smile then. "No. I haven't forgotten," she said, her voice softer. "But you weren't ever submitting to your wife."

"You want me to submit to you?"

She made a face at him. "You know what I mean. There are times, like these past couple days, when I'm going to be in charge. I don't want you screaming and yelling if I don't clear everything through you first."

"And this is a two-way street?" He didn't mean to trap her, but from the look on her face and hearing his own words, he knew he had.

Haley stared at him, then sighed. "I just want us to be equals," she said, deflating. "You were out and I needed to move on getting someone to Tijuana. I didn't leave you here and go myself." She gave him a hard look as if she anticipated his reaction to her last comment. "And trust me, you know the action is down there."

The smoldering gaze in her eyes returned as the corner of her mouth curved. He wouldn't let her lose hope, not on them. She'd taken on one hell of a challenge, but he'd accepted the challenge. He saw now how much he wanted her to know that.

"You did the right thing," he grumbled, pressing his finger under her chin and tilting her head so he could drown in her sensual eyes. "Even if you'd gone to Tijuana." Her eyes widened. "I would have been pissed as hell and more than likely completely unreasonable."

"I'm not afraid to take you on," she whispered, relaxing her head in his hand.

"No, you're not," he said, and lowered his mouth to hers.

"You just got out of the hospital." Haley was breathless when she turned her head, ending the kiss. "It was a long flight home."

"If you're too tired, just say so, but you don't have to worry about me. I always want you." Greg lifted her into his arms and carried her to the bed. He considered taking her across the hall to his own bed, which was bigger than this one, but this bed was closer and he wanted her now.

"I think you might be more stubborn than you used to be." There was a grin on her face when he dropped her on her bed.

"I'm not more stubborn. I'm wiser; like a good wine, I improve with age." He stared down at her with her bathrobe crumpled around her and her black silk nightgown twisted underneath it. "And you're more beautiful."

"You must have hit your head pretty hard when you passed out," she said, laughing and wrinkling her nose. "I definitely look my age."

"You're perfect." Greg grabbed her bathrobe, tugging until she allowed him to pull it off of her.

She started to pull her nightgown over her head. "Leave it on," he instructed.

If Haley noticed he took his time getting out of his clothes, she didn't say anything. She rolled over to her side, resting her head on her hand, and crossing one leg over the other, presenting a provocative pose that made it damn hard to move. She had a perfect hourglass figure.

The curve of her hip sloped down into her narrow waist. The lace bordering her nightgown only partially covered her breasts and his mouth watered at the sight. But then every inch of her was hot as hell.

"Need some help, cowboy?" she asked, her soft, sultry tone flowing over his senses and turning every inch of him into one incredibly sensitive nerve ending.

Haley came to her knees and eased to the edge of the bed. She wrapped her legs around his and reached for his boxers. If he hadn't just stepped out of his jeans he probably would have fallen over when her fingers brushed his dick. He ached for her touch, anticipated where her fingers would move next.

If she ever discovered the power she had over him when he was turned on like this, he would be in serious trouble. Right now, he probably would submit.

"What exactly is it you would like to help with?" he drawled, fighting for some semblance of control as he dragged his fingers through her hair.

"Let's see what captures my interest." She pulled down his boxers, shoving them down his legs until he stepped out of them. When she wrapped her fingers around his shaft Greg pulled her hair until her head fell back and she stared up at him. "What do you want?" she asked.

"All of you, sweetheart. Every single inch." He bent over to kiss her and felt the room spin. There was no way he was going to let her see he wasn't completely recovered yet. Part of him was in fine working order, and that was the only part he wanted to dwell on right now.

"Every bit of me, huh?" she purred, nipping at his lower lip, then reaching for him.

Haley used him to pull herself up. When she stepped out of her robe, she pushed him backward, causing her strap to slip provocatively off her shoulder. *God.* He loved straps.

"Sit," Haley ordered, backing him into the chair at her desk. "I'm going to ride my cowboy."

Haley pushed against his shoulders, not that he would fight her, and made him sit in the chair. He pulled her other strap down and lowered her arms to her sides as she moved to straddle him. Greg hissed in a breath when her gown fell to her hips, revealing her beautiful breasts.

"A feast for a starving man," he murmured, wrapping his arms around her waist.

He groaned with pure pleasure as he found a nipple and latched on.

"God, yes, Greg," Haley cried out.

She was soaked. She rubbed her pussy up and down the length of his shaft, coating him with her cream.

"You're harder than stone," she purred, rubbing her cheek against his, then scraping his earlobe with her teeth.

He reached for her waist, wanting to bury his face in her breasts. Haley slapped his arms, then pushed his hands to the armrests on the chair. "Don't touch," she whispered into his ear.

Haley began an erotic journey, licking, nipping, and kissing his flesh, searching for the most sensitive places on his body, while refusing to let him touch her.

"Sit there and enjoy it."

He grunted his response, feeling her moist, perky nipples stroke his chest when she kissed and licked her way down his neck. Every time he tried moving, she'd grumble for him to stay put. She moved her body against his, rubbing him, stroking him, sending her soft, smooth skin against his and creating an erogenous journey that might very well take him over the edge.

Greg wasn't the only one being tortured into a lustful state of bliss. Haley's breathing grew louder. She would moan as she rubbed against him, or kiss her way along his collarbone. Her movements grew more sensual, her slender body slinking along his as if she were a cat in heat. If he tried moving any part of his body, though, Haley immediately straightened and playfully slapped him back into submission.

His hot little wife was definitely getting off on controlling him. Greg wasn't sure if he would voice this out loud or not. Although he probably wouldn't have to. Her actions and behavior were so damn hot, he couldn't wait to sink inside her.

Greg wondered if he'd be able to let her continue to control him once she sank down on his dick. It would possibly be the toughest challenge he'd ever taken on.

Goose bumps raced over his body, her lithe body moving against his like a sensual goddess, teasing her prey. She arched into him, then grabbed his wrists and brought his hands to her breasts. When he gripped them, squeezing and tugging, Haley whimpered. "Get me off. Play with them."

Greg moved from one nipple to the other, biting gently. She was already so close. It took another minute of adoring her to make her come hard. His seductress melted in his arms.

"Mount me, sweetheart," he said, his mouth full of nipple. He lashed his tongue around the puckered flesh. "I want to fill you."

"Hm." Haley didn't argue and apparently relinquishing control, raised herself over him, pressing her soaked entrance down on his swollen dick.

Greg thrust upward, impaling her. It didn't bother him that muscles were tender and parts of him still a bit too stiff. When her hot pussy wrapped around his cock, clenching him and pulling him deep into her heat, the only thing on his mind was how damn good she felt.

"That's it, baby. Ride me."

Haley's thighs quivered as she lifted and sank. She created an easy rhythm, taking him slowly and dangerously, the pressure building as lust simmered into raging desire. Immediately the urge to explode inside her filled him, making it damn hard to think of anything else.

Haley gripped his shoulders, her breathing growing harder when he picked up the pace. Her pussy tightened around him.

"Greg," she cried out. "Oh my God! Greg!" she whimpered, coming hard as she quivered and collapsed on top of him.

His dick filled her when she relaxed over him, catching her breath. He was so swollen and his balls tightened painfully as his own urges consumed him.

Greg grabbed her waist and lifted her just high enough to give him room. Then picking up the pace, he adjusted himself in the chair and took over.

"I'm going to come," he informed her, the strength to hold out escaping him when she damn near constricted the life out of him.

"Okay," she gasped, digging her nails into his arms as she held on to him.

He thrust deeper and deeper. Her heat scorched him alive. Haley's soft gasps added to the intensity of the moment. She loved what he did to her, how much she could feel his love for her. When he finally came, all of his feelings exploded along with his physical release.

"I love you, sweetheart," he whispered, holding her close.

"I love you, too," she murmured, and collapsed, fitting perfectly against him.

Chapter 16

Haley's muscles had turned to jelly. Greg's heart beat steadily against her and she brushed her fingertips over the bruised flesh on the side of his neck where he'd been shot.

"Are you okay?" she asked, her voice gravelly. God. She hadn't made too much noise during their lovemaking, had she?

"Never felt better." There was a grin in his tone.

She reluctantly lifted her head off his shoulder and stared at him. "Like you would tell me otherwise," she complained, although she couldn't help smiling back at him.

Greg cupped her cheeks and kissed her, his lips soft as they teased hers. His dick stirred to life, growing inside her overly sensitive pussy. Haley shifted and he groaned in her mouth.

"Keep moving like that and I'll show you how great I actually feel."

More than anything she would love to make love to him again. But staring at his wounded neck reminded her that Greg was still mending. He would always be the macho he-man and push himself sometimes beyond his means. It meant she would have to be the stronger of the two, especially in situations like this one.

"The only place we're moving is to the shower," she informed him, smiling against his lips when he groaned. And since misery loves company, she moved, and felt him slip out of her. She instantly hated the emptiness and wished she could hold him inside her just a little while longer.

"I can make love to you there, too." He stood, gripping Haley by her waist and guided her into the bathroom.

Greg pulled the towel off of the shower curtain rod where it had been hanging. He dropped his arm without grabbing the towel and instead grabbed the side of his neck.

"Greg," she gasped, ignoring the towel and reaching for him.

"I'm fine." He sounded strained, and remained where he was in the middle of the bathroom.

She studied his injuries, ignoring his scowling expression. "I remember the first time you took a bullet," she mused, memories she'd forgotten surfacing as she stared at the discoloration around where he'd been shot. "Listen to me saying that so candidly."

When she met his gaze she knew at least his pride was intact.

"It's the life we lead. I wasn't hurt, or permanently put out of commission." Greg's gaze turned haunted when he stared down at her. "If you want me to admit I'm not as strong as you, I'll do it. I won't be able to handle anyone shooting you. They will die. I swear it. I made a vow to myself years ago that I would never allow you in harm's way."

She believed him and prayed he would never have to prove himself right. "Do you think I shot Torres where I did on accident? Greg, he took a bullet in the leg, incapacating him. No one shoots my man and walks away unscathed."

When Haley reached the bottom of the stairs, her hair still damp from showering, Marc, Jake, and Natasha were standing in the kitchen, drinking beers.

"Is your father down here?" Haley asked, but then smiled at Natasha. "Would you look at you!"

"He went up after you a while ago," Jake said.

"He hasn't come back down." Marc frowned. "Is something wrong?"

"No. Not at all." She put the laptop down and pulled Natasha into a hug. "You're so beautiful."

"You look great, too." Natasha still had those captivating golden eyes.

"I thought your dad came back down here." Haley rubbed Natasha's arm as she glanced at her boys.

"What is it?" Marc asked, putting his beer down and helping her with the laptop cord.

Natasha jumped in and took the cord and crawled under the table to plug it in. Her niece was breathtaking and obviously still very much a part of their family.

"Well, we should probably discuss it with your father here."

Jake headed for the hallway leading to the stairs. "I'll find him," he announced, then bounded up the stairs.

"Oh wait," Haley said, but Jake was already gone. "I need the camcorder out of my room, too. I'll be right back."

"I'll go get it," Marc said, placing his hand on her shoulder and then following his brother up the stairs.

"You look mighty happy." Natasha leaned against the counter and studied Haley with those stunning golden eyes of hers. "What were you two talking about up there? Or were you talking?"

"Natasha." Haley was surprised. "I can't believe you asked me that." Although her niece was now in her early twenties, Haley still saw the little girl.

"Uncle Greg is very much my business. I don't want him hurt." Natasha shoved her thick, long hair behind her shoulder and narrowed her gaze on Haley. "And I don't mean physically. He can take wear and tear on his body a hell of a lot easier than on his heart."

Haley stared at her niece. She'd helped raise Natasha, but being gone six years obviously had helped shift her loyalties to her uncle. It was a stab at Haley's heart, which she quickly covered up to protect it. "You don't know everything your uncle and I have been through," she said quietly yet firmly. "I don't want to see him hurt, either."

"I believe you. I also know you'll put your own wants before his. Just don't hurt him again." Natasha took a long drink of her beer, apparently done with her lecture.

Marc and Jake headed back down the stairs. Haley told Natasha with a look that they would discuss this another time.

"Do you want a beer, Aunt Haley?" Natasha wasn't swayed by Haley's look.

"No thanks." Haley watched her niece move easily around the kitchen. Natasha had made this her home after Haley left and she would be very protective of "her men." Haley took this piece of enlightenment in stride. "But ice water sounds great."

Marc and Jake entered the kitchen with Greg in tow.

"I didn't realize you were going to talk to them right now," he said quietly when he moved in next to her. "I would have helped haul everything down."

"Marc and Jake got it. It's fine." Haley searched Greg's brooding expression. "Are you tired? Greg, we can wait until morning."

"Uncle Greg, sit down," Natasha encouraged, pulling one of the chairs out from the kitchen table.

"I'm fine," he said, moving away from both of them and helping himself to a beer.

"Is this the recording you told us about?" Jake asked, flipping the small cassette around in his fingers.

"Yes," Haley said, taking it from him and putting it in the camcorder. She pushed the button to rewind it. "This is what recorded when Torres and his men showed up."

Greg sat when Haley did and took the camcorder from her. She saw the strain in his face when he held it for everyone to see and didn't comment when Marc slipped it out of his father's hands and propped it up so he and his brother and niece could see the picture better.

"Son of a bitch," Marc snarled when Arnold accused Torres of wanting to fuck Haley.

"These bastards are in jail, right?" Jake asked, his hands fisted at his sides.

"Locked up good and tight," Greg grumbled. His mouth was twisted into a cruel frown as he glared at the camcorder.

Haley waited until the recording played through and Natasha pushed "stop" on the camcorder.

"I know Tijuana," Natasha offered, standing between her cousins on the opposite side of the small square kitchen table. She put her half-drunk bottle of beer on the table and crossed her arms over her waist. "My girlfriends and I go down there to shop. If you know where to go, there are some awesome shops."

"We aren't talking about going down there to shop till you drop." Marc made a face at her.

Natasha was captivating with her beauty, but she could get a look on her face that bordered on dangerous. She blessed Marc with that look now. "Haley isn't the only woman in this family who knows how to take care of herself," she sneered.

"Oh-h-h," Jake said under his breath, drawing out the one word for dramatic effect as he made a show of trembling. "Better watch out, Marc, or she might kick your ass."

"You both better behave," Natasha ordered. She turned her attention to Greg, her expression completely serious. "Haley's boss is somewhere in Tijuana."

"I've already sent a bounty hunter from Omaha, Seth Gere, down to Tijuana."

"You've given someone else this job?" Natasha asked, shocked.

Haley wouldn't be intimidated by her niece's abrasive nature. Another time Haley might be proud of how Natasha had turned out. One might think, with her sultry good looks, that Natasha wasn't someone to take seriously. Haley realized at that moment many might think the same about her. King women were blessed with good looks, which made it imperative they be tough as nails. Natasha was a lot like Haley.

"No, dear," she said calmly, smiling at Natasha's scorn.

"Seth asked to head down there when Greg was in the hospital. He is merely checking things out down there. We're heading that way as soon as Greg is ready to travel."

"We should head down to Tijuana in the morning," Marc announced.

"Definitely as soon as possible," Haley said.

"Not you," Marc said, looking serious. "Mom, no! We might have to go to some seedy places. You and Natasha can get to know each other. She can show you how to run the office," he finished, as if implying the importance of them being here would compensate for his behaving like a chauvinist.

"I thought I raised you better than that," Haley said quietly, and shot a side-glance at Greg. Natasha stiffened, too, definitely looking pissed. Not only was her gender insulted, but Marc had just implied that Natasha's job would be on the line.

Greg leaned back in his chair, folded his hands on the table, and studied his oldest son.

"Don't you dare support your sons' thinking like this," she said. Haley wagged her finger at Marc and Jake. "You two go around thinking women can't work in the field and you're going to be humiliated each time a lady kicks your ass."

"You know better, Marc." Greg didn't raise his voice. "Don't make me count how many times Natasha has taken you down."

Natasha snorted and ignored her cousins when they scowled at her. "So when do we leave, Uncle Greg?"

"You don't agree with her on this, do you, Dad?" Jake demanded.

Haley gave Greg her attention and the others looked at him, too. She realized a couple things in that moment. They'd raised their kids well. And their boys weren't bigots. Greg had used Natasha as an example in showing how equal they all were. Greg leaned back in his chair and stared at his hands. He looked so incredibly sexy in spite of his pinched expression.

After a long moment of silence he pushed himself away from the table. "I'm heading to bed. Maybe by morning your bounty hunter will have checked in with new leads."

"Well," she began, but Greg left the room.

A silence fell over the kitchen after Greg left, his heavy footsteps on the stairs making her worry he might not be ready for traveling for a few days.

"He's not happy at all that you hired someone else," Natasha announced.

"You should have contacted us," Marc informed Haley.

Haley reached underneath the table and yanked on the cord to unplug the camcorder. "Seth asked to go down there. He was already up to speed on everything. You have to understand how much John Payton means to him."

"That's not how Dad sees it, Mom." Jake leaned against the counter, scowling. "If you think he's a better bounty hunter maybe you should go back to Omaha. You can't care about him and care about us."

Haley gawked at her younger son when he marched out of the kitchen. She gave it a second before storming after him, ignoring the wary looks Marc and Natasha gave her.

"Now you wait one minute, mister," she snapped, finding Jake in the living room. It was dark with no lights on, but she didn't bother turning them on. Instead she stepped into Jake's path as he stalked the length of the living room. "When you're running a case and new, strong leads pop up, you know you have to move on them quickly. You two were too far away and definitely not briefed. Your dad was lying flat on his back in the hospital. When Seth showed up to visit your dad at the hospital, I decided to send Seth. It was the right thing to do."

"He visited Dad at the hospital?" Marc said behind her.

Jake looked past her at his older brother with a haunted, tormented expression lining his handsome face. He returned his attention to Haley, searching her face for a moment.

"Dad's cool with Seth Gere?"

Haley didn't hesitate. "Seth is about your age, Marc. But he'd heard of your dad and was so star-struck I thought for a moment he'd ask for an autograph."

"That made Dad like him?" Jake sounded incredulous.

Haley let out a breath and took her son's hand in hers. "Your dad understood I called the right shot. I made the best of the resources I had to keep the case moving forward."

"Are you in charge of this case?" Natasha stepped around Marc and stared at Haley.

"Yes." Haley didn't hesitate. "John Payton was my boss in Omaha." She noted the different expressions on both of her sons and Natasha. She saw admiration, hesitation, and skepticism.

"Don't think for a moment that I don't know how good your father is. I know there's a lot he can teach me." And she hoped there were one or two things she could teach him.

Haley stepped out onto the back porch later the next afternoon. After Seth checked in that morning, she'd made arrangements for him to meet with Jake and Marc in Tijuana. The two of them left an hour later. Haley piddled around the office and even answered the phone a couple times. Natasha didn't seem to mind Haley being around, but at the same time Haley couldn't help feeling she was in the way. After an hour or so of helping out, she left Natasha to do her job. Clerical work had never been Haley's thing. Not to mention, Natasha wasn't thrilled to be stuck at home base while her cousins were off having an adventure, as she'd put it. This case hit a bit too close to Haley's heart to be an adventure.

Greg joined her for breakfast, hung out in the office while she was in there, and made a show of answering e-mails and discussing with her a few other cases they'd been handling. By lunchtime he disappeared into his bedroom, announcing he was going to do some research on his computer. Haley wasn't sure if he was worn out and not up to par but afraid to admit it or if he was hiding out.

Sam Wilson was supposed to stop by sometime that afternoon, having left to stay with family. According to Marc,

Sam hightailed out of there when she found out Haley was staying at the house, too. Apparently after her most recent phone call and hearing Greg had been injured and was at the house recuperating, Sam was descending on her prey once again.

The warm, salty air filled Haley's lungs and clung to her bare flesh as she stood out on the screened-in porch. Haley padded barefoot into the backyard, feeling the heat from the stone path as she wandered closer to the edge of the yard. She was surprised to see Greg on the beach and pushed open the gate, letting it latch behind her as she walked gingerly on the hot sand to join him.

"Penny for your thoughts." She focused on his bare back. A sheen of perspiration made his tanned flesh glow. Muscles rippled under his smooth skin. And the faded jeans he wore today, with no shirt, added to his roguish appearance.

"You haven't heard from your boss lately, have you?" he asked. When he turned, the bruising on his neck running down over his shoulder distracted her.

"No, and it's making me nervous. At least when he calls I know he's alive."

"Maybe you can't help whoever has him if you're here in California."

"So I should go back to Omaha?"

"No," Greg said firmly. He stared beyond her for a moment before once again shifting his attention to the ocean. "I'm not convinced helping his captors is to our advantage."

She itched to reach up and touch the spray of curls that spread across Greg's pecs, to inspect his bruising with a meticulous touch and determine for herself how well he was mending. "I want to know everything there is to know about Marty Byrd."

"What do you want to know about him?" Greg asked.

"You mentioned checking with some of your contacts, seeing what you could learn about him."

"I've already done that."

Haley placed her hand by the bruising just under his shoulder. His chest hair tickled her palm. She dragged her fingers over the coarse hairs, feeling his muscles twitch under her touch. "Is there something about The Bird you don't want me to know?" she asked.

Greg grabbed her wrist so quickly she jumped. "There are many things about him I don't want you to know," he grunted, barely moving his mouth when he spoke.

She stared into his sky blue eyes, the intensity of emotions she couldn't decipher so strong in them it gave her a chill. "Why do you sound angry?" she whispered.

"There is history," he said, continuing to speak under his breath. "Things that happened in the past."

"That would be history," she agreed, feeling her insides tighten when she studied him. Those emotions she saw swarming in his eyes were ghosts, trying to haunt him and succeeding in annoying him.

He scowled, letting her know her humor didn't sit well at the moment.

"What history are you talking about?" she asked.

"Eleven years ago I was involved with an investigation of a California politician and a lieutenant in the Air Force." He sounded pissed. "They were charged with espionage."

She searched her memory. "I vaguely remember that." He hadn't always discussed his cases with her and she'd been so busy with the boys, running the household, and getting involved with volunteer work. "What about it?"

"I brought in the politician, Ed Brown. He was rumored to be preparing a campaign to run for Governor." Greg got a faraway look in his eyes when he stared over her head and down the beach behind her. "I'd heard rumors that there was a mark on his head and was as much his bodyguard as the arresting officer on the case."

"Marty Byrd tried to kill him?" she guessed.

Greg placed his large hand in the middle of her back and started them down the beach, walking alongside her.

"I was the hero at the precinct for a few weeks," Greg said.

Haley glanced up at him, the memory haunting him coming back to her. "I remember that," she mused.

"I was bringing Brown into the station and was helping him out of the squad car. I spotted a man. He was in the shadows and I don't know what helped me to see him, but I did. I reacted on instinct, pulling my gun and aiming and firing at the man who was trying to shoot Ed Brown."

"So you stopped him from killing Brown."

Greg nodded, his pained expression bordering on anger when he met her gaze. "Rumor has it to this day that I am the only man who has ever prevented Marty Byrd from hitting his target and that I better watch my back. For a while I was more nervous than a cat, but nothing ever came of it. Honestly, I started believing the rumors were wrong and whoever I shot wasn't really the renowned hit man."

"He got away?" Haley realized how much of their lives over the years they hadn't shared with each other. Although she had vague memories of what he shared with her now, she didn't know details.

Greg's look was menacing when he focused on her. She didn't feel anger directed at her but understood that recalling what happened pissed him off. "We never found anyone. For a while they claimed I shot at a ghost. There was blood on the pavement where I saw the shooter. That was the only proof there was that I wasn't hallucinating."

"You think Marty Byrd harbors resentment for that?"

Greg shook his head, blowing out a loud, exasperated sigh. "I'm just trying to connect us to this picture."

"That connects you, not me."

"You're my wife."

"Yes, I am."

Greg stopped walking and pulled her into his arms, holding her against him. He hugged her, his warm, large powerful body wrapped around her.

"I love you," he whispered into her hair.

"I love you, too." She couldn't raise her face to his. He held her too tight against his muscular torso. If it hurt him holding her, he gave no indication.

"You don't remember any of that happening, do you?" he asked.

"Not really."

"I always thought the less you knew about my cases, the safer you would be."

"We aren't your parents, Greg," she said, bringing up the most taboo subject there was with Greg.

He held her, not letting go, and buried his face in her hair. If the pain over losing his mom as a teenager resurfaced, Haley doubted he'd mention it. One of his father's perps had shot and killed his mother. It had been a terrible time. They took chances in their line of work. Nonetheless, she didn't want any of them shot again. If that meant toughening down on Greg and possibly making a sacrifice or two on her end, Haley would see it done.

"We will never be my parents," Greg whispered into her hair.

"I know," she answered, stretching her body against his. "And we will work together, not fade apart."

"We've already proven we don't fade apart. Nothing will ever split us up."

Chapter 17

Greg found Haley in her room later that day. She sat hunched over her laptop, her fingers dragged through her hair, and appeared lost in whatever she was reading.

He glanced at her cell phone, lying on her bed, when it started ringing. Haley jumped from the sound as if she'd been a million miles away.

"I'll get it," he told her.

"Crap," she mumbled, twisting in her chair. "I didn't even know you were standing there."

"Must have been a good article."

"I was reading about assassins," she admitted.

He could suggest some good articles if she'd ask him about it. Greg was quickly learning his wife liked to learn things for herself. Maybe later he'd pick her brain and see what she'd learned.

Picking up her phone, he looked at the small screen. "It's Seth Gere," he told her, and pushed the button to accept the call before she could complain about him answering her phone. "Greg King," he said, speaking softly.

"Greg, this is Seth Gere. I've been trying to reach Hannah."

"She's doing some research online," Greg said, meeting Haley's gaze when she looked at him curiously. "You got news?"

"It's probably best that I caught you," Seth said, sounding as if he stood outside along a fairly busy street as he spoke. "Are you familiar with a man named Peter Langston?"

Greg stiffened. He'd told Haley he'd put out some feelers on Marty Byrd, which had been a phone call he'd placed earlier that day to Pete Langston. It was rather ironic Greg would try to call someone he hadn't sought out in years and later that day be asked about the man.

"I know of him," Greg said, his curiosity piqued. "I know he and Byrd were once close."

Haley stood, walking across the room to where Greg stood by her bed. She stopped in the middle of the room, facing him. "Put it on speakerphone," she whispered.

Greg pulled the phone from his ear. Haley reached and pushed the button on her phone to send it to speaker just as Seth continued. "I'm hearing his name being brought up in quite a few circles down here. When is the last time you talked to him?"

"What have you heard?"

Seth had the good sense to acknowledge that in the world of bounty hunters Greg outranked him, and this time didn't hesitate in offering what he knew.

"He's probably the closest The Bird has to a right-hand man."

"Correct," Greg confirmed.

"Rumor has it he's down here."

Greg hadn't thought to confirm Peter was in his Sacramento home when he'd spoken to him on the phone earlier. It had been a brief call, part of it playing catch-up, since Greg hadn't talked to the man in a couple years. But he had been able to confirm Marty Byrd wasn't at his home.

"Do you know what he's doing down there?"

"Watching." Seth made a grunting sound. "Langston appears to be everywhere I go, not doing much, just hanging out. My guess at this point would be he is rounding up anyone who has ever associated with The Bird."

"Why do you say that?"

"Call it a hunch," Seth said. "Langston doesn't know who I am, but he's making it clear that he's noticing me at the cantinas. Bounty hunting is against the law down here, as it is in many places."

"Your point is?" Greg ignored Haley when she scowled at him.

"My point is that Langston gives me a not-so-subtle once-over if I enter a cantina and he's already there. It appears he is watching, waiting. Twice now I've seen him meet with the same men. I tracked them this morning to the airport."

"What did they do there?"

Haley sucked in her lower lip and stared at Greg wide-eyed. There wasn't any doubt she was remembering Torres's and Arnold's comments they'd recorded in Payton's office. Apparently there were others flying to Tijuana on The Bird's behalf.

"I camped out in my car when they parked in the parking garage. Langston returned less than an hour later with a couple men. They went to a rather low-class motel downtown and have been there ever since."

"Did you know the men who were with Langston?"

"No. Should I have? You know something?"

"Not enough." He was worried, though.

Talking to Peter might have been a big mistake. Greg had told Peter he was at his house in LA. Peter had told him The Bird didn't check in after his last assignment almost a month ago. Although Peter didn't appear overly worried about it, Greg wouldn't be surprised if that had been an act. Finding a man on Peter's side of the tracks who spoke openly and without reservations was close to impossible.

"Any idea what he might be up to?" Seth asked, pulling Greg out of his thoughts. "I can't shake the feeling Langston is working with Byrd. If they abducted John, do you think they're abducting others? And if so, why?"

"I don't know."

Seth was closer to the truth than he realized. He hadn't

viewed the tape Greg and Haley had watched. Greg wouldn't bring it up on the phone, though.

"I can offer a hunch," Seth added.

"What's that?" Greg focused on Haley when she moved closer, leaning into him as she focused on her phone.

"Marty Byrd didn't disappear. He's relocated of his own accord. If he's abducted Payton and any of the others who have disappeared, hauling them down here where U.S. officials can't touch them is a smart move."

"Point well taken." Greg had considered the same possibility. "So any word on where any of these men might be?"

"I have a possible location where Peter Langston might be staying. I'm going to need backup, though, when I check it out. I can provide my own posse."

"Negative. We'll head down there. I want a low profile on this. A very low profile. I'll call you at this number first thing in the morning."

Greg gripped the steering wheel and squinted against the morning sunrise, wishing for more coffee. Haley sat next to him, humming under her breath to the CD in the CD player.

"Get your passport ready," he announced, slowing further as they neared the booths at the border.

They were in for a tough day, and round one was coming up on them. Bounty hunters weren't allowed in Mexico. The National Guard, who now monitored the borders, weren't idiots. They'd made crossing into Mexico for business a lot harder than it used to be. He wasn't worried about crossing the border, though. It was once he and Haley were in Mexico that he would need to watch his ass.

"I've got both of ours right here," Haley said, pulling them out of her purse. Her hair was still damp from showering and her bright blue sundress and freshly made up face added to her distracting good looks.

"Good girl," Greg said, offering her a tight smile.

"I'm better than good and I'm not a girl," she drawled,

her smile innocent as she straightened her dress over her thighs.

Greg did smile then. They were heading for anything but a vacation and he'd take advantage of moments like this when he could. Grinning, he tugged at her hair and didn't mind a bit when she slapped at him.

Traffic wasn't as heavy today as it usually was entering Mexico, and Greg stopped when they reached the booth, rolled down his window, and let the heat from the morning roll into the air-conditioned truck.

"Paperwork, please," the guard requested, glancing past Greg at Haley. "Roll down the windows in the back," he added, frowning at the tinted windows he couldn't see through. "Would you mind opening the back so I can see what you're hauling?"

"Not hauling anything other than all of my wife's luggage," Greg offered, although he knew the guard wouldn't appreciate his humor.

"Step out of your truck please," the guard told Greg.

Greg put his truck in park and eased out of the truck, looking down at the young guard, who couldn't possibly be six feet tall. Appearing intimidating right now wouldn't work to Greg's advantage, which wasn't always easy for him to avoid when he stood well over six feet. Another guard stepped out of the booth, joining the guard who held their passports, and looked over both of them before squinting at Greg.

"Where you headed?" the second guard asked.

"Taking the wife into Tijuana for a short vacation."

"So you aren't staying the night?"

"We might be. We packed just in case we decide on a room." Greg knew getting sweet with the guards wouldn't work but added anyway, "It really depends on how much shopping she decides to do."

"You don't shop?" the guard asked.

"If I find something I like I might buy it," Greg offered. "Most of time my wife shops and I carry her bags."

The guard nodded, taking the passports from the first guard, and walked around the Avalanche. "You want to show me what you have back here?" he asked, nodding to the hard black covers that were over the back of the truck.

Greg didn't say anything but released the gate on the back of the truck and lifted the first flap that covered the bed. He'd cleaned and waxed his truck before they'd left, so the bed was neat and shiny. A handful of suitcases were leaning against one another. Otherwise there was nothing else back there.

"You packed a lot for a possible day trip. Sure you don't plan on staying longer?" the guard asked as he reached and pulled one of the suitcases toward him.

"If we decide on a room, we're ready," Greg said, keeping his voice calm. "I'm not going to tell you we're staying the night and then we don't do it."

The guard opened the suitcase and glanced at the neatly folded clothes that were all Haley's. He ran his fingers over a lace negligee that Greg hadn't seen before. It pissed Greg off. The guardsman was out of line. If they were trying to get a rise out of Greg they'd just figured out how to do that.

The guard closed the suitcase, pulled out the other bags, opened each one until he appeared satisfied. Then, walking with Greg back to the front of the truck, he handed the passports back to him and nodded for Greg to drive through the booths. He then walked away from Greg not giving any indication he knew he'd pissed Greg off.

"I thought I was going to melt sitting here," Haley complained after they'd rolled their windows up and headed across the border.

"At least you weren't standing outside." Greg glanced in his rearview mirror at the booths as they drove into Mexico.

"The Fiesta Inn is just a few minutes from here." Haley held her phone in her hands and pushed buttons. "I can go ahead and book a room there now."

Greg was pretty confident they would be staying the night, although he hadn't been inclined to let the guards at the border know that. It was doubtful he'd learn everything he needed to know in an afternoon. More than once his name had preceded him. Greg wouldn't chance suggesting he and Haley would be in Mexico for a while. The authorities would hunt him down, assuming he was in their country to track someone.

"We can get Internet access in the rooms," Haley said. "As soon as we're checked in we'll set up the laptops and meet with Seth. Whatever connections he's got ready for us we'll research online."

"I'd rather use our air card we have through our cell phones," Greg explained. "Don't use the hotel's Internet. It isn't secure and I'm not going to have anyone questioning the work we're doing online while we're down here."

"Who would have thought you'd become so computer savvy?"

"The kids taught me."

Haley laughed as she reserved their rooms. She had everything taken care of by the time they'd parked and entered the lobby. Greg had to admit her skills with cell phone apps probably exceeded his knowledge on a computer.

"The less time we spend in the lobby, the better," she explained when they rode their elevator to the third floor alone, having declined the bellhop's services. "You never know who might be watching, or how much Seth has been talking, or to whom."

"I thought you trusted him." Greg was surprised Haley questioned Seth's abilities to be discreet. He wasn't as suspicious of the young punk anymore.

"And the last thing I need is to have to get you out of some Mexican jail for being a bounty hunter," she continued, and slid the key card out of the envelope. "I do trust Seth, with my life." Haley was calm and serious when she stared up at Greg with radiant deep green eyes. "If there's one thing I've learned in this business, it's to never get too cocky. None of us are perfect and we all slip and make mistakes."

An overwhelming surge of pride swelled inside him. Haley

was truly perfect, and definitely all his. God. He was one lucky son of a bitch. Had she been this good of a detective before she'd left him?

There were two very large beds in their room and a highly polished desk. A couch and upright chair faced a flat-screen TV. Greg pulled back the curtains and stared at one hell of a view of the city. He set their luggage on one of the beds. He doubted Haley thought they would sleep in separate beds, but he made sure they wouldn't.

"You'll have to show me how you use the Internet through your cell phone," she said, taking both laptops out of his hands and carrying them over to the large desk.

"That's actually Natasha's area of expertise," Greg admitted, and unzipped his suitcase. He reached under his clothes to open the false bottom where he'd packed a few gadgets he was pretty sure would make it across the border without being detected. "She set it up through our cell phone service. Give her a call and she can walk you through it."

"I'm familiar with the plan but don't have that service." Haley opened both laptops and pulled out cords to plug them in. "It's a really good idea, though. You're wise to stay off of unsecured access ports."

"As long as we both stay on our toes we should get through this."

"I know." She booted up the laptops, then watched him walk through the room with his bug detector. "I didn't reserve this room until half an hour ago. Do you really think it might be bugged?"

"We aren't taking any chances."

"And I put the room under 'Hannah McDowell,'" she informed him.

"Hannah is Payton's secretary and might have a mark on her head, too."

"You're right," she admitted, worry lining her face. "And I've thought of that."

He finished sweeping the room and returned his bug detector

to his suitcase, concealing it once again under the false bottom. Haley was busy with the laptops, but he sensed her nervousness. It was one thing anticipating the hunt but another completely once the hunt began. Hell, he'd been doing this for years and still felt a spike of anxiousness now that they were here.

"I need to call Natasha to put us online," Haley announced when he stood next to her.

Greg cupped his hand under her jaw, and kept it there when she slowly stood and faced him.

"I'm done having you under the same roof as me and not in my bed," he began, speaking slowly and waiting for her reaction. Just a bit of a distraction would lower the tension he knew both of them were feeling.

Lowering his mouth to hers, he watched Haley's lashes flutter over her eyes before he brushed his lips against hers. She tasted so good. He deepened the kiss and his brain went feverish with a passion he couldn't quite extinguish. She made a soft sound in his mouth, turning the heat inside him to molten lava. Then imagining her in that lingerie she'd packed damn near did him in.

Just then Haley's phone started ringing. They ignored it as he continued to devour her mouth.

"My phone," she gasped, finally turning her head. "It's Natasha. I texted her to call me."

There was a knock at the door and Greg let go of Haley with a groan.

"You started the torture session, not me," Haley said with a smile before answering her phone. "And later you may ask me if I would like you to share my bed."

Greg wanted to kiss that sly smirk right off her face. Instead he sauntered over to the door and leaned down to look through the peephole. His heart came to a standstill when he saw who was standing there.

Greg looked over his shoulder at Haley.

"What?" she asked, holding the phone between her shoulder and cheek.

"We've got company," he told her seriously. "Mexican cop," he added under his breath.

Haley straightened, instinctively closing his laptop and sliding it off the desk. It was a really smart move on her part. Mexican police would look at anything they could find to try to weasel Greg into a crime. She mumbled something to Natasha on the phone and ended the call, then nodded to Greg that she was ready as she slid her phone into her purse.

He opened the door and stared at the man in uniform facing him. Two other officers stood off to the side, their hands resting on their guns.

"Greg King, long time no see." Jefe Gonzalez, a Tijuana officer he'd dealt with in the past, took a step to enter the room, his thick Mexican accent making the phrase sound broken.

"Jefe Gonzalez." Greg didn't move to allow him into the room. "Are you here to personally welcome me to your fair town?" He wouldn't insult the officer by asking how he knew he was here, although Greg would have loved to know, especially with the room booked under Hannah McDowell.

"If you wish a greeting, then welcome," Gonzalez retorted. "Will you do the same and welcome me into your hotel room?"

There really was nothing to hide. They hadn't brought weapons over the border. Nothing was unpacked. The room was clean.

"Of course. Come in. My wife is relaxing after our drive here. It's very hot outside, as I'm sure you know. And as our hotel room isn't large, please ask your men to remain in the hallway so that so many uniforms don't intimidate her." Greg didn't doubt for a moment he'd get an earful for implying his wife was weak and scared by anyone in uniform. But leaving the officers in the hall would warn anyone else who might show up unannounced that Greg and Haley had company.

Gonzalez nodded to his two men, who straightened and stood along the wall. Greg's phone buzzed against his hip a moment later and he pulled it off his belt as he stood to the side, allowing Gonzalez to enter and the door to close behind him.

He stared at the message on his cell telling him where Marc and Jake were in Tijuana. Marc knew Greg sucked at texting. His fingers were too big and the buttons on his phone were too damn small. His son would just have to wait a bit.

"So what brings the infamous bounty hunter, Greg King, to our fair city?" Gonzalez asked, clasping his hands behind him and rocking up on his heels as he gave Greg the once-over. Already Gonzalez looked as if he'd busted Greg and couldn't wait to gloat to all of his men.

"I promise the only thing my husband will be hunting for while here in Tijuana is a party dress for me," Haley said, moving to wrap one arm around Greg's waist and extending her other hand to Jefe Gonzalez in greeting. "I was just trying to figure out where to go to this evening. Maybe you could suggest a nice nightclub."

Gonzalez studied Haley, obviously not expecting to find her in the room with Greg. Previously when Greg traveled to Tijuana, he'd come alone. Gonzalez hesitated long enough to give Greg the edge.

"We're taking some much-needed time off," Greg offered easily, working to sound as relaxed as Haley did. The last thing he needed was a Mexican cop becoming his shadow while he was trying to hunt down Byrd and find Haley's old boss.

"I don't think I ever knew you had a wife." Gonzalez shifted his attention to Greg, ignoring Haley's extended hand.

"The truth is, Senõr Gonzalez," Haley said, speaking before Greg could, "we've been separated for six years and have decided to try and work things out. You obviously know my husband and so understand he is always very busy. Since your town doesn't allow bounty hunters and arrests them if they are caught chasing a fugitive into your town—"

"You're right. We do," Gonzalez sneered.

His cruel grin didn't faze Haley a bit.

She continued on, holding her pleasant smile. "Which is why I thought this was the perfect place to spend time together. Greg can't work while he's here. Do you know of a shop where I can buy a nice dress?" she asked, cleverly changing the subject before Gonzalez could decide whether to question her story or not.

"I'm sure you'll have a fine time finding a shop to spend your American money," he grumbled, unwilling to advise her on shopping or where the best nightlife was. Gonzalez backed up, his eyes sweeping the hotel room before he reached for the door. He narrowed his dark eyes on Greg. "I know you're here, Señor King. Any business conducted in my town I will take as a personal offense and make sure you are charged with the full arm of the law."

Greg gave Gonzalez a curt nod, reaching around him and opening the door, aching to tell the officer not to let it hit him in the ass on his way out. Haley's people skills ran circles around Greg's and he didn't mind letting her know that. In fact, he could think of quite a few ways to thank her for getting the cop off his back as quickly as she did.

"Threats aren't needed," Greg informed Gonzalez, meaning it. Greg wasn't fooled for a minute. Gonzalez managed to find Greg every time he came into Tijuana and had yet to bust him in the act of hunting down a criminal. It rubbed Gonzalez the wrong way and that was just too damned bad.

Greg let the door close behind him, exhaling and gathering his thoughts before turning around. It was very curious that Gonzalez knew Greg was checked in under Hannah McDowell. The reason might just be as simple as Gonzalez being notified King had crossed the border then following him to his room.

They weren't followed to their room, though. He would have noticed. Not to mention, Gonzalez would gloat if he'd learned an alias. Why would he not mention it?

Haley opened the laptop in front of her and grinned. "I guess we showed him, huh," she offered, her green eyes glowing with amusement.

Greg stared at her triumphant grin and how her cheeks

glowed. Her hair was still slightly tousled and the way she pursed her lips reminded him how wonderful it was to kiss them. Now the local police knew she was his wife. Maybe that was why Gonzalez didn't gloat. He'd just found Greg's Achilles heel.

"Do you find it curious that the local police found us so quickly?"

Something flickered in Haley's eyes, but she sucked in a breath, fisting her hands at her side. Then standing, she pressed her finger against her lips as she sauntered toward him. Greg swore her walk was more provocative than usual. Her hands slid up his chest, moved to his shoulders, then she wrapped them around his neck as she leaned into him, pressing every inch of her hot, sultry body against him.

"Do a search for bugs again," she whispered into his ear, her breath torturing his flesh as badly as her body did.

Greg had an image of that little bit of lingerie she had packed in his brain when her words filtered through his thoughts and hit him. Damn, that little outfit was driving him crazy ever since he'd seen it. He stiffened, circling her waist with his hands and pushing her away a few inches so he could gaze into her eyes. They were bright, alert, and all business.

Nodding once, he let go of her and her hands slid back down his chest before falling to her sides. She remained where she was, watching him while he ran his bug detector over every inch of the room where Gonzalez had been. He was on his hands and knees, covering every inch of the floor by the entryway. He spotted something at the same time his equipment began beeping.

Greg picked up what looked like a small, silver ball bearing and took it into the bathroom. Haley was on his heels. Neither of them spoke when he set it on the counter. Haley moved quickly, finding tweezers and Kleenex and a small butter knife. Tools of the trade could be found in so many places.

Haley used the butter knife to hold it in place. Greg used

the tweezers to pick it up. He brought it to eye level and the two of them stared at it. Without some kind of magnifying glass, Greg couldn't tell what it was equipped to do. What fascinated him, though, was that he'd never seen this type of device before. That the Mexican police had access to equipment he didn't was rather interesting.

He placed it on the Kleenex. Haley placed the flat edge of the knife on top of it, then covered the knife with the other half of the Kleenex. Greg made a fist and came down hard, hitting the bug underneath the Kleenex. Haley revealed what was left of it. It looked like a smashed bug.

"Good call," he told her, finding it was getting easier to sing his wife's praises on the job. She was a top-notch detective.

"Damn shame," she said, bending over to peer at it. "I would love to find out what that was. Have you ever seen anything like that before?"

He shook his head. Gonzalez must not have known as much as Greg worried he might. He'd planted a bug in hopes of grabbing information he could use to arrest him, and Haley if she'd been with him. He watched her bundle it up in more Kleenex, then reach under the counter, pull out the Kleenex box, stuff the damaged bug at the bottom, and return it to the case that held it in place against the counter.

"Something isn't right," he mumbled, leaving the bathroom and sitting on the edge of the bed closest to the desk.

Haley joined him, returning to the desk and booting up the laptop. "Because he knew what room we were in?"

"Yup. And I know Gonzalez. If he'd learned your other name, we would have heard all about his superior detective skills, even if someone had tipped him off with the information."

Haley made a snorting sound although her face didn't look as if she found any of this humorous. "You think someone tipped him off and told him to come here? I booked the room over their website fifteen minutes before we got here, and under a name not that many people would know."

"John Payton would know it."

"True." She looked over her shoulder at him but then moved in her chair, rubbing her bare legs against his as she resituated herself and faced him. "And if he told whoever has him my name, they would know to watch for that name if it entered their city." She snapped her fingers, her eyes opening wide. "It didn't have anything to do with us just crossing the border. Because I used the Internet to get us a room and didn't do it at the front desk, whatever phishing program they might have set up alerted them immediately I had checked in." She slapped her forehead with her palm. "I should have thought that through before making the reservations."

"You're doing great, sweetheart." He took the hand she'd just used to slap herself and brought it to his lips. "It's a challenge keeping up with all new technology and what our computers and phones allow bad guys to do. For now, we're going to assume whoever it is we're after already knows we're hunting them. They know more about us than we do them."

"That's often how it is, my dear," she said softly, her smile making her eyes glow even more.

Greg put her hand between his and gave it a gentle squeeze. "Another thing. While we're down here. You're not in charge."

Chapter 18

Haley tried not to let Greg's overthrow of power get to her. She instead reveled in how easy it was to use an air card to get her laptop online. Natasha had told her she would order one for Haley's laptop.

"I like the idea of meeting Gere while out shopping," Jake said, sitting at the desk with Haley after she'd successfully brought both laptops online. "It will appear a lot more natural and not cause suspicion."

"Agreed," Marc said.

The two of them had showed up after Greg informed Haley he was taking command.

"In fact, we should make it a family outing. The streets are crowded, and with all of us together none of us risks getting hurt, or worse." Marc looked to the rest of them for their agreement.

Haley glanced at Greg, who was stretched out on the hotel bed with his hands clasped behind his head. He stared at the TV, which he'd turned on the moment that Marc and Jake arrived. He hadn't said a word to his sons, not even to tell them he was heading up the case.

Her phone rang and she stared at it, leaning closer on the second ring to read the small screen. Her stomach twisted in knots. It was Seth. As anxious as she was for the action to begin, she wouldn't admit to any of them that she was also more than a bit nervous. Her men were used to the danger of the hunt. She had handled dangerous situations before, but there was something different about sneaking around alone. No one saw or judged her mistakes.

"Hello," she said, and stared at the wall, ignoring the curious stares all her men were giving her. She felt as if she were in the spotlight, her every move being critiqued.

"Did you two make it down here?" Seth asked, sounding more jovial than usual.

"We checked into our hotel a bit ago," she offered, knowing Greg had talked to Seth on her phone but also knowing if they were closing in, the amount of people wanting to listen in would definitely increase. It was best to keep her comments vague.

"Good, good," Seth said. "I know you can't wait to go shopping. Did you decide where we should meet?"

"Let me see where everyone wants to go and I'll call you back." She ended the call and shifted in her chair, not surprised Greg gave her his full attention.

"Where does he want to meet?" Greg asked.

"He didn't say."

Greg shifted his attention to Marc and Jake. "We need a place with good visibility where we can see all approaching, but not too noisy so we can hear ourselves talk."

"Seth will be providing us with guns," Marc cut in. "We met him before we came here."

"Good. We need to be armed," Haley said, curious what her sons thought of him. "It might be better for appearance's sake to go window shopping until we find a good place to meet. Seth can trail us and enter whatever shop we do."

"Give Gere a call back," Greg said. "And good thinking," he added, then pushed himself off the bed and headed into the bathroom.

The streets were congested with people. They had walked several blocks when they reached a line of ladies' clothing stores. Haley had talked to Seth on the phone about shops in the area and nightclubs when she'd called him back, the same conversation she'd tried having with Jefe Gonzalez. Being acutely aware of how easily their cell phones could be tapped into, as well as the fact that probably more than one person watched them as they walked down the street, created a fierce knot in her gut. She was drenched in sweat by the time they had reached the stores Seth recommended.

Greg slipped his hand around hers, giving the appearance to anyone watching that they were enjoying a day of shopping. Haley knew he was also keeping her close to him with so many locals and tourists moving around them. Marc and Jake were behind them. They talked amongst themselves, commenting on some of the shops, discussing what they might buy while here. To anyone watching, or listening, the Kings truly appeared the family enjoying some time away, visiting Tijuana without a care in the world other than finding some good deals.

As much as nervous anticipation continued twisting and churning in her gut, Haley knew if she kept a clear head, John would be safe with them soon. She watched waves of heat rise from the street and sidewalk in front of them. What they were doing was very dangerous. It was a high she got a taste of years ago and had no desire to give up. Not only were they searching for whoever had abducted John, but they also were in a country that arrested bounty hunters. She'd never been behind bars before and didn't want her first time to be in Mexico. Nonetheless, as nerves continued twisting in her gut, a thrill of excitement shot through her, too.

Haley let out a heavy sigh and Greg glanced down at her. He gave her hand a slight squeeze, which was oddly reassuring. She wished she could talk to him about this.

When they got home, somehow, Greg would open up to her. It might be a lot to ask right away after they'd been apart six years. Haley remembered Greg used to share his deepest, darkest thoughts and feelings with her. It didn't happen very often. And if someone were to guess a man as tall and powerful-looking as Greg King wasn't the type of man who would get all emotional and sobby, they'd be right. Even as a teenager, he never showed deep dark emotions. Haley wasn't sure Greg ever cried over his mom's death, and he'd been such the mama's boy. Haley remembered Greg telling her once that he wasn't expected to think and feel the way she was, so he didn't do it. He claimed he never allowed the intense emotions to develop inside him since it wasn't manly to experience them. After years of marriage, she'd learned all of that was bullshit. Greg knew fear, terror, panic, sorrow, and happiness the same as anyone else did. Once this case was over and they were able to settle in and start living as a married couple again, she would get him to open up to her and discuss how it felt when he knew he was going in for the bust. She'd have to be told a really good story to believe the great Greg King never experienced a bit of anxiety and fear once in a while.

Haley glanced around at the many people moving around them. Those coming toward them would take one look at Greg and move out of the way. Those behind them kept a fair distance. She didn't have to look up at Greg to know the hard, serious expression that would be on his face. He intimidated those around him to get out of the way. She glanced over her shoulder at her sons. It didn't surprise her Jake had turned out to be the tallest. It also didn't surprise her both her sons had that same dangerous look on their faces. No wonder they had company fifteen minutes after arriving in town. Haley wondered if these three could sneak anywhere. Or maybe the King confidence level was so high they didn't feel a need for low profiles.

She forced her attention to the shops. If she let so much weigh her thoughts down, they would make a mistake. Haley didn't need Greg, or anyone else, telling her one mistake in this line of work could cost lives.

As she fought to get her thoughts focused, she also battled a growing unease that something was seriously wrong. It was more than knowing the pending danger surrounding them, but she couldn't put her finger on it. Dwelling on it, especially in this heat, only seemed to make it harder to narrow down why she sensed something was about to go wrong.

Haley turned her attention to the stores, picking up on the conversation Marc and Jake were having behind her. It helped distract her from her thoughts. They commented on different styles of clothes and how cheap things were down here. They were in this business, too. Marc and Jake knew they were walking into a dangerous situation yet made light conversation. They had been trained by the best in the business. Greg hadn't trained her, though.

"Let's go in here," she suggested, pointing with her free hand to a clothing store that had some cute dresses in the display window. If she continued worrying about everything she'd be a mess. It was time for action.

Greg put his hand on her back as he guided her to the shop entrance. "You'll put everyone in this town to shame if you wear something like that out tonight," he said in her ear, and nodded at a snug-fitting, brightly colored dress a mannequin wore in the window display.

"Looks like they sell men's clothing, too," Jake announced as he pulled the door open and held it for Greg and Haley. "Maybe this won't be so boring after all."

Haley grinned and patted Jake's cheek when he gave her his infamous crooked smile. "Don't tell me you wouldn't have fun helping your mom shop for a dress."

"I can't think of anything I would rather do," he drawled, giving her a mock bow.

Haley rolled her eyes and at the same time gave quiet thanks for the blast of air-conditioning that greeted her as she stepped into the shop. It seemed to work magic on her frazzled thoughts. Haley calmed almost immediately.

"I worry about you, son," she murmured, but then smiled easily when he appeared noticeably wounded.

Jake was so much like his father, well built and incredibly

handsome. She prayed that whatever lady stole Jake's heart would be strong enough to tame the playboy in him and not be swept off her feet and follow him blindly.

Haley sifted through dresses as she took in the layout of the store. The dresses were priced very reasonably. She couldn't remember when she'd last purchased something for herself that was so nice. Well, other than the lingerie outfit she'd packed at the last minute. If their hunt proved successful, there would be an overwhelming adrenaline rush they would need to burn off afterward. More than once over the years Haley had come home to an empty house after helping solve a case and wished she could discuss her successes with Greg. And too many times she'd lain in bed, masturbating, crying with need for him, and aching for satisfaction she couldn't give herself.

Thoughts of making love to Greg wouldn't help her focus on what she was supposed to appear to be doing. Haley glanced around the store, taking in the few other customers. Greg took his time approaching her as he was immediately detained by an overzealous salesperson who spoke in such quick Spanish Haley couldn't keep up to understand. At the same time, Seth entered the store. Marc and Jake were closest to him but didn't acknowledge his entrance other than giving him a once-over as any man might do when another enters a domain he's already claimed.

Haley made eye contact with Seth and noticed how tense his expression was. He looked nervous, almost scared. It gave her an unsettling feeling, and she worried Greg would interpret it as Seth not being professional. She knew he'd successfully solved every case John had given him. Although she'd never worked with Seth before, she held on to that knowledge and reminded herself Seth knew what he was doing.

"This dress would look perfect on you, senõra," a middle-aged saleslady said, taking the black, strapless dress in front of Haley off the rack and holding it up to her. "You really should try it on."

"Okay," Haley said, responding without thought.

"Maybe there are others you wish to try on, too." Her accent was thick and her voice husky.

Haley regrouped her thoughts quickly, scanning the dresses in front of her. "This one," she decided, reaching for a shimmering green dress made out of very light material.

The saleslady started chattering in Spanish as she gestured toward the back of the store where the dressing rooms were. Haley wanted to know why Seth looked so stressed. She didn't want to be occupied too long with changing clothes and miss out on anything important.

"Go try them on," Greg encouraged, having managed to make his way to her side and walking with them to the back of the store. "Come out and model them for me," he said, resting his large, warm hand on the middle of her back. "I'll be right outside the dressing room waiting for you," he added, speaking softly. Greg gave her a quick, barely noticeable nod that was enough to assure her he didn't plan on leaving her alone.

Haley entered the small dressing room and closed the door. She was attacked by a rush of claustrophobia she couldn't kick and fought to catch her breath as she stared at herself in the full-length mirror. Somehow she managed to try on the green dress and even get it zipped up her back before stepping out of the dressing room, barefoot, to find Greg leaning against the opposite wall, listening and staring at the floor, as Seth spoke quietly to him.

When he glanced up at her, Haley thought for a moment he didn't see her. He looked as stressed as Seth did when he first entered the store. She managed a smile as she walked past the overzealous saleslady and up to the two men.

"What do you think?" Haley asked, turning around and holding her hands out as she tried to appear the happy wife, excited to shop and not caring about anything else.

"You're beautiful," Greg told her, his gaze sweeping down her body before returning to her face.

"I'd have to second that one," Seth offered, smiling at her.

His expression transformed so quickly it would have been hard to believe he'd looked as stressed as he did a moment ago.

Greg ignored Seth and nodded to the saleslady. "My wife will take this dress," he decided.

Haley hurried to change and then handed both dresses over to the saleslady, hoping the other one would fit her as well. "I'll take both of them," she told the middle-aged woman.

There was no time to try it on right now. Haley had to know what Seth had just told Greg.

Greg stood in front of a row of leather belts hanging on the wall. When he glanced down at her, his blue eyes looked so haunted she frowned.

"What's wrong?" she whispered.

"Seth has a lead on John."

"He does?" It was all she could do to keep her voice at a whisper. Haley focused on the belts, staring at the sizes but not seeing them as she ran her fingers down the length of one of the belts. "Where is he?" she asked. "What does he know? Is John okay?"

It took forever to get out of the store. The sales ladies fussed around her and Greg, trying to sell more items to them. Haley wanted to scream. By the time they left the store, she and Greg both carried bags stuffed with dresses, a new belt, earrings, and a necklace. Marc and Jake bought several items, too, although Haley didn't have a clue what. Her patience was running thin. She needed to hear Seth's news. Her thoughts were distracted when they walked out of the store.

"We're going to have to drop these bags at the hotel room," Greg decided, reaching to take her bag from her.

"Where are we going after that?" she asked, looking up at him as she spoke quietly.

Seth was with them now, walking in front of them with Marc and Jake. All the years she'd compared the young bounty hunter to her sons proved accurate. They were built the same, moved the same, and fell into an easy conversation as they strolled ahead of Haley and Greg.

Greg didn't look at her but focused on people ahead of them as he spoke. "We're getting the truck and driving across town," he said, without elaborating.

Haley swore the walk back to the hotel took twice as long as it did to get to the store. When she and Greg reached their hotel room, he tossed the bags carrying their purchases on the bed. Marc and Jake had taken off with Seth, not coming up to the room with them. Haley barely remembered what they said they were going to do. All her thoughts were focused on John. Something was wrong. Her premonitions from earlier seemed too strong now.

"What did Seth say to you?" Haley demanded, feeling perspiration bead between her breasts and down her spine. She needed a shower but wasn't budging until she was brought up to date. This was one reason why she preferred being in charge. Any news came to her first.

"Apparently your bounty hunter has a few contacts down here," Greg began, although he didn't sound as if he were complaining.

"Good. And?"

"A maid at one of the motels on the other side of town said she's seen an American who fits John's description. We're going to go check it out."

"Let's go!" Haley hurried for the door, pressure constricting around her chest so fiercely she could hardly breathe. There would be time to shower later.

It had to be John. In spite of how many times she told herself not to get her hopes up, she didn't listen very well. The way Greg glanced at her repeatedly once they were in the truck, she knew her fidgeting was too obvious.

"There are a lot of Americans in Tijuana," he said as they idled in traffic.

"I know." Haley blew out a breath, glancing out the street at the buildings alongside them. "What details did the maid give Seth to make him think it was John?"

The address Seth gave Greg was to a small motel, privately owned and in a part of town where not many tourists went.

Greg parked the truck in a gravel-covered circular drive off the road. "Seth was told an American man had been at this motel who didn't look good."

"You're right. It could be anyone." Haley entered the motel with Greg, reciting the steps involved when going over a crime scene in an effort to keep her mind from thinking the worst.

"Let's hope my Spanish works," Greg mumbled under his breath.

"Hopefully that maid you mentioned speaks some English." They walked across a lobby that once might have been rather upper-class. Cracks in the cement ran up to the oval ceiling. The walls were a pale peach, but as Haley squinted she noticed very faded paintings. "This was once a beautiful place," she whispered.

Ceiling fans squeaked as they worked to create a breeze in the stiff, musty room. Haley glanced around as Greg walked to the counter and tapped a bell sitting to the side with a sign next to it in Spanish. Haley guessed it said something to the effect of "ring for assistance."

A heavyset man appeared in a doorway and moved to the counter warily. "*¿Puedo ayudarte?*"

"A friend of ours is staying here," Greg said, tilting his head to study the man. "John Payton, an American, is here. We don't know what room."

"*No hay americanos aquí,*" the man grunted, and disappeared behind the door.

"Shit," Greg hissed under his breath.

"He said there aren't any Americans here," Haley translated, although she guessed Greg understood. "Someone else might have checked into the room, though."

Greg stared at her and she knew he was thinking the same thing she was. Marty Byrd wasn't Mexican. So either they had followed a false lead or the man behind the counter simply didn't want to help them.

"We can't give up this easily," she said, searching the empty lobby as she spoke. "Maybe we can find that maid Seth said told him about John or the American," she added, correcting himself.

"Maybe." Greg turned his attention to a wide flight of stairs that curved along the wall and disappeared before they saw the second floor.

Haley started toward the stairs, guessing the rooms were upstairs, since there weren't any entrances to rooms outside the building. Her shoes echoed across the bare floor, making it impossible not to announce her intentions before she reached the stairs.

"*¡Espera! ¿Adónde vas?*" the man behind the counter yelled, his deep voice echoing off the high ceiling.

"*Lo siento,*" Haley said, reaching for the banister but turning quickly when the man yelled at them. "My friend is here. I know he is. I need to find him. *Por favor, senõr.*"

"*¡No hay americanos aquí!*" the man yelled, his black eyes glowing as his cheeks turned red in outrage. He pointed to the door. "*¡Licencia! ¡Ahora!*"

"Now wait a minute, mister—," Greg began.

The man pulled a large gun from underneath the counter and aimed it at Greg.

"Oh shit," Haley said, moving quickly to grab Greg by his waist.

He twisted and took her by the arms, shielding her with his body. "We're leaving. It's cool," Greg said, pushing her out into the heat.

Haley's heart pounded a mile a minute, but the man's determination that they leave convinced her even more that there was something or someone here he didn't want them to see. Greg opened her door for her and she slid into the hot cab. He came around and started the engine, cranking the AC, then staring ahead as he rested his hand on the steering wheel.

"Marc and Jake went with Seth to get guns," he said.

Haley stared at him. His expression was lined with worry, and possibly regret. Possibly, even though Greg swore by his line of work, he worried more than he let on. Her sons were committing a serious crime in a foreign country. She nodded, understanding. In a world where people shot first and asked questions later, they needed to be armed, regardless of the danger.

"*John is in there, Greg*," she stressed. "I can feel it. I know you would rather us be armed. I agree, but . . ."

"But we need to get him out of there," Greg finished for her. "What's this?" Greg nodded ahead of them.

Haley looked out the front window at a woman standing alongside the motel building. She watched the two of them and gestured with her hand when she thought she had their attention.

"Maybe that is our maid." A rush of excitement washed over Haley.

"We'll find out." Greg made a show of leaving the parking lot.

Luck was on their side. "Over there." Haley pointed at the same time Greg turned off the narrow road and pulled in on the other side of the motel.

A thick grove of palm trees lined the edge of the parking lot, offering some privacy as Greg pulled his truck in alongside them. They blocked her and Greg's view of the back of the old motel, giving Haley hope no one inside noticed them park.

"There she is," Haley pointed out, opening her passenger door at the same time Greg opened his.

She barely noticed the heat this time when she moved to stand alongside Greg.

"*Senõr, senõra*," a young lady said, her accent as thick as the black hair that tumbled down her back. "I overheard you in the lobby. Your friend is in room six." She nodded once, then turned, hurrying back to the motel.

"Come on," Greg said, pressing his hand on Haley's back

and hurrying her across the parking lot. He grabbed the door the maid had used to reenter the building before it closed.

"No! No!" An old, very petite woman began waving her arms, gesturing for Haley and Greg to turn around the way they had come. She continued yelling at them in Spanish, speaking so quickly it was impossible to understand anything she said. Her meaning wasn't missed, though.

"*Lo siento. Lo siento,*" Haley mumbled several times, hurrying behind Greg as they worked their way through a cluttered kitchen that smelled thickly of spices.

Greg hesitated for only a moment at a pair of swinging doors before pushing through them into an empty dining room. There was an odd mixture of mustiness and cleaning supplies creating a strange odor in the room. Haley followed Greg around tables and chairs to a staircase along the wall. This one wasn't half as glamorous as the one in the main lobby.

"Room six," Haley said under her breath, and followed Greg up the stairs.

The staircase wasn't stone, either, but wood, and creaked and groaned against their weight, sounding a few times as if it might give out. Haley reminded herself how long the building had been standing and that if it had withstood so many others climbing it, it would hold them.

They hesitated at the top of the stairs for a moment. There wasn't a sign indicating which rooms were in which directions. The hallway was narrow and dark and smelled from lack of use. Haley doubted many cleaning supplies were used on this floor. Which was odd, since it was the floor where guests stayed. She took one look down each direction of the dimly lit hall, though, and wondered how often anyone stayed here. The place was gloomy and it smelled.

"The doors aren't numbered," Greg said.

"How many doors are there?" Haley started to her left, counting three doors. Then turning and looking around Greg, who stood directly behind her, she counted three more. "Six rooms. So he's at one end of the hallway, or the other."

"We try them both." Greg moved in behind Haley.

She turned, leading the way to one end of the hallway. Although their footsteps were loud and floorboards creaked underneath them, no one appeared at the stairs. As odd as it was that they had been forced to leave at gunpoint earlier, now no one showed up to escort them out of the motel.

"It's hard to believe no one knows we're up here," Haley whispered, shooting a furtive look behind Greg at the hallway when they stood at the hotel room door that was either number one or number six.

"They know we're here." There was an edge in Greg's voice.

She looked up at him, feeling a wave of unease hit her.

"Knock," he told her, nodding at the door.

Haley's stomach lurched to her throat as she rapped on the door. Greg gripped her arm the moment she knocked and pulled her to his side, as if someone would fly out the door in the next moment. She stood there, not breathing, and stared at the wooden door that had once been painted a color that could no longer be distinguished.

"No one's answering," she said unnecessarily after what seemed like an eternity of standing and staring at the worn-out-looking door.

Haley glanced down the hallway at the same time Greg did. It was as if they were suddenly alone in the hotel. It reminded her of one of those scenes in a horror movie where any moment someone would pounce out of the corner and she'd start screaming.

"Let's try the other door," Greg said, sounding tense.

This time he led the way. Focusing on his broad back, on the muscles that flexed under his shirt as he moved, didn't help soothe her nerves any. Haley couldn't be with a better protector. Greg would probably beam with pride knowing she thought that. All the strength and predatory skills he possessed at the moment wouldn't help them if John was hurt, or worse. Her legs grew shaky as she and Greg headed down the hallway.

"God, it stinks."

Haley drew in a breath and about gagged. "They don't clean this floor much, do they?"

"That isn't the smell of filth."

It took a moment for his words to register. Greg had slowed and come to a complete stop before they reached the last door at the other end of the hall.

"What's that sound?" Haley tilted her head. "Do you hear it?"

"Maybe you should wait here." Greg's pinched expression hardened when he turned and stared down at her.

Haley shook her head. She brushed a strand of hair from her face that was stuck from perspiration. The air was so thick it was hard to breathe. The disgusting stench made her not want to breathe.

"I have to do this." She moved around him, sucking in a deep breath as she searched for strength to carry out their mission. She dragged the foul smell into her lungs and almost gagged. "I'm fine," she said to herself as much as to Greg.

Acid filled the back of her mouth when she walked around Greg and stood in front of the door at the end of the hall. The sound she'd heard, a repetative humming, had grown louder. Instead of knocking this time, she reached for the door handle. It was sticky. She pulled her hand back quickly as if she'd been bitten.

"What's wrong?"

"It's just dirty," she said, and made herself grab it again.

The door opened easily. It wasn't locked. It opened into the room, and as Haley pushed it the stench they'd been smelling grew tenfold.

"Oh my God," she cried out, gagging. Her eyes were watering so badly she couldn't focus.

She jumped when Greg touched her. He moved his arm around her, one hand gripping her waist while he felt for a light switch with the other.

"What's that noise?" Speaking dragged the disgusting smell into her mouth, allowing her to taste it.

Haley choked and covered her mouth as her eyes continued watering. The room was tight, way too warm, and the humming sound made her skin crawl. When Greg found a light switch and turned it on, Haley started screaming. She couldn't stop and she couldn't look away.

Chapter 19

"Oh my God! Oh my God! No!" Haley was across the dingy motel room before she realized it.

Flies were everywhere. She swatted them away from John's body. They quickly descended again, as if after a moment deciding they would fight for the right to feast on his body. The humming was too loud. No matter how hard she tried the flies returned.

"Get away from him!" Haley gagged and fought the repeated urge to throw up. "John!" she cried, and could barely see from flies swarming in her face.

After a moment she gave in to her physical panic and staggered backward from the bed. Greg was right there, on the phone, offering comfort as he pulled her against him, shielding the flies and blocking her view of the corpse.

"I take it this is John Payton?" he whispered above her head.

All she could do was nod. She didn't want it to be. She told herself if she looked at him one more time she would realize it wasn't John. He was still missing, alive somewhere, and would call her soon with further instructions. They would find John and everything would be okay.

"Yes, it's John." Her voice sounded foreign to her.

"Go on outside, sweetheart. There isn't anything else you can do here."

She wanted to agree, to run, to get the hell out of that room and never come back. "No," she heard herself say. "I need to go to him."

Haley endured the flies, swatting them away as she stared down at her boss. "What happened to you?" she asked, choking on the words as she stared at John's tormented expression.

His eyes were closed, his lips a thin, pale line. He lay on the bed, dressed in slacks and a short-sleeved, button-down shirt. They were clothes he would wear into the office. Maybe part of the stench came from him being here in this room all this time and unable to change or possibly even shower. There was a bruise going down the side of his face, but she didn't see blood.

"It's hard to say by looking how he died." Greg was right behind her. "His hands and feet are bound. But his expression is relaxed, as if he didn't struggle."

"I'll find out who did this, John," she said, having a sudden urge to touch him but knowing she couldn't.

"The police will be here soon. We'll get our answers."

Time seemed to float by, leaving her in a surreal world. Somehow she ended up in the hallway, and then later outside by Greg's truck in the smoldering heat. Sweat trickled down her back, but she didn't care. There were police everywhere, uniforms moving around, doing their job efficiently and professionally. She answered questions, heard her voice offer explanations, and barely remembered a thing she said.

John was dead. It was wrong. Someone would pay dearly for taking such a good man's life.

Haley sat with Greg and Seth at a small, round table, cool drinks in hand, although none of them drank. The small café where they'd agreed to meet was as far from the grungy hotel as day from night. Flowers were in full bloom in pots. The air smelled sweet and clean. Even the temperature seemed more comfortable and the sky bluer.

Not that any of it mattered. Haley's drink didn't seem to have any taste. Everything around her seemed fake. John was dead. It just wouldn't sink in. Although it explained her fear all morning that something wasn't right. Seth sat on the other side of the small, round table, facing her and Greg. He kept his voice low so it wouldn't carry even though there were only a few other people in the café.

"I have a few friends in town. We'll know before the day is out who killed John," Seth was saying while fingering the cold Mexican beer and staring at the dark, longneck bottle. "I also heard you were paid a visit at your hotel by the local police shortly after checking in."

"Good news travels fast," Greg growled.

"I'm not staying at quite as nice a place as you are," he added, although it didn't sound as if he were complaining. "I'd hoped with the drug wars going on right now between the local government and the drug lords in the area that we would be left alone."

"There's nothing a Mexican police officer loves more than arresting an American bounty hunter," Greg told him, whispering under his breath. Seth nodded.

"I'd just headed out, shortly after the sun was up, to get some breakfast when one of my friends called me and told me an American had been found dead in another nearby hotel."

"They already knew he was dead?" Haley snapped, gripping her cocktail glass hard enough that it almost slipped out of her fingers. She glared at Seth, although his expression remained impassive. "Why didn't you tell us that part?"

"I didn't have proof and didn't want to upset you if it weren't the case," he offered, but then shook his head. "I'm as sorry as you are, Hannah. Or may I call you Haley, now?"

Haley didn't care if Seth appeared put out that she'd withheld her true identity from him. Or maybe his tone reflected the fact that he hadn't found out sooner.

"'Haley' is fine," she said without emotion. "And how sure was your housekeeper that John was dead before we got there?"

"She wasn't sure at all. Since all she was doing was speculating, going on the fact she hadn't seen him come or go in a few days, it wasn't enough to suggest the idea to either of you."

"It doesn't matter now." Haley waved her hand in the air, her fingers damp from holding her drink. "John is dead and none of this will bring him back."

Greg rubbed her back. "My guess is he's been dead at least a couple days. I don't know if we'll be able to get any reports out of the local law enforcement. We need to get him back into the States for an autopsy."

Haley nodded, fighting the lump that started swelling in her throat. Her eyes burned, although she refused to cry. More than ever she needed a level head. This had just gotten incredibly personal, and for John's sake they had to find out who killed him.

"There was no indication of a fight or struggle of any kind. John was lying on the bed, fully dressed, his body fine other than a bruise along the side of his face. I took pictures with my phone."

"Good," Haley said, suddenly frustrated that she hadn't thought to take pictures. In spite of her effort to remain calm, obviously she was forgetting things.

All she could offer was what she knew. "There were a few items in the bathroom. A toothbrush, toothpaste, and a razor on the counter. Only one of each. He was either staying there alone—and if so, why?—or those items belonged to someone else." Haley rubbed her head, aware of both men watching her. For a moment her mind went blank, but she forced herself to gather her thoughts. "The door was unlocked, as if he could come and go as he pleased. Or it was left unlocked for us to find him after he was dead."

"There was no cell phone in the room," Greg added, cutting in when Haley paused for a breath. "If that is where they kept him this whole time, someone came to him to have him call you. He wasn't calling from his cell phone."

"Yes. It was a track phone. We couldn't trace it."

"I would have been surprised if they'd used anything else," Seth muttered. "Did you find a feather anywhere in the room?"

"A feather?" Haley and Greg asked at the same time.

Seth nodded. "I thought maybe The Bird would leave a calling card."

"I didn't notice any feathers," Haley said, and glanced at each man's grim expression when they stared at her. "I think we were supposed to find him, though. How did you know this maid who told you about him?" she asked Seth.

"Honestly, I met her in a cantina the other night." Seth cleared his throat before taking another drink of his beer. "This is the first time in my life I haven't been a single man. And I was damn proud of myself for turning down her advances. This morning, though, she found me at my motel and told me of this American who was staying at the motel where she works. She hadn't seen him in a few days and thought I should take a look and make sure he was okay."

"We were set up to find him." Greg continued rubbing Haley's back. "Think you can find your maid again and see if you can learn who encouraged her to tell you about him?"

Seth nodded. "That shouldn't be too hard."

"It also suggests he'd been staying in that room for a while, apparently coming and going, since the maid reported seeing him." A shudder ransacked Haley's body. If only she and Greg had come down here sooner. If only she'd spotted John on the streets. "Why did he die?" Haley asked, shifting her attention from one brooding expression to another. "Tell me that. There has to be a reason why he died."

"Sweetheart," Greg said, his incredibly low baritone causing the air to sizzle around him.

Haley yanked her hand from underneath his when he tried clasping it in his. "Don't feel sorry for me. I don't want sympathy. I want answers."

She rested her elbows on the table and dropped her head in her hands. "And don't either one of you promise me we'll get those answers. I don't want to hear that anymore. We didn't find him in time. We didn't save him."

She didn't mind the silence that followed for the next few moments. Lifting her head, she nursed her drink, staring out to the street at people walking up and down the sidewalk. For the most part she loved her work, loved thinking she did what she did so people like those strolling outside the café could do just that, enjoy their lives and not worry about bad guys destroying them. Then there were other times when she ached to be one of them, without a worry in her head, simply enjoying life and oblivious to anything bad.

"I might head over and join Marc and Jake." Seth slid his chair back.

If he was put out that she had snapped at him he would just have to get over it. Haley sipped her drink, feeling the alcohol fumes float around in her head. Maybe she should just get trashed until all her inhibitions were gone, find Marty Byrd herself, blow his head off, and end his life as he'd done John's.

"They're at the bar down the street seeing if they can hear anything from the locals," Greg offered.

"Peter Langston is here in town somewhere, too," Seth said, keeping his voice low so only she and Greg heard. "He might be easier to find than Marty Bird. I have some friends who would know where he is, if he's here."

"Let's talk to them." Greg downed his beer and placed the empty bottle on the table with a thud. "Where do they live?"

"The streets don't have names," Seth told him. "But I can take you to them."

Haley heard the men talk but was still lost in her thoughts about John. Just over a week ago he'd been in his office, business as usual. She could only imagine what this past week might have been like for him. And the more she thought about it, the more it made her sick to her stomach.

"Let's go." She pushed her drink to the middle of the table, done with it. Getting drunk wouldn't help matters. She wanted to be clearheaded when she learned who killed John, whether it was Marty Byrd or someone else. And she really wanted to be the one who pulled the trigger when they found him.

Greg's smile didn't reach his eyes when he put his hand over hers. "We'll get whoever did this to him."

"Yes, we will," she agreed. "And we're going to get him, or them, before anyone else dies."

Greg brought her fingers to his mouth, his lips moving against her flesh when he spoke. "I promise you, darling. You'll be there when I put the cuffs on the asshole who killed John. I know how much he meant to you. I will personally see to it that you get your pound of flesh."

Something quickened inside her. The pain over losing John tore her apart, but as she stared into Greg's eyes the warmth and concern filling them created a heat inside her she couldn't ignore. Very soon, she'd be the one to put the cuffs on, as soon as she got her license.

It took some effort to look past Greg to Seth. "I want to go meet these friends of yours now. No more sitting and promising each other we'll get the bad guy. We're taking him down now."

"I'll make a phone call." Seth grabbed his beer as he reached for his phone and stood from the table, leaving the two of them alone as he walked up to the bar and purchased another beer.

"I'm so sorry, Haley," Greg told her, pulling her into his arms and holding her, not saying anything else for a moment.

Haley relaxed and felt the tension ease from Greg's body as well. She leaned her cheek against his shoulder, letting him hold her. Greg wasn't the most demonstrative man, but he cared about her with all his heart and had most of his life. She rested her hand over his heart and wasn't surprised the beat matched her own. They were soul mates and always would be.

Haley didn't focus on anything, but when she blinked, bringing her surroundings into view around her, Seth leaned against the bar, talking on his phone and watching her. He'd never known she was married, or even her real name. They hadn't been close, but during the many times over the years he'd come into the office or seen her around town, she'd grown to like him. There was a mystery about Seth. And she believed he liked getting people to think that about him. But she'd pulled off the bigger mystery, being someone she wasn't. The look on Seth's face was a mixture of frustration and admiration when he made eye contact with her. Her life as Hannah McDowell had been real, but it was over now.

As she remained cuddled against Greg, Haley knew she was where she belonged. She wouldn't say John's death had a purpose. There was never logic behind murders like this, other than corrupt men believed taking lives made them more powerful.

"We're going to meet with my friends," Seth announced when he returned to the table.

"When?" Greg asked.

"Now."

Greg let go of Haley, standing and pulling a few bills out of his wallet to pay for their drinks. Haley stood as well, gripping her purse and pulling out her phone to make sure she hadn't missed any calls. When they walked out of the café, her phone started beeping, as did Greg's.

"I missed a call," she announced, checking to see when the call came in. "I must not have had a signal in there," she mused. "The call came through several minutes ago."

"I missed several calls," Greg said, squinting at the small screen on his phone. "Who called you?"

"Marc," she said, pushing the button to return his call.

"He called me a couple times. Are you calling him back?"

Haley nodded, standing outside the café with Greg and Seth watching her. The phone rang in her ear and she didn't hear what Seth murmured to Greg. But Greg nodded and wrapped his arm over her shoulder, starting down the street as she continued waiting for Marc to pick up.

"Hello," he said, finally answering. The background noise coming through the phone made it really hard to hear him.

"Marc, it's Mom," she said, aware that Seth shot her a side-glance but then looked ahead as he continued walking next to her. Greg was on her other side, his arm still around her, and also glanced down at her. "We must not have had a signal where we were, but your dad and I just noticed you tried calling."

"Yeah, I was trying to reach Dad. You're still with him, right?"

"Yes."

"Natasha called and Samantha Wilson has been trying to reach Dad."

"Oh?" Haley asked, refusing to allow any concern that the brazen hussy wanted Greg.

"Apparently Samantha is hysterical about something. She insists on talking to Dad immediately."

"I'm sure," Haley muttered.

"I don't think it's like that, Mom."

Haley wanted to ask him, *Like what?*

"She came to Dad because her brother skipped out on his court date. She offered to pay us more than the bonding agency to bring him back in. But then he skipped out of Orange County. We suspected her immediately when she showed up at the office before you came to town, but when she came back she blew her own cover, admitting she showed up because she was sent to us. You might already know the details on her, but anyway, apparently she went over to her brother's apartment where he was staying before he disappeared and found some papers that terrified her."

"What papers did she find?" Haley was aware of Greg and Seth both glancing down at her as they continued walking. She couldn't help but feel incredibly dwarfed between the two large men but stared straight ahead of them as they walked slowly along the broken sidewalk, crowded with people. They continued toward the edge of the shopping district. Already she could see endless shacks stretching over the flat desert land ahead of them.

"She was really adamant about talking to Dad in person. Sam isn't as stupid as she tries to make the world think and she didn't trust the cell phones she and Natasha were on. But I think she might be in trouble."

"So let me guess, she wants to come down here."

"Yup." The noise around Marc faded and she guessed he had stepped outside or into a bathroom, where he would have more privacy. "I find it interesting that Sam keeps coming up with clues to guide us in a certain direction. She wanted to hire us to find her brother but continually admits to doing her own investigating, then providing us with clues to lead us the way she wants us."

"Other than not trusting her, what do you think she's up to?"

"I think Dad needs to meet with her, see what she has for us, then pay attention to the direction it takes us. She might be leading us into a trap."

Chapter 20

Greg touched the Glock Seth had gotten for him. It was a nice gun, clean and loaded. They entered a neighborhood that was cluttered with homes that were often no more than shacks, built in no particular order, with no yards, and stacked along either side of the narrow, twisting road that didn't have a name. They were definitely no longer in the tourist part of Tijuana, nor were they in a good part of town.

Haley had yanked a small notepad out of her purse and jotted something down, then ended the call with Marc. Greg wanted to ask her about the call. It didn't sound like good news. But they were being escorted through this neighborhood by a group of small children and at least as many dogs. The chattering in Spanish and barking of the dogs made it rather difficult to have a conversation at the moment.

There weren't any more sidewalks, and walking on the road pretty much meant walking alongside different families' front doors. Greg, Seth, and Haley stayed in the middle of the road, which was so broken most cars wouldn't be able to drive along it. There wasn't any way Greg would take his new black Avalanche into this part of town. Even if the locals didn't try stealing something off of it, the children, who appeared to be a mass of their own, would climb all over it simply out of curiosity and something new to play with.

"We're almost there," Seth offered when Haley stopped to get a pebble out of her sandal.

She clutched her purse to her chest, and nodded, pushing a strand of hair behind her ear.

"You hear about people living like this, but you never truly believe it until you see it," she said under her breath.

"This is the nicer side of this part of town," Seth told her, patting the head of a boy who was a bit more persistent than the others in attempting to get change out of the three of them. "Okay, this is it," Seth said, nodding to the left side of the street.

Greg wasn't sure which shack Seth meant, since several were almost on top of one another, with narrow pathways between each home. He dug into his pocket, pulling out what change he had, and held his hand out to the group of children who'd stuck close to them since they'd entered this neighborhood. He almost thought he might be pulling his arm back without his hand. The kids were incredibly greedy when they dove at his hand, practically ripping the change from his fingers.

Seth took the lead, walking between two shacks, the smell of a variety of spices and fried foods hanging heavy in the smoldering heat around them. Haley walked behind Seth and in front of Greg, looking down and watching her footing as they stepped with caution over the packed but uneven dirt path. The dress she wore clung to her slender figure. In spite of being sweaty and dusty after walking there, Haley still looked damn good.

Greg put his hands on Haley's shoulders, pulling her back against him when Seth stopped in front of a solid wooden door and knocked. He glanced around them, aware suddenly that there was no one in sight, not even kids. The dogs still lingered, most of them small, brown dogs who appeared to be related by their similar appearance. They were all underfed but wagged their tails, as if it were their job to greet all newcomers and they took their job very seriously.

"*¿Quién está allí?*" a man asked from the other side of the door.

"Seth Gere," Seth said seriously, keeping his voice low. "I bring guests."

The door opened inward and Seth ducked to enter the small wooden structure. Greg held Haley close, acutely aware that he had to trust Seth as they walked into a shack when he couldn't tell who opened the door. Keeping one hand on Haley, Greg patted the cold metal of his gun with his other hand. Sometimes the hardest part of his line of work meant trusting someone he barely knew in order to secure leads that would result in an arrest. For the most part Greg preferred not using weapons if he didn't have to, but it was nice knowing the gun was there.

"We weren't sure you would make it back," a tall American man with a healthy tan said as he held the door, speaking to Seth but giving Greg and Haley a curious once-over. "Margarita heard about the American found dead in the motel this morning."

"These are my friends," Seth said, standing in the middle of a surprisingly clean living room with nice, modern-looking furniture. Whoever lived here intentionally chose this neighborhood to keep a low profile. By the looks of their surroundings, they could afford a lot better. "Greg King and his wife, Haley King."

Haley adjusted her purse in her arm and offered an easy smile, turning her attention to the couple who moved to stand next to each other.

"Bret and Margarita have been good friends of mine for quite a few years," Seth offered. "They've lived down here for at least a year now."

"Margarita isn't an American citizen, so we chose to live down here," Bret offered, wrapping his arm around Margarita and extending his free hand to Greg. "Welcome to our humble home, though. I bet you'd like something cold to drink."

Margarita was a petite although full-figured woman with skin the shade of milk chocolate and thick black hair she had piled on top of her head. She was barefoot and wore a tank top with no bra, which showed off her ample breasts. Her cutoff blue-jean shorts barely covered her ass when she left the group and hurried into another room, speaking too quickly in Spanish for Greg to catch everything she said. Something about cold iced tea and that it was too hot for *cerveza*.

"*¿Quieres una cierta ayuda?*" Bret called after her, wanting to know if Margarita wanted help.

"No. *Que él quiere y si su digno de confianza.*" Margarita must have thought leaving Bret alone in the living room with the three of them would make it easier for him to determine if they were trustworthy.

Greg stared at the ground, finding it interesting that Margarita believed he and Haley wouldn't know her language. It said something about Margarita's nature, and her opinion of Americans. For the time being, he would remain quiet, as well as deciding to learn how trustworthy this couple was. His Spanish wasn't the best, but he could pick up on enough to understand if they didn't use too much slang.

Seth apparently disagreed with Greg's gut reaction to the couple. "*Somos sonidos y el suena bueno,*" he called out to the other room, informing Margarita that Greg and Haley were trustworthy and that iced tea sounded perfect.

"You are a smart man," Bret told Seth, and gestured to the three of them to sit in the living area. There were long, narrow windows that had almost see-through screens hanging over them, possibly to offer privacy and probably to keep the glare of the sun from making it hotter inside. A ceiling fan rotated at a decent speed in the middle of the room, creating a breeze. But the window air-conditioning unit that hummed quietly at the end of the room dubbed this couple as one of the wealthier households in this part of town. It was also a godsend, as the group made themselves comfortable on the small couch and upright chairs that faced each other. His clothes quit clinging to him as sweat dried on his body.

Margarita appeared a minute later with a tall glass pitcher, which perspired heavily while ice cubes clinked inside it. It was on a tray with glasses that she set on the coffee table.

"*¿Soy supuesto asumir que estos dos no hablan español o no son que fingen entenderme?*" Margarita asked as she picked up the pitcher, poured tea into a glass, and handed it to Bret.

Greg knew he was being tested. Unless Haley had managed time to perfect her Spanish in the six years she was in Omaha, she was fairly bilingual but not as good as him. One glance at her and the quick frown she gave him let him know she'd probably gotten the gist of what Margarita just said but wasn't certain. Greg understood completely, and if they were going to learn anything during this meeting he would honor Margarita by answering her question, even though it was directed to Bret.

"My Spanish is okay," Greg offered. "Haley, however, is going to be at a disadvantage."

Haley smiled humbly, the humidity creating soft waves in her hair that bordered her face. "I admit I've been trying to follow what you've been saying. If I'm right, you just asked if we possibly spoke Spanish and were just pretending not to understand."

Margarita grinned broadly and Bret glanced down at his drink, looking as if he hid a smile. He remained quiet as Margarita stood facing them. It offered more insight into both of their personalities. Margarita was a tricky woman and also head of this household.

"You understand better than you thought," Margarita said in English, her accent sounding melodic. She was a very pretty woman but apparently a bit conniving.

"Now that we all understand each other," Bret said, taking the next glassful of tea from Margarita and handing it to Haley, "let's get down to business."

"*Gracias,*" Seth mumbled when he was handed his glass. "And yes, I want you to tell Greg and Haley what you learned this morning."

"Correct me if I'm wrong," Bret said, standing and letting Margarita take his chair, which faced the couch where Greg and Haley sat. Bret stood behind Margarita, resting his hand on the chair as he focused on Greg. "But are you Greg King of KFA in Los Angeles?"

"Yes," Greg said.

Margarita shifted quickly, looking up at Bret as she started whispering frantically in Spanish. This time Greg didn't catch what she said.

"My wife is concerned that your line of business is illegal in her country."

"We came down here to find John Payton, my wife's boss," Greg told both of them. "Just this past hour we learned he was dead, which has upset my wife greatly. We want to find out who killed him. I'm not trying to find someone to turn them in for the bounty. No one has hired me and I'm not on the clock. Therefore, I'm not breaking any of your laws."

"It's a fine line in the eyes of the cops here in Tijuana," Bret told him gravely.

"Trust me, I know." Greg had no intention of sitting in any Mexican jail. "Do you have any information about our friend's murder?"

"The Ramoses own the motel Senōr Payton was found in. Margarita's brother works at that motel. He told us there wasn't a John Payton checked into that room, or any room in that motel."

"Who was that room reserved to?" Haley asked.

"Now see, this is where I think it is very interesting," Margarita said, leaning forward on her chair and resting her elbows on her knees. She offered one hell of a view of her large breasts as she shifted her attention from Greg to Haley, then Seth. *Mi hermano,* Miguel, has worked the front desk there now for almost two years. He has worked every day this week and he knows he reserved that room, room six, for an American man who was in his fifties and almost bald, with silver sunglasses, the kind you can see yourself in when you're talking to someone who is wearing them," she said, taking a breath and nodding, causing her thick, black hair to slide slightly from its clips that held it in place. Margarita raised her hands over her head, arching her back and putting a little stretch into it as she adjusted her hair. "*Mi hermano* swears the *hombre*'s name was Pablo or Peter. One of the saints, although he swears this man was no saint."

"Peter Langston," Haley whispered, searching Greg's face when he looked at her.

Greg nodded, returning his attention to Margarita. He took a sip of his tea. It was cold, sweet, and very strong.

He leaned back, placing his arm along the back of the couch and behind Haley. Margarita watched him while shifting on her chair. If he didn't know better, he'd swear she was doing her best to show off as much of her hot little body as possible. Either she was a seductress by nature or this was another of her tricks in her effort to learn more about them.

Quite possibly Margarita flaunted herself simply to see what their reaction might be. If Greg reacted, she might conclude he wasn't an honorable or trustworthy man. Beating her at her own game would be no problem. He refused to look anywhere other than her face.

"Why did he say this man was no saint?" Greg asked.

Margarita smiled, showing off very white teeth that almost appeared to glow against her soft-looking brown skin. "This *hombre* has been staying at the motel for over a week. He paid cash in advance and made arrangements for one of the barmaids down the street to bring him his meals. One night *mi hermano* said she ran from the motel crying. That was a few days ago and he didn't see her after that. When *mi hermano* asked the *hombre* about it the next day the *hombre* told him to go to hell."

"Nice guy," Haley muttered. "That wasn't John, though. He wouldn't act like that."

Bret pressed his lips together, shaking his head as he rested his arms against the back of Margarita's chair. "Miguel says he never saw John Payton before he was found dead in the bed in this man's room. He's already confirmed he wasn't the man he saw going in and out of the room."

"Why doesn't your brother remember this guy's name?" Seth asked. "Wouldn't it be in their computers?"

Margarita laughed and twisted on her chair, batting her long, thick black lashes over her dark eyes as she focused on Seth, who sat on the other upright chair alongside the couch.

"This motel doesn't have computers, at least not at the front desk. *Mi hermano* wouldn't know how to turn a computer on," she added, still smiling. "He has a logbook at the front desk where he writes the name of anyone who stays at the motel and how much money they pay. His books always have to match the money in the drawer or he has the difference docked from his paycheck."

"We need to look at that logbook," Greg decided.

"It won't do you any good," Margarita told him. "Miguel told Bret and me he would swear on a stack of Bibles he checked this American into room six over a week ago. He collected the cash from the *hombre* and his drawer always matches the logbook. But today, after John Payton is found, and we look at the logbook, there is no name registered in room six. His book shows the room is vacant."

"Interesting," Greg muttered, leaning forward for his iced tea and gulping the rest of it down. "We should probably head back to our motel. If your brother remembers this man's name, please let us know."

"I couldn't tell you about Marc's phone call earlier," Haley said after they left Bret and Margarita's home. She struggled with her purse as they walked. "Here it is," she said, handing him the piece of paper she'd written on earlier. "Samantha Wilson needs you," she added, looking up at him with an incredibly innocent look on her face as if she didn't intend to imply she meant anything by her comment other than he should return Sam's call.

"Do you know why?" he asked, deciding to take Haley's comment seriously.

"She called Natasha earlier today. I guess she went to her brother's house and found something over there that scared her and she needs to talk to you about it."

Seth walked on the other side of Haley, as he had when they'd come to this neighborhood. He glanced at Greg when Haley explained the phone message, his serious expression contemplative when he shifted his attention to the piece of paper in Greg's hand.

"I'll call her when we return to the hotel," Greg decided. He focused on Seth, knowing he walked on the other side of Haley to offer her more protection from people downtown. "Do you want to see if you can get a look at that ledger that doesn't have Peter Langston's name in it?"

"I figured I would check out the other motels in the area. I'm willing to bet Langston isn't at that motel anymore."

"Wherever he is, he can't be working alone," Haley said, once again clutching her purse against her body when they reached the sidewalk and started through the downtown area. "I wish there was a way to know if anyone else is missing under similar circumstances."

"You mean how John disappeared?" Greg asked.

"Yes. We still don't know why John was taken, but the reason has to be pretty intense. This is more than one man. It's an organization. We know others are involved from what Torres and Arnold said on that tape."

"What tape is that?" Seth asked, lowering his voice as they walked slowly along the sidewalk.

"We haven't had a chance to show it to you," Haley offered, glancing up at Seth.

"We need to find out who is helping Langston. But above and beyond everything else, why are they doing this? What was John's involvement with Marty Byrd? And if they're after Haley, what was her involvement?" Greg asked.

Seth nodded once but stared ahead, appearing to focus on

the people moving around them and going in and out of the shops downtown.

"John worked a case for Marty Byrd," Haley offered, but didn't say anything else until they'd passed a group of people. "I don't know what my involvement is, unless he thought to challenge my investigative skills," she added when no one else was around them on the sidewalk.

Seth grunted his response and Greg had to agree.

"I doubt it," Greg muttered. "I'm going to make several phone calls once we reach the hotel." Haley glanced at both of them. It didn't surprise Greg when Seth didn't say anything. Greg had no intention of telling his feisty wife she might be wanted simply because she was hot as hell.

Seth pointed to a side street when they reached an intersection in the heart of downtown near their hotel.

"I'll start here," Seth said, nodding to the side street. "I'm going to head back down to that motel where you found John's body. Then I'll check out anywhere else where a person might be able to pay and get a room. I've got a hunch Langston won't be in a motel room anymore. He's going to keep a lower profile from here on out."

"If he even remained in town," Haley muttered.

Seth squeezed Haley's arm. "Go kick back for a while. We'll figure out who did this to John and we'll nail the mother-fucker to a cross," Seth hissed; then looking past her to Greg, he nodded once and trotted across the street.

"He's not a bad young man," Greg decided.

"I wouldn't have agreed to let him come down here if I didn't think he could handle it," Haley said, focusing ahead of her as she clutched her purse. "He's not nailing anyone to a cross, though. When we figure out who killed John, I get the right to swing the hammer first," she added, squinting as she glanced up at Greg.

Greg let Haley shower first when they returned to the room. More than likely their hike into a nearby neighborhood in the intense heat wore her out. On top of that, finding John as they had would haunt her for a while. Haley disappeared into the bathroom without saying a word.

Greg ran his bug detector throughout the room, making sure it was clean before relaxing back in the office chair, and waited for the laptop to boot up. The sounds of the shower distracted him, however, and produced images of Haley arching beneath the water, suds streaming down her body. It was damn hard to focus on the matters at hand. He considered joining his wife in the shower, but the sooner they had answers the better off Haley would be. He knew from experience when a hunt hit too close to home, it got harder and harder to think straight.

The afternoon after Haley's appearance in court, she'd entered the Witness Protection Program. They'd both known it would happen, even though Greg wasn't supposed to know anything. Haley had told him. It had made it even tougher. They took her away from him. He couldn't say anything to anyone, not to the U.S. Marshals, who stood by to take her after her testimony, or to her lawyer, or to any of the cops who were also part of the investigation or court process. Greg had been left on his own, and obsessed.

Marc and Jake hadn't been old enough to stop him. They didn't know what was happening to their mother and Greg never planned on telling them. Instead of focusing on them when they went through losing their mother, he had to know where Haley was. There was no one to stop him. He'd gone from obsessed to insane, finding Haley, seeing the house she now lived in, watching her go to work in a car she bought under her new name, and not being able to touch her. Any good psychiatrist would have told him this wasn't a healthy way to move on, not that he would have listened back then anyway.

All it did, a good few months later, was give him a very small amount of peace of mind knowing exactly where she was. He still had to live with his world thinking that she'd run out on him and that Greg didn't have a clue where she was. He never talked to anyone about her and refused to let anyone in his home mention her name. He'd never healed, but simply covered up the nasty wound from his immeasurable pain as he attempted living without her. He had a couple years before Marc and Jake considered themselves grown men and started trying to dictate his life. If they'd been older when Haley had left, they would have seen the cases he'd fucked up and the mistakes he'd made in his personal life. For whatever reason, no one would ever know how terribly he'd lived those first couple years.

Now Haley endured something very similar. Greg knew it wasn't an exact comparison. John Payton wasn't her lover, but he had been a boss she'd cared dearly about. Greg saw her pain. He'd be there for her, when she wanted him. He'd cover any mistakes she might make while working through her grief. And he'd never say a word to her about her work not being up to par during this time. It had been hell going through it, but Greg knew if anyone had tried taking him off a case, or told him the best way to grieve the loss of his wife, or pointed out every time he made a mistake because he wasn't thinking straight, he probably would have leveled them to the ground. Greg would give Haley what he had had: a full, busy life to lead to keep her occupied while she worked through the pain of losing someone close to her.

Greg pulled the piece of paper Haley had given him out of his pocket and stared at Samantha Wilson's number. He really wasn't in the mood to speak with Sam. She was annoying at best. But something didn't ring right about her and, unfortunately, the only way to learn what it was was to give her the attention she wanted.

He glanced toward the bathroom, again thinking of scrubbing Haley's back.

"Focus on the job," he told himself, dropping the paper on the desk next to Haley's laptop. If it became harder for Haley to focus, he would need to be on top of his act, get this case solved, and give Haley closure. Getting more comfortable, and having something cold to drink, would make it easier to make the phone call. Comfort came with security.

Greg changed into shorts, putting the Glock Seth had obtained for him into the false bottom of his suitcase. He would have to dispose of it before returning across the border.

Greg called the LAPD, then called Room Service. He returned his attention to the laptop when Haley came out of the bathroom, dressed in clean shorts and a blouse, with her damp hair curling in waves past her shoulders. Her cheeks were flushed and her face glowed, causing her sensual green eyes to look even prettier than usual.

It hit him he'd been waiting for her to get out of the shower to talk to her about the case. "We've got Room Service on its way up," he told her as means of starting the conversation. "I was just getting ready to call Sam Wilson."

"You haven't called her yet?" Haley paused in front of the mirror on the wall that faced the beds and ran her fingers through her hair, turning slightly as if admiring her reflection.

She looked damn good to him.

"Not yet," he said. "But I did put in a call to my friend with the LAPD."

"You're down to just one friend on the force?" Her grin was impish when she stared at him through the mirror.

Greg really liked the idea of grabbing her and pulling her down onto the bed. "Pretty amazing, huh," he grunted, feeling his cock twitch in his shorts when she ran her hands over her ass.

God. The woman was taunting him.

"He's going to make arrangements to have John Payton's body transferred back to the U.S.," Greg told her, watching her ass sway when Haley walked into the bathroom. "He'll be shipped to Omaha, where an autopsy will be done. We're going to need next of kin."

"Thank you," she said, peering around the corner with a mascara stick in her hand. "And John never mentioned family, but I'll see if I can find any relatives once we're home."

"We'll need to know if he left a will, and there is his business to tend to."

"I've already thought of all of that," she said, disappearing into the bathroom again.

Greg never remembered her wearing makeup so often before, but he liked that she did now. Although with Haley, she looked good either way.

"Did you discuss the rest of the case with him?" she asked. "Who is your contact, if I can ask? Anyone I knew?"

"Yes, I did, and probably. You remember Bernie Osborne, don't you?"

"Yeah, I do," she called out from the bathroom. "How's he doing? Still a bachelor?"

"Married to his work," Greg told her.

"Some of the best men are."

Greg decided not to touch that comment. Although the more he'd thought about it the last day on so, have Haley by his side day in and day out would be a damn good way to live.

"He's going to get in touch with Frank Roster in Omaha, let him know about John. When you make your phone calls see if Roster will launch a full investigation on Payton. If this becomes a police issue, we can override any will, or any relative who might not want the business messed with. I want to find out where that e-mail came from that Torres claimed to receive."

"The one he said he got and printed the note he left on my desk?" Haley came out of the bathroom again, her eyes nicely made up, complete with black eyeliner that finished her seductress appearance.

"Yes. Osborne is going to get back with me as soon as they have anything concrete from the Omaha PD."

His phone rang and he glanced down at the screen. "It's Natasha," he offered as he took the call.

"I just got home and thought I'd call you before showering and figuring out what I'm doing for supper," Natasha said in form of greeting, sounding as if she was out of breath.

Natasha was on the work line, which, although it was a cell phone that he allowed her to carry on her when she wasn't in the office so she could still answer the phones, had a scrambler in it. Anyone trying to tap into their phone conversation would be blessed with a high-pitched whistle in their ear for their efforts. Yet another wonderful device his smart niece had discovered, then had installed in all their phones. As soon as they returned home, he'd have Natasha install one in Haley's phone.

"I was just getting ready to call Sam," he told his niece when she mentioned her calling.

"She insisted on knowing where you were. I told her Tijuana just to make her quit nagging me about it. Man, Uncle Greg, that woman can throw a fit. She got downright rude when I wouldn't tell her the name of the hotel where you were staying."

"Something tells me our dumb bimbo could find me if she wanted." Greg glanced at Haley when she leaned back on one of the beds and reclined on her elbows while stretching her legs out in front of her. She shot him an inquiring look at his comment.

"She definitely has an agenda. I'm still trying to figure out what it is." Natasha seldom went out in the field, but she was damn good when it came to brainstorming. He credited himself for her being such a computer geek instead of a party monster like her father. "She called me again right before I called you to tell me she has driven to Tijuana. She is at a coffeehouse right now waiting on your call. She sounds really upset."

Greg held back his sigh of exasperation. It wasn't Natasha's job to shield him from annoying clients. "I want you to do a favor for me."

"What's that?" she asked.

"Do you have Seth Gere's number?"

"No."

"I have it," Haley offered, jumping up to get her phone, then returning, scrolling through numbers until she pulled it up, then handing her phone to Greg.

"Okay, write this number down," he said, reading it off to Natasha. "Call Seth and find out Bret and Margarita's last name. Then I want you to run a background check on them. Find out everything you can for me."

"Who are they?" she asked.

"A couple we met today. I'll fill you in when I can," he said; then promising to call Sam, he hung up. "Apparently Sam Wilson is now here in town," he informed Haley as she returned to the bed. Greg dialed Sam's number, deciding to get her call over with. He was surprised, yet grateful, when it went to voice mail, and left a brief message letting Sam know he was calling her back, then hung up his phone.

Tossing his phone on the bed next to Haley, Greg moved over her, pressing his fists into the bed on either side of her. He came down on top of her and forced her to lie flat on her back. "You're beautiful," he whispered, keeping his face inches from hers.

Haley's slow smile was pure seductive magic. "Thank you," she said. "I was dripping with sweat and swore I could still smell the stench from John's room on me. I really needed to scrub the day off of me and look nice."

"You look better than nice." Greg was more than impressed with how well Haley held herself together after finding John. If a shower was all it took to keep her sane from the grotesque scene they'd witnessed earlier today, she was stronger than most. "Was today the first time you'd seen a dead body?"

"No, but it was the first time I'd seen someone dead whom I'd known and cared about." She brought her fingers to her eyes, blinking several times. "Don't make me ruin my eye makeup," she snarled, making a face at him. "Today was terrible. And if this is the only time I find someone dead that I knew and cared about, I'm cool with that."

"It's the worst thing in the world," he admitted, easing in next to her, then stroked her damp hair. "It won't ever get easier, but you were amazing. I wanted you to know that. You didn't fall apart."

"Oh, believe me, I fell apart," she confessed. "For a while there I really thought I could get rid of those flies. Then I swore if I looked one more time I would realize it wasn't John."

His phone rang and he glared at it, then recognized the number on the screen. Sam had really lousy timing

Greg rolled to his back and answered his cell. "Hello," he growled into the phone.

"Hi, Greg. I didn't recognize your number or I would have taken the call," she purred, her sultry whisper sounding as sweet as maple syrup, and just as sticky, too. "I really need to see you, *now*," she stressed before he could say anything.

"Where are you?" he asked. "Natasha says you're in Tijuana. We'll come meet you."

"This conversation would be better held in private. Where are you staying? I'll come to your room."

If she thought he was staying in a hotel room alone, she would soon learn otherwise. Reluctantly, Greg told her the hotel name and room number and hung up the phone.

"I think I'll hop in the shower," he announced.

"Going to spiff yourself up for our guest?" Haley asked, rolling to her side and showing off one mouthwatering view of cleavage.

Greg tangled his fingers through her damp hair, gently forcing her head back. She pursed her lips into the perfect pout.

"If you'd rather I entertain Samantha Wilson in just my shorts, I could do that," he offered.

"Yeah, right." Haley's eyes twinkled with amusement. "Her hands would be all over you."

"Actually I was thinking about soaking and hiding in there as long as possible so you could entertain her."

"You do that and I'll send her in after you," Haley threatened.

"Somehow I seriously doubt you would do that. However, you're more than welcome to come in and let me know when she's here," he offered, and slid his hand to Haley's neck, reaching for her and pulling her on top of him.

Her nipples hardened against his bare chest. Greg stroked her silky soft hair as Haley leaned forward and kissed him. He almost didn't notice the sharp knock on the door until Haley turned her head, breathing hard as she relaxed on top of him.

"Where was she calling from? The lobby?" Haley complained.

Greg rolled Haley off of him and stood quickly. Sam couldn't have been that close. Letting the overbearing blonde enter his thoughts was enough to get rid of his hard-on, though. He reached for a shirt, pulled it over his head, and went to the door. "It's room service," he told her, having forgotten the burgers and beers he had ordered. Greg held the door as the young waiter placed a large tray with covered plates and two bottles of beer on it on the desk next to the laptop.

After tipping the young man and watching as he drooled over Haley, Greg sent him on his way, closing and locking the door.

"I'll hurry with that shower. I'm sure Sam isn't far behind him." And the sooner he dealt with her and got her to leave, the better. It would be fun hiding from everyone for a few hours and making love to his wife until she couldn't stand.

Chapter 21

The look on Sam Wilson's face when Haley opened the hotel room door was classic. Her toothy grin faded for just a second but then turned almost vindictive.

"I'm here to see Greg," she said, a cutting edge in her tone making her voice sound harsh. Her glare was as cold as her words. "He asked me to come over."

"I know. I was here when you two spoke." Haley managed her sweetest tone, opening the door farther to let Sam enter. "You look like you're melting. Would you like some ice water? Greg will be out in a moment," she added, watching Sam walk into the hotel room and give it a quick survey. She focused on the two beds, probably trying to determine whether Haley and Greg would sleep together or not.

"My conversation with Greg is rather private. Do you have your own room?" Sam offered Haley a sweet smile, but her eyes were cold enough to chill the room.

"This is my room, too," Haley told her, shrugging. "But Natasha mentioned you were terribly upset over something. Are you okay? You really don't look good."

Sam plopped down in the chair by the laptop and started primping, leaning forward to see herself in the wall mirror.

"I'm sure I look a wreck," she confessed, her tone softening somewhat.

Haley could only kill the bitch with kindness. Maybe Sam figured out the game, because when she flashed another smile at Haley it damn near looked sincere. Haley took one of the glasses off the tray by the coffeemaker and filled it with ice. Without a word, she left Sam sitting there and entered the bathroom where Greg was, closing the door behind her, and filled the glass with water at the sink.

"Is she here?" Greg asked, peering around the shower curtain.

Haley couldn't see him from the steamed-over mirror, but when she turned, the droplets clinging to the tight curls on his muscular chest, as well to his eyelashes before he wiped his hand over his face, damn near made her drool.

"Yes, and she looks terrible, the poor thing," Haley purred, matching Sam's breathy tone as she drawled out the words. It was impossible to keep a straight face when he scowled at her. "You better hurry. She just can't wait to see you."

"Come here," he growled.

Haley stepped forward before giving a thought to him getting her wet. Which he did when he grabbed the side of her neck with his hand and kissed her.

"You have nothing to worry about," he whispered, keeping her face inches from his as he spoke.

Her face would be wet when she returned to Sam, but Haley really didn't care. "If that kind of woman appeals to you, then you're right. There's nothing to worry about. Because there is no way I could be anything like that," she told him, and held up the ice water. "I'm going to take her a drink before the poor thing melts," she added, again mocking Sam's breathy drawl.

"You do that. And go show me how good of a detective you are and do your girl-talk thing. See what you can get out of her."

Haley was ready to tell him she didn't need to prove to him, or anyone, how good a detective she was. She was up for the challenge. Brainstorming and plotting out the case got her almost as hot as being in his arms when he grabbed her for that passionate kiss. Greg was an incredibly intelligent man, but compliments and praise never came easy for him. Haley had no problem showing him how good she was.

"Hurry," she said. "It won't take me long to get her talking." Greg raised one eyebrow but Haley headed out of the bathroom with Sam's ice water.

"This is all I have to offer right now." Haley held the glass of water out to Sam, who sat upright in the chair, her hands pressed on her bare knees, and smiled too sweetly at Haley.

Haley would have sworn Sam snapped herself into that pose the moment Haley came out of the bathroom. She was trying to snoop around on Haley's laptop. The screen wasn't black anymore. It was a damn shame Sam would have been blocked by the password-protected screensaver.

"You're a dear, thank you," Sam purred, taking the water and drinking greedily.

Haley sat on the edge of the bed closest to Sam, scooting back and pulling her legs up, getting comfortable. It was time for girl talk, and she created the intimate setting, getting close and in Sam's face as she took the lady in.

Sam wore a tight-fitting dress and open-toed shoes. Her feet were dusty, and her painted toenails looked rather dirty. Haley could only imagine the reception Sam would have received walking down the streets of Tijuana dressed like that. Possibly Sam enjoyed men gawking at her, if not doing more.

Focusing her thoughts, Haley searched Sam's face, watching her down most of the water and run her fingers over the moist outside of the glass before putting it down. She dabbed her wet fingers over her face and ran them along her neck, lifting her hair and patting her skin. The large curls in her hair were sprayed into place so well the heat from outside and her damp fingers barely made them move.

"I'm a worse wreck than I thought," Sam confessed, still staring at herself in the mirror. "But I promise I wouldn't have come down here if it weren't an incredible emergency."

"What's happened?" Haley asked, catching her own reflection in the mirror along with Sam's and deciding she didn't mind a bit looking incredibly refreshed while Sam looked a disaster.

"Like I mentioned, it's terribly personal," Sam informed her, continuing to primp and appearing indifferent to the fact that she worked to make herself as presentable as possible for Haley's husband right in front of Haley. The woman had no morals or values, although there was something else about her Haley couldn't label that made her seem not trustworthy.

"Did you learn something about your brother? You didn't get another threatening letter, did you?" Haley asked, lowering her voice so she almost whispered. Sam turned, looking down at her with an assessing gaze as if surprised Haley would know anything about why Sam had hired KFA.

The bathroom door opened and Greg appeared, fully dressed in a nice blue and white pullover, short-sleeved collared shirt, and a pair of knee-length tan shorts that gave him the appearance of being ready to head out for a round of golf, or at least to the country club. His short hair was still wet but combed back. He approached them, glancing from one woman to the other as he sat on the bed opposite Haley.

"Where did I pack my socks?" he asked Haley, his concerned expression seriously making it look as if he had been hunting and couldn't find them.

Haley didn't have a clue, since she'd never looked inside any of his suitcases. "I'll get them," she offered, hopping up and heading to their bags, which Greg had moved to the luggage rack outside the bathroom. "You're just in time. Sam was just telling me what has her so upset," Haley added, moving around the wall and opening Greg's suitcase. There were several pairs of socks on top of his other clothes. She grabbed a pair and came back around the wall, holding them out to him.

Greg looked at her as if she were a lifesaver. If Sam weren't watching the two of them a bit too closely, Haley would have made a face. She bit back the urge to ask if he wanted her to bring his shoes to him also, or kneel at his feet and beg. He would like that last one a bit too much, and she doubted Sam would get the humor.

"You know, I'm not stalking you," Sam announced, pushing out her lower lip in a perfect pout. "I went over to the house where my brother had been staying before his arrest and I found these." She reached into her purse, pulled out several folded pieces of paper, and shoved them at Greg. "They scared me to death. My brother is in way over his head and you need to find him."

Greg took the papers and unfolded them. Haley came up behind him, reading alongside him without looking at Sam. She dared the woman to say a word.

They were e-mails sent to Jason W. from Bobby T. Haley forgot all about Sam as her insides tightened and excitement made her heart pound erratically. She read the first email a second time before Greg flipped to the next page.

"You printed these off his computer?" Greg asked, looking at the second e-mail, which was a follow-up to the first.

Sam shook her head. "There isn't a computer in his house anymore. The cops took it. These were at the bottom of a shoe box under an old pair of shoes in his closet."

Greg gave Sam as curious a look as Haley did. He obviously wanted to know what Sam was doing looking underneath old shoes in shoe boxes as much as Haley did.

"Jason owes me a lot of money," Sam offered, straightening and folding her hands in her lap as she gave both of them a haughty stare. "I was looking for things to hawk, or sell at secondhand stores. I paid you a lot of money to find him and I need to survive, too," she told them, her tone turning defensive as she looked at each of them with a determined, cold stare. The woman could change her mood faster than the weather changed in Omaha.

"What date was Jason arrested?" Greg asked, holding up the first e-mail. "This e-mail is dated February sixth and explains who will contact him once he's in jail to help him get out."

"He was arrested on February fourteenth, Valentine's Day." Sam looked as if arresting anyone on that date were more astonishing than the information in the e-mails. "My poor brother didn't get to enjoy the holiday of love," she added, her sultry, breathy tone returning.

"Do you know where this house is?" Haley asked, reaching over Greg's shoulder and taking the second e-mail out of his hand. He glanced at her, but Haley focused on Sam. "It says here that Jason will be taken to a safe house south of Tijuana. The instructions in this e-mail are so clear on missing his court date and being picked up to leave town. I'm shocked the LAPD didn't pick this up off his computer. Do you know anyone who lives down that way?"

"No one." She rubbed her hands down her dress, smoothing the material over her tanned legs. "But my brother is there. I bet you he is. You've got to go get him. He's in way over his head. What kind of people make plans to take someone who is out on bail out of the country?" she wailed.

Greg didn't answer her but placed the printed e-mails next to him as he sat on the edge of the bed to put his socks on.

"I think I'll get a room here in the hotel," she decided, focusing on Greg and talking to him as if Haley weren't standing right there. "I'll be closer to you and will know when you go down to get my brother."

"We'll keep you posted," Greg said, standing and moving to the door then opening it for her.

If he looked rather anxious to get Sam out of the room she didn't appear to notice but instead strolled up to him, brushing her fingernails down his cheek as she faced him with her back to Haley.

"I know you'll bring my brother back safe and sound," Sam purred, letting her fingernails linger along Greg's jawbone longer than she should have. It was a blatant display of her lack of respect or consideration for someone else's man. "But I'll probably check in with you really soon just to find out if you've made a game plan or figured anything new out."

"Do you not want the e-mails?" Haley asked, picking them up off the table where Greg had put them.

"Those are for Greg." Sam dropped her hand from Greg's face as she half-turned and let her gaze travel up and down Haley before taking only a moment to make eye contact.

"Actually, I do want them," Greg said.

"See," Sam acknowledged, her grin triumphant when she returned every bit of her attention to Greg. "I knew you were the man to have on my case. Bring my brother back to me as quickly as you can, okay?"

"I'll see what I can do," he said, focusing on Sam and not once looking past her to Haley.

"When are you heading south to get him?" Sam asked, her voice turning sweeter than sugar.

"We'll have to investigate the matter a bit before heading anywhere."

"Well, how long will that take?" she demanded, suddenly pouting.

"I'll let you know." Greg put his hand on Sam's shoulder and led her into the hallway. He turned to Haley and missed the pensive look Sam had on her face when the door closed. It clicked as the lock secured itself. "Our food is probably cold," he grumbled, heading straight to the tray Room Service had left.

"Maybe you should have pushed her out the door a bit sooner," Haley suggested. "I can't believe that woman."

Greg moved the large tray to the bed and sat on one side of it. Haley slid on the other side of the tray, crossing her legs and accepting her covered plate from Greg.

"Did you notice how incredibly interested she was in knowing how quickly we would run to the south of Tijuana looking for her brother?"

"What are you saying?" Haley asked, taking the cover off her burger and French fries.

"And that she found the e-mails under an old pair of shoes in a shoe box in her brother's closet," Greg added, picking up his burger and taking a large bite of it.

"Do you really think she was looking for things to sell?" Haley reached for the small bottle of ketchup.

"Maybe she was inspecting the quality of the shoes," Greg suggested, picking up several fries. "That is, if she was planning on hocking them."

"If the cops confiscated Jason's computer, they would have been able to pull that e-mail off the computer with most programs even if it was deleted," Haley said, putting her burger down and reaching for the e-mails. "It's even more odd that for someone so intent on hiding them and burying them under shoes in a shoe box that the computer path would be printed right here on each e-mail."

"Not everyone is computer literate," Greg pointed out

"Or possibly they want us to be able to trace it."

Haley reached for her beer. Greg grabbed it first and opened it, then handed it to her. "So you thought her behavior was odd, too?" he asked.

"I thought she was rude as hell," she said, still feeling the personal stab from when Sam had groped Greg before leaving, as if Haley's feelings or reactions didn't matter at all to her. "I honestly don't think she cares about anyone but herself. But yes, I think she has more of an agenda than just pissing me off."

"She could be coming on to me to upset you so that we'd argue over her instead of taking time to figure out what she is really up to."

Greg's phone rang and Haley balanced the tray between them, grabbing the beers so they wouldn't topple when he slid off the bed and reached his phone. He had made a good point just now. She watched Greg look to see who called, thinking how she might have griped about Sam for a while and allowed possible fresh evidence to grow stale or, worse yet, miss it altogether.

Haley grabbed the e-mails and read them again as Greg answered his phone.

"Hello," he said, his baritone deeper than usual. "This is Greg King." Silence followed and Haley looked at him. Greg looked pissed as hell. "I'll be down there in a few minutes."

For a moment she worried he'd throw the phone.

"What was that all about?" she asked.

"Marc and Jake are in jail."

Twenty minutes later Greg and Haley pulled up in front of the jail. She got out on her side before Greg made it around the truck. Although evening was setting in, the heat from the pavement was intense and Haley hurried with him to the sidewalk leading to the building.

"Tell me you don't make a habit of doing this?" Haley asked when he reached for the door to the jail.

"This is the first time either of them have been arrested."

Her stomach twisted at the thought of trying to get her boys out of a Mexican jail. "And they didn't tell you the charges?"

Greg didn't answer but rested his hand in the middle of her back as they entered the jail.

"I'm here to get Marc and Jake King." Greg said when he and Haley moved in front of a cage where the officer on the other side studied him warily. "I got a phone call they were here. What have they done?"

Haley gave silent thanks that Greg kept his cool in front of the officer. In spite of the nightmares spread about being arrested in Mexico, she knew most of the time the arrests were legitimate and prayed her sons weren't in serious trouble.

"*Senõr* King," Jefe Gonzalez announced, coming through the door but holding it open as he smiled at first Greg and then Haley. "I see you bring *Senõra* King. Is this more effort to show me you are here simply to enjoy our fair city?"

"What are you talking about?" Greg demanded. "Why are my sons here?"

"Are you going to tell me now your sons go to the nightclubs simply to pick up on our *senõritas*?"

"Last I heard that wasn't a crime."

"It depends on how they pick them up," Jefe drawled, wagging his thick black eyebrows as he grinned.

"What have they done?" Greg roared, his fierce tone vibrating off the white, dingy walls surrounding them.

Jefe quickly picked up on the fact that Greg wasn't in the mood for games, which was a good thing for him. Haley didn't want Greg attacking a cop because the asshole pushed him too far.

"*Senõr,* I'd like to see my sons," she told Jefe, stepping in front of Greg and facing the officer.

Jefe ignored her request and looked past her at Greg. "They were picked up for propositioning several of the *senõritas* at one of the clubs."

"They tried to buy prostitutes?" Haley couldn't believe it. They might have changed in six years but not that much. Neither of her sons needed help getting a lady.

Officer Gonzalez gave her a smile that chilled her blood.

"Many American boys come to Tijuana thinking they can buy a prostitute for nothing when they would pay her three times as much in your country."

"Have they actually been arrested? Was money exchanged?" Greg demanded. "Let me see these charges or release Marc and Jake to me now."

"I will release them to you," Jefe said, waving his hand as he continued holding the door open.

Another officer appeared and Marc and Jake were behind him, escorted by two other cops behind them. Her boys looked fit to be tied.

"Don't give anyone here a damn dime," Marc hissed under his breath. "We didn't break any laws and they goddamn know it."

"You really should teach your sons to control their tempers," Jefe said, rocking up on his feet as he continued grinning. "We don't go for violence in our jails."

"Like hell," Greg grumbled under his breath, although fortunately Jefe didn't appear to hear him.

Haley hurried to Marc and Jake, fighting an overwhelming urge to inspect every inch of them and make sure they weren't hurt. They weren't boys anymore, though, but men, and when she suddenly found herself in the middle of her sons and husband it was almost impossible to see anyone else around them.

"What charge did he give you?" Marc asked, his body tight as he fought to control his temper.

"We weren't doing anything illegal. And I seriously doubt the ladies we were talking to were prostitutes." Jake sounded just as pissed.

"We escorted them outside the club so they could get a taxi," Marc explained, his back to the officers as he focused on his father. "We were having a rather interesting conversation with them. But as soon as they left in the taxi, suddenly we're surrounded by cops. Kind of hard to say we were buying hookers when they left before we did. All we did was talk."

"And maybe now you will tell us about this interesting conversation," Jefe suggested, easing his way along the wall until he stood where he could see both Greg and Marc.

"What we were talking to them about is none of your business," Jake snapped.

Haley didn't remember her youngest having such a harsh side to him, but as she stared at the young man who used to be her baby, she saw a grown man who wouldn't be pushed. He had almost been a man when she'd left, but now, with muscles rippling under his shirt and a shadow covering his jaw, Jake was a man to to be reckoned with, just like his father. In spite of the seriousness of the situation, Haley felt a wave of pride rush over her as she watched her sons handle a serious situation with style and confidence.

"Now you see!" Jefe pointed his finger at Marc and Jake as if he'd just received a confession. "They were not cooperative and already we have statements from the young ladies."

"Now they are young ladies?" Haley snapped, putting her hand on Jake's arm and attempting to move around him. "A second ago they were prostitutes. Did you follow these ladies in their taxi in order to question them?"

"Maybe it isn't a profession you approve of, *senōra*." Jefe gleamed. "I always make it a habit not to judge anyone until I know where their heart is," he added, punching his chest.

His smile bordered on evil and she didn't like it. "We're leaving now," she informed the cop, fighting to keep her cool when she ached to yell at him. "It doesn't sound to me as if there is a crime here at all. They both told you they escorted the ladies to their ride, and obviously didn't go with them, as you know yourself. Yet you get statements from ladies who were gone before you brought my sons here? It doesn't sound like they were partaking in anything illegal, unless you have another charge you'd like to throw out?"

"As you know, *senōra*, bounty hunting is a crime," he said, his smile fading.

The room grew quiet, and at the same time Haley swore all three men around her grew in size. The anger and tension surrounding her could be cut with a knife. Suddenly Haley understood and it sickened her. Greg would never have agreed to come down here on charges too weak to stand, but call and tell him they had his sons and Greg was here in a second. Jefe Gonzalez had the King men right where he wanted them.

"I think I've made it perfectly clear we're here on a family vacation," Greg snarled, sounding so dangerous that even the smug look on the cop's face disappeared. "If this is how we're going to be treated maybe we should go spend our money in another city."

"Maybe you should," Gonzalez growled, making it clear he wouldn't be intimidated. "We're on to you, and your family, *Senōr* King," he added, straightening, his expression and tone remaining harsh. "I know you're here on business and you won't convince me otherwise. You and your *hijos* better watch yourselves because we're watching you."

"Maybe we should be asking what you're hiding," Jake snarled, gently removing Haley's hand from his arm, although she didn't miss how his entire body tightened before he let go. "I don't care too much for you suggesting that my father is lying to you."

"I suggest you take your sons to your hotel," Jefe said, his voice suddenly too calm, as if getting a rise out of one of them pleased him very much. "I'll be in touch."

Greg moved between Jake and Jefe, giving both of his sons a harsh look and a quick nod toward the door. Marc and Jake moved to leave, Jake once again touching Haley, this time to take her arm and escort her to the door.

"The only reason you need to contact me is if you're inviting my wife and me out to enjoy your nightlife," Greg informed the cop, his tone matching the calm, smooth baritone Jefe used. The only difference was that Greg made his suggestion sound like a threat.

Haley sat next to Greg, and Marc and Jake climbed in back. The moment the doors were closed, Marc and Jake began talking at once.

"They came after us," Marc announced when Jake tried explaining what happened.

"You notice they didn't have any charges," Jake added.

"I noticed," Greg said, raising his hand to quiet both of them. "They think we're here hunting someone, which really makes me think they know of someone who needs to be hunted and don't want him found."

"I'm sure that list is rather long," Marc grumbled.

"I'm sure it is." Greg started the truck and kicked the AC down to a lower temperature, causing cold air to blow on all of them.

Haley shifted so she could focus on all three men. The AC felt good but immediately chilled her. Greg didn't put the truck into drive but instead rested his arm on the steering wheel, turning to look over his shoulder at his sons. So much muscle bulged against his shirt. His cold, hardened expression leaned toward violent, as if the thought of causing someone bodily harm at the moment really appealed to him. Haley needed her head examined. Watching him as he looked ready to explode caused every inch of her to sizzle with need. She'd showered and primped a bit in hopes of spending time with Greg alone tonight. They would get their time. And when they did she hoped some of that raw energy still existed inside him. Right now, though, she wanted to understand what had motivated the local police to haul in her sons.

"I want to hear everything that happened, but not with both of you talking at the same time."

"I'll tell you what happened," Marc began.

"I was trying to explain," Jake said at the same time.

"Stop," Haley announced, holding up her hand and silencing both of them. "Start with the women you escorted out of the bar. Who were they and how did you meet them?" Her sons were as wound up and pissed as Greg. The sooner they were out of the truck the easier it would be for all of them. "Let's go," she told Greg.

"I started talking to them first," Jake explained when Greg put the truck into gear and left the police station. "Their names were Angela and Evelyn. We didn't work on a last-name basis," he added. "They don't live here in Tijuana but were out for the night. Apparently they are from a small town south of here and wanted to enjoy the big-city lights."

"Were they prostitutes?" she asked.

"Hell no!" Jake snapped. "Far from it. Mom, we wouldn't have been escorting them to their ride away from us if they were," he added, chuckling as the fierceness in his expression relaxed a bit. "I found Marc and had him join us when Angela and Evelyn started talking about the man who has their village in an uproar."

"Jake introduced me to the ladies and we bought a couple

drinks for them, offering a sympathetic ear as they continued to complain about the *hombre* who'd moved to their village and was making demands of all of them. And neither woman liked him being there at all."

"They tell you what his name was?" Greg asked.

"The ladies told us that the villagers simply refer to him as *El Pajaro.*"

Haley struggled with her Spanish, trying to remember what a *pajaro* was. Fortunately, everyone else's Spanish wasn't as rusty as hers.

"The Bird," Jake and Greg said at the same time.

Chapter 22

Greg didn't like it. He stood in the parking garage, watching his Avalanche disappear around the corner before he backed into the shadows. Reminding himself this was his idea didn't help.

Natasha showed up that morning and took the Avalanche. Before leaving Tijuana, she would drop Marc and Jake off at the motel where the girls they had spent time with and who had inadvertently gotten them thrown in jail were staying. Jake had managed to find out where the ladies were staying and had contacted them this morning to arrange a breakfast date. He was a player. Sometimes his skills worked to their advantage, although that knowledge didn't settle Greg's nerves any. He didn't doubt for a moment that someone would be watching his truck like a hawk every minute it drove along the city roads. If the Tijuana police brought any of them in again he swore he would wreak havoc on this town.

Glancing around the parking garage, Greg didn't see anyone and turned toward the service elevator. He used it to return to his floor. There wasn't anyone in the hallway and he slid his card down the lock and entered the hotel room. Haley glanced up from her laptop as he entered.

"You left your phone here," she said, holding it up as he approached.

"You tried to reach me?" He took the phone and put it back down on the desk. Then dragging his fingers through her hair and cupping her cheek with his other hand, he eased her out of the chair until she stood against him. "Couldn't wait for me to get back up here, could you?"

"Well . . ." she began. "It's just if you don't have your phone and I need you, what am I supposed to do?"

"Did you need me?" He rested one hand on Haley's hip and toyed with her soft, silky wave of hair that wrapped around his finger.

She took her time looking up at him, her lashes hooding her gaze when she offered a small smile. "I might have. You'll never know since you left your phone here."

"Forgive me." He moved his hand down her hip to her bottom, cupping her perfect curves in his palm. "I must have been preoccupied in making sure my new truck made it out of the parking garage in one piece."

Haley shook her head. "I offered to walk down with all of you, but I'd already given Marc and Jake and Natasha too many hugs. We'll see Natasha in a day or so and the boys probably later today."

She made a face and started laughing. Greg was inclined not to tease her for referring to her very grown men as boys.

"I know. They sure aren't boys anymore," Haley said, her smile turning warm. "They are both incredible men."

"You raised two awesome guys."

"You picked up where I left off."

Greg snorted, knowing if he lied at some point, his sons would turn him in. "I stumbled my way through at best," he grumbled, then ran his hands over her body. "But, for now, they are gone. Natasha is dropping Marc and Jake off at the hotel where the girls they met last night are staying."

"Gluttons for punishment, are they?" Her laughter was so melodic. The way her eyes lit up, glowing and offering a view into her soul, showed how beautiful Haley was, not just on the outside, but on the inside, too.

He wasn't worthy of her yet here she was, leaning against him, every sensual and incredibly appetizing curve touching him.

"Those two went over to the hotel where the girls who got them thrown in jail are staying?" She was laughing, shaking her head. "I can just see Jake using that as his opening line to grab a bit of their attention. Although I guess it's pretty original telling a young lady she has to have breakfast with you since she got you thrown in jail."

Haley was making light of it, and he knew she wanted a grin out of him, at least. He had other ideas on how to stay in a good mood. "They want to learn more about that town the ladies were from where they said Marty Byrd was staying."

"I really hope that is what those ladies meant." Her smile slowly faded. "And that it isn't some kind of trap."

Marc and Jake wouldn't do anything stupid. Granted, if they had sexy young ladies tantalizing them, they might stumble a bit but they'd realize what the smartest move would be, women around or not. He'd trained them and they were his blood. Regardless of whether they were young or not, his sons were smart enough to always watch their asses.

"Don't worry about them," he said, lowering his face to hers and nudging her cheek until she tilted her head to kiss him. "They'll call as soon as they know something."

Her lips were so appetizing. He couldn't think of anything he'd rather do than devour his wife.

"Greg," she gasped, letting her head fall back and exposing her neck to him.

He bent over and dragged his lips past her jaw and began nipping at her warm flesh. "What?" he whispered, placing his lips where her pulse throbbed just above her collarbone. "Tell me, Haley," he whispered, his voice raspy as he moved his lips against her soft, smooth flesh.

For years he'd dreamed of having the woman he had lost back in his arms. But feeling her silky hair tickle his arms, inhaling her scent that had always been a combination of her soap, powders, and perfume, and pressing his lips against her soft, smooth, warm flesh, was better than any fantasy.

"Is there something you want?"

Haley stared up at him, her cheeks flushed as she nibbled at her lower lip.

"Oh, most definitely, my dear," he said.

"Why do you want it?"

Greg dropped his attention to her blouse, unbuttoning each button and spreading it open, then damn near drooled over the sight of her pink lace bra. Haley inhaled sharply, forcing her breasts over the curve of the lace. He had to kiss that swell of flesh, first on one side, then on the other. His cock was so hard and his brain in such a fog, figuring out a good answer for her was almost an impossible task.

"Because I can't live without you," he told her, nipping at the small strap of material between her breasts that held the bra together.

Haley moaned, grabbing his shoulders. "Yes, you can," she reminded him and pressed her fingertips into his muscles as she massaged his shoulders, then his arms. "You seem very much alive to me." Already her breath was coming stronger.

Lifting her into his arms, he turned for the nearest bed, which wasn't the one they'd slept in the night before. They might as well mess the other one up, too. "I don't ever want to live without you again," he said, looking down at her face cradled against her shoulder. "That wasn't living."

"I want to be with you, too," she whispered.

"Damn good thing." He sounded cocky. Haley would make their conversation mushier and mushier if he didn't stop her. She always wanted to know his feelings and thoughts, but when she pushed too far, Greg wasn't sure what to say.

Greg hugged her closer, praying no one would ever take her from him again.

"We really do belong to each other." She held on to his gaze as he laid her on the bed, then stretched out next to her.

Greg reached between them, undoing her shorts and pulling down the zipper. He slid his hand inside and felt her smoothly shaved pussy and the heat generated between her legs. His heart pounded harder. All the blood drained to his crotch until his balls tightened and his cock stretched painfully against his jeans.

"Are you just now figuring that out?" His voice was scratchy, rough.

When he met her gaze, saw the glow in her glazed-over green eyes, pride swelled inside him. Haley smiled and damn near made him light-headed. This was his woman. His wife. Daring, intelligent, beautiful, so damn sexy—Haley was the perfect package. He was definitely one lucky son of a bitch.

She ran her fingers over his chest and pushed his shirt up so she could touch him. As she dragged her nails over his skin he straightened, making it easier for her by pulling the shirt off and tossing it to the side. Backing off the bed, he slid out of his shoes and stripped out of his jeans.

"You better get out of those clothes," he warned her. "If I take them off they might not end up neatly folded, and I doubt you want them messed up."

"You've become such a romantic over the years," she grumbled under her breath, although she grinned as she slid out of her shorts. She wore a lacy thong that matched her pink bra and made no effort to remove either. "This really is better than teasing and torturing me while taking forever to undress me," she said as she stretched on the bed, then rolled to her side, facing him and propping her head up with her hand.

"That's because I was always too busy willing your clothes to disappear," he confessed, stepping out of his boxers, then crawling back onto the bed. "And who is torturing whom?" he whispered into her mouth as he kissed her again.

Haley chuckled but it turned into a groan. She draped her arms over his shoulders and deepened their kiss. Her nipples hardened through her lace bra, turning into hard little beacons.

She pressed against his chest, making him very aware of all that lace as he felt it rubbing over his flesh. His insides tightened, creating a need that swelled into a pressure more intense than he'd known in years.

"I thought you'd like the lingerie." Haley cupped his cheek, her gaze probing his. "Whenever I really missed you," she whispered. "I would go buy a piece of lingerie and pretend you bought it for me."

"I have incredibly good taste."

"Yes, you do," she said, and leaned into him for a kiss.

Her lips were soft and warm and she tried angling his face to deepen the kiss. Greg lifted his head. "You're it for me, sweetheart. I don't need anything other than to love you." He stared at her parted lips, which were moist and swollen from his kiss.

But it was the flush in her cheeks, the glow in her eyes that drew him into her the most. He saw the emotions he wished he could label along with the feelings he couldn't describe harboring in her expression.

"Did you ever think of moving on during those six years?" Her expression didn't change but she watched him, her gaze never wavering from his. She wanted to catch his first reaction to her question.

Greg worried she'd see the torture and pain he'd successfully suppressed while she was gone. "Honestly, Haley," he began, for a moment letting his attention drop to the swell of her breasts and how the lace stretched over her full, round mounds. He paused for barely a second, but when he returned his attention to her face, worry clouded her pretty eyes. "Haley," he breathed, reaching between them and rubbing her cheeks with his knuckles. "I died inside without you," he admitted, knowing she was the only person on this planet he could speak his mind to, share his deepest, darkest, scariest thoughts with. "No one mentioned your name. I couldn't bear the pain of thinking about you. I buried myself in KFA, and as long as I didn't remember you, I made it from one day to the next."

He'd opened up, given her what he knew she wanted. Her worried expression didn't change, though. Haley didn't pull away. Her warm, soft body remained cuddled into his. Greg gave her time to digest his confession while a knot started twisting in his gut. Haley had told him she wanted to know his thoughts, but maybe she didn't, not really.

"You never thought of trying to replace me?" she asked, her voice soft and filled with concern.

"Not once. Not even for a second."

The knot dissipated faster than it had appeared when she smiled. Some doctor somewhere would probably tell him it wasn't healthy to allow someone else to control whether he was happy or not. With Haley, though, it couldn't be helped. She was his world and had been almost his entire life. He wasn't happy if she wasn't happy, and he was filled with joy when she blessed him with one of those satisfied smiles, as she did now.

"God, darling," he growled, gripping her chin as he brushed his lips over hers. "I'm so glad you're back," he muttered into her mouth. Haley tried saying something, but it turned into a luscious moan when he parted her lips and began making love to her mouth.

He wanted to touch her everywhere, to caress and adore every inch of her.

He pulled her bra straps farther down her arms until the lace cups slid off her full, round breasts. They were perfect! He cupped her in his hands, rubbing her nipples between his fingers and watching as her green eyes turned smoky and her long lashes fluttered over them.

"I love you, Greg," Haley said on a breath.

She stretched her legs and lifted them around his thighs, then crossed her feet, tightening her grip on him. The heat from her pussy reached his cock and her lace thong brushed against the length of his shaft. Blood boiled in his veins, blurring his vision and his mind as the need to penetrate her overwhelmed him. If he was supposed to say something to her there was no way he would be able to pull it off. Lowering one hand, he found the thin strap to her thong and pushed his finger underneath it pulling it from her body.

"Don't you dare tear that," she whispered, her voice rough and her words drawn out.

He toyed with the thong strap, dragging it across her ass. "Remember, darling, I got these for you. I would never want them damaged."

Her chuckle added to the heat already tearing away at his senses. "Would you like me to take them off?" she asked. "Or are you content just to play with them?" she added, and moved her hips, grinning as she continued torturing him.

Greg nipped at her nipple, taking it between his teeth and tugging until she cried out. "Do you want to take off your thong, my love?" he asked.

Haley scraped her nails down his back, digging into his flesh as she arched into him. "You don't like it?" she purred.

"I love it. You're easily the most sexiest woman alive," he grumbled, and moved to the other breast to torture that nipple with his teeth.

Haley jumped when he lightly bit her puckered flesh. She moaned when he lashed at it with his tongue. Her fingers moved to his head, holding him in place and burying his face in her breasts. Greg couldn't think of a better place to be. He ran his hand down her hip, taking the thong with him. When he'd pushed it to her thighs, he moved his hand between her legs, cupping her pussy, and continued adoring her breasts.

"Now! Greg, I need to come," Haley gasped, speaking in between pants.

"My sweet lady knows what she wants." Greg raised his head in spite of the pressure she applied with her hand to keep him where he was. She was already watching him when he met her gaze. "Don't look away," he instructed, and her eyes opened a bit wider when he cupped her pussy and pressed the ball of his hand against her clit.

Haley opened her mouth, her gaze burning into his, but then cried out when he pressed into her clit again. This time moisture soaked his fingers. He burrowed into it, unable to stop himself until his fingertips slid over her creamy entrance.

"My God, you're so wet," he informed her, and groaned with pleasure as his fingers slid into her heat. "My sexy lady really is close to the edge. Tell me, dear, what brought you so close, the lingerie?"

Haley reached between them and grabbed his dick. "I want this," she demanded, ignoring his query.

Greg hissed in a breath but managed to cup her pussy. The thong stretched around her legs, out of his way. Her skin glowed with her need for him. And the way she panted, her nipples harder than small pebbles, not to mention her hands on him, doing her best to keep him where she wanted him, showed him all he needed to know.

"What," she began, but then cried out when he grabbed her, moving too fast for her to get her bearing and try to stop him. "Oh God," she moaned when he flipped her over, lifting her until she was on her hands and knees.

"That is one soaked, swollen pussy, sweetheart," he drawled, sliding his fingers inside her as he moved her thong further down her legs.

He left it draped around her knees. Haley wouldn't break it, and if she spread her legs it would snap. Pulling out of her as easily as he glided in, Greg grabbed her hips, his fingers damp and sticky. Haley tossed her hair over her shoulder and did her best to look back at him, which caused her to arch her back and push her ass up toward him.

"If you could only see what I see," he said, his voice tight as he stretched his fingers over her ass and opened her up to him. "Damn, darling, you are offering a view that could kill a man."

Haley's laughter was deep, sultry, and as enticing as her hot, perfect body. He positioned his cock at her entrance, unable to speak as his balls tightened painfully. His insides simmered over as the pressure that had already created waves of need inside him threatened to explode. Greg gritted his teeth, fighting for the control needed to enjoy the moment and give her the pleasure he wanted her to have. Haley was like a magnet, luring him inside her.

As he watched his cock disappear, sinking deeper into her soaked heat, he fought to focus and enjoy the view.

"God damn, darling," he drawled, wishing he could find the words to share with her how incredible she was. Haley would render him useless, completely incapable of doing anything but drowning inside her, letting her take him over the edge. "Is this what you need, sweetheart?" he asked, wanting her to know perfection.

"Yes," she groaned. "It's perfect. So thick and long. But you're moving so slow."

Greg gave her what she asked for and might as well have had the wind knocked out of him. He moaned as she cried out. There was no stopping it. He took her hard and fast, drowning in her again and again. And with each thrust she tightened around him, dragging him even deeper, suffocating him with her velvety, hot perfection.

"Greg! Oh my God!" Haley stiffened, clawed at the bed, then arched her back further until she was partially off the bed. She went rigid, then began trembling as a low moan surfaced from deep inside her.

"That's it, baby. Come for me," he growled, his jaw so tight he could barely move his mouth to speak. "Let go and enjoy it."

He kept her ass stretched, watching her pussy continue to constrict around him as he sank inside her heat, increasing the momentum with each thrust. The friction was so intense, the heat overwhelming. And when she cried out, she screamed loud enough that anyone on this floor would know what they were doing. All those soaked muscles inside her clung to his dick, tightening until he feared she would drain him with her orgasm.

Even as she gasped for breath, dragging her nails over the blanket and crinkling it around her, Greg continued fucking her with everything he had. He thrust deeper, feeling her wrap around him, her come soaking his balls. She had the most incredible pussy.

"You're so perfect," he murmured, needing her more than his next breath. "So damned perfect."

"Why am I perfect?" she gasped, tossing her hair over her shoulder again. "You're the one who just gave me the best experience of my life," she told him in between breaths and as a thick sheen of perspiration made her skin shiny, almost glowing.

Brown strands of hair streaming down her slender back added to the incredible view. He ran his hand up her spine, gripping her neck, and leaned into her, taking her hard and fast as he hit a different angle this time. The way her muscles adjusted, gripping at him like velvety heat, had him aching for the strength to make love to her like this all night.

"Every inch of you, darling," he groaned, his brain as feverish as his cock.

"Does that feel good?" she purred.

"Yes."

"You like my body?" She was so breathless her husky tone simply made his insides boil more.

"All of you," he growled.

"You like all of me?"

"Yes." He leaned forward, pressing his lips against her shoulder and tasting her flesh. It had a salty edge, and he wanted to kiss her everywhere.

"Just like me?" she grunted.

His brain swirled in a thick haze of lust and desire. His cock was swollen. His balls were so tight they burned with the need to release. Even as his world tilted, there wasn't any doubt in his mind.

A fire released inside him, tearing at his insides, rushing through him so hard it was as if a tidal wave destroyed his dam of resistance. Greg roared, coming so hard that everything around him spun out of control. There was no holding back, no strength to think through how to answer her. All he could do was say what he knew to be true.

"I love you," he moaned, and released all he had until he barely pulled off the strength to keep from completely collapsing on top of her. "I love you with all my heart and need you with all my soul."

Greg stepped out of the bathroom almost an hour later after showering with Haley. If he had the strength to strut around like a peacock, he would have done it. He felt so good that the dull ache in his neck from where those assholes had dosed him up with horse tranquilizer didn't bother him a bit.

He walked across the hotel room with a towel wrapped around him as his phone rang. Haley wanted to soak in a hot bath for a bit and he didn't have a problem giving her time to do that. He'd worn his wife out, he thought with a grin, and picked up his phone.

"Hello," he said quietly.

"I didn't wake you, did I?" Jake sounded surprised.

"Hardly," Greg said, and cleared his throat. Maybe he had bragging rights but not to his sons. "What's up?"

"We never could find those ladies," Jake said, the connection fuzzy enough that it was hard to tell whether that disappointed him or not.

"Maybe they found better," Greg offered, heading back to the bathroom and stepping into steam that drifted around him.

"Maybe."

Haley opened one eye and stared up at him as she lay in the full tub. Suds clung to her breasts and she lazily ran a finger through the water as she gave him an incredibly sated look. Greg grabbed his shorts and stepped out of the bathroom, knowing he wouldn't hear a thing his son said if he continued admiring his wife.

"It might not hurt to take another look at these women of yours. How exactly did you meet them? And what about this village?" Greg dropped his towel and stretched as he appraised his naked body in the mirror. "These ladies leave and suddenly you two end up in jail. Are we looking at coincidence, or not?"

"It's a possibility. We've been discussing that." Static erupted and it was impossible to hear what Jake said next.

"Where are you now?"

"We decided to head south, see what there is to see." The signal faded in and out as he spoke. "There's public transportation for tourists, if you want to call it that. We paid to take a bus down here."

"Oh yeah? Where are you?" Greg asked again, understanding now why the connection sucked.

"This place is actually called Aldea," Jake said, laughing. "It's where Angela told me she lived, and where they complained about The Bird."

"Doesn't that mean 'village'?"

"Yup. Some of the things here match what Angela told me. We think we're in the right town, or Aldea," he added, chuckling again. "So far, though, we haven't found either lady. No one seems to know an Angela matching her description."

"You aren't drunk, are you?" Greg would hand both of them their heads if they were drinking and ended up arrested again. "Please tell me you aren't stalking this lady because she stiffed you."

"Hell no. Give me some credit, Dad. And for the record, Angela didn't stiff me. I've got this feeling about her. Maybe she knew who I was and thought if she got me down here I could help her town, or village."

"If she knew who you were, why wouldn't she just ask for your help?" Greg shook his head, doubting any woman would be able to tolerate his son's cockiness. "How far south from here are you?"

"It took a couple hours to get here. The roads aren't great, but at least we didn't break down. The public transportation isn't great but it's reliable." Again a pop of static made it hard to hear. "This town shuts down in the middle of the day. Wait, I mean 'village'—Aldea. There's a gas station here that sells gas several times a week and that's it. Damn good thing we didn't try bringing the truck down here."

"There's still places like that." It sounded as if there wasn't a lot to Aldea, which might make it the perfect hiding spot for a world-renowned assassin to do his dirty work. "Is there a place to stay?"

He glanced at the digital clock on the nightstand between the beds. It was almost three. Greg couldn't remember when he had last spent the day having sex, and wondered why he gave up such a wonderful pastime.

Jake said something, but it didn't come through.

"So no signs of your lady friends?" Greg pressed.

"Nothing, and there isn't much to Aldea." Jake suddenly sounded as if he were next door.

"I can hear you."

"We're standing outside." Jake lowered his voice but remained easy to hear. "No one down here knows an Evelyn, and the only Angela is an old woman. We haven't heard any mention of *El Pajaro* yet. But we thought we would check in and see how you're doing before getting a room."

Greg had no intention of telling Jake how good he was doing. "We haven't left the hotel yet."

"Good. You two spend time together. It's too late to get a ride down here today anyway."

"Keep yourselves out of jail. I'll call you in the morning to see how you're doing and we'll probably head down that way and join you if you think the village is worth our time."

"We'll see what we can learn. We're going to wait for it to cool down a bit, then do some exploring."

"Be safe and keep me posted."

Jake commented about something, but Greg didn't catch what his son said. Reminding him once again to keep his nose clean, Greg ended the call and returned to Haley.

It was still dark the next morning when Greg's phone rang. Climbing out of bed without disturbing Haley, he padded over to the desk where his phone sat next to hers, both of them charging. She rolled over in the large bed, blinking and moving strands of hair away from her face as she looked at him. God, she looked good when she first woke up. He fought not to grin at her disgruntled expression as memories of her not being a morning person flooded through his mind.

"Greg King," he said formally when he recognized the caller.

"Greg, it's Bernie. I know it's early," Bernie Osborne said, his deep baritone making it sound as if he were whispering. More than once he'd been told he sounded just like Barry White.

"I just crawled out of a very comfortable bed," Greg grumbled. "And I wasn't alone."

Bernie took the comment just as Greg anticipated.

"Hell, man. I don't even want to talk to your ugly white ass on the phone if you don't have clothes on."

Greg chuckled along with his old beat-stomping friend and glanced at Haley, who'd rolled to her side and tucked the sheet under her arm as she slowly woke up. He strode into the bathroom, setting the phone on speaker, and pulled on his boxers.

"So what do you have for me?" he asked.

"The morning news," Bernie told him. "Pedro Gutierrez broke out of jail during the night."

"What the fuck? I brought that motherfucker in." Greg stalked out of the bathroom, reached down and grabbed a clean pair of shorts, and headed back into the bathroom. "Has he been brought back in yet?" he asked, closing the door so as not to disturb Haley.

"Nope. But here is where it gets weird. I didn't work the night shift, but he was in a holding cell according to the report."

"You'd think he would have been processed already." Greg didn't push for explanations of details. He wanted the whole story first.

"I clock in this morning and there aren't any formal searches that have been organized. It's like we're just letting the guy walk."

"So are you going after him?"

"I have orders to bring him in if I find him on my beat."

"Damn," Greg hissed, rubbing his head as the beginning of a dull headache set in. He needed to eat. This was too much to process on an empty stomach. "Are you telling me someone slipped him a get out of jail free card?"

"There aren't any crooked cops in my shop," Bernie growled, immediately defensive.

Greg held back, knowing the loyalty behind wearing the uniform. They covered each other's back. If Bernie thought someone had dropped the ball, he would say something. There would always be crooked cops and politicians. Bernie wasn't one of them, though.

"Got anything else for me?" he asked. Gutierrez and Jason Wilson were connected, but that didn't mean Gutierrez disappearing was related to Marty Byrd. He needed more information before he could make that connection.

"Actually, yes. I talked to the detective in Omaha, Nebraska, right before I called you," Bernie said, then paused. There were sounds of papers shuffling. "You got to remember it's a few hours later out that way."

"That's right. Did they find out where that e-mail Torres claimed to have received came from?" Greg pictured Bernie moving around in the break room at the station, probably getting his morning coffee going and doing his best to keep his conversation with Greg as private as possible.

"That's why he called me. Detective Frank Roster is the guy's name. And yes, Roberto Torres received an e-mail. Torres goes by Bobby T. on the Internet. Roster called asking me a favor because the e-mail's ISP is right here in Orange County."

"No shit," Greg said under his breath, and glanced up when Haley opened the bathroom door, her hair tangled and her right cheek rosier than her left. "Do we have a physical address?" he asked.

"That was the favor. We got a response back from the Internet provider pretty fast. But here's the kicker. The e-mail was sent from Jason Wilson's house."

Haley started to walk around him but stopped, almost tripping over herself as she gawked at Greg's phone, which was still on speaker on the bathroom counter.

"I'll be damned," Greg muttered as his mind raced and he played back the events over the past few weeks. "Wait a minute."

"You've got it!" Bernie interrupted, his deep baritone growing excited through the phone. "The e-mail was sent from Jason Wilson's computer, which according to paperwork here had been confiscated before the date on the e-mail. And Jason was already in jail."

Chapter 23

"Sam!" Haley said, suddenly excited and looking a lot more awake than she sounded.

"What did you say?" Bernie asked.

Greg put his finger over her lips, frowning as he mouthed for her to remain quiet. "I said, 'Damn,'" he said to his phone. "So someone set up shop in his house and used his IP?"

"Now that I don't know. I'll look into it. At the moment that would be my best guess."

"I thought ISPs varied from computer to computer, kind of like a unique signature."

"Something like that. But I'll find out and let you know. You're still down in Tijuana?"

"Yup. The boys and I are going to do some sightseeing today."

"Watch your ass."

"You know I will."

"Because you know those cops down there are watching yours."

"They've already let me know that," Greg said, turning his back on Haley.

Haley scowled at the roped muscle bulging under his smooth, tanned flesh and walked around him, heading for the shower. Greg didn't want Bernie knowing she was in the hotel room with him. She tried figuring out why and couldn't think of a reason. Everyone thought they had split up six years ago when she entered the WPP. It probably tore at Greg's ego letting everyone think he couldn't find her. Regardless of what explanation he offered, Greg could have told Bernie they were back together and Bernie would have been happy for them.

"Hell, man. Don't get your ass thrown in jail. And they'll do it, too. You following a lead?"

Greg hesitated for a moment and Haley glanced over her shoulder, curious as to why he did. They'd both known Bernie a good fifteen years and she couldn't possibly accept that Greg might think he'd gone dirty.

"Yeah, I am," Greg admitted. "But do me a favor and keep that under wraps."

"You don't even have to say that, man."

"You're right. I'm getting paranoid in my old age."

"Just cautious," Bernie said, his deep, bellowing laughter lightening the mood.

Greg smiled. "A hell of a lot more than we were in the old days."

"Don't even get me started. We raised some hell back in the day."

"You know it," Greg agreed, glancing in her direction and winking.

Immediately her body reacted to his attention, brief as it was, which annoyed her. Greg returned to his call, taking a minute to reminisce with his old buddy from the force. Not once did Greg mention her. They were going to talk if Greg had any thoughts of keeping her homecoming a secret. If Greg wasn't ready to announce to the world they were back together, she had a right to know why. Did Greg already believe he couldn't meet her terms on being equal in their professional and personal lives?

A quickening started in her gut and she turned on the bathwater, although it didn't completely drown out the conversation.

Tears threatened to stream down her cheeks. She couldn't catch her breath. She'd been a fool thinking she could saunter back into Greg's life and he would accept her newfound assertive nature when for years he'd been happy with his submissive wife. She hadn't asked to change, but living on her own for the first time in her life had helped draw it out of her.

"Well, I'd love to chat and rehash the old days, but some of us are on the clock," Bernie said.

"Better earn that paycheck." Greg looked at her through the mirror when she glanced over her shoulder.

"You know I will," Bernie said. "And you will, too."

"Yup." Greg's attention drifted up and down the mirror, as if he took in all his brawn and muscle. His look wasn't one of approval, though. Maybe he focused on the small scars, the puckering of skin here and there over his torso. War wounds, as he'd always called them, were trophies from the job. "Stay in touch, my friend. And thank you for the update."

"You know it," Bernie drawled. "Give me a call if you get any leads on Jason Wilson."

"You do the same. I'd be real curious to know if we're right about the computer in Wilson's house after his arrest or not," Greg said, picking the phone up and staring at it as he cupped it in his palm.

"You know something?" Bernie was quick, a damn good cop.

Greg didn't bat an eye at the question, or appear as if he'd said more than he should. Haley wasn't sure why he held back on mentioning Sam's name. But at the moment, she was definitely their strongest suspect. Even if Jason's computer was confiscated, she'd admitted to them that she was in her brother's house after the arrest.

"Honestly, I don't know yet. The information you've given me definitely raises some strong questions, though. They need to be researched a bit and I'll get back with you."

"What strong questions do they raise?"

Greg disappeared around the corner toward the beds, taking

his phone with him. "Give me a day and I'll get back with you on that one." He reappeared with a T-shirt in hand.

They said their good-byes and Greg hung up his phone. "I'm going to go get food," he announced, pulling on his shirt.

"Let me hop in the shower and I'll go with you." Haley made sure she had a fresh towel and put her clean clothes on the closed toilet seat.

"I need to eat now. A dull headache is kicking in. If I don't eat it will get a lot worse. I can bring you back something, though."

Greg slipped his wallet into his back pocket and disappeared out of her sight again, reappearing with a key card in his hand. There wasn't any arguing with him. He seemed adamant about hurrying out of the room as fast as he could. Haley really didn't feel like rushing her bath just so she could exist on his schedule. She needed some answers and if he was running out the door to avoid giving them to her, she'd be here when he got back.

Greg gave her a crooked smile, not looking upset or concerned. "Don't open this door for anyone," he instructed, then was gone before she could argue.

"What the hell?" Haley was confused, and even more so when Greg didn't appear to know he'd upset her.

Haley managed to enjoy her bath, shaving and taking her time soaking in fragrant water. She argued with herself over the pros and cons of her relationship with Greg, and when that threatened to ruin her bath she switched gears and methodically outlined in her head what they knew so far about their case.

When her bathwater started to cool, Haley toweled dry and dressed. Greg still hadn't returned. She'd brought some more lingerie, a snug-fitting teddy with matching thong. The teddy fit perfectly under her peach-colored tank top, with only the two straps over her bare shoulders giving any indication she wore something under her shirt. She put on hip-hugging blue-jean shorts, which showed off a bit of her tummy under her shirt.

The final package looked rather sexy. At least she thought so as she surveyed the results in the mirror.

Even as she stared at herself and took her time applying just a bit of makeup, she continually played over the bits and pieces of knowledge they had around John's death. It was frustrating and a feeling she'd experienced before with other cases. There wasn't any proof that all of it connected. She couldn't get rid of the gut feeling she had all the pieces to a puzzle, though, and simply had to fit them all together.

It was easier to see the big picture when she drew all of it out, or wrote everything down. Haley got comfortable at the desk with pen and paper but kept glancing at the clock on the nightstand between the beds. She'd taken her time with bathing, dressing, and applying makeup. Her hair was drying on its own and falling into soft waves just past her shoulders. Over an hour had passed and Greg wasn't back yet.

"Like you can concentrate when you keep wondering what's taking him so long," she grumbled, tossing her pen on her paper where she'd written a few notes.

Grabbing the second key card, she stuffed it in her purse and slipped into her sandals. Haley took the elevator to the dining room. It wasn't hard to spot Greg or Sam Wilson, who sat opposite him at a corner table in the large, airy dining room. Haley waved off the hostess who approached her and marched across the room, her temper spiking when Sam spotted her and leaned forward, whispering something to Greg, whose back was to Haley.

Sam tried putting her hand over Greg's, and to his benefit, he prevented the act by turning and standing when Haley approached.

"I guess I took too long, huh," he said, actually sounding apologetic.

Haley couldn't stifle her anger that quickly. "Is this why you didn't want me joining you?" she hissed under her breath.

Even when he sincerely appeared surprised at her question and immediately started shaking his head, it was hard to cool her temper and not make a scene. She hadn't noticed when she first entered how busy the restaurant was but saw now that almost every table was full.

"I needed to eat, Haley. It was the only way to stop the headache that was coming on," he explained, his voice calm and quiet as he spoke under his breath, facing her with his back to Sam, blocking her view of the woman. Greg searched Haley's face, his blue eyes bright when he reached for her. "You don't have anything to be angry about, sweetheart."

"I can decide that for myself," she snapped, moving around him and taking the chair between Sam and Greg. "Have you finished your breakfast?"

"Actually, we just got served. They're pretty busy. Do you want me to order you something? Or you can share mine." Greg sounded as if he were falling all over himself trying to calm her down.

Haley wasn't the only one who noticed, either. Sam appeared rather upset, leaning back in her chair and crossing her arms under her large boobs, pushing them together and showing off way too much cleavage. Her skin was leathery and freckled from tanning too much and the amount of perfume she wore was nauseating. She picked up her coffee, the cup stained on one side from the pink lipstick she wore, and sipped, her attention shifting from Greg to Haley, appearing anything but pleased.

Greg had ordered a lot of food and made quick work of sliding a fair bit of it Haley's way. He placed toast in front of her and gave her several packets of jelly. "It would do you good to eat, too, sweetheart." His deep, soft baritone was filled with concern.

"Maybe I should leave you two alone," Sam began, putting her cup on the table.

"Did you want to eat with Greg alone?" Haley asked, more than willing to clear the air. Sam was wrong to assume she had any right to Greg and it was time to make that clear. It appeared the woman had lied to them about what she'd done while at her brother's, and possibly how many times she'd actually been there after he'd been arrested. How many other lies had she told? And if she was a liar then she very well could be a cheat. There was only one way to treat a person like that.

When she met Haley's gaze, Sam appeared anything but remorseful. Her cold green eyes flared with emotion as she stared at Haley, as if contemplating whether to answer truthfully or not. The truth was plain to see on her face.

"Sam was just starting to tell me about her evening last night. It sounds as if she had a run-in with trouble." Greg adjusted his chair so he sat close to Haley, and draped his arm over the back of her chair while picking up a piece of bacon and shoving it in his mouth. Then, as if on an afterthought, he put a couple pieces in front of Haley, on her small plate with the toast. "Go ahead and tell us what you started to say," he encouraged.

Haley was ready to set Sam straight. Especially when she gave Greg such a grateful smile and once again reached across the table and squeezed his hand. He pulled his hand out from under hers, patted the back of her hand, then reached for his food.

"Go ahead," he prompted, reaching for another piece of bacon. "Go on with your story."

"I was scared to death," Sam complained, cupping the curls at her neck and making sure her heavily hair-sprayed hair remained in place. "I was coming home last night and someone jumped out of the bushes as I walked up to my house and tried to attack me."

"They tried attacking you outside your house, where you live, or outside the hotel?" Greg asked. "You went back home and drove down here again?"

Haley stared at the pieces of bacon on her plate next to sliced, buttered toast. She had no appetite. Sam's low, sultry tone and her too-sweet perfume were enough to turn Haley's stomach. And it seemed Greg either didn't mind Sam as much as Haley did or was a better actor than she'd imagined, which were skills needed to be a bounty hunter. He chewed his bacon, giving Sam his undivided attention, which only made her run her hands over her body even more, shifting in her chair and trying her best to strike the most alluring pose she could manage.

"Yes, but it wasn't a they, just one man. A Mexican," she added, lowering her voice and leaning forward. "He had a thick accent and dark skin and coal black hair."

"First of all, where is this home? And why would you return home then come back here?" Greg asked.

"My brother is down here. I know he is," she said, her tone suddenly sharp. "I went to my home, in San Dumas, to pack a few more things so I could stay down here longer."

Greg barely acknowledged her response before shooting out his next question. "What did this man say to you?"

Sam wasn't as quick at answering his questions as he was at asking them. She shook her head, her hair barely moving.

"We didn't exactly have a conversation. He leapt at me in the dark and I fought with everything I have." When she grinned, her glossy pink lipstick sparkled against her white teeth and leathery tanned face. Wrinkles appeared in her cheeks and by her eyes, showing off her age. "I know I don't look it, but I can hold my own in a fight."

Haley fought to keep from reacting to Sam's comment. She wondered what the woman thought she looked like. Sam batted her lashes at Greg, not once looking at Haley, as if she weren't sitting at the table with them. Haley managed a relaxed facial expression as she picked up half a slice of toast and took a bite, glancing at Greg. He was nodding, his attention still completely on Sam.

"You said he had a thick accent. He must have said something to you if you knew how he spoke."

Sam puckered her lips, looking as if she'd blow Greg a kiss. If it was her contemplative look, she didn't appear to be thinking too hard.

"Like I said, we didn't exactly have a conversation. He said something like 'you aren't going anywhere, bitch.'" Sam faked an accent when she repeated the words of her assaulter. "And when I kicked him in the nuts, right before I ran away from him, he screamed a few choice words at me in Spanish." She smiled triumphantly.

"Do you know who he was?"

"No. But I'm sure I could pick him out of a lineup."

"So you called the police."

"No. I am telling *you*," she stressed, twisting her torso slightly as if she already knew that particular pose would show off her over-sized breasts the best.

"Why did he attack you?"

Sam shrugged. "Maybe he wanted some," she suggested, grinning suggestively. She was hardly displaying the behavior of a victim who'd recently been sexually assaulted.

Haley had spoken to too many women over the years who had been mugged, raped, or sexually attacked in one way or another. They were shaky, distraught, and anything but flirtatious, even if the horrible act had happened days before. It was a traumatizing experience to be attacked by another human being, no matter what the reason. Haley almost felt more sorry for Sam's attacker than for Sam, if she was in fact attacked. And if she wasn't, why was she sharing this story with them? Something told Haley that Sam did very little that she didn't plot out and decide would work in her favor.

"Did he try to take your clothes off?" Greg asked, his calm baritone remaining sharp as he continued eating and asking questions in between swallows.

"Darling, I didn't give him the opportunity."

"Where had you been before you went home?"

His question surprised Sam, and Haley wasn't sure she followed his line of thinking, either. He met her gaze when she studied him, looking at her for only a moment before glancing down at his plate.

"I told you I returned home to gather a few things so I could stay down here longer," Sam told him.

"So you'd driven straight across the border and then to your house?"

"No," she said slowly.

Greg glanced up from his food, watching Sam and waiting for her to elaborate. Haley tried to focus on his line of questioning, needing to get ever Sam's incredibly rude and insulting behavior. No woman could force Greg to do anything and Haley knew she could trust him. Sam was blatantly rude to Haley whenever she was around. If Greg was right and Sam did this to distract them, Haley couldn't let her win. Already she suspected Sam was more involved in all of this than just a concerned sister. Haley needed to be the top-notch investigator that she knew she was and pay attention.

Haley exhaled, feeling her anger fade. Greg was being nice to Sam simply to get more information out of her. He was trying to figure out Sam's role in all of this. Haley needed to do the same.

"I went by my brother's house first," Sam offered, glancing down at her plate of food for the first time since Haley had joined them. Sam seemed a bit more reluctant in sharing that information.

Haley reminded herself that she doubted Sam said anything she didn't want to say, and that she would make up a good story before sharing the truth if she thought it would get her further with her own personal agenda, whatever that was.

"What were you doing over there?" Greg asked.

"I was attacked and you're more concerned about what I was doing beforehand?" Sam asked, her tone accusatory.

Greg didn't hesitate, nor did his expression appear apologetic or sympathetic.

"You should have called the police when you were attacked," Greg offered easily. "Since you didn't, all I can do is determine why you were attacked and if the man followed you from wherever you were before going home."

Haley shot Greg a quick glance. He didn't believe Sam's story. He was damned good at keeping Sam on track and getting her to answer his questions. Granted it didn't hurt that the woman was lusting over him big-time and maybe he was using that to his advantage, but he kept the questions coming, milking as much as he could out of Sam. The look she suddenly gave him suggested she'd just figured that out.

"Do you think he was someone who might be connected with my brother?" she asked, lowering her voice to a whisper and once again leaning forward, causing her large breasts to press against her low-cut shirt.

"I'm not sure. Why were you at your brother's house?"

Sam shrugged as if the reason weren't important. "Because he isn't there. It's not exactly a secret that he didn't run with the best of crowds."

That was an understatement. It also wasn't an answer. Haley gave up on her toast, which was way too dry, and reached for Greg's ice water. He moved as if knowing she would want it, and handed it to her, his gaze warming for a moment when he met hers.

"Why would you go there if you knew he ran with a bad crowd?" Greg pressed, asking the question before he'd fully pulled his attention from Haley. He focused on Sam when he asked his next question before she could answer the first. "Why would you want to intentionally put yourself in danger by being over there?"

"I've been trying to keep an eye on it," Sam added, her expression darkening when Greg handed Haley his water.

"Did you take anything out or put anything in the house?" Greg asked, his expression shifting and becoming all business the moment he focused on Sam.

"Of course not."

"And you didn't notice anyone following you to your home from your brother's house?"

Sam sighed. "I wasn't paying attention. But no one was obvious about it if they were."

Greg nodded, then gave his attention to his food, reaching for the small container of syrup and pouring it over his pancakes. Sam watched him, her focus so intent it was as if she wished she were those pancakes. The thought of Sam getting kinky with any man, let alone Greg, created a stiff, hard knot in Haley's gut she doubted she would be able to get to go away any time soon.

That annoyed her almost as much as Sam's blatant drooling over Greg, even when he'd positioned his chair close to Haley's and had his arm draped behind her throughout his questioning. He moved it to tend to his pancakes, though, and Sam seemed to see that as her cue to pounce while he was distracted.

"I know the man was taller than me, and I was wearing heels. His hair was gelled back and he had black eyes. And he wore way too much cologne," she added, making a face.

Haley was surprised Sam would notice what anyone else might wear with the amount of perfume she had sprayed over her body.

"What about his age? And how he was dressed?" When Haley asked, Sam shot her a look as if she were eavesdropping on a private conversation and had a lot of nerve interrupting with questions. "You really should call and report the attack," Haley pushed. "You don't want whoever it was attacking someone else and being more successful with them than he was with you."

"Of course not," Sam spit out, pressing her lips into a thin line. The moment she shifted her attention to Greg her entire persona changed, the hostile bitch disappearing and a helpless female surfacing. "Do you think I should call the cops, Greg?"

"You should have last night," he said, without looking up from his food.

"You're right." She sighed, fluttering her fingers in front of her face and showing off her long red dagger-like fingernails. "I guess I was just so upset. Living alone and all. I just wanted to get out of there and return here as quickly as I could. I feel so much safer when I know you're nearby," she finished, and added a melodramatic sigh.

"It's not too late to call them and give them all the information you've just told us," Haley said, deciding she could play sweet and concerned, too, just to annoy Sam even further, which it appeared to do. Maybe if she got Sam upset, the woman would slip. "Did you take time to find more stuff to sell while at your brother's?"

"No," Sam snapped.

"What did you do?"

"I cleaned." Sam's cold smile was venomous. "I don't want the place ransacked for when you find my brother and we bring him home." Once again Sam was all smiles as she stared at Greg.

Haley walked with Greg, neither of them saying a word to each other after having escorted Sam to her room, which she'd almost begged Greg to do. Haley knew Sam would have preferred he escort her alone, which was why she had no problem walking with them, even when Sam did her best more than once to snuggle into Greg and push Haley out of the way. Greg slipped his card down the lock and pushed open the hotel room door. Haley entered and Greg followed, closing the door behind him.

Greg began pacing the length of the room as he pulled out his phone and placed a call.

"Bernie, it's Greg King," he said after a moment. "I need you to confirm a couple things for me. Give me a callback as soon as you can. I might have a solid lead for you."

When he hung up, he tossed the phone on the desk by Haley's laptop, then stared at her a moment, as if there was something he wanted to say and he wasn't sure how to say it.

"Do you think someone really attacked her?" she asked, moving to the edge of the bed they hadn't slept in the night before and sitting. She let her sandals slide off her feet and stared at her painted toenails before giving Greg her attention.

His brooding manner made her uncomfortable. She didn't know what it was about, but when he stared at the floor, not answering her right away, she decided brainstorming herself was better than enduring the silence.

"I'm also wondering why she is going over to Jason's house as often as she is, if she even told us the truth about that. Sam doesn't strike me as the kind of person who would be a compassionate and concerned sister. Although she's incredibly determined to be here when you find Jason. That doesn't make sense, either. She didn't seem concerned that you would find him last night while she was parading back and forth across the border. Also, did you hear her say she couldn't wait for you to bring her brother home, and not return him to jail? Isn't that odd?"

"I don't know," Greg said slowly, his back to Haley as he opened the curtains and stared out the window, sounding distracted enough that she doubted he heard everything she'd just said.

When his cell rang, Greg grabbed it on the first ring, taking only a second to glance and see who the caller was before answering it. "Bernie," he said, suddenly animated. "I need you to check Jason Wilson's house out for me."

He paused, listening when Bernie said something. "I know, but can we put a rush on that?" he asked, continuing to stare out the window with his legs slightly spread and one hand fisted against his hip. "A woman named Samantha Wilson, who claims to be his sister, sought me out over a week ago and asked me to find her brother because he'd skipped out on his court date, then vanished, and she feared for his life." Greg's laugh was stiff. "I know. And I told her that. Relatives don't hire bounty hunters to put their family behind bars. But that is what she did. She swore the people he was mixed up with would kill him and he was safer behind bars. Shortly after she asked me to do this for her, I got another job searching for a missing investigator from Omaha, Nebraska."

Haley stared at Greg, biting her lip hard enough it hurt. She wasn't sure if she was trying to suppress anger or hurt feelings. She'd never hired him and he knew that. Why was

Greg keeping her presence a secret? It hurt, and it bugged the crap out of her.

Greg didn't look at her but stared at the floor and nodded. "Yeah," Greg said. "Yes. Exactly."

She studied his backside, his collared shirt untucked over his shorts, his broad shoulders, and how his muscular back slimmed down to his waist. There was a lot more silver in his brown hair than there used to be, but it added to his sex appeal. She was falling in love with him hard and serious all over again, and Greg remaining quiet about it to Bernie was a stab to her heart, which was already too vulnerable from so many emotions and feelings coming to life now that they were together again.

"There is an assassin who is missing as well. His name is Marty Byrd."

Haley swore she heard Bernie through the other end.

"You're right. An assassin at his level doesn't disappear without people getting nervous. I put a call in to a friend of mine who is closer to The Bird than I am and he confirmed the guy disappeared from his home. No one knows where he is." Again there was a slight pause. "So we've got Jason Wilson who has vanished, Pedro Gutierrez breaking out of jail, a well-known assassin disappearing, a private investigator in Omaha who disappears and shows up down here dead, and a known Mafia leader, Roberto Torres, who was arrested and admitted leaving a threatening note in our private dick's office that apparently came from a computer in Jason Wilson's house. All of these guys are connected somehow."

Haley would bet good money on that. She was sick of being left out of the conversation, though, and stood, moving barefoot around her sandals, until she stood behind Greg. It made it a bit easier to hear Bernie, although she didn't catch everything he said. It sounded as if he asked about a solid lead.

"Yeah, I might have something. Samantha Wilson, or Sam as she calls herself, is here at the hotel right now. She told me she returned to LA last night, stopped by her brother's house to make sure everything is okay there, then went to her house in San Dimas, which is a good hour away. Apparently she was attacked when she got to her house. And no, she didn't call the police about it, her reason being she needed to return here so she'd be present when I found her brother."

"What if you'd found him last night?" Bernie asked.

Greg sounded anything but amused when he laughed. "I had that same thought," he said dryly, glancing at Haley. His pinched expression was all business.

"Why is she going over to Jason Wilson's house? Sister or not, he's an escaped convict. She's tampering with evidence being at his house."

"You don't have to tell me that," Greg muttered. "I don't think she is on the level. Honestly, I'm starting to think she might be involved with at least some of these men's disappearances."

"How so?" Bernie asked, his baritone rough through the phone.

Haley moved closer.

"The other day Sam brought a couple printed e-mails to me. They were e-mails exchanged between Jason Wilson and Bobby T. The e-mails explained to Jason how he would get out of jail once he was arrested and that he would be taken to a safe house south of Tijuana."

"So you're down there to bring him in?" Bernie asked. "Fax those e-mails to me," he added on an afterthought.

"Will do and I wasn't at first." Greg met her gaze and his sky blue eyes glowed as he moved a strand of hair behind her ear. "But I think I might be ready to break up an assassin's sick game."

Chapter 24

Everything was happening so fast Haley's head was spinning. Sitting in the backseat next to Margarita, she shifted her attention from the view out the window to Greg, who sat shotgun. His jaw was set, adding to his masculine profile. More so than usual, his hard focus and the way his eyes glowed proved his brain was wrapping around a puzzle, methodically putting all the pieces together in his mind.

The great Greg King was at work. She'd seen him like this too many times. But in the past when a case blew open and the predator who always lay in wait inside Greg roared to life and got ready to pounce, Haley had been left behind.

It was hard accepting that being away from Greg for six years while in the program could possibly be a good thing, yet, today, on this case, she entered the scene armed and ready and capable of being Greg's partner. He never would have been able to train her. Although his not training her had been his argument all along for why he didn't want her to be part of KFA.

"Aldea is down in the valley," Bret announced, pointing with one finger as he continued holding on to the steering wheel and navigating over the rough, uneven road. "There really isn't much there."

"Which would make it the perfect hiding spot," Greg mused. "MapQuest doesn't even pick it up."

Bret laughed. "You'll see why."

Possibly if Haley had insisted when they'd been a lot younger that Greg teach her everything he knew about catching criminals, things might have turned out differently. Instead, John Payton had taught her. She would always honor his memory for teaching her everything he knew about the P.I. business.

Maybe she didn't know everything about how Greg investigated a crime, but his intense way of interrogating Sam showed how he'd already started piecing everything together. It wasn't until they took time to talk to each other that the puzzle really started coming together.

"There won't be any way you can get a room here without everyone knowing within an hour or so that you're here," Bret pointed out, pulling her out of her thoughts and ending the silence in the car.

"I don't plan on keeping my presence a secret," Greg said, his expression chiseled in stone.

Greg glanced over his shoulder, meeting Haley's gaze. She felt the rush of adrenaline with Greg. Once they were alone with Marc and Jake they would plot out how to find Marty Byrd, if he was down here.

"What do you plan on doing?" Bret asked.

Greg turned his attention to Bret. His smile bordered on sinister. "Putting a bird back in his cage."

Haley focused on her fingers, which were crossed in her lap. Her stomach began twisting in knots as her nerves tingled throughout her body. Danger was closing in on them. She could feel it. Haley still didn't know what Greg experienced when they closed in on the bust. And it was impossible to tell by looking at him what he thought.

"Well, folks, we're here," Bret said, and turned off the rough road.

When they pulled in front of a small building, which was so nondescript she wasn't sure what type of establishment it was, she felt a tingle of excitement zap at her when Greg climbed out of the front seat, then helped her out of the back.

"We appreciate the ride," Greg told Bret, who got out of the car as well and shook hands.

Margarita climbed out of the backseat but then moved to the front, immediately closing herself back into the heavy AC.

"Good luck to both of you." Bret smiled, but his expression was serious. "We can wait here for a bit if you like."

"We're good." Greg waved as Bret climbed back into his car and rolled down his window. "Hopefully our paths will cross again sometime."

"You're always welcome in our home." Bret rolled up his window and took off, leaving the two of them standing outside the small building.

Children and dogs were in as much abundance as they had been in Tijuana, but these youngsters were a bit more leery and didn't flood around them begging for spare change or food. Greg and Haley stood out as the only people along the wide dirt road who obviously weren't from around there. Haley tried meeting the gaze of several women and men who were unloading crates out of the back of a pickup truck. None of them would look at her, although she was overly conscious of being watched.

"Friendly people," she whispered.

Greg led her across the street to a store with a front porch and barrels stacked along both sides of the wooden stairs leading to the doors.

"They know why we're here," he said under his breath.

"What?"

Greg gave her a slight squeeze and looked down at her, his expression softening for the first time that day. "There's nothing to worry about. I doubt they'll treat us with any hostility. But at the same time, they don't want their bread and butter taken away from them."

"Sounds like we need to find out where their bread and butter is coming from," she suggested.

Greg grabbed her shoulder and started them around the

side of what appeared to be a general store. The smell of spices and leather hung heavily in the hot, dry air.

"We aren't going inside," he told her, glancing around them as he spoke under his breath. Every inch of him was tense. The protector and predator dominated his senses. "Marc and Jake should be around back."

"Oh." She glanced past Greg at two older men, their leathery dark skin and faces deeply grooved with wrinkles. She wasn't about to test how well they understood English by asking Greg why he forget to tell her Marc and Jake had told them where to meet.

Haley headed around the side of the building. She kept up with each long stride Greg took as he moved silently by her side. Her insides were so tense any movement around her grabbed her attention.

"What's wrong?" he whispered, pacing her as they rounded the back side of the building.

"It seems as if everything is overly charged with energy," she whispered.

"That's the craving for the hunt," he told her, speaking under his breath, his mouth barely moving as he searched her face.

"I'll do better once I have a set game plan."

Something changed in his expression. "Soon."

The doors to an old, beat-up-looking pickup truck opened. Haley snapped her attention that way. Marc and Jake got out, leaving the truck running and looking as sweaty and dirty as the locals.

"It's not exactly the Avalanche," Marc announced, moving to the passenger back door when Greg stalked to the front. Marc took his father's scowl as meaning he wasn't thrilled with the ride. "It looks like hell but seems to run fine. Oh, and we're not renting it. I had to buy it."

"I don't suppose it has air-conditioning?" Haley asked when she slipped into the front passenger seat, catching her shorts on the torn interior.

"Once we get going the breeze through the windows isn't so bad. Here you go, Mom." Jake sat behind her and leaned forward, handing her an unopened bottle of water.

"You're a godsend! Thank you!" Haley gripped the cold bottle of water, greedily twisting off the lid.

"Where are we headed?" Greg asked after all four of them were in the extended-cab pickup truck, which appeared to be at least ten to fifteen years old and not in that bad shape, considering.

"Get back on the road and head south," Marc said, pointing over Greg's shoulder. "We're pretty sure we've found the house where The Bird is staying."

The temperature dropped substantially once it was dark, in fact more so than Haley thought it would. As well, it seemed there was no twilight. It was light outside when they arrived at the small, dilapidated motel where Marc and Jake had stayed the night before. After washing up in the dingy bathroom and cooling off a little bit, she peeked out the window, and it was dark.

Haley met Greg's attentive gaze when she joined her men, who took up most of the space in the worn-out-looking motel room. Thick gray-green curtains covered the window and off-color, almost yellow walls looked as if they hadn't been painted, or cleaned, in years. Seth had supplied them with some state-of-the-art weaponry. She wasn't familiar with every handgun spread out on one of the two beds but picked up a Glock and checked the chamber.

"So let's hear your thoughts," she said, taking the edge of the bed next to Greg.

Greg finished cleaning a Glock and placed it on the bed between them. He picked up a small box of bullets. "Load that gun. You'll need it."

"Okay," she said slowly. "Since Marc and Jake think they know where Marty Byrd is staying, we should probably go scope it out."

"It's less than ten mile from here." Marc said. He and Jake knelt on the floor, going through some rather dangerous-looking weapons. The black, hard metal looked deadly, mean, and vicious, and reminded her how many felony charges they might be facing if anyone caught them with all these black-market weapons. "We can do a drive-by fairly easily now that it's dark."

"Arm yourselves," Greg said, standing and walking around all of them to the window, although he didn't move the curtains. "And let's get all of this cleaned up."

Jake pushed himself off the floor. "Are we heading out?"

"Not yet." Greg headed to the bathroom, turning the water on and causing a loud humming sound to rise from the pipes.

Haley sat there, the cold metal resting in her palm, and stared at the gun, deciding how best to do this drive-by. Hairs prickled on the back of her neck. A nervous energy charged the room. One look and Haley guessed all three of her men felt that sinking pit in their gut. The sooner they got on the road the better all of them would be.

"Haley," Greg said, his low baritone yanking her out of her meandering thoughts.

Jake and Marc glanced up as Greg gestured for her to come to him.

"What?" she asked, placing the gun on the bed.

"Keep the gun. Come here," he said, his tone so soft he almost whispered.

When she reached the bathroom door, Greg stepped out of it and put his arm around her, having her face the small room as he pointed.

"Think you can get out that window?" he asked.

"What?" Haley stared at him. "What are you talking about?"

"If you need to get out of this room without using the door I think you can fit through that window." He ignored her last question and glanced at Jake and Marc. "What's on the back side of this building?"

"Nothing." Jake shrugged. "Why?"

"You can drive the truck around back?"

Marc frowned at him. "Probably. What the hell are you talking about, Dad?"

There was a hard knock on the door and Haley jumped. Marc and Jake were on their feet in a minute, both of them scrambling to hide the guns they hadn't chosen in the suitcases they came in. Haley's heart swelled into her chest as she stared at the worn-out-looking door. It wouldn't keep a child from entering.

"Were you expecting someone?" she whispered.

Greg pushed Haley into the bathroom.

"Go. Now," he hissed, closing the door on her.

Haley tried opening the door, but he was stronger than she was. "Do it now, sweetheart. Trust me. Please."

The knock came again, this time louder, more determined. Someone yelled something she didn't understand, but it didn't sound good. A cold sweat broke out over her flesh as her heart slammed in her chest. She stared at the bathroom door, which looked greasy and worn out. She shifted her attention, taking in the closet-like room, staring at the disgusting sink, the shower stall, and a toilet they wouldn't be able to pay her to sit on. Haley forgot about her surroundings when yelling broke out in the other room.

God. Whoever was out there was pissed!

She gripped the gun so hard it pinched her flesh, Haley yelped when the bathroom door opened and Greg shoved her purse in her hand.

"Go," he whispered, then grabbed the side of her head, pulling her face to his and kissing her soundly on the lips before letting go. "I love you," he told her.

She barely managed to keep her balance when he let her go, this time shutting the bathroom door and leaving her standing there staring at it. Several men started talking at once. It seemed complete chaos broke out all at once on the other side of the door.

"Mighty convenient of you to come to us," a booming male voice announced.

"Make sure they aren't armed," someone barked.

"I thought you'd appreciate it," Greg said, sounding too calm considering the level of excitement in the other man's voice.

"Put the gun down, son. You are outnumbered." It was a different man speaking this time, someone with a thick accent, although it wasn't Hispanic.

Haley almost puked when she heard the sound of flesh hitting bone. There was a loud grunting sound and someone yelled. She stood there, holding the gun, and stared at the door, frozen, unable to fathom what was happening.

When something crashed, Haley's heart kick-started into action.

She looked at the window Greg was talking about, her brain racing as she frantically tried to figure out how the hell she was supposed to get out of it. She yanked at the lock on the window frame and pushed it up, actually surprised when it moved. The window slid up a few inches, but then it stopped. Haley fought with the dilapidated window frame until it moved almost to the top. There was barely enough room, but it was either shove her way out the small window or get captured. Greg and her boys were in trouble!

The window became her life source. She didn't try to rationalize her thoughts but accepted that everything that was dear to her depended on her getting outside. Everyone would be too close if she charged into the motel room.

There was no way she could ignore the sounds coming from the other side of the bathroom door. She fumbled with her purse and the gun. It seemed her fingers wouldn't release the gun to drop it in her purse.

Focus, she ordered herself. She could do this. She had to do this.

Haley clutched her purse under her arm and pushed herself onto the bathroom sink, praying it would hold her weight, then reached for the open window. She lifted one leg into the open window and then the other.

Splinters ripped at her flesh as she slid out the window. She hit the ground hard, dropping her purse and her gun. The cool night air didn't help calm her nerves. She hurt all over and her bare skin burned. Haley crawled to her purse and gun, feeling the pain intensify in her knees. The pain cleared her head and she stood, then did her best to close the window. It wouldn't go all the way down.

When the bathroom door flung open inside, Haley jumped out of the way, pressing herself against the wall and running sideways to the end of the building. There was still yelling going on, but she couldn't tell who was doing it or what was being yelled.

A gun fired. It might as well have been aimed right at her heart. Her insides exploded and Haley couldn't breathe, couldn't move. She aimed her gun toward the bathroom window she'd just climbed out of, determined to shoot the first thing that moved.

More shots rang out. Haley spun around and aimed at the corner of the building. She continued aiming her gun as she ran around the corner. Sliding to a stop when she rounded the front of the building, her arm locked straight in front of her, she aimed at two figures who were shooting repeatedly at several vehicles that were leaving quickly.

The two men standing in front of her turned around, guns still aimed. Haley stared at her sons, outrage and fury burning in their eyes and etched in their expressions. She barely shifted her attention to the two guns pointed straight at her when they lowered their weapons.

Greg wasn't with them. The two cars were disappearing from sight.

"They took your dad," she said, wanting it to be a question, but something in her mind already told her it was the truth.

"I don't get it. He didn't fight them." Jake's voice shook with anger.

"Get the truck. Hurry!" Her brain clicked into overdrive with enough strength she swore she would have floated off the ground if her sons weren't clinging to either side of her. "Move!" she yelled, straining to still see the taillights disappearing into the darkness. "We can't lose them. Let's go. Now!"

Haley ran with her sons to the truck and jumped in the passenger seat as Marc took the wheel. Jake slid in the backseat and Marc spun the tires, taking off before she had her door shut.

"Who were they? What happened?" Haley struggled with her seatbelt as she tried to make sense out of the last few minutes.

Greg's odd behavior started making sense. None of it calmed her down any.

"Your father got captured on purpose," Haley said, coming to the conclusion as she spoke.

"I'd never seen those men before," Jake said.

"They were Americans, although one, I think, was European. I didn't recognize the accent," Marc added as he continued driving too fast in complete darkness. Without streetlights or lit-up signs and buildings, they were engulfed in an inky blackness, the light from the truck headlights like narrow tunnels ahead of them.

"That way." She pointed, not at all sure if it was the right way but thinking she saw taillights in the darkness, although it could also be wishful thinking. "Where is Marty Byrd from?"

Her sons didn't answer her right away. Haley didn't dare take her eyes off the windshield and the darkness outside. She would find Greg. It was what the stupid jerk wanted her to do. He was leading them to Marty Byrd, and more than likely all the other people who'd disappeared in the recent past.

They needed backup.

"He's got a home in Northern California." Marc was white-knuckling the steering wheel.

Haley only gave him a moment of her attention. "Jake, do you know Bernie Osborne's number?"

"Who?" Jake leaned forward from the backseat, gripping her seat and snagging a few hairs from her head.

She leaned forward, running her hand down her hair. "Bernie. He's a cop with the LAPD. Your dad has been talking to him the past few days. I've known him forever and so has your dad."

"Oh yeah, okay." Jake exhaled loudly, obviously trying to get his own head in gear. It was a tense moment for all of them and the adrenaline and nervous energy sizzled in the cab among the three of them. "Sorry, Mom. Yeah, I know who he is, but I don't have his number."

"Wait." Marc leaned to the side, gripping the wheel with one hand and driving even faster on dirt roads that were barely marked or visible in the dark. "Dad asked me to hold on to this. I didn't get why. I figured because he was going to try to shower, or something, but it still didn't make sense to give me his phone."

He pulled it out of his pocket and held it out in his palm. Haley and Jake stared at it, neither of them moving for a second.

"That idiotic son of a bitch," she hissed, almost ripping the phone from Marc's hand.

"No reason to insult Grandma. It's not her fault Dad is a pain in the ass," Jake muttered, his humor not appreciated at the moment.

"He gave you his phone because he knew they would come get him. They tried taking him in Omaha and failed, and your father decided this time he would let them capture him. He prepared all of us without telling us because he knew we wouldn't allow him to do it." Haley wanted to wring the bastard's neck. How dare he use himself as bait! He had no right to make that decision without consulting with her first. If he wasn't hurt when they got him back, she would pound his pompous nature into submission for pulling a stunt like this. "This way they don't have access to any of his contacts."

"So he's a smart son of a bitch," Marc grumbled, once again gripping the steering wheel as if he would rip it from the steering column in the next moment. "And you're right. He didn't want us fighting the men but told us to put down our guns. Which we did. We were all armed and could have taken them out. But we were also still holding guns we couldn't put away fast enough when Dad answered the door. So when they disarmed us, they didn't take all of our weapons. The moment they took the guns they saw in our hands, Dad stepped forward and went with them. He let them believe it was all we had."

Haley's fingers shook when she scrolled down the phone book in Greg's phone. She didn't recognized a lot of the names, but it was also hard focusing on who they might be when she was continually glancing up at the road ahead of them and the stream of light from the headlights that created tunnel vision and limited what they were able to see.

"Damn it! Crap!" Marc yelled, slamming on the brake when a clump of trees and rocks appeared in the headlights. He skidded the truck to a stop, barely managing not to hit them. "That would have been your fucking fault, Dad," he howled, slamming the steering wheel with his hand as his adrenaline peaked and hit an overload. "Goddamn it!" he yelled as loud as he could. "Which fucking way did he go?"

"Hold on a minute," Jake announced, and jumped out of the truck.

"What are you doing?" Haley wailed, twisting in the seat and straining against her seat belt, which had constricted against her painfully when Marc brought the truck to such a quick stop.

"Back up and focus the headlights this way!" Jake yelled from outside the truck.

"What the fuck are you doing?" Marc was screaming. "Get your ass back in this truck before I leave you here."

"Do what I say!" Jake's deep, authoritative tone stilled Haley and Marc. Her son sounded just like Greg. "The road is dusty and not paved. We'll see tire tracks if those cars just came through here."

"Do it," Haley said.

Marc stared at her a moment, his eyes bloodshot and his expression strained.

He backed up the truck and positioned the headlights in one direction, then aimed the light in the other direction as Jake looked down both roads that T'd off from the road they'd been on.

"That way!" Jake jumped back in the backseat, pointing to their left as he slid into the middle of the seat. The truck door squeaked loudly, desperately in need of a good oiling, as Jake yanked the truck door shut. "It looks like the two cars slid to a stop almost as quickly as we did. The grooves in the dirt from several tire tracks are really visible headed in that direction."

"Good job," Haley said. "Hit the gas and let's pray there aren't a lot more forks in the road."

"Thanks," Jake muttered, and squeezed her shoulder. "We'll find him. He's put himself in worse situations before."

"I'm sure." Haley tried for a laugh, but it came out sounding more like a grunt. They had just re-bonded. Haley had thought they were a team. She'd believed Greg wanted her as a partner. But making decisions without discussing options first made for a bad partner. "Okay. I have Bernie's number. Did your father say anything to either of you that you think might mean anything? Anything at all. I want to give Bernie all the information I can. We're going to need serious backup right now and honestly, I don't trust the Mexican police."

"Some of them aren't so bad," Marc muttered. "And you know he doesn't have jurisdiction down here."

"I'm sure most of them are very good," she admitted. "Right now I don't know who to trust and so I am going to call Bernie, since Greg has already briefed him on what's going on. We'll leave it in his hands to know who to send in for backup."

Haley placed the call and held Greg's phone to her ear, staring at the darkness out of the windshield and willing taillights or something else to come into view that would help them. As scared as she was for Greg's safety, she was pissed, too. She could have been his backup. Obviously Greg didn't trust her to protect him.

"What's up, old man?" Bernie Osborne asked as he answered on the third ring.

"Bernie, this is Haley King."

There was silence for only a moment before Bernie acknowledged her. "Haley. How in the hell are you doing?" he asked, but then his tone changed. "What's wrong? Where is Greg?"

"I'm not sure, but I can probably say absolutely everything is wrong. And I know this isn't your jurisdiction, but we need some serious backup right now."

"Son of a bitch," Bernie growled.

Chapter 25

The sunrise was magnificent. Greg probably would have taken time to enjoy it if it weren't for the man sitting opposite him at the nicely dressed table on a very large stone patio. It hadn't surprised Greg as much as it should to learn such a mansion existed in the middle of absolute nowhere.

"Was your sleep comfortable last night?" Marty Byrd was dressed casually in very expensive brand-name clothes and looked like he might be heading to the golf course after breakfast. He was also younger than Greg would have guessed, possibly in his mid-thirties. The Bird had created one hell of a reputation for himself in a lot fewer years than it took the average man to go bankrupt.

"As comfortable as a prison can be," Greg acknowledged, making eye contact with the man across the table but then taking his time taking in his surroundings. "You've been here awhile," he guessed.

"Not as long as it looks. This house belonged to someone else. Let's just say I inherited it." Marty smiled at him. He was a good-looking man; dark hair and deadly blue eyes would make him the kind of guy who probably got a lot of what he wanted simply by charm. Where that didn't work Marty Bird didn't hesitate in using violence.

"So you killed the previous owner," Greg acknowledged, once again staring into those focused blue eyes.

"I heard you didn't resist us last night. You were expecting us," Marty said instead of commenting on Greg's speculation.

"It was a hunch." Greg saw right away that Marty wasn't the kind of man who was accustomed to someone not telling him exactly what he wanted to hear.

Marty's eyes narrowed on Greg as if he waited to hear the details around his hunch. He reached for his fork but didn't stab his food with it. Instead he ran his finger over the prongs while studying Greg.

"How did you know we were coming for you?"

"Because you didn't get me in Omaha." Greg felt he stated the obvious but spoke it anyway.

Marty nodded. "You're a smart man. Which is why I want you on board. You're already aware, I believe, of most of the men I've recruited. Maybe not all of them. I'm taking the game very seriously and this is a project where knowledge is on an as-needed basis."

"What is it you need me to know?" Greg asked.

Marty smiled and put his fork down. Greg began thinking the food on the table was there simply for decoration. Neither of them was eating. And after he had been here for what he guessed was probably around nine hours, the fireworks would probably start soon. He just hoped his family was smart enough to call for backup and not try to spring him out of here by themselves. As beautiful as his surroundings were, they were also incredibly well monitored and guarded. From where he sat there were two visible cameras, and he doubted the men standing just outside the door behind Marty were there to refill coffee.

"I need you to know you are here because you are the best at what you do," Marty said slowly, taking time to search Greg's face when he finished speaking.

Greg supposed he was to appear flattered at this point. When he didn't say anything, Marty continued.

"Do you know who I am?" Marty asked.

"We've never met before," Greg said unnecessarily. He saw no point in flattering the man by telling him all he knew about The Bird. "But I heard your name mentioned a time or two over the years."

"And you knew I was coming to get you. So we're going to work with the knowledge that you already knew I was behind several select individuals disappearing." Marty poured more coffee for himself and offered Greg a refill. "It's a very good blend," he added.

Greg obliged, lifting his cup so Marty could fill it. "I'll agree with you there. The coffee is the best I've ever had."

"You are the last on my list of men and women, I need for the game. As I mentioned, you won't be aware of all details. I find when I work with a team, things go smoother if each person is focused only on the task at hand."

"What is this game?"

Marty took his time sipping his coffee and hummed his approval, smiling over his cup at Greg. His handsome features were grossly misleading. There wasn't even a cold edge in the man's eyes. A killer with no remorse. Greg fought a chill as he stared at Marty. He was a very dangerous man indeed.

"The details are privileged for now. We'll work with you for a while, confirm that all the skills you possess are as finely tuned as I believe they are. Once I'm confident you are part of our team, you'll learn your assignment. I already own several portions of the world. It's too early yet to know where I'll send you. But if you can't conform to the game, I'll kill you." He said his last sentence with such relaxed conviction, there was no doubt he meant it. And no doubt at all he thought very little of human life.

Marty's phone buzzed, vibrating on the table next to his plate. He picked up the phone, glanced at the screen, and pushed a button. "If you'll excuse me," he said, and stood, leaving without preamble.

Greg sipped at the coffee. It was good. The morning air was warm but nice, and he took in the surroundings past the large patio. He didn't bother focusing on the two men at the door. They were like statues, but he didn't doubt for a moment they would move if he did. And there really wasn't anywhere for him to go. This house, as huge and incredibly beautiful as it was, was out in the middle of nowhere. Beyond the patio was a tall iron fence that probably surrounded the home. Past that the dry, arid land spread out as far as he could see. There wasn't even a road. It would be really hard for anyone to approach from any direction and not be spotted.

He'd intentionally left his phone with Marc. There was no way Greg would let Marty Byrd have access to his personal phone book. And he knew when he was strip-searched the night before they weren't pleased at all to find absolutely nothing on him.

Haley and his sons would use his phone to call for backup. All of the necessary numbers were on it. It would take some time to organize a force to come out here and take down this place. The house was more than a fortress. It was an anomaly sitting in the middle of nowhere, sticking out worse than a sore thumb. Which confirmed his belief that the locals knew about Marty Byrd and tolerated him because they had little choice. It wouldn't surprise Greg at all if Marty paid the local law to be quiet, and killed those who refused.

Greg prayed Haley would forgive him for not sharing his plan of action with her last night. If he'd explained to Haley and his sons what he anticipated happening once they arrived in Aldea, they would have wanted to talk it out, if not argue how it would proceed. There wasn't time for that.

And now he was on the inside.

While he was here he needed to learn as much as he could about this project Marty was undertaking, or game, as he continually referred to it. Greg was just a bounty hunter. It wasn't in his line of work to research international crime or figure out what plots criminals had in mind. He found people.

That was his job and it was what he did best. But he was here. The more information he could give to the proper authorities once he got out, the better.

He shifted his attention to the men at the door when one of them reached for something on his belt. The man farthest from Greg pulled what appeared to be a phone from his waist and listened for a moment before replacing it on his belt and saying something to the man next to him. Greg stiffened when they approached.

"You're going inside," one of them said without preamble.

Neither appeared to be armed, at least not visibly. Greg nodded, taking another drink of his coffee, then set the cup on the table and stood. He walked between them to the doors and waited as one of them pushed several buttons on a panel next to it. Both men were about the same size as him and appeared to be in good physical shape. They were definitely younger. He continued sizing them up as a beep sounded and the man to his right opened the doors just as a helicopter flew over the house.

"Let's go," the same man ordered, pushing Greg inside.

Greg hesitated, smiling at him. "No need to push. I'm not fighting you." But he procrastinated long enough to see there was more than one helicopter, black and unmarked.

"Get inside!" the other man roared, shoving Greg hard enough that he almost stumbled forward into the heavily air-conditioned room.

Gunfire broke out, splintering across the patio. The table where he'd just been sitting blew up, shattering into many pieces when it was directly hit by the attack from the helicopters. It appeared Haley's backup had arrived. At least that was who he hoped was here.

The men dove past him, knocking Greg to the ground as glass shattered around them from the windows when parts of the table came flying inside.

Greg landed flat on the floor, instinctively covering his head with his arms when another round of gunfire exploded outside.

A voice sounded from a loudspeaker, but he didn't catch a damn thing said as more glass exploded and chaos erupted around him.

Apparently it was every man for himself. The two guards scurried to their feet, no longer worried about him as they raced across the room farther into the house. Since he guessed that was probably the direction to go in order to stay alive, Greg raced after them.

He hurried through rooms, avoiding any with lots of windows, until he heard voices and followed them into a large office. Marty stood in the middle of it, talking on the phone. Seeing Marty completely pissed off didn't surprise Greg as much as seeing Sam Wilson standing next to him, clinging to him, with makeup streaming down her face as she cried in his arms.

"Get him out of here!" Marty barked, pointing at Greg.

Several men approached him at the same time and Greg braced himself, knowing he needed to decide quickly whether he should continue to be compliant or if attacking was the smarter move.

"This is all his fault!" Sam screamed, pointing one of her dagger fingernails at him. "If you hadn't insisted he come here none of this would be happening." She sneered at Greg with enough hatred it was hard to believe she was the same woman who had shamelessly come on to him.

"Shut up and let me think," Marty bellowed, shoving her away from him.

Sam fell onto a nearby couch. "You need to kill him!" she screamed, leaping off the couch and looking as if she might attack Greg herself.

Marty pulled a gun out of his side holster and aimed it at Greg. There was a loud explosion and a piercing pain that ransacked Greg's entire body in the next second. His legs didn't want to cooperate when he turned toward the door. Running was the better decision but no longer seemed to be an option. The wall came up alongside him when he reached the hallway and Greg slid down it, feeling the pain take over as blackness set in. As long as he didn't die, he was pretty sure he would be okay.

Haley squinted against the glare of the sun and rubbed sand against her skin in an effort to wipe sweat off her forehead. She was filthy and exhausted, and really didn't have time to care about either. Marc and Jake were on either side of her, leaning against the old truck they'd purchased and watching the happenings going on around them.

Her guard went up when a man dressed in a suit approached them.

"You three need to head out now," he said stiffly. "This is a secure area now and you need to leave. I'll provide an escort." As he spoke he glanced over his shoulder, snapping his fingers.

A younger suit hurried to join them, his cheeks flushed and sweat dripping down his face. Both men had to be dying from the heat in the suits they wore. Haley needed to remind herself she'd called them in for help.

"We're not leaving," she said firmly before Marc or Jake could say the same. "I called you out here and I'm not leaving until Greg King is out of there safely."

She watched as several helicopters flew into the air, arriving from different directions off the horizon.

"Let me remind you, bounty hunting is illegal down here. You can leave freely or we can have the three of you arrested and taken out of here by force." He raised his voice as he spoke, working to be heard over the third helicopter coming from behind them.

Haley ignored the man threatening them and instead hurried around him to where a group of officers in uniform stood around the back of a van. She couldn't even guess what equipment was housed inside.

"What's happening?" she demanded.

"Mrs. King," the suit behind her demanded, trying to grab her arm.

Haley stepped away from him, avoiding his dragging her back to their truck. She listened to the men in front of her. None of these guys were cops, Mexican or American. This chase had turned from dangerous to deadly and incredibly overwhelming. But they wouldn't send her and her sons away.

"They're going in," one of the uniforms told the suit behind her. "We have orders to take no prisoners."

"I want Marty Byrd alive," the suit pressed, his face turning redder as he moved around Haley and took on the uniform who appeared to be in charge. "We've had an ongoing investigation on this for over a year and if you check you'll see I outrank you."

His argument fell on deaf ears when a loud explosion sounded across the field. Ground blew up to the side of the structure, causing dirt to fill the air and make it even harder to focus on their target. From where they stood, Haley could barely see the incredibly large mansion set out in the middle of nowhere. It sprawled over a flat terrain with desert spreading around it in all directions. Heat waves rolled off the ground, mixing with the dirt clouds rolling toward them until her entire world turned a smoky gray. Greg was inside that house, and it looked like the whole thing just blew up.

"I want Greg King alive, too!" she yelled, determined they wouldn't ignore her or send her away. "You just said you've been investigating this for over a year. We found Marty Byrd for you. I don't care if bounty hunting is illegal here or not. You get my husband out of there alive."

Another explosion sounded and Haley jumped, turning and almost tripping over her feet as she stared at fire and dark clouds filling the air where the large mansion was.

"Oh God," she cried out, hugging herself and stumbling backward, unable to take her eyes off the horrific sight growing across the desert.

"What the hell is going on?" the suit in command demanded.

The men in front of her were all talking at once. Fire shot into the air, the explosion followed by several more and the whirl of helicopters sounding overhead making it all a surreal nightmare. They'd waited so long for this moment and now fear gripped Haley that she'd done the wrong thing. All she could have done was call Bernie. And all he could have done was report the matter to his senior officer. Everything was out of her hands now and it was the most sickening feeling she'd ever experienced.

Maybe Marc, Jake, and she should have tried entering the building on their own. After calling Bernie they'd parked the truck and waited, waited for hours in the growing heat as daybreak had turned into afternoon. She hadn't minded the heat, didn't care about the dirt clinging to her clothes and skin. Bernie had called them several times as they waited. Although hunger had gripped her and she knew Marc and Jake were starving as well, none of them was going to leave this site and risk missing out on saving Greg. She hadn't anticipated this kind of action, though.

"What are you doing?" she screamed, terror attacking her as she watched another explosion erupt. "Why are you blowing the place up?"

No one heard her. The uniforms were arguing with the suits and more men were working frantically inside the van. Haley leapt forward, ready to attack all of them until they quit and focused on what mattered: getting Greg out of there.

Strong arms wrapped around her and Haley slapped at them, determined to make all these men listen to her. She hated not being in control, hated even more not knowing what was going on. None of these men had bothered to introduce themselves when they'd pulled up less than an hour ago. They all seemed to know who everyone was and all of them were intent on Haley and her sons leaving.

"Mom, calm down." Marc held her in his arms, pressing her back against his body. "There's nothing we can do now."

"How dare you!" There wasn't anyone else to release her anger against, so she turned on her son. Pounding his chest with her fists, she glared up at him. "Don't you ever, ever give up on your father, or on any of us. Do you hear me?" she shouted.

When Marc pulled her into his arms, ignoring her attack, but embraced her in a hug fierce enough she couldn't move, Haley had time for the dirt clouds and black explosions to clear from her brain. She collapsed against him, feeling the tears burning in her eyes. No way would she break down right now. Taking a moment, she fought to regain control of herself and sighed heavily against Marc's steel chest.

"I'm sorry," she whispered.

"It's okay."

She was amazed Marc heard her, but he began rubbing her back, comforting her and keeping her in his arms. It was a safe place, secure and filled with love. As much as Haley wanted to remain there, shoving all the ugliness out of her head, she wouldn't allow herself to do that.

When she turned in his arms, Marc didn't stop her. Jake stood next to them, focusing on the black clouds filling the sky across the desert terrain with a fierce, condemning look etched on his dirt-smeared face. Haley turned her attention there as well, shifting only to watch the men in front of them who continued to surround their equipment and talk on their phones. At least they were all ignoring the three of them and not trying to make them leave. Although by the looks on all their faces, the situation wasn't stable, not by a long shot.

The heat around them was overwhelming, suffocating, and made even worse by the dark clouds that now engulfed them. The men in suits and uniforms looked like crap, dirt smudged on their faces from wiping off sweat and dirt. Haley couldn't say if an hour or a day passed as she stood there watching, the feeling of helplessness mixing with an overwhelming sense of doom that all of this would end with incredibly bad news.

Life was full of making decisions. Haley began pacing, letting her mind wander, as she worked to keep hysteria from building in her again. She'd made major decisions with the intent of helping others, making this world a better place. When she'd agreed to testify and enter the Witness Protection Program, she'd believed taking such a deadly drug dealer off the streets would help keep so many people alive. She'd made the decision to walk away from Greg and her sons knowing she'd done the right thing. Her boys were grown. She and Greg would get through her leaving. It would be temporary. Her thinking had been righteous, her convictions strong.

But the decision to call Bernie. She hadn't thought that out but acted on instinct, moving at full speed because she knew they didn't have much time. If she had taken time to weigh the odds, factored in the possibility of her and Marc and Jake going in alone, would they have pulled it off?

There was no knowing now.

She hated staring at the massive black cloud closing in around them. It signaled death, the end, total and irreversible destruction. It existed because of her actions. Her eyes burned from the smoke. The air stank, making her eyes water even more. It wasn't tears she slapped off her cheeks. There wasn't time to cry.

Enough time had passed. She didn't hear or see helicopters anymore. In fact, it seemed unnervingly quiet when she walked past her sons and once again joined the men standing around the equipment behind the van. Even they seemed quiet. No one talked on a phone. They all seemed to be standing there, doing nothing.

"What's going on?" she asked, her voice sounding too calm and foreign to her ears.

The suit in charge held his finger up, either silencing her or telling her to wait a minute. She gave him his minute.

"Do you have men in there?" She shifted her attention to the man in uniform who appeared to be in charge.

Wrinkles on his forehead and under his eyes were lined with black dirt. "Yes. We have men in there. The building is secure, but I don't have a count yet on who is alive and who is dead."

It might have been her imagination, but she thought she saw some compassion in his eyes.

"Do you know how many people were in there?" She needed to keep talking. The more facts she could gather, the more grounded she felt.

"Not yet, ma'am." He turned to his equipment, his back to her as he picked up a satellite phone. He stretched out the curly cord attached to the receiver before putting it to his ear. Haley listened as he spoke to someone on the other end. When he hung up he glanced her way, then at the suit in charge.

"We've got a few injured. Ten dead bodies found so far." He spoke matter-of-factly, not looking at her as he continued reporting to the suit who had tried sending them away. "I've got medical choppers flying in now. Your team can probably go in soon."

That satisfied the suit. He turned from them, hurrying over to his car parked alongside the truck, and climbed inside. Haley saw him talking on his phone a minute later.

"I need to know if Greg King is alive," she pleaded with the uniform.

"Ma'am, I honestly can't tell you that right now. The best thing for you to do is return home. Leave your number and we'll contact you as soon as we know anything."

"We'll go up to the building. My husband is in there. We followed him this far," she pleaded, needing the officer to understand. "He turned himself over as bait while we held back and contacted all of you. We'll follow you up to the structure, and if he's one of the injured I'll fly to the hospital with him."

"No, ma'am."

It was the perfect plan. Haley stared at the man, certain she didn't hear him right. "You don't understand. Greg intentionally went in there without identification or his cell phone. I can identify him. You will need to know who he is to treat him."

"Give me your cell phone number. I will personally call you once we have the injured loaded."

He wasn't going to budge. Haley didn't feel the hysteria

mount this time. Instead everything inside her deflated. She was suddenly aware of how long it had been since she'd eaten, or slept. There was no energy left. Nothing to fight him with and nothing to move. She really must have looked like crap. Marc was there again, putting his arm around her and giving the uniform their number. Her son murmured reassuring words as he escorted her to the truck.

Chapter 26

There was a hell of a lot of pain when Greg blinked his eyes, squinting against bright lights and way too much white surrounding him. He'd never really bought into the white lights and tunnel appearing when it was his time to meet his maker. Nonetheless, Greg tried his damndest to focus, wanting to see exactly what was around him. If he were dead, he wouldn't still be in so much fucking pain. The hallway in Marty's mansion wasn't this white, either.

"Oh good, you're waking up. Mom is going to be so excited. She can't wait to talk to you." The voice speaking sounded like Marc.

Greg tried swallowing, but his mouth was too dry. Speaking sure as hell wasn't an option. But he was pretty sure now he was very much alive. Soon he would figure out where he was. First he needed some of this pain to go away. He drifted back into the blackness.

When he blinked again, Haley was sitting next to him looking at a magazine. She glanced over it, smiling as he brought her into focus.

"How are you doing?" She looked tired.

Greg glanced at the hospital room and at the IV going into his left arm. "I'm thirsty," he said, his voice cracking. He managed to clear it, then accepted the plastic cup with ice chips in it when she handed it to him. "Thank you," he muttered, testing his voice. He spoke more clearly this time. "Where am I?"

"In the hospital." She took a damp washcloth to his forehead. It felt really good. "In LA," she added. "How are you feeling?"

"What happened? How long have I been here?" His body didn't want to cooperate at first when he tried scooting up on his pillows.

"Here, let me," she offered, putting down the washcloth and doing her best to reach underneath him and help adjust his body. "You're probably just stiff from lying here for so long. You lost a lot of blood. It was touch-and-go there for a few days," she added, smiling, although now he understood why she looked so tired.

"How long have I been here?" he asked again.

"Over a week." She brushed hair from his forehead. "You need a haircut," she decided, her grin broadening as she stared down at him. "I'm glad you're awake," she whispered, her voice cracking with emotion when she leaned down and kissed him.

He did his best to kiss her back. It seemed his body wasn't fully cooperating with him yet.

"So what happened? I remember Marty pulling a gun on me." It came back to him slowly. "Did he shoot me? I don't remember. There was an explosion, but I don't think it was from his gun. I fell in the hallway. Everything went black."

"They wouldn't let us go down there." She picked up the washcloth and started caressing him with it again. He would give her a day or so to stop that. "But the FBI went in and took down his entire operation. There were very few survivors. And we had to sit here and wait almost a day without any news until they finally informed us you'd been flown in here to ICU." She smiled and looked like she was seriously paraphrasing everything for him. "Apparently we tapped into an investigation that had been going on for over a year," she added, leaning closer and whispering. "If it weren't for us, the FBI might have wasted a year's worth of work."

"Am I in ICU?" Everything she was saying swam around in his head. "What's in that IV?" he asked, curious how drugged he was.

"They moved you this morning." Haley glanced at the tube going into his arm. "And I'm not sure what they have you on. I can find out."

Greg tried out his arms, pushing on the bed and struggling to move to more of a sitting position. The IV needle moved as he did, aggravating his arm. Otherwise, he was a bit weak, but nothing a good solid meal wouldn't fix. He moved his legs under the sheet, and they cooperated. More than likely all other body parts would wake up and respond appropriately with a little time.

Greg shifted his attention to Haley's breasts. The green sleeveless vest-type sweater she wore hugged her shapely figure and offered one hell of a view. His body didn't react, though. She continued stroking his forehead, the side of his head, and his neck with the washcloth. He lifted his arm, moving it slowly until he could brush his fingers across her breasts. Immediately her nipples hardened and grew visible through the sweater. At the same time his cock jerked under the sheets.

"What was that for?" she asked, frowning, although her pretty green eyes twinkled with amusement.

"Just making sure all parts are still in good working order," he told her seriously. "How much longer do I have to be here?" He knew he'd be a lot better off once he could get up and move around. "Let's get a nurse in here and get me unhooked."

Haley's laughter was melodic. "Slow down, cowboy," she teased, leaving his side and walking into the bathroom, where she doused the washcloth, then brought it back to him. The cold water on the cloth felt better than she would ever know. "We almost lost you, and whether you like it or not, I'm very much in charge." She let her gaze travel down his body. "We have to wait for the doctor to give you a clean bill of health, and honestly, I doubt that will be today."

Greg was reminded why he didn't like hospitals. The doctor seemed very content to torture Greg for as long as possible. He didn't go home that day, or the next. The physical therapist who came to visit him the third day he was awake wasn't bad looking, but her good looks faded when she pushed him physically until he damn near crawled back into his bed.

He was lucky. Although the bullet went through his chest, it missed his lungs and heart. Apparently he had lain in the hallway of the mansion, damn near bleeding out, for quite a few hours before medics got to him. When he finally was wheeled out of the hospital, almost a week later, the paperwork in Haley's hand reminded him of the amount of therapy he would endure before he was back on track.

The meds they sent him home with helped. Greg was damned if he could remember much of the first few days he was there, though. Physical therapy was wearing him out worse than he wanted to admit, although he doubted he was fooling anyone when he hobbled to his room and crawled over his bed, barely managing to reach for the remote before dropping his head on his pillows.

"Are you okay?" Haley asked, peeking her head in through the doorway.

"Come here and I'll let you know," he suggested, patting the bed next to him. "I admit lying on my own bed, with my own remote and my own TV, is better than you could possibly know."

Haley smiled, approaching slowly. "Bret and Margarita called to make sure you were okay."

Greg nodded. Natasha had run a background check on the two of them, and neither had a criminal record. Bret was an American citizen; Margarita wasn't. Greg still thought there was more to the couple than they let on, but they appeared to be good people and he was glad to hear they were concerned.

"I'll try to remember to give them a call sometime this week." He took Haley's hand when she sat down on the edge of the bed, brushing his thumb over her fingers while he tried putting into words the thoughts that had been plaguing him recently.

"You haven't really asked yet what happened after you were shot," she prompted, searching his face with a worried expression when he met her gaze. "Honestly, all of us are concerned you might not be as well off as you're trying to make us think you are. If you were, you would want to know what happened with the case."

"No. I feel fine." He'd caught bits and pieces on CNN after the FBI raided Marty Byrd's home, and knew enough to realize the case was closed. "Go ahead and give me all of the details. I know The Bird is dead."

"Very few people made it out alive. When Marty Byrd wouldn't respond to orders to surrender and leave the home that is when the air raid began. There were several teams on foot, but apparently the home wasn't easily approached. Marty Byrd picked a very good location strategically where he could see anyone approaching without needing to worry about a lot of monitoring devices outside of the property. I admit I was in the worst panic of my life waiting for over twenty-four hours just to hear if you were alive or not."

"I made a promise to you when we married that I wouldn't let my work kill me."

She made a face. "This was bad," she whispered. "I think what surprised me most was learning Sam's involvement with all of this. I don't have to tell you I didn't like her."

"I might have noticed that," he said, enjoying the look Haley gave him. "I didn't trust her, either. And you know any attention I gave her at all was simply to try and learn the truth about her."

"I know."

He didn't want Haley to see how tired he was. Studying her determined expression, the glow in her eyes, Greg knew Sam's involvement had to be something good. "I doubted she would be the mastermind behind all of this. She didn't have what it took. But she handed clue after clue to me and seemed to know more than she should. My guess would be she was the mastermind's slut."

Haley's jaw dropped.

"I'm right?"

"That was just a guess?"

"Sure was."

"Damn. I already knew you were good, but damn," she said, shaking her head. "Samantha Wilson was Marty Byrd's girlfriend. He was feeding her information and sending her to us to pry intel out of you. Sam didn't make it out of the mansion alive, but Jason Wilson did. He and the few others who weren't killed were in the hospital while you were there."

"I'm sure they wish they didn't make it out alive."

"I don't know what charges will be pressed. Marty Byrd is being blamed for John's death." She pursed her lips together, dropping her gaze for a moment and focusing on her hands. "We couldn't find next of kin on John, but Seth is already back in Omaha. He's helping with arrangements for a funeral."

"I'm sorry you lost your friend." Greg clasped both of her hands in his and brushed his thumb over her smooth, warm skin. "We'll go to his funeral."

"Yes," she said, and sighed. "It's hard losing someone you care about, but I think I admired John even more when I learned he died refusing to conform to Marty's plan. There were quite a few people abducted from different cities around the world. If they didn't agree to do what Marty said, they were killed."

"I'm sorry about John." Greg remembered breakfast with Marty, and that raised more questions when Haley said John wouldn't conform. He hated seeing the pain in her face and didn't want to push for information he could learn on his own later. Right now he needed to be there for his wife. "I can't imagine he would have been any other way. You've always had a great eye for finding the good in people, and knowing when someone is bad. At least now no other good people will be abducted."

Her smile didn't quite reach her eyes. "Yes," she said softly. "It's over."

"Are you okay?"

"We can discuss it later." Haley patted his arm.

"Let's discuss it now."

Haley sighed, staring at her hand resting on his arm.

"What is it?" Greg's senses cleared and he suddenly felt very alert. Marty had mentioned his plan and had said something about Greg needing to be ready. That's when Marty had received the call telling him they were being attacked. Greg never got a chance to learn the truth. "What was his plan?" he asked.

"There's no way to prove it." Suddenly Haley looked angry. "And God knows we won't get anything out of the FBI on what their investigation entailed."

"What did you hear?" He frowned at her, knowing the aggravation of never being able to prove a truth but at the same time wanting to know what she knew.

"It was a game," she hissed.

"A what?"

"Like Risk. You gather your players, build your armies, strategize, and arrange them where they are the strongest, then attack."

"What the hell?" She wasn't making any sense. "What are you talking about?"

"That's what Jason Wilson told the cops and what Seth told me. Marty Byrd was building his army. It was a warped, sick game designed by killers who feel they've mastered every aspect of their line of work and so therefore need to move to the next level, which is making others kill for them."

"But if it was a game, there would be more than one player."

Haley looked at Greg without saying anything. When she suddenly exhaled, looking defeated and upset, he reached for her, stroking her cheek. "Sometimes we find who we're hunting, complete our task, and still don't get all our answers."

"Greg, I instigated the raid. I knew when I spoke with the police, then afterward with several agents, how dangerous this would be," Haley said, pressing her fists into her lap and giving him a hard stare. "You went in there using yourself as bait without letting me have any part of that decision. But I put your life in danger and I had no choice. We'll never know all the answers."

"You had to put my life in danger, sweetheart. You did the right thing. And I had to let them take me. If I hadn't, they would just have continued abducting people. Enough families and loved ones had suffered."

"So you made a decision that took you away from me but you didn't regret doing it because you were saving people, right?"

Greg shook his head, wanting anything but to argue with her.

"Yes, but I wasn't gone for six years," he said, seeing her point right away.

Haley sighed, glancing down at her hands. "I know. It killed me letting go and leaving my men. I didn't know it would be six years, but I knew we'd get through it."

"It better never happen again." He tried pulling her down on him.

"It won't if we both agree we're a team. We always keep each other informed."

"I'm game if you are," he said gently, knowing it would be the best team he'd ever been part of.

"It's a deal then," she said, but her voice cracked. "Darling, I love you so much."

"I love you, too," he said, focusing on her happy expression. "It won't always be easy."

"I know. I've got my work cut out for me."

"I'm a stubborn pain in the ass." Greg had his work cut out for him, too. But he wouldn't have it any other way.

"I've never stopped worrying about you," she whispered, her eyes watering with tears once again.

"Welcome to KFA." He reached for her and she collapsed into his arms. Greg held on to her, holding her and terrified he'd be unable to hold up his end of the deal. Haley meant too much to him to risk losing her to a bullet. She was good, damn good. She could brainstorm and plot and knew her way around a shotgun with the best of them. Greg was scared to death that the first time anyone aimed a gun at her, he would lose it. Then where would they be?

Greg always found solace in his garage. It was never changing, solid, reliable. It was the one constant in his life, the one thing he knew would never change no matter how many different projects he took on out here. Whatever he worked on, when he had time to return, it would be exactly as he'd left it. Accepting how little else he really had control over sometimes scared the living crap out of him.

When he realized he wasn't alone, he didn't bother looking up but continued wiping his bike down with a clean cloth, removing every bit of dust. Haley didn't say anything as she cautiously entered his space, although her fresh scent, the smell of her shampoo and soap and perfume she always wore, wrapped around him. It was an aroma he never wanted to live without.

"I thought I might find you out here," Haley finally said, staring at his bike when she stood on the opposite side of it from him. "Is everything okay?"

"I'm scared, Haley," he admitted, knowing there wasn't another soul on the planet he could say that to. "I know you know how dangerous this line of work is. And I know how you've suffered all the years I left the house to go to work. You're one hell of a good investigator. I see how much you love it, the passion in your eyes right before a hunt, and the excitement sizzling through you when you brainstorm. How could I deny the woman I love with all my heart something that makes her so incredibly happy?"

"You couldn't."

When she touched his arm, his flesh tingled, causing a sizzling sensation to race over him and burn him alive. He stopped wiping down his bike and stared at her small hand as it rested on his arm.

"They came after you," he stressed. "With the feathers in the room. Marty Byrd was letting me know he knew what you meant to me. It was a warning."

"He didn't catch me," she whispered, running her hands up his chest.

"I don't want to live another day without you," he admitted. "I'm not saying I can't live without you. We both pulled it off for six years, but I don't want to. You're an incredible investigator. I don't know if I ever told you how proud I was when you helped bring down Perry Pierre, then testified against him in court. Not many would have the courage to do that. You're amazing, Haley, absolutely amazing."

When she squeezed his arm, he sensed so much more strength in her small grip than he ever would have guessed a woman of her stature could possess. She wasn't a large person by any means. And, damn, was she beautiful. A woman like her should be adored, cherished, treated like the goddess that she was. Greg saw today that Haley didn't want any of that. Oddly enough, he wanted her by his side, too, not carefully set on some pedestal for all to admire. He would most definitely adore her, cherish her, and treat her like a goddess. He would just have to do it while protecting her as they ran together, taking down whatever bad guy it was that week.

"You're amazing, too," she said, smiling up at him. The tears were gone and her eyes glowed. "You are my protector and always will be, cowboy. I know how hard it is for you to accept me as a partner. But you are strong enough, stronger than you think."

"No. You're wrong. Now you aren't listening," he stressed, reaching to wrap a strand of hair behind her ear. "I'm not strong. I'm not fair. And I'm incredibly selfish." He sighed, wishing he could hide his imperfections from her.

"Okay. I'm listening," she said, clasping her hands behind her back and watching him patiently. She was going to make him share every one of his tortured thoughts.

"You are so much my equal in every way. You always have been. I think that's what I adore about you the most. I know I'm accepting you as my partner. But it's going to take some training on my part to learn not to leap in front of you when a perp pulls a gun instead of leaping at him, or her." He would have given her half the business, let her take over the office, but that wasn't what Haley wanted. She wanted half of the action.

"I have no doubts you'll make it through your training with flying colors. You'll protect me and I'll protect you.

"I love you, Haley." He pulled her into his arms, feeling the strain on his body and wishing he had more strength to show her how much.

"I love you, too," she said, grinning up at him. "Come on inside and let me fix you some dinner," she encouraged, turning toward the opened garage doors.

"Wait." Greg pulled her back against him. "Don't you want a ride on the Harley?"

"Oh." Haley had always had an odd sense of awe when it came to motorcycles. If he remembered right, it had something to do with some kid in junior high taking her for a ride and flipping his bike. Neither had been hurt, but Greg was pretty sure Haley had never been on a bike since.

"I promise I won't flip the bike."

She shot him an odd look, as if surprised he remembered. "How long have you had it?" she asked, and after staring at the motorcycle for a moment, reached out and gingerly touched the seat as if believing if she had moved any faster, somehow the motorcycle might strike out and harm her.

"I bought it three years ago, right after I finished building this garage." He grabbed the handlebar and turned it, then pushed with his other hand, testing his body as he walked it out of the garage. "I paid it off three months ago," he added, a sure selling point, he thought, as he looked over his shoulder at his wife.

"Your pride and joy," Haley muttered. She followed him out of the garage, and the setting sun immediately picked up the highlights in her hair. "You've wanted a motorcycle as long as I can remember."

"And you always told me no."

The look she gave him was classic. "You pulled a fast one, Mr. King," she scolded, although her grin was contagious.

Greg was going to make her fall in love with his Harley. "Stay right there." He hurried to the back of his garage and grabbed two helmets, then pulled his leather jacket off the hook it hung on. "What do you say we go buy you a sexy biker's jacket?" he asked, returning with everything and handing her his jacket. "Put this on."

"You sure you're okay to ride?" She frowned, giving him a stern once-over as if she would know the answer by looking at him.

"Are you kidding?" He grinned at her. This would be the best therapy in the world. "I'm taking my lady for a ride on my Harley. This might possibly be the best day of my life."

"You're grinning like a schoolboy," she said, and started laughing as she put his coat on, which she immediately drowned in.

He helped her with the helmet, then showed her the proper way to get on the bike.

"Something tells me this case might not be over," he said as he climbed on in front of her. She wrapped her arms around him and rested her body against his back.

The evening sky was beautiful. Incredible shades of blue and pink faded into lavenders and deep colors of red. For now, they had downtime. "You're the one who said it takes more than one player to play a game," he added.

There would be cases that came and went, bondsmen wanting men and women brought in who missed court dates, or got jittery and ran. It was their bread and butter. But it was the larger cases, the ones they stumbled onto every now and then, that kept him alive. Once he had thrived on those, but now he waited for the next one with an odd sense of trepidation. Those were the dangerous cases and Haley was as hooked as he was.

"This case is over," she stressed. "We found John Payton and then we found his killer."

"But if it's a game . . ."

"Then we take our time building our pieces on the board, too."

Greg shook his head. She was absolutely amazing.

"I need to get certified in California."

"I have a feeling you'll be on that in no time." He started the bike, loving the deep rumble of the engine and the confident vibration underneath them, proof of the power they were about to embark on. "We're going to fight," he said over the sound of the engine as he looked at her over his shoulder. "I know I'm not perfect."

"I can handle you." She squeezed her arm around his waist. "And I'm far from perfect, too."

"We won't always see things eye to eye."

"We'll have to remind each other from time to time that we aren't always right."

Greg ignored the slight physical pang in his chest when he shifted the bike into gear and started out of their driveway. His Haley was back. Nothing else in the world mattered. He would give her the moon if she asked for it. And all she wanted was to work with him. He was one hell of a lucky son of a bitch; a day wouldn't pass when he wasn't fully aware of that.

"Sounds like we need to get you started on your certification," he said.

Haley scooted further into him and with the higher passenger seat was easily able to rest her chin on his shoulder.

When she spoke, her words tickled his ear. "I think that can wait a little while."

"Oh?"

"Not too long, but there are some things I would rather do first."

"And what is that, my dear?"

"When we get back home, I'll show you."

"I have to wait until we get home to be shown?"

Haley laughed. It was the most beautiful sound in the world. "I might get to like these motorcycle rides," she said, and lowered her hands until she rested them on his thighs.

Read on for an excerpt from
Lorie O'Clare's next book

GET LUCKY

Coming in April 2011

London didn't relax against him as easily as she had the last time he'd kissed her, but she tasted so good Marc didn't care. Gripping the side of her head, he tilted her so he could devour her better. She tasted of their dinner and the wine. But it was the heat that greeted him, slowly drifting to his brain, that made him slow the kiss and pull her closer. London groaned and he dragged his fingers through all that thick, tangle-free silk down her back until he clasped her rear end.

More than anything he wanted to explore every inch of her. He was acutely aware of the zipper down her spine and forced himself to instead caress her smooth, round ass as he continued feasting on her mouth. If he moved too quickly, she'd make him stop. He wasn't sure how he knew that but didn't doubt it for a moment.

"You really don't want your dishes washed," he murmured into her mouth, knowing he could stop now but if he held her in his arms much longer, he'd be carrying her in search of her bedroom.

"Huh," she gasped, letting her head fall back and her eyes remain closed when he raised his head. The slight grin on her face added to the vision of beauty Marc stared down at. "Soap is in the cabinet under the sink," she said, holding her position.

"You are wicked," he accused, letting his gaze drop to the

view of her breasts with the material of her dress stretched over them.

London relaxed even more in his arms. If he let her go, she'd fall backward, not that he would ever let her go. Marc blinked, suddenly realizing this wasn't casual sex, or friends with benefits. They'd known each other a week. They'd had well over a month with him at the lodge. If this was how he felt about her right now, where would they be when it was time for him to leave?

He was wicked. He was a selfish bastard. Marc would take what London offered, and worry later about where it might lead them. He wanted London too much to start analyzing something as serious as a relationship.

"I tell you what," he said, squeezing her ass and pulling her dress up until he felt the edge of the material in his hands. That was enough to open her eyes. "I'm going to wash your dishes and then I want more of this," he said, lowering his head and nibbling at her lower lip.

"You drive a hard bargain," she informed him. When she straightened, London appeared a lot more sober than she had a moment before. "And we'll see. No promises."

London couldn't remember when she last had more fun washing and drying dishes. Marc jumped into the task, making her feel obligated to get out a hand towel and dry.

"You see," he told her, "I learned at a young age washing the dishes was the much better task than drying them. My brother and I had to do this every night. It was our chore, before we got a dishwasher."

"Oh, yeah? Sounds like you were so tortured." She enjoyed hearing about his childhood and trying to imagine what it would be like being in a family where there were actually chores given. Any time her parents had told her to do something, they forgot they'd told her before she found time to do it. Although for the most part, her parents had ignored her. She kept whatever house they were living in clean because they didn't. They were always too busy plotting their next venture, or "business deal," as they liked to call them.

"Most definitely," he told her, grinning and showing how little he was tortured. "Washing is the easier half of the task. When you dry, not only do you have to dry the dish, but also put it away. Usually the dish towel is too wet to keep drying dishes and so you have to get another one. Yet another part of one task. When you wash, that is all you do. This is the easier half of the job."

"Sounds like you put a lot of thought into the matter," she said, laughing.

"Yup. I was all about making sure Jake did more of the chores. I lived to see to that fact."

"So you were the oldest?"

"Yup. And definitely the better of the King men," he told her, as if there might be a competition if she were to meet the other brother. "Jake is a player."

"And you're not a player?" She twisted her damp dish towel and aimed it at him. "I might be the judge of that."

Marc shifted his attention from her face to her towel. "I'd think twice before doing that," he said, his voice lowering into a challenge.

London let the towel go, releasing it with one hand and aiming low. The towel slapped against Marc's waist before he ducked backward, his blue eyes suddenly glowing as his mouth twisted into an ornery grin. London's heart skipped a beat and started pumping too quickly in her chest. She reloaded as fast as she could, aiming higher when he straightened and started for her.

"You think I'm a player, do you?" He tried grabbing her towel.

London jumped out of his reach, letting the towel fly again. It made a slapping sound against his chest. "What would you call it?" she asked, laughing even harder when he lunged at her.

She barely made it out of his grasp and darted out of the

kitchen. There wasn't time to twist her towel again and reload before he pounced on her, lifting her off the ground. Her back was pressed against all that steel muscle and his arms were all bulging muscles. London lost her towel and gripped his arms but couldn't budge his grip on her.

"You would attack an unarmed woman?" she asked, barely able to get the words out as she laughed harder than she had in ages.

"You attacked an unarmed man!" he accused, his voice a deadly growl in her ear.

Her heart exploded in her chest. A warmth stretched over her body, causing immediate swelling between her legs and a tingling to start over her flesh. She'd had a few glasses of wine but not enough to make her drunk. As she continued laughing and twisting against his impossible grip, fumes flooded her brain. London might blame it on the wine, but suddenly she wanted him.

Did someone say HOT?

If you enjoyed this Bounty Hunters novel, you won't
want to miss the dangerous and sexy FBI series
from award-winning author

LORIE O'CLARE

STRONG, SLEEK AND SINFUL
ISBN: 978-0-312-94344-8

LONG, LEAN AND LETHAL
ISBN: 978-0-312-94343-1

TALL, DARK AND DEADLY
ISBN: 978-0-312-94341-7

Available from St. Martin's Paperbacks